THE SONG RISING

The
Song Rising

Samantha Shannon

B L O O M S B U R Y

NEW YORK · LONDON · OXFORD · NEW DELHI · SYDNEY

Bloomsbury USA
An imprint of Bloomsbury Publishing Plc

1385 Broadway   50 Bedford Square
New York   London
NY 10018   WC1B 3DP
USA   UK

www.bloomsbury.com

BLOOMSBURY and the Diana logo are trademarks of Bloomsbury Publishing Plc

First published in Great Britain 2017
First U.S. edition 2017

© Samantha Shannon-Jones, 2017
Map copyright © by Emily Faccini, 2017

ISBN: HB: 978-1-63286-624-0
            EPUB: 978-1-63286-626-4

Library of Congress Cataloging-in-Publication Data is available.

2 4 6 8 10 9 7 5 3 1

Typeset by Integra Software Services Pvt. Ltd.
Printed and bound in the U.S.A. by Berryville Graphics Inc., Berryville, Virginia

To find out more about our authors and books visit www.bloomsbury.com.
Here you will find extracts, author interviews, details of forthcoming events,
and the option to sign up for our newsletters.

Bloomsbury books may be purchased for business or promotional use.
For information on bulk purchases please contact Macmillan Corporate and Premium Sales
Department at specialmarkets@macmillan.com.

For the silenced

Silence is all we dread.
There's Ransom in a Voice—

Emily Dickinson

Contents

THE REPUBLIC OF
SCION ENGLAND
*also known as the
Republic of Scion Britain*

Inverness

HIGHLANDS

Edinburgh

LOWLANDS

ULSTER

Belfast

CONNAUGHT

NORTH
WEST

NORTH
EAST

LEINSTER

Dublin

Leeds

Manchester

MUNSTER

Feirm na mBeach Meala

MIDLANDS

WESTLANDS

Birmingham

THE REPUBLIC OF
**SCION
IRELAND**

Cardiff

SOUTH EAST

Bristol

London

SOUTH WEST

	Capital
	Citadel
	Paige's Family Home

The Mime Order

The UNDERQUEEN, Paige Mahoney,
also known as the Black Moth *or* the Pale Dreamer

Her MOLLISHERS, Nicklas Nygård,
mollisher supreme, *also known as* the Red Vision,
and Eliza Renton, *also known as* the Martyred Muse

THE HIGH COMMANDERS
of the Unnatural Assembly

I Cohort – Ognena Maria – Strategy
II Cohort – The Glym Lord – Recruitment
III Cohort – Tom the Rhymer – Communication
IV Cohort – Minty Wolfson – Proclamation
V Cohort – Wynn Ní Luain – Medical
VI Cohort – The Pearl Queen – Provisions

THE HIGH COMMANDERS
of the Ranthen

Terebellum, Warden of the Sheratan – Resources
Arcturus, Warden of the Mesarthim – Instruction

NO SAFE PLACE, NO SURRENDER

Prelude

November 2, 2059

The lights scalded my borrowed eyes. I was still inside a different body, standing on the same floor, but everything had changed.

There was a smile on his lips. That old gleam in his eye, like I'd just brought him good news from the auction house. He wore a black waistcoat embroidered with interlinked gold anchors, and a scarlet cravat was tied at his throat. One silk-clad hand grasped an ebony cane.

"I see you have mastered possession at a distance," he said. "You *are* full of surprises."

The cane's handle was porcelain, shaped like the head of a white horse.

"I believe," Nashira said, her voice soft, "that you are already acquainted with my new Grand Overseer."

I let out my first breath since laying eyes on him.

He had tried to stop me. The scheming worm had silenced me for weeks, kept me from telling the world about the existence of the Rephaim. Yet here he was, looking as easy with them as he was with his own shadow.

"Oh, dear. Have you swallowed that pilfered tongue?" Jaxon let out a deep laugh. "Yes, Paige, I am here, with the Rephaim! In the Archon, wearing the anchor! Are you aghast? Are you oh-so-scandalized? Is this all a terrible *shock* to your fragile sensibilities?"

"Why?" I whispered. "Why the hell are you here, Jaxon?"

"Oh, as if I had a choice. With you as Underqueen, my beloved syndicate is doomed to self-destruction. Consequently, I have decided to return to my roots."

"Your roots?"

His smile widened.

"You have chosen the wrong side. Join this one, darling," he continued, as if I hadn't spoken. "I can't tell you how it hurts me to see you in the pocket of those despicable Rephaim who call themselves *Ranthen*. Unlike the Rag and Bone Man, I have always believed you could be saved from their indoctrination. From Arcturus's . . . seduction. I thought you had more sense than to blindly obey the man who was once your master."

I stared at him coolly. "You're asking me to do that now."

"Touché." A fresh bruise stained his cheekbone. "To Terebellum Sheratan, you are a convenient pawn in an age-old game. Arcturus Mesarthim is nothing but her lure. Her bait. He took you under his wing in the penal colony on her orders, to entice you into the Ranthen's net. And you, my darling—you fell for it . . . and everyone but you can see it."

A chill warned me that something was wrong. Elsewhere in the citadel, someone had touched my body.

"This is a fight you cannot win. Don't mutilate the syndicate, O my lovely," Jaxon purred. "It was never meant as a weapon of war, and you were never meant to rule. Step back from the brink. All any of us in the Archon wants is to protect you—you, and the wonder of your gift. If we must pull off your wings to stop you casting yourself into the fire, so be it." His hand reached out. "Come to us, Paige. Come to me. All this can be avoided."

He had shocked me. We both knew it. If he thought he could scare me, he would have to try harder.

Another shiver. I felt myself falling out of the stranger's dreamscape, back into the æther's embrace.

"I'd rather burn," I said.

My brain was liquid, slithering out through my nose and down my front. I had to get out, get air into my lungs . . .

A hand took hold of my arm. Someone was talking to me, saying my name. I clawed off the oxygen mask, got the door open, and spilled out of the car in a jumble of limbs, gasping. The jolt peeled open the stitches in my side, wetting my shirt.

Jaxon Hall was many things, but I couldn't believe he had gone to Scion. He had made his career out of living in their shadow, not their arms.

My wounds from the scrimmage flared, white-hot in my torso, deep and throbbing in my back. I pitched into the night, down the moss-slick steps to the Thames, and fell to my knees at the water's edge, where I gripped my head between my hands and cursed my own stupidity. How, *how* could I have not foreseen this? There must have been some clue. Now he would be our most formidable enemy, a vital asset to the anchor.

I will find other allies, he had told me after the scrimmage. *Be warned: you have not seen the last of me.*

I should have killed him in the Rose Ring. The blade had been against his throat, but I'd been too weak to cut.

A very old ally, Nashira had said. *One who returned to me . . . after twenty long years of estrangement . . .*

A shout in the distance stopped time, or started it again. I hunched over the water, holding myself.

I have decided to return to my roots.

"No," I breathed. "No, not you. Not you . . ."

He had been standing so comfortably alongside the Sargas. Not like someone who had only laid eyes on them for the first time a few hours ago. And there were other things I had brushed off, that I hadn't seen from behind the blindfold. He had always been wealthier than other mime-lords. Absinthe alone cost a fortune on the black market, and he drank it almost nightly. How had he leaped from pauper to prince? Surely not just from his writing; there was no money in pamphlets. Then there was the fact that he had spearheaded my rescue from the colony with no exit plan—senseless. It wasn't in his nature to go blindly into anything. But if he had left the colony once before . . . if he had *known* there was a way out—or if the Sargas had *allowed* him to take me away . . .

An old ally. Twenty long years. Those were the only words I needed to work out who Jaxon Hall had once been, and who he was. I had no absolute proof, but I knew—I knew, in my heart—that my instinct was right.

He wasn't just a traitor.

He was *the* traitor.

The man who had betrayed the Ranthen twenty years ago to buy his freedom from the Rephaim.

The man who was responsible for the scars on Warden's back.

The man who had left his fellow prisoners to die in the colony.

And I had been his mollisher. His right hand.

The crunch of footsteps broke through the white noise in my ears. Out of the corner of my eye, I saw Warden sink into a crouch beside me.

I had to tell him. I couldn't carry this knowledge alone.

"I know who betrayed you twenty years ago," I said. "I know who gave you the scars."

Silence. I realized I was shivering.

"It is not safe out here," Warden finally said. "We can discuss this at the music hall."

The thoughts tangled like barbed wire in my head. I was everybody's puppet, caught in a thousand strings.

Nick ran to the railings above us. "Vigiles," he shouted. "Warden, bring her up here!"

Warden stayed where he was. I was afraid he would lack the ability to read my expression—that I might have to say the name myself—but as the moments ticked past, I watched it dawn on him, just as it had on me. A fire rose in his eyes.

"Jaxon."

PART 1

God in a Machine

1

Underqueen

War has often been called a game, with good reason. Both have combatants. Both have sides. Both carry the risk of losing.

There is just one difference.

Every game is a gamble. Certainty is the last thing you want when you begin. If you are guaranteed to win, there is no game at all.

In war, however, we crave certainty. No fool ever went to war without the cast-iron belief that they could win, that they *would* win; or at least, that the likelihood of losing was so small as to make the bloody price of every move worthwhile. You don't go to war just for the thrill, but for the gain.

The question is whether any gain, any outcome, can justify the way you play.

November 27, 2059

In the heart of its financial district, London was burning. On Cheapside, Didion Waite, poet of the underworld and bitter rival of Jaxon Hall, was howling over the remains of a derelict church.

Once a fixture of the capital, it was now a mass of charred and smoking rubble.

In his powdered wig and tailcoat, Didion was eye-catching even by Scion London standards, but everyone was too engrossed in the drama to take notice of one madman—everyone but those of us who had answered his call. We stood at the mouth of a lane, masked and shrouded, taking in what was left of St. Mary-le-Bow. According to reports from local voyants, an explosion had obliterated its foundations around midnight. Now several of the nearest buildings were on fire, and graffiti had been sprayed across the street.

ALL HAIL THE WHITE BINDER
TRUE UNDERLORD OF LONDON

A sunset-orange flower had been painted beside it. Nasturtium. In the language of flowers, it meant *conquest*, or *power*.

"Let's get the poor man out of there," said Ognena Maria, one of my commanders. "Before Scion does."

I didn't volunteer to help. Didion had demanded that I come here in person, but I couldn't risk speaking to him, not when he was in this state. He must expect me to compensate him for the damage from the Underqueen's coffers, and I knew from experience that he would have no qualms about exposing me to the whole street if I refused. Better not to let him see me at all, for now.

"I'll go." Eliza checked that her hood was fastened. "We'll take him to Grub Street."

"Be careful," I said.

She hurried toward Didion, who was now pounding the cobblestones with his hands and screaming incoherently. Maria followed, motioning to her hirelings to come with her.

I stayed behind with Nick. We had taken to wearing the winter hoods that had come into fashion in recent weeks, which could be worn so they covered most of the face, but by now I was so recognizable that even that might not protect me.

After the scrimmage—when I had fought Jaxon Hall, my own mime-lord and mentor, for the right to rule the clairvoyants of London—Nick had quit his job with Scion and vanished from their view, only staying long enough to steal a few cases of medical supplies and take as much cash from his bank account as he could. Within days, his face had appeared on the screens alongside mine.

"You think this was Jaxon?" He nodded to the wreck of the church.

"His loyalists." The heat of the fire baked my eyes dry. "Whoever's leading them is starting to gather a following."

"It's a tiny group of troublemakers. Not worth your time."

His tone was reassuring, but this was the third assault on a syndicate landmark in as many days. The last time, they had raided the Old Spitalfields Market, scaring the traders and looting stalls. Those responsible considered Jaxon to be the rightful Underlord, despite his conspicuous absence. Even after I had told them the facts, they refused to believe that the White Binder, the glorious mime-lord of I-4, could be involved with Scion.

In the grand scheme of things, this was a minor nuisance; the majority of voyants did support me. But the message this attack sent was clear: I had not yet won all of my subjects' hearts. That came with the territory, I supposed. My predecessor, Haymarket Hector, had been widely despised. Those who had obeyed him had done so out of fear, or because he paid them well.

Didion wailed as he was hoisted to his feet and led away by Maria and Eliza. He was drowned out by the siren of a Scion fire engine. It might be able to douse the neighboring buildings, but anyone could see that the church was beyond saving—as was the Juditheon, the auction house beneath it. We retreated, leaving another part of our history to be swept away.

Once I might have mourned. I had whiled away many an hour at the Juditheon, shelling out extortionate amounts of Jaxon's money for spirits Didion had no right to sell—but since the revelation of Jaxon's true nature, all of my memories of life as his mollisher had gained a taint, a film of scum that smeared their surface. All I wanted was to scrape them all into a pit, close the earth on top of them, and build again on the new ground.

"Nearest safe house is Cloak Lane," Nick said.

We slipped into another backstreet, away from the ring of heat around the church. I kept us clear of other people. Nick checked for security cameras. Since the scrimmage, we were no longer just unnatural criminals, but nascent revolutionaries, with ever-growing bounties on our heads. Even if we hadn't yet made a move against Scion, they knew our objective.

I had to wonder how much longer we could survive in the capital. It was dangerous for us to be out this late at night, but when Didion had sent for me, I had wanted to come, to convince him that we were on the same side. He was, after all, Jaxon's long-time adversary, which now made him a potential ally.

The Cloak Lane safe house was a studio apartment rented by an ex-nightwalker, who was keen to help the Mime Order in whatever way she could. Unlike most of our buildings, it had heating, a fridge, and a proper bed. The warmth was a relief after a long night on the streets. Over the last few weeks, the temperature had plummeted and snow had fallen almost every day, leaving London as thickly iced as a birthday cake. I had never experienced a winter so ruthless. My nose and cheeks were almost always a raw pink, and my eyes streamed every time I stepped outside.

When I refused it, Nick dropped on to the bed. He, at least, got a few hours' rest. A hint of moonlight shone on his pale face, drawing out the crease that pinched his brow even in sleep. I lay on the couch in the dark, but I was too restless to close my eyes for long. The image of the burning church, a promise of devastation, was scorched on to my mind. A reminder that while Jaxon Hall was gone, he wasn't yet forgotten.

In the morning, I took a buck cab to the Mill, an industrial ruin in Silvertown—one of several abandoned buildings we had recently occupied across the citadel. It was home to our largest cell.

Changing the structure of the syndicate, with the view to eventually turning it into an army capable of fighting Scion, had been far from easy. I had ended the traditional system of territory and dens, though I had tried to keep gang members together where possible. Syndicate voyants were now organized into cells. Each was based in one location, known only to cell members and the local mime-lord or mime-queen, who received orders through a high commander. Forcing my subjects to limit contact outside their cells hadn't pleased them, but it was the only way we were going to survive. It was also the only way to evade Jaxon, who had known the old syndicate inside-out.

Now anyone who was captured would only be able to betray the whereabouts of a certain number of people to the enemy. We were going to war with Scion, and in war, we took no risks.

When I arrived at the Mill, I climbed the stairs. Leon Wax, one of the few amaurotics who worked with the Mime Order, was at the end of the upper hall in his wheelchair, handing out packs of essentials, like soap and water bottles, to two newly arrived soothsayers. Leon was sixty and losing his hair, and his skin was a deep, rich brown.

"Hello, Paige," he said.

"Leon." I nodded to the newcomers, who were staring at me. "Welcome to the cell."

Both of them looked slightly awestruck. They must have heard plenty of talk about me: the mollisher who had stabbed her mimelord in the back, the dreamwalker with allies from the æther. I wondered faintly how I matched up to their expectations—all they would be seeing now was a woman with dark circles under her eyes. My hair was back to white-blonde, with a single streak of black at the front. The only evidence that I had been in the scrimmage were my fading bruises and the conspicuous welt on my jaw, where my skin had been split open by a cutlass. Proof that I could fight and win, written on my face.

One of the newcomers—a pale redhead—actually curtsyed. "Th-thank you, Underqueen. We're honored to be part of the Mime Order."

"You don't need to curtsy."

Leaving them in Leon's capable hands, I made my way to the top floor. My deepest injuries still throbbed, but we had just enough medicine to keep the pain under control.

The surveillance center was eleven floors up. When I entered, I found Tom the Rhymer and the Glym Lord—two of my high commanders—eating breakfast and poring over a map of the citadel, which showed the positions of newly installed Senshield scanners: our latest concern. Numa were spread among the paperwork and laptops on the table: shew stones, keys, a knife, and a fist-sized crystal ball.

"Good morning to you, Underqueen," Glym said.

"We have a problem."

Tom raised his bushy eyebrows. "Now, that's no way to greet anyone at this time of the morning. I've not even finished my coffee." He pulled out a chair for me. "What's the matter?"

"Jaxon's supporters burned down the Juditheon."

He sighed. "Maria told us. They're small fry."

"Even so, it's not something we can ignore for much longer." I poured a coffee for myself. "We need to consolidate the syndicate, and fast. A replacement for Jaxon would be a good start." I said it more to myself than to them. "How are you both getting on?"

"New recruits are arriving daily," Glym said. "We need far more, of course, but I have no concerns at this stage. Many voyants seem to be taking to the idea of the Mime Order, and the more of them that join us, the more will feel emboldened to follow them into our ranks."

Tom nodded. "We rescued a pair last night—mediums. They were caught by a Senshield scanner. I had a vision of it happening; Glym sent some of his people to where we knew they would be hiding." He cleared his throat and glanced at Glym. "They had an . . . interesting story. Said the scanner went off, but they couldna *see* it. They just heard the alarm."

I frowned. Scion had started to put Senshield scanners in the Underground—an unwelcome development—but they were so big that it was fairly easy to avoid them. "They must have seen it—they're huge. Where was this?"

"I havena heard all the details yet."

"Send your mollisher to investigate. I don't like the sound of it."

I purloined a ginger bun before I left, causing Tom to gather the rest protectively into their box.

Downstairs, in the training room, daylight spilled through the broken windows, dappling the concrete and the disused machines. At some point, a cave-in had taken out most of the ceiling; you could see up to the pearl-gray sky. There were rings for cell members to train in physical and spirit combat, as well as a knife range.

At Terebell's command, the Ranthen had taken to regularly visiting cells to help our recruits hone their skills. Pleione Sualocin was in the ring on the left side of the room, teaching spirit combat. The voyants around her were transfixed by their instructor.

"When the spool makes contact with your opponent's aura, the spirits will unleash a disturbing sequence of images, disorienting them. However, a weak spool can be deflected or broken. To hold true, spools must be tightly bound. In the fell tongue, we call this art *weaving*." She cast a gloved hand in front of her, lacing the spirits together. When she saw me, she let them go and said to her students, "There are enough spirits in this building for you to practice with. Go."

The class raced off. Some of them mumbled "Underqueen" as they passed me. Pleione watched them leave.

"The sovereign-elect has asked me to inform you that she will be carrying out an inspection of the I Cohort cells tomorrow," she said to me.

"Fine."

The light in her irises burned low; she was hungry. I had forbidden all the Ranthen from feeding on the voyants in my care, forcing them to lie in wait for those who lived outside the syndicate. It hadn't done much to improve their temperaments.

"Terebell is disappointed," she continued, "that you have had no success in erasing the influence of the arch-traitor from London."

"Trust me, I'm trying."

"I advise you to try harder, dreamwalker."

She gave me a wide berth as she left. I was used to it by now.

Mutual hatred of Jaxon was holding us together, but barely. All of the Ranthen knew now that he was the human who had betrayed them the first time they had revolted against the Sargas, the ruling family of Rephaim. I wasn't wholly sure that I had been spared from guilt by association. After all, I had worked for the arch-traitor, their sworn enemy, for three years—it was hard to believe that I had never noticed anything, never learned his dirty secret.

There were voyants sparring nearby. An augur rolled a spool together and hurled it at the other Rephaite instructor, who was standing in the middle of the ring.

Warden. A quick motion of his hand shattered the spool and put the spirits to flight.

Arcturus Mesarthim is nothing but her lure.

His head turned slightly. I hung back, nursing my coffee.

Everyone but you can see it.

The augur sighed and retreated. After a moment, Warden beckoned two more voyants from the line.

First was Felix Coombs, one of the other Bone Season survivors. He stepped into the ring and filled a bowl with water for hydromancy. His opponent was Róisín Jacob, a vile augur, whose plaited hair was dark with sweat. Since I had ordered the release of the vile augurs from the Jacob's Island slum, she had given herself, heart and soul, to the cause, training for hours every day. Warden stood with his arms folded.

"Felix," he said, making him start—he was still jumpy around Rephaim, "you are slouching. I assure you, a Vigile will still see you."

Felix squared up to Róisín, who was a head taller than him.

"Róisín, strike true," Warden said, "but give him a chance to attempt the technique."

"A small chance," Róisín agreed.

Clearing his throat, Felix beckoned several spirits and spooled them. Warden paced around the ring.

"Turn your backs." They did. "Now, take three steps away from one another." They did. "Good."

He always made combat a duel, a dance, an art form. A train of observers wound around the outside of the ring. As Felix and Róisín waited for their cue, the audience called encouragements.

"Three," Warden said, "two, one."

Felix sliced his arm downward. The spirits wheeled after it in a smooth arc and dived into the bowl of water, making its surface tremble and the æther strain. I raised my eyebrows. As the spirits rose again, carrying a chain of sparkling droplets with them, Róisín put a sudden end to the grace period and sprang toward Felix.

She knocked his arm upward with her fist and threw him against the ropes before her fingers bit into his shoulder. His body gave a violent jolt, causing the spirits to panic and flee. Water sprayed everywhere as he slid into a heap on the floor.

"Yield, I yield," he yelled, to gales of laughter. "That hurt, Róisín! What did you do?"

"She used her gift against you," Warden said. "Róisín is a talented osteomancer. Your bones responded to her touch."

Felix recoiled. "My *bones*?"

"Correct. They may be enveloped in flesh, but they will always answer an osteomancer's call."

Applause smattered for Róisín's victory. I put my coffee down and joined in. With a little fine-tuning, Warden had transformed her osteomancy into an active gift—something she could use to defend herself. Even what Felix had done was nothing like the hydromancy I had seen before.

"Told you we should never have released them," a whisperer hissed. Trenary, I thought his name was. "Vile augurs don't belong here."

"Enough." Warden kept pacing around the ring. "The Underqueen has forbidden that sort of talk."

Several people started. Rephaim, as it turned out, had keen hearing. Anyone else would have quailed at his tone, but the whisperer recovered quickly.

"I don't have to do what you say, Rephaite," he sneered. Felix swallowed and glanced at Warden. "I'll take my orders from the Underqueen, if she ever shows up."

"Then listen to this, Trenary," I called. Heads turned in my direction. "We don't hold with that attitude any longer. If you can't let go of it, take it elsewhere. Outside, perhaps, where the snow is."

There was a pause before Trenary stormed out of the hall, leaving Róisín to grind her teeth.

"Warden, what can you teach me?" Jos Biwott piped up, snapping the tension. "All I can do is sing."

"That is no small gift. All of you have the potential to use your clairvoyance against Scion, but my time is short today." Groans of disappointment rang through the hall. "I will return next week. Until then, keep practicing."

I watched them disband. On the other side of the hall, Warden reached for his coat.

It had been weeks since we had spoken more than a few stiff words to one another. I couldn't put this off any longer. Trying to shake off my apprehension, I crossed the hall to stand beside him.

"Paige."

His voice had the same effect on me as wine. The heaving, clumsy weight behind my ribs was still.

"Warden," I said. "It's been a while."

"Indeed."

I tried to appear as if I was observing the knife range, but I couldn't concentrate. I was too aware of the eyes on us, of those who were regarding the Underqueen and their Rephaite instructor with open curiosity.

"That was very impressive," I said frankly. "How did you teach Felix to use hydromancy that way?"

"We call it *fusion*. An advanced form of spirit combat for certain types of soothsayers and augurs. You saw the Wicked Lady use it during the scrimmage." He watched as a medium allowed herself to be possessed. "Some voyants can learn to command certain spirits to carry their numen. The art can be used to manipulate fire, water, and smoke."

This could give us a real advantage. Before the Ranthen had come along, soothsayers and augurs could only really use spooling against an opponent; it was part of why Jaxon thought them so weak.

"That one has been speaking against the vile augurs." Warden nodded in the direction Trenary had left. "And, less openly, speaking in favor of Jaxon as the rightful leader of the Mime Order. Apparently he often quotes the more incendiary passages from *On the Merits of Unnaturalness*."

"I'll ask Leon to keep an eye on him. We can't have anything leaked to Scion."

"Very well."

There was a brief, uncomfortable silence. I closed my eyes for a moment.

"Well," I said, "I have business to attend to. Excuse me."

I'd already taken a few steps toward the door when he said, "Did I do something to insult you, Paige?"

I stopped. "No. I've just been . . . preoccupied."

My tone was too defensive. It was clear to both of us that something was wrong.

"Of course." When I was silent, he said, softer, "The company you keep is yours to decide. But you may always speak to me, if you ever desire counsel. Or someone to listen."

Suddenly I was aware of the hard line of his jaw, the caged flame in his eyes, the warmth I could feel from where I was standing. I was also aware of the tension in my back. The flutter in my stomach.

I knew why it was there. What was keeping me from opening up to him. It wasn't anything he'd done. He had accepted me as the woman who had spent years working for Jaxon Hall without realizing who and what he was. Unlike the other Ranthen, he had treated me no differently. He had excused my ignorance.

It was the warning about him that Jaxon had given me. Words that still played on my mind. And I couldn't tell him so; I couldn't admit to him that Jaxon Hall, a serial liar, had poisoned my view of him. That Jaxon Hall had made me doubt that he was anything but a vessel for Terebell's will.

"Thank you. I know." Conscious of the interest we were attracting, I turned away. "I'll see you soon."

I spent the rest of the day taking stock of our supplies. As I left the Mill at dusk, Nick and Eliza were on their way in, looking for me. They had taken an urgent report from a mime-queen in II Cohort, who was convinced there was a Vigile squadron watching a phone box in her section.

"She says a few of her voyants have been to make calls. Half of them never come back," Nick told me as we trudged through the snow. "When she tried it herself, she was fine, but she wants hirelings posted around it."

"Didn't we have something like this last week, with the medium who went into a pharmacy and was never seen again?" I said tersely.

"We did."

"Did you go to the phone box yourself?"

"Yes. Nothing."

I lowered my head against the wind. "Don't waste any more time on it, then."

"Right. Back to the den?"

I nodded. We had been out for too long today, and we needed to assess our finances.

We caught a rickshaw to the Limehouse Causeway and went on foot from there, keeping our heads down and our scarves over our faces. Partygoers were already out in force, high on Floxy and excitement, weaving past dockworkers from the Isle of Dogs. Oxygen bars were always busy in the run-up to Novembertide, especially the cheap ones that dominated this part of the citadel. Eliza stopped at a cash machine and covertly took out a pickpocketed bank card.

Stolen cards were useful, even if they only lasted as long as it took for their owners to realize they were missing. Terebell often refused my requests for money, something I was convinced she took pleasure in. Nick glanced over his shoulder, checking for observant passersby, as Eliza fed the card into the machine and tapped her foot.

An alarm shrilled.

Nick and I stiffened; Eliza flinched back with a sharp intake of breath. The ear-splitting wail drew the eyes of everyone in the vicinity. For a moment, we just stared at each other.

I knew that sound.

That was the sound a Senshield scanner made when it detected the presence of a clairvoyant, a sound that portended arrest—but it was coming from *inside* the cash machine.

And that wasn't possible. Senshield scanners were cumbrous, full-body contraptions. You could see one from the other end of the street. If you stayed alert, you might never encounter one. They weren't *hidden*.

Were they?

I thought all of this in the split second it took me to react.

"Run," I barked at the others. As one, we fled from the machine.

"Unnaturals," someone shouted.

A hand snatched at Nick's coat. His fist swung up, striking the man away. I looked back to see a squadron of night Vigiles swarming from the bank, flux guns at the ready, bellowing "halt" and "get down," their voices gnarling into a roar that made people scatter in panic around them. The telltale *click-hiss* of a flux dart made me drop into a roll and veer into the next street, hauling Eliza along with me. Shock had already ramped up my heartbeat; now terror carved my body, cutting my breaths short. I hadn't felt fear like this in a long time, not since the day I had been captured and taken to the colony by Scion. The three of us were the highest-ranking members of the Mime Order—we could not be detained.

We sprinted in the direction of the dockworkers' shantytown, where we could vanish into the close-knit labyrinth of shacks. Just as it came into sight, a van screamed into our path. We turned, like cornered animals, only to find ourselves face-to-face with the squadron. Their uniforms were a blur of black and red.

"Oh, *shit*," Eliza murmured.

Slowly, I raised my hands. The others echoed my position. As the Vigiles formed a half-moon in front of us, shock batons glowed to life and flux guns were leveled at our torsos, no doubt loaded with the newest version of the drug. I glanced at Nick. His aura was changing, reaching farther into the æther.

I couldn't dreamwalk. After overusing my spirit in the scrimmage, I was too rusty. Too slow.

That didn't mean I couldn't kick some Gillies to the kerb.

Nick's gift exploded out of him. He blinded them with a torrent of visions; Eliza chased them with a string of spools. Complex weaves of spirits twisted all around them, trapping them in a gyre of hallucinations. In the confusion that followed, I clubbed my knuckles into an unprotected chin and snatched a flux gun with my other hand. The ballistic syringe sprang free, hitting the commandant between the shoulder blades.

We were fluid, working as a team, as we had in the past when we'd fought rival gangs. Nick made a grab for one of their shock batons and snapped his elbow into a nose. With a sizzle of electricity, a Vigile dropped to the ground. Eliza rammed her shoulder into another and ran, tossing one of our precious smoke canisters over her shoulder. As it broke open, swathing us all in a dense gray cloud, I fired off one more dart and raced after her, keeping hold of the empty gun. Nick's footfalls soon caught up with mine.

One leap took me over a low wall. We crawled under the graffiti-coated fence that marked the boundary of the shantytown, closed in on the first shack we came across, and flung away the tarpaulin that served as a door. Even as we crashed through occupied dwellings, even as the dockworkers swore at us, we didn't slow down. It was only when we emerged from the south-western end of the shantytown, on to an oily ribbon of sand beside the Thames, that we stopped. A stitch was biting into my side, but it was nothing in comparison to the abyss of dread that was opening inside me.

We had always been so careful, so sure of our ability to blend in. I had thought nothing could touch us. Yet we of all people had been taken by surprise—almost to fatal effect.

"What the hell was that?" Eliza said, between gasps. "A *concealed* Senshield scanner?"

I felt too shaken to speak. We had to move, but every bone and muscle protested my return to combat. Nick shook his head, panting. Finally, I gathered enough breath to say, "Come on. We have to warn the Mime Order. This could—this could end everything."

2

Emergency

I called a meeting at once. By the time we reached a hideout north of the river, the Glym Lord, Tom the Rhymer and Ognena Maria were already seated, bickering over the rest of the ginger buns. Opposite them was Danica Panić, the other member of the Seven Seals who had stayed with me after the scrimmage. I would usually have asked all six commanders to attend a gathering like this, but I didn't want all of us under one roof.

When I entered, they stood. My ribs ached as I lowered myself into a chair beside Nick. The bitter cold wasn't helping my injuries from the scrimmage.

"What's going on, Paige?" Maria said. "Is this true? A hidden Senshield scanner?"

On the other side of the table, one seat was vacant.

"Should we wait?" Eliza asked, taking her place on my left.

"No," I said curtly.

Terebell's absence was beyond frustrating. She knew what time the meeting was due to start, and nothing could be more important than this. We had always expected Scion to increase the number of Senshield scanners—they had advertised their intention to install them—but we had also expected to be able to see them.

"Thank you all for coming at such short notice," I said. "I'll get straight to the point. Eliza just tried to use a cash machine, and an alarm went off. It seems a Senshield scanner was . . . built into it." I paused, letting them take it in. "We barely escaped."

Breaths were drawn. Glym lowered his face into the palm of one hand.

"The implications for the Mime Order could be catastrophic," I said. "If we can't see the scanners, we can't avoid them."

"In a cash machine." Maria scraped a hand through her hair. "Such an ordinary thing . . ."

"This might explain the mysterious phone box," Nick murmured. "And the voyant who disappeared from the pharmacy."

I had been too quick to brush off those reports. "This is the greatest threat to voyant-kind we've ever faced," I said. "Depending on how many hidden scanners have been installed, the first three orders—the only ones that can currently be detected—may have to go into hiding temporarily until our numbers are great enough to overcome the Vigiles. It could be too dangerous on the streets."

"No." Eliza stared at me. "Paige, we can't just *hide*."

"As a fellow medium," Glym said, lifting his face, "I agree. Despite the danger, it would be impractical to freeze most of our foot-soldiers."

"It would also be impractical to allow Scion to capture them," I said. "We have voyants from the other orders to do the footwork."

"Not many."

"Enough," I said, but I could tell that they weren't having this. Maria shook her head. "Fine. Then we'd better get damned good at avoiding the scanners. And it's time we actually tackled the threat head-on. Hector buried his head in the sand about Senshield, but we have to face the facts about how serious this is. This is a god in a machine. An all-seeing eye."

"And you're going to find it hard to blind it," Danica said.

She was sitting uncomfortably at the other end of the table with her arms folded. Her hair was a thatch of auburn frizzles, her eyes bloodshot from overtime. With her job in Scion's engineering department, she was our best source of information on Senshield.

"Dani," I said, "did you have any idea this was coming?"

"I knew they planned to install the large scanners across the citadel, which is why I tried and failed to build a device to block our auras—we all knew that. We also knew that they would eventually target essential services. I did *not* know, however, that they had created a version that could be concealed."

"Let's cut to the chase, then. Do you have any idea how we can get rid of them?"

"Well, you can't destroy or remove the large ones by hand. Aside from the fact that they're clearly being watched, each scanner is welded in place."

"Do you know how they work?" Glym asked Danica, tersely. "Do you know anything about them at all?"

"Obviously."

"And?"

She shot him a dark look. If there was one thing Danica Panić hated, it was being rushed.

"According to the engineers' grapevine, the scanners are powered by a central source of energy, which they call the *core*," she said, with deliberate slowness. "I don't know what it is, but I do know that every single scanner is connected to it."

"So if we get rid of the core, we disable the whole thing," I said.

"Hypothetically. It would be like removing the battery."

Tom stroked his beard. "And where do we find it?"

"The Archon, surely," I said.

"Not necessarily," Danica said. "Senshield is a ScionIDE project, so it's most likely in a military facility."

ScionIDE. Scion: International Defense Executive. Scion's army. I had encountered them once before, thirteen years ago, when they had broken into Ireland through Dublin.

"ScionIDE," Maria repeated.

I looked at her. Wearing an odd expression, she took a leather cigarette case from her jacket.

"I didn't know Senshield was a military brainchild. That's very interesting." She removed a cigarette and lit up. "A link to the army gives its increased presence an even more sinister touch."

A tremor scuttled across my abdomen. We had security measures in place to protect us from Vigiles and enemy Rephaim, but I hadn't seriously considered the army as a prospective threat at this stage. Most of it was stationed in Scion's overseas territories.

"I'm all for going after Senshield, but if we bait the beast, we have to be prepared for one hell of a bite," Maria said, "and that bite might well include a certain Hildred Vance, Grand Commander of the Republic of Scion and authority maximum of ScionIDE."

Tom muttered some choice words.

Vance . . . I had heard that name before.

"Vance," Glym said. "She spearheaded the invasion of Bulgaria."

"That's the one. The mastermind behind Ireland *and* the Balkans." Maria blew out a fine mist of smoke. "She may well be sponsoring Senshield's expansion. For military use."

Eliza's knee bounced. "What does it mean if she comes here?"

Maria drew on her cigarette again, eyes closed. "It means," she said, "that we will be fighting one of the most intelligent and ruthless strategists alive. One who is used to dismantling cell-based rebel groups."

There was a long silence. Our movement wasn't strong enough to deal with the army yet.

"Well," I said finally, "whether or not it *is* linked to Vance—"

I stopped when Warden appeared in the doorway, wearing his heavy black overcoat. The commanders observed him with apprehension, taking in the ice-blue irises, the statuesque build.

"Apologies for my lateness, Underqueen," he said.

The color of his eyes betrayed the reason for it—he had stopped to feed.

"Where's Terebell?"

"She is engaged tonight."

I was aware of his every movement as he took the seat beside Glym. His eyes were unnerving, reminding me of exactly what he had to do to survive, but I couldn't resent him for it. For his sake, I briefly explained again about the hidden scanners and the threat they posed.

"We could use your advice," I said, "if we're going to have any chance of disabling Senshield. You were close to the Sargas. What do you know about it? About what powers it?"

"Knowing the Sargas, the core is likely a form of ethereal technology, which harnesses the energy created by spirits," Warden said.

Tom raised his eyebrows. "Technology that uses spirits? I've never heard of such a thing."

"Even most Rephaim know precious little about it. The Sargas are the only family to have spliced the energy of the æther with human machinery. Many of my kind consider it obscene," Warden said. "Unfortunately, I do not know the workings of Senshield's core."

I nodded slowly. "Do you think it might be in the Archon?"

"I will ask our double agent if he has any idea, but I imagine that if it was, he would already have told us."

Alsafi Sualocin, the Ranthen's most valuable spy in the Archon. I had known him in the colony as Nashira's brutal and loyal guard. It had been a shock to discover that he was Ranthen, working in secret to undermine her.

"Although we do not know the location of the core, this may be the time to consider something we do know about the scanners." Warden glanced around the table. "As you are all aware, Senshield can currently only detect the first three orders of clairvoyance. Hard as they have tried, Scion has been unable to tune it to detect the higher four."

Maria tilted her head. "How do they do this . . . tuning, exactly?"

"No one knows, but I have long suspected that exposure to aura is involved. It would be logical for Senshield to recognize what it has already encountered." He paused. "It is possible that any of you could be used to improve its ability to detect aura."

That was all we needed. If walking on the streets could not only get us arrested, but potentially increase Senshield's power, then going into hiding had to remain an option, even if we only used it as a last resort.

"On the subject of the core—do you think it can be easily replaced?" I said. "If we destroyed it, would they just build another?"

"Unlikely," Warden said. "Not being a Sargas, I am no expert in ethereal technology—but I know it is complex, volatile, and delicate. If you destroyed the existing core, I imagine it would take them many years to return it to its current operational state."

I could hear in his voice that this was educated guesswork, but it was something to go on, at least.

"Something else to bear in mind," he said, "is that an improved Senshield will pose a great danger to the Night Vigilance Division. If it can be adjusted to detect all seven orders, there will no need for sighted clairvoyant officers. They will be redundant, and would consequently be . . . disposed of by Scion in the same way as other unnaturals." He looked at me. "Some of them may well be willing to help you imperil the core."

"Absolutely not," Glym harrumphed. "The syndicate does not work with Vigiles."

I had always thought Glym was a bit of a prankster, like Tom, but I had learned that he was quite the disciplinarian. He was taking the revolution seriously, at least, which was more than I could say for some of the Unnatural Assembly.

"If you do not extend the hand of friendship," Warden said, "the night Vigiles will be eliminated."

"Good," Glym said.

"They *are* traitors." Eliza pulled at one of her ringlets. "They chose to work for Scion."

She received an approving look from Glym for this observation. It was a good one.

"Warden makes a salient point." Maria shrugged. "They're potential recruits. Why waste them?"

"It would only be a temporary alliance," I said to Warden. "Once Senshield is down, there's no risk to their jobs."

"A temporary alliance may be all that is needed."

There was silence while I mulled it over. I could listen to counsel all I liked, but in the end, this would be my call. I was beginning to understand why my predecessor, Hector, had been able to abuse his power to such an extent: syndicate leaders were handed a lot of it. The voyants in this organization bowed before strength, and in the scrimmage, I had proven mine. That didn't make me an expert in starting revolutions.

My instinct had always been to steer well clear of Vigiles, but what they could offer might be worth the flak I would get for giving them a chance. It would also drain numbers from Scion's ranks.

"It's something to bear in mind," I concluded. "If we find ourselves in a situation where help from the Vigiles would be vital to our success, we'll reconsider the matter. Until then, I don't think we should risk approaching them." Everyone seemed satisfied by the response. "For now, we need to decide on a course of immediate action. Dani, I want you to do your utmost to find out what Senshield's core is—and *where* it is, more importantly. That's our number-one priority."

"Hang on a second." Tom gestured to Danica. "Doesn't the White Binder know that you work for Scion? And you're still happy to work there?"

"Yep," Danica said.

Nick looked troubled. "It's strange, but he doesn't seem to have given her away. I don't trust him, so I left, but if he hasn't said anything after three weeks—"

He trailed off.

"Warden has already checked with the Ranthen's double agent," I explained. "As far as we can tell, Dani isn't being monitored. He'll let us know if the situation changes."

Tom's brow relaxed out of its frown.

"While we work out how to disable Senshield, I want all of you to inform your mime-lords and mime-queens of the threat of these hidden scanners, as a matter of urgency," I continued. "I want them sending reports to you about any they encounter. We need to work out which kinds of places have been targeted and keep the syndicate aware. I'll have Grub Street distribute maps of all the known locations." I tapped the table. "We also need to deal with the few who still support the White Binder. Bring them to heel."

"They will forget any lingering fondness for him when I-4 has a new leader," Glym said.

"No one has declared themselves to me."

"They think Jaxon's coming back," Eliza said. "They're all too scared to take his place."

Of course. Even now Jaxon was gone, his shadow still lay across the citadel, as it had for decades.

Usually, the only way to change the leader of a section was if the current one was killed, and if no mollisher came forward to claim the title. There would be a power struggle within the section before someone declared themselves to the Unnatural Assembly.

I didn't know if Jaxon had chosen a new mollisher before he left, and in truth, I didn't care. I also didn't want chaos while the syndicate tried to work out who was the best replacement.

"One of you must have a candidate in mind. I'd like you to encourage them to present themselves at the trial tomorrow. So we can put an end to this." I stood. "I'll send orders within a day."

With murmurs of "goodnight," the commanders left the hideout. As Nick and Eliza went to secure the building, I cleared away the papers.

Warden was the last to stand. For the first time in weeks, we were alone together. I kept my head down as he stepped toward the doorway.

"Are you leaving?"

"I must," he said. "To speak with Terebell about what you have learned."

I couldn't stomach this atmosphere between us. The golden cord—the fragile link that had connected our spirits for several months—was supposed to tell me what he was thinking, what he was feeling, but all I sensed was an echo chamber for the void inside me.

"You must remove Jaxon's remaining supporters, Paige." He had stopped. "It is Terebell's desire. Fail to do this, and you risk dissatisfying her."

"You just heard me—"

"I was not referring to his supporters in general. You know which two I mean."

Zeke and Nadine. I glanced at him from behind my hair. "Have you told Terebell that I haven't evicted them from I-4?"

"Not yet."

"But you will."

"I may have no choice. She will ask."

"And you'll tell her."

"You seem exasperated."

"Do I really, Warden?"

"Yes."

I rubbed the bridge of my nose. "Terebell is obsessed with the tiny minority who support Jaxon," I explained, calmer. "She needs to stop. I know she hates him—I know it's personal for her, and for you—but having to think about it is distracting me from things we *need* to focus on, like Senshield."

"She views your unwillingness to replace him as a sign that you are secretly loyal to your old mime-lord. That you await his return. Your refusal to expel Zeke and Nadine will only increase her suspicion."

"Oh, for goodness' sake—" I shrugged on my jacket. "I'll deal with it. Give me a few days."

"You have delayed the matter because of Nick's feelings for Zeke."

"You might know Terebell's mind, Warden, but don't presume you have any insight into mine."

He fell silent, but his eyes burned.

Heat fanned across my face. Before I could say anything more, I snatched up my bag and headed for the door.

"You may think me subservient to the Ranthen. Perhaps my respect for duty disappoints you," he said. I stopped. "Terebell is my sovereign-elect. I owe her my service and my allegiance—but do not think me some mindless instrument of her will. I remind you that I am my own master. I remind you that I have defied the Ranthen. And still do."

"I know," I said.

"You do not believe me."

A long breath escaped me. "I don't know what I believe anymore."

Warden's gaze darted across my features before he lightly touched the underside of my jaw, lifting my face. My heart thumped as I looked him in the eye.

The contact awakened something that had lain dormant for weeks, since the night before the scrimmage. As we watched each other, linked by the barest touch of his fingertips, I didn't know what I wanted to do; what I wanted *him* to do. Leave me. Talk to me. Stay with me.

My hands moved as if by instinct—smoothing up to the rounds of his shoulders, settling at the nape of his neck. His palms stroked down the length of my back. I searched him the way I might search a map for a path I had known long ago, chasing the familiar, learning what I had forgotten. When our foreheads met, my dreamscape danced with the flames he always set there.

We were quiet for a while. My fingers found the hollow of his throat, where his pulse tolled—and I wondered, as I had before, why an immortal being had need of a heartbeat. I willed it to calm me, but it only made my own run faster. His hands rasped through my curls; I felt his breath flit over them, felt warmth race and rise beneath my skin. When I couldn't stand the separation anymore, I wound an arm around his neck and closed what space was left between us.

It was lighting a fire after days in the rain. I pressed my mouth to his, feverishly seeking a connection, and he answered in kind. I tasted wine first, a hint of oak, then him.

The strain of staying away from him had almost snapped me in half. Now I was cradled to his chest, I had thought that strain would ease, but I only wanted him to hold me tighter, closer. We kissed with a hunger that was almost a hurt, an ache deepened by weeks apart. I felt for the door handle, found no bolt or key to protect us from discovery—but I couldn't stop. I needed this.

His lips unlocked mine. Our auras intertwined, the way they always did. My heart pounded at the thought of Terebell or one of the other Ranthen walking in; the uneasy alliance being torn apart. "Warden," I breathed, and he stopped at once—but now I had him back, I couldn't bring myself to end this. I brought him back to me, his hands back to my waist. As I caught my breath, his lips grazed over the scar on my jaw and turned my skin as delicate as paper. Gently, he opened the top of my jacket and kissed my throat, brushing over the pendant that rested between my collarbones. A low sound escaped me as a shiver worked its way down my body.

I only sensed the dreamscape when it was far too close. With a jolt, I broke away from Warden and threw myself into the nearest chair. Maria strode in a moment later.

"Forgot my coat. Still here, Warden?"

He inclined his head. "Paige and I had a private matter to discuss."

"Ah." She grabbed her coat from the back of a chair. "Paige, sweet, you look . . . feverish."

"I do feel a little warmer than usual," I said.

"You should see Nick about it." Maria looked between us. "Well, don't let me keep you."

She slung her coat over her shoulder and left.

Warden stayed where he was. My blood was hot and restless in my veins. I felt tender all over, like his touch had stripped off armor I hadn't known was there. There was no one else close, no one else coming.

"I almost forgot about the hazards of being in your company," I said, trying to sound light.

"Hm."

Our eyes met briefly. I wanted, needed, to trust that this was real—but I was frozen by the reminder of the danger, and by the memory of Jaxon, that mocking laughter in his eyes. *Arcturus Mesarthim is nothing but her lure. Her bait. And you, my darling—you fell for it.*

"I should . . . get some sleep." I stood. "It's Ivy's trial tomorrow."

Her trial for being part of the gray market; for helping the Rag and Bone Man sell voyants into slavery.

"You will come to the right decision," Warden said.

He knew, somehow, that I wasn't sure what to do with her. "Is Terebell sending someone to witness the trial?"

"Errai."

Great. Errai was about as friendly as a punch in the mouth. "Do not give me that look," Warden said softly.

"I'm not giving you a look. I *love* Errai." My smile faded almost as soon as it appeared. "Warden, I—never mind. Goodnight."

"Goodnight, little dreamer."

The other three didn't ask why I had taken so long to join them. Nick knew about Warden, and I had a feeling Eliza suspected. I sometimes caught her looking between me and Warden, eyes astir with curiosity.

We set off into the blizzard. As we fought our way through the wind, I tried not to think about what had just happened. Maria had come so close to seeing the truth, and while I doubted she would have gone to Terebell, she wouldn't have been able to resist telling at least one of the other commanders. Our secret could have been out. No matter how much of a weight off my shoulders it had been to be close to him again, it was just too dangerous.

But I missed talking to him. I missed just being near him. I wanted him—but what I wanted might be an illusion. It had seemed so much simpler before I had become Underqueen.

When we passed a pharmacy at the end of a line of shops, Eliza stopped dead. Nick and I turned to look at her.

"It's okay," Nick said gently. "Come on. We'll keep away from—"

"Everything?"

"You'll be fine."

Eliza hesitated before pressing on. We walked on either side of her, as if our auras could shield hers.

We never stayed long in our safe houses, but my favorite was the neglected terrace in Limehouse we arrived at now, which overlooked the marina. Once we were locked in, Danica went up to her room while Eliza retired to the cellar. I made myself a cup of broth.

One side of my head was beginning to throb. I didn't know what we would do if we couldn't get rid of Senshield. The location of its core must be top-secret, and the information that would help us was unlikely to seep into Danica's department. It was hard not to give way to dread.

When I drank the broth, I hardly tasted it. I was exhausted from doubting everyone and everything. Suddenly I realized that no matter what I did next, I had to resolve my relationship with Warden. For three weeks, Jaxon's words had sunk hooks in my mind and spread a poison of misgiving there. I had started to question Warden's motives. To wonder if he was manipulating me on behalf of the Ranthen. They had chosen me to lead their rebellion, but they needed me to be willing. Pliable. Perhaps they thought a love-struck human, overcome by emotion, would be easy to influence. Perhaps they thought that if I wanted Warden badly enough, I would do anything for him.

Now paranoia swelled at the back of my mind every time I caught sight of him. More than likely, this was just what Jaxon wanted; more than likely, I was playing into my enemies' hands.

There was only one thing to do about it. I could come right out and tell Warden what Jaxon had accused him of. Give him a chance to defend himself. It would take courage, but I wanted to be able to trust him.

In the parlor, Nick was sitting before the fire, leafing through reports. I could smell the wine on him from the doorway. He had always refused to touch alcohol until recently.

"You miss him," I said quietly, dropping on to the couch beside him.

His voice was hoarse when he replied: "I miss him every minute. I . . . keep expecting to look up and see him."

My conscience had stopped me throwing Zeke and Nadine out of Seven Dials. I had sent them an offer of shelter, regardless of their feelings toward me, but received no reply.

"Have you told Warden what Jaxon said to you?"

I glanced at him. "How did you know?"

"Same way you knew I was thinking about Zeke. I always know."

We exchanged tired smiles. "If only Rephaim were so easy to read," I said, sinking back into the couch. "No. I haven't told him."

"Don't leave it too long. You never know when the chance to say things will just . . . disappear."

We sat together in the gloom. He stared into the fire like he was trying to find something. I'd always thought I knew Nick Nygård's face, down to the dent in his chin and the way his nose dipped slightly at the end. I had memorized how his pale eyebrows sloped upward, giving him a look of perpetual concern. But when the light found him at this angle, I sensed the unfamiliar.

"I keep imagining what Jaxon might have planned for him," he said. "Look how badly Jax hurt you in the scrimmage."

"Zeke isn't trying to steal his crown."

He grunted, but I couldn't blame him for worrying.

"Terebell wants them gone, doesn't she?" When I didn't answer, he shook his head. "Why haven't you done it?"

"Because I'm not heartless."

"You can't risk appearing to have sympathy for your old gang. Jaxon's gang." His voice was softened, on the cusp of slurring. "Do what you have to do. Don't take my burdens on to your shoulders, *sötnos*."

"I'll always have room on my shoulders for you."

Nick smiled at that and draped an arm around me. I didn't know what I would have done without him on my side. If he had chosen Jaxon, his friend of eleven years, instead of me.

Neither of us wanted to be alone with our thoughts, so we stayed there, resting in front of the fire. Night had become a perilous time, when I sifted endlessly through paths I could or should have taken. I could have shot Jaxon in the Archon. I could have cut his throat in the scrimmage. I should have had the mettle to tell Warden the truth. I should have done better, done more, done otherwise.

I needed to consider what had been said at the gathering, but I was so worn out that I lost my train of thought and drifted back to sleep when I tried. Every time I woke, I thought Warden was with me. Every time I woke, there was less light in the fire.

Arcturus Mesarthim is nothing but her lure. Her bait. I remembered that long night when our dream-forms had touched for the first time. How easy it had been to laugh when I danced with him in the music hall.

And you, my darling—you fell for it. It felt real when he held me, but I might have been too trusting. Did he do it all on Terebell's orders?

Was I a fool?

At some point Nick fell asleep, and then it was his words on my mind. *I keep imagining what Jaxon might have planned for him.*

I imagined, too. And so imagination became my nemesis; my mind created monsters out of nothing. I imagined how Scion would punish us if they found our nests of sedition. How Nashira would hurt those I loved if she ever got her hands on them.

I had sent people to check the apartment complex where my father lived. They had reported Vigiles outside. He might be in there, under house arrest. Or perhaps they were waiting for me.

A burner phone was in my jacket pocket. Carefully, I slid it free.

I hit the first key, lighting up the screen. My thumb hovered over the next number. Before I could press it, I replaced the burner and put my head down. Even if he was alive, Scion would have tapped his phone line. He had to forget me. I had to forget him. That was how it had to be.

3

Judgment

"The Underqueen's court recognizes Divya Jacob, a chiromancer of the second order, also known as the Jacobite. Miss Jacob, you stand accused of a most abominable crime: assisting the Rag and Bone Man and his network in the capture and sale of clairvoyants to Scion, resulting in their detainment, enslavement, and, in some cases, death, in the penal colony of Sheol I. Tell us how you plead, and the æther will determine the truth of your words."

The Pearl Queen, leading the proceedings, was standing on the stage in a suit of black velvet and pearl embroidery, a dainty pillbox hat perched on her hair. Seated behind her, I was also dressed more elegantly than usual: a shirt of ivory silk with long, belled sleeves; beautifully cut trousers; and a sleeveless jacket of crimson velvet, richly embroidered with gold roses and fleur-de-lis. My curls were arranged in a sort of ordered chaos around my shoulders, and my face was painted. I felt like a doll on display.

Ivy stood before the stage in a moth-eaten blazer. One sleeve hung empty where her left arm had been folded into a sling. The other was bound to a brazier by a length of lapis-blue ribbon.

"Guilty."

Minty Wolfson's pen scratched in the record book, which looked as if no one had touched it in a century. Apparently, all syndicate trials had to be chronicled for posterity.

"Miss Jacob, please tell the court about your involvement with the Rag and Bone Man."

I hadn't seen Ivy since the scrimmage. She had been staying in a cell north of the river, kept in her own room to prevent revenge attacks. She had gained a little weight, and her hair, which had been shorn off in the colony, was coming through soft and dark.

With composure, she repeated the story she had told at the scrimmage of how she had been taken in by the Rag and Bone Man, made his mollisher, and ordered to send him talented voyants for "employment."

He had vanished after the scrimmage, as had all his allies. Ivy was the loose end. Our last clue as to where he might have gone.

We were in another neglected building, a music hall near Whitechapel that had been closed down for showing free-world films. The high commanders and my mollishers were fanned out in seats on either side of mine, listening to Ivy describe the voyants' suspicious disappearances. Errai Sarin stood in a corner at the back of the hall, while above us, in the gallery, were eighteen observers, who would report the trial to the rest of the syndicate.

"You observed that these voyants were disappearing, and you became worried. You tipped off Cutmouth, who was mollisher supreme at the time," the Pearl Queen said, in her clear, fluting voice. "You must have thought her trustworthy. Will you describe your relationship?"

"We were close. Once," Ivy said. "There was a time when we couldn't have lived without each other."

"You were lovers."

"Objection, Pearl Queen," Minty piped up. "That is your insinuation. The accused has no obligation to—"

"I don't mind," Ivy said. "She fell in love with Hector when she joined the Underbodies, but yes. Before that, we were lovers."

Minty shot the Pearl Queen an exasperated look, but noted down the information.

They combed through Cutmouth's investigation of the Camden Catacombs, the imprisoned voyants she had found there, and her report to Haymarket Hector. How Hector's lust for easy gold had persuaded him to join the gray market instead of suppressing it.

My gaze flitted toward Errai, who wore all black, as the Ranthen usually did. I knew he had little patience for syndicate politics, but I felt his scrutiny. He would report every word of the trial to Terebell.

"Were you aware that the missing voyants were being sold to Scion for your master's financial gain?"

"No," Ivy said.

Minty continued scribbling as if her hand would drop off.

"Who else was involved in the ring?"

"The Abbess, obviously. Faceless, the Bully-Rook, the Wicked Lady, the Winter Queen, Jenny Greenteeth, and Bloody Knuckles. Some of their mollishers, too. Not Halfpenny," she added. "He didn't know about it."

A small relief. Halfpenny was well-liked, and I hadn't wanted the evidence to force me into banishing him.

"At any point," the Pearl Queen said, "did you see the White Binder, mime-lord of I-4, associate with the group?"

"No."

Murmurs from the gallery. I gripped the arms of my chair.

It was tough to believe that Jaxon, if he had been associated with the Sargas for two decades, hadn't known about the gray market.

The Pearl Queen hesitated. "To your knowledge, did any members of the gray market have dealings with the White Binder or speak of his involvement?"

"I wish I could say 'yes,'" Ivy said darkly, "but I won't lie. It's possible he could have been involved without my—"

"No speculation, please," Glym rumbled. "This is the Underqueen's court, not one of your palm-readings."

She dropped her head. "For what it's worth," she said, her voice a notch higher, "I'm sorry. I should have done more. And earlier."

"Yes, you should have, vile augur," someone bellowed down at her. "You earned your name!"

"Scum!"

"Enough," I barked at the gallery.

Some of them shut up at once, but after a lull of about five seconds, the abuse started again. The deep-seated hatred toward vile augurs was never going to disappear in a matter of weeks. Another one of Jaxon's glorious contributions to the syndicate.

"Silence." The Pearl Queen banged her gavel. "We will have *no* disruptions from the observers!"

Hearing the story for a second time had made it no less disturbing; I wondered how much more there was to it than Ivy knew. From the sound of her account, she had only been a pawn.

"Now," the Pearl Queen said, "the æther must determine if any lie has passed the accused's lips."

Ognena Maria sprang down from the stage. She was a pyromancer, a kind of common augur that used fire to reach the æther. She struck a match and tossed it into the brazier, which was already piled with wood and kindling. Once a fire was burning, she said, "Come here, Ivy."

Ivy shuffled toward the brazier. Maria placed a hand on her good shoulder and drew her closer.

The æther quavered. Maria leaned so close to the flames that sweat dewed her upper lip.

"I can't see a great deal," she said, "but the fire is bright and strong, and it was easy to light. Her words were truthful."

She patted Ivy's arm before leaving her. Ivy shied away from the flames.

"The high commanders will now cast votes," the Pearl Queen said. "Guilty?"

She raised her own hand. A moment passed before Maria, Tom and Glym also held up theirs. Nick, Eliza, Wynn, and Minty kept theirs down.

"Underqueen, the deciding vote is yours."

Ivy kept her head down. Scars were hatched into the smooth brown of her skin. The marks of Rephaite cruelty. I remembered her so clearly from the first night in the colony, with her electric-blue hair and trembling hands. She had been the most fearful of all of us, this woman who had helped sell other voyants into slavery; who had been with me in the darkest time; who had survived to cast a light on the corruption.

I had also spent years grafting for a mime-lord whose true nature I hadn't known. I had carried out his orders without question. If I could work in the service of a traitor and end up as Underqueen, I had no right to deprive Ivy of a place in the syndicate for committing the same crime.

"I have to find you guilty."

She didn't flinch, but Wynn did.

"Under my predecessors, a crime like this would have been met with the death sentence," I continued. Wynn stood with a screech of chair legs. "However . . . these are exceptional circumstances. Even if you *had* known about the trade with Scion and sought help, you would have found none from the Unnatural Assembly. I also believe your crimes have been punished enough by your time spent in the penal colony of Sheol I."

The scrabbling started again. Tom leaned toward me.

"Underqueen," he whispered, "the lass was brave to come forward, but to have *no* sentence—"

"We must send a message that sympathy with the gray market will not go unpunished," Glym said. "Clemency will show contempt for your voyants' suffering."

"I wouldna go that far," Tom said, knitting his brows, "but a soft hand, aye. And you canna afford that."

"Hector would cut people's throats if he was in the wrong mood," I pointed out. "In comparison to that, any punishment I give will seem weak. I can't win this."

Glym glanced at Ivy. "Death would be too extreme," he said, "but she must serve as an example. Too much mercy, and your voyants will assume that mercy will be your answer to all crimes."

Wynn's gaze was boring into me. Whatever I did next would estrange someone, whether on the stage or in the gallery.

"I'd like you to be a part of the Mime Order, Ivy." My voice resounded through the hall. "I'm giving you another chance."

She looked up. Maria cursed under her breath, while Glym shook his head and angry mutters rolled from above.

"Underqueen." The Pearl Queen was quivering. "This is an extraordinary decision. For the sake of the gallery, may I confirm that you intend to give no punishment at all?"

"Her confession was instrumental to exposing the gray market." The fury on the observers' faces was already making me doubt my decision, but I couldn't backpedal now. "Without it, the Abbess and the Rag and Bone Man might still have influence over this citadel."

Shouts rained from the gallery. "Who cares?" I heard them say. "This bitch sold us out!"

"Hang her!"

"Let her rot!"

These people were the ones who would spread news of my first trial as Underqueen. If they went away dissatisfied, the syndicate would soon rally against my verdict.

"Ognena Maria deems her honest," I said, "and I see no reason why the accused would continue to have loyalty to the Rag and Bone Man—but there is a risk. She'll remain under house arrest at one of our buildings, or in the company of a commander, for the next three months, at the very least."

The commanders seemed placated, if disgruntled, but the observers still clamored for a harsher judgment. Ivy, who looked close to passing out, recovered enough to give me a small nod.

"The trial is over." The Pearl Queen banged down her gavel. "Divya Jacob, the æther absolves you!"

A roar of outrage went up. Glym sliced the ribbon that bound Ivy to the brazier. As it fell, Wynn hurried down from the stage, enveloped Ivy in her arms, and guided her away from the bellowing in the gallery.

She had the right idea. Best to lie low while things cooled off. I was about to get up when a newcomer strode from the sidelines, ending the commotion.

I recognized that easy gait, the heeled leather boots, the hooded cloak of forest-green silk. This could only be Jack Hickathrift, the new mime-lord of III-1, who was usually shadowed by a doting admirer or ten. He had taken over from the Bully-Rook after the scrimmage. Maria clicked her fingers to get my attention and pointed to herself.

Jack Hickathrift bowed low. "My queen." His voice was soft and honey-smooth. "With your permission."

"Please," I said.

He lifted an elegant hand and lowered his hood, revealing a smooth, chiseled face, white as milk. Thick dark-red hair coiled over one eye. The visible one was clear hazel, more amber than green, framed by long lashes. He smiled at the gallery.

"Thank you, Underqueen. I saw you for the first time at the scrimmage, knowing you only by reputation before it," he said. "I thought I would be struck down by your beauty."

My face must have said it all. Nobody had commented on my beauty in my life, least of all in such a public setting.

"You *were* struck down, if I recall correctly," I said, almost without thinking, "though I doubt my beauty was to blame."

Laughter echoed through the music hall. Jack Hickathrift grinned, showing that his perfect teeth had survived the scrimmage intact. He carried an array of bruises from the fray, like all the survivors, and it was common knowledge that he was now missing his left thumb.

"Jack, you scoundrel," Maria said, in mock outrage. "Are you trying to seduce your way into the Underqueen's good graces?"

"I would *never* do such a thing, Maria." He placed a hand over his heart. "I'm far too in love with you."

"I should think so, too."

Wolf-whistles rang from the gallery. I sat up straighter and threw on a coolly amused expression.

"Tell me, Jack," I said, "did you open your meetings with Haymarket Hector in this manner?"

"I might have done," he shot back, unperturbed, "had Hector been as exquisitely lovely as you, my queen."

He had caught me by surprise at first, but now I relaxed into my chair, trying not to smile at his cheek. This was nothing but a performance, a power play. "For the sake of your ego, I'll allow you to believe your flattery has worked," I said in a jaded tone. "What do you want?"

More laughter. Jack winked.

"I have come here to declare myself before any other can," he said. "I wish to rule I-4."

"You already rule a section."

"I have greater ambitions."

"And what makes you think you can control such a key territory?"

"I survived the scrimmage in one piece. That should prove my strength. I ran III-1 for six years while the Bully-Rook soaked himself in drink and debauchery." He dropped on to one knee. "I will be devoted to you, Underqueen, and to your cause. I slew the Knife-Grinder in the Rose Ring to stop him striking you, knowing you would make us a good leader."

He had done that. I didn't believe for a moment that it had been to protect me, but he also hadn't attempted to fight me—not even when his mime-lord had been out for my blood.

"Let me prove myself to you," Jack said. "Let me bring I-4 under control."

I looked to my commanders. Maria nodded vigorously, Tom gave me a thumbs-up and a grin, while the others appeared ambivalent, which I took to mean they had no serious objections. I would be left with the problem of who would rule the section he left behind, but I-4 needed a leader far more.

"Very well," I said. "Jack Hickathrift, I declare you mime-lord of I Cohort, Section 4, there to reign unchallenged for as long as the æther allows." Applause thundered from the gallery. "Who is your chosen mollisher?"

"I might have to get back to you on that front, my queen. Not that I haven't considered it," he added, "but I have, ah, a few options to contemplate."

"Hm." I arched an eyebrow. "I'm sure you have."

Jack went straight to I-4 to assess how it had changed since Jaxon had left. At my behest, he promised to give Zeke and Nadine an ultimatum: relocate to a Mime Order safe house and join us, or fend for themselves. Either way, they had to leave I-4. I had delayed the inevitable for too long.

Several of my commanders had eyed me with displeasure as I stepped down from the stage. Over the last few weeks, I had learned that the Pearl Queen and Glym had the toughest approaches, and the utmost respect for tradition. Tom had a softer heart than he let on. Maria was fairly unpredictable, while Minty tended to do whatever she thought would cause the least offense. Wynn tried to protect the vulnerable.

Usually, they produced a good mix of views, but only Wynn, out of all of them, had shown real approval of my verdict on Ivy. She had taken my hands and promised that my kindness would not go unnoticed.

Elsewhere, kindness was not seen as an admirable quality. News would be spreading through the syndicate now, warning my voyants that their Underqueen was weak.

It couldn't be helped. Ivy had been through too much for one lifetime.

Back at the hideout, Nick set about making supper while I tended to my injuries from the scrimmage. The slash along my side was itching as it healed, driving me spare. It blazed from underarm to hip in a trail of pink and red. A token from my old mentor. Warden had far deeper scars, his punishment for betraying the Sargas—punishment he would never have received if not for Jaxon. I had never seen them, but I had felt the wales of scar tissue that laddered his back. Jaxon Hall had left his mark on all our lives.

One day soon, he would pay for it.

I faced the mirror and sluiced the greasepaint off. Beneath it, my dark lips looked bruised, and my eyes were steeped in shadow. Weeks of living on broth and coffee had urged my bones against my skin.

This was not a leader's face.

As I turned, something glinted in the mirror. I touched a finger to the necklace I wore, the one Warden had given me, with the pendant shaped like wings. It had saved my life after the scrimmage.

Downstairs, Nick was at the wood-burning stove, stirring whatever was steaming in the pan, and Eliza was head down over a piece of paper. As soon as I entered, she looked up.

"You," she said darkly, "are one lucky woman."

"Yes, I often reflect on how very *lucky* I am. Lucky enough to be detained by Scion and taken to a prison city for half a year. Let's bottle my good luck and sell it. We'll make a killing."

She pursed her lips. "Jack bloody Hickathrift flirted with you, and you're not even a tiny bit hot and bothered. Do you know how long I've been in love with that man?"

I sat down. "You're welcome to offer yourself as his mollisher, but I think you'll have to queue."

"No, thank you. I'd want to be his one and only lover," she purred.

I raised a faint smile at that, but it faded when I saw what she was working on. A list, she told me, of everywhere the new Senshield had been reported as being used. Cash machines, phone boxes, Scion taxis, and the doorways to oxygen bars, hospitals, schools, supermarkets and homeless shelters had all been reported as potential death-traps. No voyant could go about the citadel for long without encountering something on that list.

Nick handed us each a mug of tea and a bowl of barley soup. The wan light from the oil lamp made his face look pinched.

"There's discontent in the syndicate, Paige," he said. "They're not pleased with the outcome of the trial."

Surprise, surprise. "Hector gave them a taste for bloodshed," I said, "but they don't have a right to it. Ivy needs protection, not more punishment."

"I'm glad you weren't hard on her. I'm just warning you that some of your voyants aren't."

"Well, if they could handle Hector's decisions, and heaven knows they were piss-poor, then they can handle mine."

"Your piss-poor decisions?"

I gave him a look. He smiled a little, the first genuine smile I had seen from him in days.

"Sorry."

"You're not funny. When's Dani back from her shift?"

"About one," Eliza said.

I checked my watch. Half past eleven. The chances that Danica had been able to find anything out were minuscule, but she was the only one of us on the inside; and if anyone had the willpower to find out where the power source of Senshield was, it was Danica Panić.

"Errai spoke to me after the trial," Nick said. "He said that Terebell wants to see you tonight—at midnight. I'll go with you."

"Great. I can't wait to be belittled for an hour." Among other things, I would have to ask Terebell for money. "Do you have the accounts?"

Eliza unearthed the ledger and pushed it across the table. I scanned our streams of income. More like trickles, except for Terebell's lump sums and syndicate tax. The only reason Hector had been effortlessly rich, I imagined, was because the gray market had raked in so much extra income.

I closed the ledger. "Let's make ourselves presentable. Eliza, can you check that the Unnatural Assembly have all handed over their taxes on the syndicate rent?"

"Sure."

Terebell wanted to meet us at an abandoned building in Wapping. One of our local moto drivers picked us up from the corner of the street. We didn't get far before the screens across the citadel came to life; an announcement from our glorious Inquisitor was imminent. I called for the driver to stop, and the moto swerved to the side of the road. Across the river, Frank Weaver appeared on the transmission screens.

"*Denizens of the citadel, this is your Inquisitor,*" he said. "*For security reasons, due to a threat that cannot be discussed at this time, a curfew will be imposed in the capital from eight P.M. to five A.M., effective immediately. Scion employees on night duty are exempt but must be in uniform and in possession of ID when they travel. We ask you to trust that this extraordinary measure has been put in place for your protection, and we thank you for your co-operation. There is no safer place than Scion.*"

He vanished, replaced by the anchor on a white background. All I could hear was my breath inside the helmet.

"We're going back," Nick said. "Now."

As the moto drove away, I could see people on the streets pointing at the screens, anger etched on to their faces, but they gradually began to trickle back to their homes.

Our driver returned us to the docklands. My mind whirred like an overworked machine, drilling out every potential consequence of this announcement. Coupled with the hidden scanners, a curfew could do a lot of damage to the Mime Order's ability to function.

45

Eliza looked up from the taxes as we burst in.

"What's happening?"

"Official curfew," I said. "Eight to five."

"Oh, no. They can't have—" She bolted the window. "Aren't you supposed to be with the Ranthen?"

"It'll have to wait."

We set about locking down the building, with Nick doing the final check. Once he had secured the doors, he joined us at the table, where the enormity of the setback kept us all silent, lost in our own thoughts.

As we sat there, I tried to devise ways we could work around a curfew. It would be especially difficult if Jaxon was advising Scion on our movements. He was aware of most secret routes, at least in the central cohort. I could send out scouts to seek new tunnels, paths he had never found, but there wouldn't be many. His knowledge of London, built up over decades, was far greater than mine.

The best way to get about would be through tunnels *under* the citadel, but the mudlarks and toshers would stop us from going too far underground. They were homeless Londoners, mostly amaurotic, who made their living by scouring the lost rivers, drains and sewers of the citadel for trinkets and artifacts to sell. They claimed most of the tunnels under London as their territory, treating the manholes on the streets as their doors, and there was an unspoken agreement that it was their realm. No syndies would venture down there.

Someone or something hammered on the front door. We snapped to our feet, spools quavering around us.

"Vigiles." Nick was already moving. "We can—"

"Wait," I said.

Two more crashes. Those weren't human dreamscapes outside. Slowly, I released my clutch of spirits.

"No. It's the Ranthen."

Nick swore.

I stepped across the hallway and cracked the door open, leaving it on its chain. Chartreuse eyes flashed—just before the chain tore away from the frame and the door was flung wide.

The impact caught me hard in the shoulder. I had barely absorbed it before a gloved hand seized the front of my jacket and pinned me against a wall, making Eliza and Nick shout out in protest. For the first time since the scrimmage, my spirit snapped out like an elastic band—only to ping off an armored dreamscape and slam back into my body. Red-hot pain streaked up one side of my face and burrowed deep into my temple.

"I see now," Terebell Sheratan said, "that you were a poor investment, dreamwalker."

Several of the Ranthen followed her into the hallway. Nick pointed his pistol at her hand. "Let go of her. Now."

The ache was swelling uncontrollably. I tried not to let it show, but my eyes watered.

"If you were a Rephaite, I might excuse your lack of punctuality, but you are mortal," Terebell said. I made myself look her in the face. "Every second chips away at your lifeline. Do not try to convince me that you cannot tell the time."

"There's a curfew," Nick said. "In effect as of tonight. We had to turn back."

"It does not supersede your duty to meet me."

"You're being unreasonable, Terebell."

"Rich words for a human," Pleione said. "Your species is the very definition of *unreasonable*."

A storm of black flecks crossed my vision. As the iron grip tightened enough to leave bruises, I saw Warden come through the door. He hadn't observed the scene for more than a second before the light in his eyes ignited, and he barked at Terebell in Gloss. She threw me, like I was nothing but a sack of flour, toward Nick, who caught me by the arms.

"How dare you?" Eliza said hotly. "Don't you think she took enough punishment in the Rose Ring?"

"You will not speak to the sovereign-elect in that manner," Pleione said.

Eliza bristled. I pressed my hands to my forehead, willing the pain to disappear.

"Paige," Nick murmured. "Are you okay?"

"I'm fine."

"Do not affect illness," Errai sneered.

"Please, Errai, just give it a rest," I forced out.

"What did you say to me, human?"

"Stop, all of you," Warden said curtly. "This is not the time for petty disagreements. The curfew, along with Senshield, will seriously restrict syndicate activity if we cannot produce a solution." He closed the door. "The Mime Order is a union of both Ranthen and syndicate. We pose a far greater threat to them together than divided. If you cannot see that, then you are all fools."

There was a tense silence. Every hair on my arms stood on end; I had never heard Warden speak with so much authority in the presence of the other Ranthen. Nick lowered his gun.

"If everyone's cooled off," I said, "perhaps we could begin the meeting."

Terebell swept into the parlor, shadowed by the Ranthen. "Bring wine, dreamwalker."

A flush crept into my face.

"Paige, I'll get it," Nick said, but I was already heading for the kitchen.

She wanted a reaction; I wasn't going to give her the pleasure. I reached under the sink and plucked out one of the bottles she had left with us for safekeeping. I filled five glasses, sloshing red wine all over the counter, and took a few gulps from the bottle.

The alcohol scorched down my throat. In the hallway, Nick lurked like a security guard outside the parlor door. As we made to go in, Lucida Sargas barred our way.

"Alone," she said.

Nick frowned. "What?"

"The sovereign-elect wishes to speak to the Underqueen alone."

Eliza squared up to her. No easy feat, as she was a foot shorter. "We're Paige's mollishers. What she needs to know, we need to know."

"Not if you want your revolution funded."

"Don't you mean *our* revolution?"

I touched Eliza's shoulder. "Don't worry. I'll tell you everything later."

Neither of them looked happy, but they stepped away. I held out a glass to Lucida.

"I don't partake," she said, with something that vaguely resembled a smile. "I escaped the scarring, you see. You will find that they become ill-tempered without wine to numb the pain."

"And I thought it was just their personalities," I said.

She tilted her head. "Is that a 'joke'?"

"Not really."

Balancing the tray of glasses on my hip, I opened the parlor door. My head continued to hammer, and I swung on my feet. Usually, I had a chance to warm up before dreamwalking, but the shock of Terebell's aura on mine had caused an involuntary jump.

Errai stood beside the window. Pleione was lounging on the couch (she never seemed to sit, Pleione; she *lounged*), while Warden was a statue in the corner, his back against the wall. There was also a stranger among them: a female with sarx of pure silver and a bald head, like Errai.

Terebell, who stood beside the fire with her usual ramrod posture, took a glass of wine and raised it to her lips.

"Arcturus," she said, "you ought to drink."

"I will endure."

I put down the tray a little too hard. Terebell emptied half her glass at a draught.

"This is Mira Sarin," she said. "Another of our Ranthen-kith. She has been in exile for many years."

I inclined my head briefly to the stranger, a gesture she returned. Her primrose eyes, which were wide-spaced and large, like Errai's, betrayed her recent feed on a sensor.

"I summoned you to inform you that we are leaving," Terebell said.

"Leaving for how long?"

"For as long as necessary."

"Why?"

She approached the nearest window. The other Ranthen watched her. "We have found pockets of Rephaim who are willing to confront the Sargas with us, both here and in the Netherworld," she said. "They have asked us to prove our commitment to rekindling war before they will take up our cause. To do that, we must persuade an influential member of each of the six families to join us—preferably a Warden, past or present, given that they are the head of the family."

"Those who went into exile after the war may be sympathetic to our cause," Lucida said, "so we will approach them first. To begin with, we will seek out Adhara, the banished Warden of the Sarin, who was rumored to have Ranthen sympathies. Mira knows her location in the Netherworld."

I picked up a glass of wine for myself. "What if it doesn't work?"

"It must," Warden said.

Reassuring.

"It would help our cause if we could convince our potential allies that you are a loyal and capable associate," Terebell went on. "Many of our old friends are disturbed by the notion that we must work with humans, given what happened . . . last time." Her face turned colder.

"How would you like me to prove my loyalty?"

"Show us that you are willing to do whatever is necessary for this movement to make progress." She handed back her empty glass. "I understand that you have finally replaced the arch-traitor. I assume you have also expelled the remaining members of the Seven Seals, in accordance with my orders."

"Jaxon's gone, Terebell. He's not coming back," I said, hoping she would miss the evasion. "We need to focus on deactivating Senshield, or else we will find ourselves unable to leave the house, let alone start a revolution. Warden said it might be powered by ethereal technology, and we have a list of places where we know the scanners have been hidden, but we need more information." When none of them volunteered any, I pursed my lips. "Lucida, you're a Sargas. You *must* know something. Do you know why they're rolling Senshield out earlier than they originally projected? What could be powering it?"

Lucida turned away. I doubted she liked to remember which family she belonged to.

"Only the blood-sovereigns know how Senshield works," she said. "Perhaps the Grand Commander, too. As to why they are increasing the number of scanners, I can only suppose that they wish to tighten their control of the capital to counter the threat of the Mime Order."

"Senshield's core may be powered by an ethereal battery: a poltergeist inside a physical casing," Mira Sarin said. Her voice was soft and cool. "The battery contains and channels the energy the poltergeist creates. Something to consider."

Ethereal batteries. I remembered them from the colony. The Rephaim had used them to power fences that no voyant could touch without receiving a shock, or to create padlocks that couldn't be opened until the poltergeist was banished. I tried not to think of Sebastian Pearce, whose spirit had been used inside one.

"Say it *is* an ethereal battery," I said. "How could it be destroyed? By banishing the spirit—or destroying the physical casing?"

"Either, I should think."

"Desecration," Errai muttered. "Grafting ethereal energy with human machinery . . . the Sargas continue to disgrace us."

"What's wrong with human machinery?" I said.

"It poisons the air and taints the ground. Much of it feeds on fuel made of putrefying matter. It is inelegant and destructive. To force it into a union with the energy of the æther is profane."

When he put it like that, I had no argument.

"Errai speaks the truth. I approve of your proposal to rid us of the Senshield core," Terebell said to me, "but I expect you to seek my authorization before you take any action."

"Can I expect to authorize your decisions, too?"

"Not until you fund my decisions, as I fund yours." She turned her back on me. "You can contact me through Lucida, who will stay behind. The rest of the Ranthen will join me in the Netherworld."

"Warden is our best instructor," I said. "I'd prefer him to stay with the Mime Order. And I'll need him to help me if I'm planning to dreamwalk again."

"I am putting an end to your training with Arcturus."

I looked at him, then at her back. "What?"

"You heard me. If you require assistance with your ability, you may ask Lucida."

Warden kept his gaze on the fire. I was conscious of my pulse, sharp and crystal-clear. "Lucida doesn't train voyants."

"True," Lucida said airily, "but one has to start somewhere."

"I don't know how my recruits will respond to you. I do know how they'll respond to Warden—that they respect him—and I need that certainty. Things are about to get a lot harder for them, with the curfew and Senshield." I turned to him. "Warden, we need you here."

My tone was even, but it sounded all too much like an entreaty. Terebell looked at him.

"I must do as the sovereign-elect commands," Warden finally said.

Such a small number of words to drain so much strength from me. One look, and he belonged to her.

To Terebellum Sheratan, you are a convenient pawn in an age-old game. I had stifled that voice for a few days, but now it filled my ears. *Arcturus Mesarthim is nothing but her lure. Her bait.*

I should never have gone to him. He was content to see me embarrassed in front of them, to undermine my orders in front of Terebell, who was supposed to be my equal in leadership, and to abandon me to handle the Mime Order alone while they left on Rephaite business.

"We leave in four nights' time," Terebell said.

She strode away. Errai opened the door for her, and the Ranthen filed into the hallway, leaving a chill in their wake. Mira Sarin gave me a fleeting look, one I couldn't read, before she left.

Only Warden stayed. He shut the door, so the two of us were ensconced in shadows.

"Your nose is bleeding."

"I know."

I hadn't known, but I could taste the blood now.

"Errai reported to us that you chose a new mime-lord for I-4, but that the ceremony was casual and your own attitude through-out was flippant and . . . improper." He looked at me. "Would you disagree?"

I should have known that Errai would find something to criticize. "With all due respect, none of you know the first thing about syndicate politics. That's why you needed a human associate."

"How did you choose the replacement?"

"The usual way. The first candidate to declare themselves to the Unnatural Assembly is considered for the position. In this case, Jack Hickathrift declared himself to me, and I deemed him suitable." I lifted my chin. "Look, the reason Errai called it 'improper' is because Jack made his entrance by flirting with me."

Warden's eyes darkened. "I trust your judgment. Errai did not."

"If Terebell wanted me to cross-examine every candidate, she should have said." I tried to sound calm, but my insides were boiling. "I know the syndicate. I know how it works."

"That is not her only qualm. If she discovers that you have not expelled the Seals—"

A flare of resentment burned up my patience. "I'm getting really sick of pandering to Terebell's obsession with Jaxon. I'm sorry if publicly betraying him wasn't enough to show that I've rejected him. Or if risking my neck in the colony didn't already prove my loyalty to the cause. Maybe I was the wrong human to choose." I held out a glass. "Some wine, blood-consort?"

"Stop, Paige."

"You never manage to tell Terebell to *stop*, do you?" It took effort to keep my voice down. Every word quaked. "You fucking coward. She belittles me, treats me as her waitron, and you do nothing. Not only that, but you make me look like a fool for all the Ranthen to see. At least I know where I stand now."

Warden lowered his head, so we were at eye level. A quiver ran across my back.

"If I speak for you too loudly," he said, his voice rumbling from the depths of his chest, "you will pay a price far higher than wounded pride. If you suppose that I enjoy upholding the façade, you are mistaken."

His voice was no sharper than before, but there was a simmer in the softness.

"I wouldn't know what you enjoy." I stared him out. "I need you here. You know what we're facing."

"If I press the matter, she may not allow me to see you at all."

"Don't pretend you care, Arcturus. I know what you are."

His eyes narrowed slightly. "What I am," he said, an invitation in his tone. An invitation to explain.

The accusation was on the tip of my tongue. I was ready to parrot every word of Jaxon's warning.

Lure. Bait.

"If all you're going to do is tell me how much you *can't* do, then go," I said finally. "Deal with your Rephaite business. Go to the Netherworld and let me run this organization my own way."

Warden watched me. I didn't break his gaze, but my heartbeat was rough.

"I cannot tell what you think you know of me," he said, "but remember this, Paige. The Sargas want you isolated. They want the Mime Order divided. They mean to sow the seeds of mistrust. Do not prove to them that human and Rephaite cannot join forces."

"That was an order," I said.

My shoulders were rigid. There was a short silence before Warden said, "As you command, Underqueen."

When he stepped away, our auras untwined. I sank on to a chair and held my head between my hands.

4

Vance

November 29, 2059

Novembertide

I was losing him. Little by little, he was slipping out of reach. We were the bridge between the syndicate and the Ranthen, and unless I could somehow preserve our relationship, everything we had built together would begin to crumble. The Mime Order would not survive.

Danica came in at just past one in the morning, clad in the boiler suit she wore to work, and stamped the snow from her steel-capped boots. I was nursing my headache by the fire, raw-eyed.

"Give me some good news," I said.

"All right. I think I've found Senshield's core."

I sat up. "You're serious?"

"I don't really like to joke. Do you want the bad news, too?"

I was still reeling from the good news. "Go on."

"It's underground. And the facility it's stored in is probably going to be guarded to the hilt."

I went to wake the others; they needed to hear this. A few minutes later, the four of us were sitting in the parlor. Danica unlaced her boots and took her hair down from its bun.

"Right. My idiot supervisor has some role in the installation of the large scanners. Today he got news that the core needs maintenance for the first time in a year. I wasn't chosen to work on it," she said, answering the question that had jumped on to my tongue, "but I overheard him talking to the group that's been selected. I know where it is."

"Go on," I said.

"There's a warehouse in II-1, which sits on top of the facility." I wasn't too familiar with the section, but I could find people who were. "A trapdoor inside leads to the core. While they're carrying out the maintenance, the alarms will be deactivated. But there's a catch: the work will only take a day, and they're doing it immediately. Today."

"And you still have no idea what the core *is*?" Nick said.

Danica shrugged. "My guess is that it's something volatile, which is why it's kept underground. Still," she said, "now might be your chance to find out. If you can go today, while there are engineers working on it, Paige could possess one of them and see for herself."

"Dani," I said, "you are brilliant."

"Frankly, anyone could have eavesdropped on the morons in my department." She wiped her oily hands on her boiler suit. "I'm going to bed. I've got an early shift tomorrow."

The stairs creaked as she trudged upstairs, leaving us to contemplate our options.

"We have to make a quick decision here," I said. "The core might not need maintenance again for years. This could be our only chance."

Nick rubbed his chin. "I don't know. This seems too convenient."

"They don't know about Dani. The double agent would have told Warden if there was even a whiff of suspicion."

We had a lead. I needed to quash the exhilaration and think clearly, because if we did this, it would be our first direct assault on Scion's infrastructure. It was risky, but it could be decisive for the Mime Order.

"I want Maria and Glym to help us decide." I stood. "Jimmy O'Goblin, too—it's his section. Make sure he's sober."

Eliza took her phone from her pocket. In the kitchen, I dug out a detailed map of the section.

"Paige," Nick said, "should we get permission from the Ranthen?"

I hesitated.

"No," I said. "If Terebell is ever going to trust me, I need to start proving I can make decisions on my own and that they can pay off. She doesn't ask me for permission when she decides to do something."

"She could cut off the money if something goes wrong."

"If it does, I'll call her bluff. She needs us, too." I reached for my gloves. "Let's go."

We met the others in the dockworkers' slum. Maria and Glym waited in an empty shack with an ashen Jimmy O'Goblin, mime-lord of II-1. His hair was a mess and he smelled faintly of alcohol, as always, but at least he was upright.

"Afternoon, Underqueen," he rasped.

"It's two A.M., Jimmy." My breath came white and thick. "We think we've found Senshield's core."

"That was quick," Maria said.

I imparted to them what Danica had told us. Glym listened with a frown.

"We need to go for it," Maria said immediately. "It's worth the risk if we can kill this thing."

"I agree," I said. "Jimmy, it's in your section. Have you ever noticed any Scion activity around this warehouse?"

"Not usually," Jimmy said, rubbing his eyes, "but since yesterday there's been swarms of Gillies all around it."

I spread the map on the floor between us, and Jimmy described what we were up against. The warehouse, as well as being guarded, was surrounded by a fence, with only one entrance gate. It was too high to scale, the links too tough to cut, and approaching in the open was likely to get us shot.

"But there is one option, Underqueen." Jimmy flashed his wine-stained teeth at me. "One way you could get inside without being seen . . . but you'd have to be mad to try it."

I leaned closer. "Let's assume I'm mad."

"All right. You know how bleedin' cold it's been lately?" I nodded. "There's an old service ladder behind the warehouse that leads down to the Thames. Normally you wouldn't be able to access it, but with the weather being what it is, the river's frozen in that area."

I raised my eyebrows. "You're not suggesting we walk *across* the ice?"

"That is a truly mad idea," Maria said, looking impressed.

"Mad," I admitted, "but not bad."

My hands pressed together, so I felt my pulse in my fingertips. I had fought to be Underqueen so I could make decisions, but now I had to trust myself to make the right ones.

"The ladder comes up near a hidden gap under the fence. Local junkies dug said gap a few years ago," Jimmy said. A grubby finger tapped the site on the map. "I can send you a local who knows exactly where it is. Mad it may be, but I reckon it's the only way you'll get in undetected."

I was swiftly becoming convinced by the idea. "There should be back-to-back Novembertide celebrations; Weaver will have to allow a reprieve from curfew. That will give us plenty of cover," I said. Everyone nodded. "I say we send in a small, armed team— today. We get into the underground facility, locate this 'core,' do as much damage to it as we can—or at the very least find out what the hell it is—and get out of there."

"When you say *we* . . ." Eliza started.

"I'll lead the team."

Glances were exchanged. "Paige," Nick said, "remember what we agreed. About your staying behind the frontlines."

"Dani said I could possess one of the engineers to see inside the facility. I'm better up close."

"You haven't used your gift that way since the scrimmage. If you insist on going, you should ask Warden to train with you today."

"He can't."

"Why not?"

I gave him a look that said we would talk about it later. His mouth thinned, but he didn't push it.

"I need to show that I'm not just using the syndicate as cannon fodder," I said. "That I'm happy to put my neck on the line, too. I'm not going to do this like Hector did, from a safe distance. I can't."

He didn't argue anymore.

Next up was the matter of who should come with me. Maria volunteered first. Three summoners, so we could call for help from powerful spirits if we needed them, and three other voyants who had taken Warden's advanced training. A local seer, sent by Jimmy, would help us get in and out.

"I'm coming, too," Nick said.

Eliza nodded. "And me. We're your mollishers."

"I can't risk both of you being captured." I considered them. "Eliza, I think an oracle would be more useful for this mission. I'm taking Nick. You can coordinate our exit."

She folded her arms tightly.

"Right," she said.

She had been waiting weeks for a chance to shine, but I couldn't put her in the team for the sake of it.

"I will ask Tom to check for portents, Underqueen," Glym said. "The æther may be able to offer us guidance."

"And I'll try to source some explosives in the meantime," Maria said. "I owe Vance a little pain."

Morning came, swathed in mist. The sun shone like a silver coin behind its gauze of cloud, and all over London, people were singing parlor songs around their pianos and wishing each other Happy Novembertide. Images of the first Grand Inquisitor, James Ramsay MacDonald, were draped from every building. The Grand Inquisitor of France had been expected for the celebrations, but according to ScionEye he had been taken ill. I would have expected Ménard to be on his deathbed before he missed such an event, especially as his visit had been so heavily publicized, but there was no time to dwell on it.

As the day passed, we prepared for our assignment. Glym, as the commander in charge of recruitment, assembled and briefed an infiltration team. A backup group would be ready to cause a distraction if anything went wrong. I worked out the route across the ice, based on what Jimmy had told us.

Nick was right about my gift. I might need it, and I was badly out of form. I swallowed my pride and tried the golden cord—no answer.

If that was how Warden wanted to play, so be it. Even if he had come, he might have gone straight to Terebell with our plans. I spent a while practicing alone, trying to push my spirit into birds. It was late in the day when I successfully possessed a magpie and amused Nick by having the bird perch on his head. Less amusing was the headache that followed.

We set off as dusk fell. The team gathered in the district of Vauxhall, in a closed-down oxygen bar built into the railway arches. Nick handed out second-hand Scion boiler suits.

"Everything washes up in Old Spitalfields," he said, when I shot him a quizzical look. As I zipped mine up, Maria strode in.

"The bastard trader had sold out of explosives," she groused. "Because ScionIDE has never been stationed in London, there's not much military-grade weaponry around."

I tucked the legs of my suit into my boots. "Is that how it works?"

"It's the one advantage. If you have krigs nearby, you can steal their equipment. That, in turn, allows rebels to become militarized. You cannibalize one army to create another."

"Krigs?"

She waved a hand. "Soldiers. It's from the Swedish word for war, *krig*. As Nick will know, there are a lot of them in Sweden." She grabbed a boiler suit. "We'll just have to use fire."

Fire was her numen. It would do. We had one other pyromancer with us—the redhead from the Mill cell—along with two capnomancers. They might be able to use smoke to mask us if we needed a quick escape. Jimmy had sent us two augurs, who refused to show their faces, and a waifish seer with the violet-tinged lips of an aster user. Three summoners had also volunteered; the tallest introduced himself as Driscoll. As agreed, none of them said which cells they were from.

We waited to hear from Tom, who had checked with our scrying squad that there were no ill omens in the æther, but after an hour, we decided we couldn't delay any longer. I gathered the infiltration team around me.

"This is the Mime Order's first move against Scion," I told them. "We're basing this plan on intelligence stolen from them, which appears to be reliable, but I can't guarantee that the mission will be successful. Or that something won't go wrong." I looked at each face in turn. "None of you are under any obligation to do this. Just say now, and you can return to your cells."

The silence stretched on for some time. The seer gnawed her nails, but said nothing.

"We're all with you, Underqueen," one of the capnomancers said.

The rest of the team agreed.

It was utterly dark by the time Nick led the way from the safe house. Eliza sat down on a dusty barstool and watched us go. "We'll be back soon," I said.

She smiled. "Go get 'em."

A perishing wind howled by the river. There was no moonlight to betray us as we approached the ice, taking care to erase the footprints we left in the snow.

The silhouette of the warehouse loomed over the Thames. It was exceptionally rare for the river to freeze to this extent—according to the records, it hadn't happened in over a century. Most of the surface was clearly too brittle to stand on, and the middle was as swift-flowing as ever, but a vein of thicker ice jutted into the water and ran right past the warehouse, providing us with our entrance. When I tested it, a tissue of silver threads surrounded my boot. Nick hovered nearby as I risked the other foot.

"On a scale of one to lethal," I said, so only he could hear, "how dangerous is this?"

"I think we've done more dangerous things. Maybe." He joined me on the ice and rocked his weight. "It's a plan, Paige. That's more than any of your predecessors have had."

I turned to the rest of the party. "Here we go," I said. "Spread out as much as possible."

We set off. Every step ratcheted up my pulse. The cold alone could finish us off if the ice were to give way, and if it didn't, the current certainly would. This was an ancient artery of London that we walked on, one that had never been known for its mercy.

The crossing took time. Nobody dared walk too quickly. The seer, who knew the area best, led the way, delicately stepping around the thinnest patches. After what felt like days, I spotted the rusted ladder, almost hanging off the wall and missing several rungs. As we inched closer to it, Driscoll hit a weak spot in the ice. One booted foot splashed through it, into the river, before one of the others grabbed him. The impact quivered right the way along the ice shelf and turned us into statues. When it became clear that we weren't about to meet a watery end, the other summoners hurried to get Driscoll to his feet.

When we were in the shadow of the warehouse, Nick gave the seer a boost onto the ladder, causing a web of cracks to materialize. I went next. The relief at being off the ice was almost enough to tame my nerves.

At the top, the seer squatted beside the fence. When she found the shallow ditch that had been dug beneath it, which was well-hidden by a sheet of corrugated metal, she clawed her way under.

Save for a pair of security guards at the main gate, which was chained shut, the place was deserted. I scanned our surroundings. The warehouse was bordered by a desolate expanse of concrete, where a SciORE vehicle, presumably containing whatever was needed to repair the core, was parked and empty. Footprints littered the snow around it. I reached for the æther, letting my sixth sense wash everything else away.

"There's nothing below us," I said to Nick. "No dreamscapes. No activity."

"If you can't sense anything below ground, maybe it's because there's nothing here to sense." He swallowed. "This might be a dud lead."

"Warden and Mira both said the core was probably some kind of ethereal technology," I said. "Scion could have concealed the facility in the æther. Stopped voyants being able to sense it."

"Right."

Beneath my boiler suit, my skin was clammy. The seer beckoned from the other side of the fence. One by one, we scrambled into the gap and burrowed through the snow on the other side, soaking our hands and knees. The redhead and the capnomancers would stand guard outside while the rest of us went in to investigate.

We broke into a run, keeping low. When we got within spitting distance of the warehouse, I motioned to the redhead to join us and told her to wait for Nick to flash his flashlight from the doorway. One flash, and she could send in the other team members. Two flashes meant that they should get back on to the ice and out of the district.

The seer led us toward the warehouse. As she slipped inside, snowflakes drifted from above.

Our footfalls echoed as we stole into the building. As far as I could tell, it was unguarded. A draft wafted across my face, carrying the stale odor of cigarettes and purple aster. Beside me, Nick switched on his flashlight. As we walked down the length of the warehouse, Maria's boot snagged on a glass bottle marked LAUDANUM, making us all start. It rolled through threads of dried aster and unsettled several plastic bags.

The seer stopped at the end of the hall. The wall in front of her was taken up by a vast transmission screen.

"Look," I said.

Nick dipped the beam of his flashlight. There, sunk into the floor in front of the screen, was the trapdoor.

"Paige, be careful," he said, but I was already crouching beside it. Finding no evidence of a lock or bolt, I grasped the handle and heaved it up.

Beneath it, there was nothing but concrete.

Nothing.

I stared at the place where a ladder should have been. It took moments for panic to engulf me. Not a trap*door*. Just a trap. I turned to warn the team, to tell them to run—but before I could get out a single word, I found myself wrenched upside-down, high above the others' heads, pinioned in a net. Blood surged through my body. My heartbeat rustled in my ears and throbbed behind my eyes, drowning out the shouts from below. The mesh around me was so tight that my elbows dug into my waist and my knees were jammed together. Gritting my teeth, I pushed my fingers toward the knife inside my jacket, but moving my limbs was close to agony.

As I struggled, the transmission screen switched on, and a white background cast light into the hall, stretching out our shadows with it. When my eyes adjusted to the glare, I found myself looking at the face of a woman.

She had to be seventy, at the least. Lines branched through her sun-beaten skin. A pinched nose, a seam of a mouth, and a head of white hair, combed back from a raw-boned face. The eyes in that face chilled me to the heart of my being. They were black as pits.

"*Welcome*," she said. "*Paige Mahoney.*"

Her voice was calm, crisp as pressed linen. The feeling it induced in me was like nothing I had ever experienced. Detachment, numbness, followed by a rush of dread through my bones. The way she said my name was oddly thorough, each syllable sharply enunciated, as if she was determined not to let a single part of it escape her tongue.

Maria seemed hypnotized by the screen. I could see the whites of her eyes around the iris.

"*I am Hildred Vance, Grand Commander of the Republic of Scion England. As you are no doubt coming to realize, this is not where Senshield's core is located.*" She didn't blink once. "*Such information would never be allowed to fall into the wrong hands. There is no . . . underground facility.*" Nick stepped back, knocking a piece of rubble across the floor. "*This building is derelict. Tonight, however, it has been prepared for your arrival.*"

She had trapped me. Lured me here like an animal for the abattoir. I thrashed wildly inside the net.

"*As we speak, your unique radiesthesic signature is being used to recalibrate Senshield. Thank you for assisting us.*"

A white light beamed down from above, blinding me.

The æther trembled violently, pushing shudder after shudder through my body. Something skirted the edge of my dreamscape. Sweat seeped into my boiler suit as I hung there, powerless, feeling my pulse twang in my fingers and the backs of my knees and my aura flexing like a fist, reaching out and recoiling by turns. I curled around myself as if my clothes had been stripped away, suddenly certain that something was *looking* at me.

A soft *beep* sounded in the building. Warmth ran from my nose and over my forehead.

"Shoot it, Nick," Maria barked. "Paige, don't move!"

"*You have already made a grave error by coming here. Do not make the mistake of resisting detainment.*" Vance seemed to watch us, soullessly, from the screen. "*Your allies may be shown clemency if you allow my soldiers to take you peacefully into Inquisitorial custody.*"

My mouth rang with the taste of blood. The air was too thin, weak, and spidery in my lungs. I was going to black out.

Danica. Vance must know about her, somehow. Jaxon must have told her without Alsafi's knowledge.

A bullet snapped the hook that held the net, and the pressure on my head abruptly released. I barely had time to gasp before I plummeted—only to have my fall broken by Nick. He let out a faint "oof" before his knees buckled and we both slammed into the concrete, hard enough to knock the breath from my lungs and awaken all my old hurts from the scrimmage. Maria was already dragging me up by the back of my jacket.

"*There can be no escape for those who defy the anchor,*" Vance said. "*No mercy for those who pervert the natural order.*"

Chased by her voice, we sprinted toward the open doors of the warehouse, back into the snow. Floodlights were blazing at us from beyond the fence, exposing our position, but there were still no dreamscapes closing in—at least, I thought there weren't until my sixth sense vibrated, and I looked up sharply. Eight shadows bloomed in the sky above us.

It took me a moment to understand. Maria got there first.

"Paratroopers." Her hands viced my arms. "Run. Back to the ice!"

The seer was already tearing back to the fence. The redhead was waiting on the other side, shouting "Underqueen." As Driscoll and his summoners ran after her, the first of the paratroopers landed on the warehouse roof. Maria fired her pistol at the next one, nicking the parachute.

"Paige," Nick roared, "come on!"

Gunfire hailed from above. I watched as one of the summoners went down. When the second was hit, a choke of "no" escaped me. Maria pulled me down before shoving me toward Nick.

"Go," she snarled.

She flattened herself against the warehouse and reloaded her gun. I ran like I never thought I could, keeping Nick in my sights. They were amaurotic soldiers, immune to spools, but I could cover Maria. My spirit wasn't like those of the dead. I could access any mind.

Heat flared behind me. I threw a glance over my shoulder to see a string of burning spirits flying toward one of the paratroopers, who had landed on the snow close to Maria. Before the soldier could take aim, the parachute was consumed by fire. Maria ducked behind the warehouse door. Beside the two dead summoners, Driscoll stood his ground and joined in with the gunfire. The redhead scrambled back under the fence to help him. When I was near the end of the concrete field, Nick ran out to meet me and grabbed my hand.

Everything about the trap had been perfect. Vance had known, somehow, that I would sense deception if her people were waiting nearby to arrest us; that dropping assassins in would keep them off my radar until it was too late.

The snow was misted with red where the summoners had fallen. "Maria," I shouted. "Get over here, now!"

She let off one more shot before she struck out across the snow. Nick fired at the soldier on the roof, but they had armor.

I squirmed through the gap beneath the fence, scraping my hip, and hauled myself out of the ditch on the other side. Somewhere behind me, Maria let out a cry. Instinctively, I threw my spirit toward the paratroopers. I was aware of tearing through a dreamscape and lashing one of them into the æther, of hearing a rifle clatter to the ground and seeing letters stamped on its side, but my silver cord whiplashed me back to my own body before I could take full control. Through tears of pain, I saw another soldier approaching from the left, his rifle aimed at the redhead, who was focused on driving off the one who had shot Maria. I tried to dreamwalk again, but it was as if two rusted gears were grinding in my skull. Locked in place.

A spray of bullets tore through her midriff.

Nick dragged Maria underneath the fence and swung her arm around his neck. Her face was white. Driscoll just about got through before the soldiers opened fire again, and we scrambled down the ladder.

A helicopter dropped from above us and shone its light across the river, on to the ice. A voice from inside told me to surrender immediately. I thought of the three dead voyants I had left behind, and with a surge of breathless fury, I turned to face it, throwing my arms wide. I motioned for Driscoll to move behind me and made sure I was shielding Nick and Maria. My hair whipped across my face as we gathered together.

"Paige," Nick said, "what are you doing?"

"They won't shoot." I kept my eyes on the helicopter. "They can't risk breaking the ice."

"Why would they care?"

"Because they have to take me alive."

Nashira wanted my spirit. If I was swept away by the river, she would never get it.

We were deadlocked. The helicopter hovered above the water. It might not shoot while we were here, but it would follow us until we had to leave the ice—and as soon as we were on solid ground, it would incapacitate me and kill the others. Sickening fear took hold as I pictured it. We might have eluded Vance for an instant, but she had us in a corner.

I smelled something acrid on the wind and risked a look. Smoke was billowing across the ice, carried by a stream of spirits. The capnomancers—they were giving us cover. I took a step back, forcing the others into the cloud. The helicopter banked before it disappeared from view.

The cover might not last. We started moving, faster than on our journey here. Too fast. As we neared the end of the ice a deep fracture coursed beneath my boots and forked off in all directions. There was no time to think. I drove my shoulder into Driscoll, shunting him away from the splintering, just before my foothold collapsed.

For a blinding instant, I thought I was dead.

Somehow I resisted gulping as I plunged into the blackness of the Thames. I went down like a diving bell. Blades impaled my ribs and sliced along my legs, carved me open from navel to throat, but I didn't let the water in.

As I sank deeper, my lungs bayed for oxygen. I was burning without heat, on fire without flame. I wrestled with the river, screaming inside as it scourged my skin, but my limbs had turned to stone.

London does not forget a traitor, Jaxon whispered from my memory. *It will suck you down, O my lovely. Into the tunnels and the plague pits. Into its dark heart, where all the traitors' bodies sink.*

Damn him to hell. I would not die like this. Some deep reserve of strength glowed within me, warming my arms enough to get them moving. My hands tore my boiler suit open; I freed myself from it and clawed through the foul-tasting water, but the darkness was disorienting. Frantic, I kicked and scrabbled, not knowing which way was up, until my head shattered the surface. White breath plumed from my mouth. A vicious current roared against my body, carrying me faster than my shocked muscles could fight.

I was too far from the bank. I was too cold to swim.

I wasn't going to make it out of this alive.

My head slipped under again. The river took hold of my body with greed.

That was when I felt an aura against mine, and an arm scooping me back to the surface.

My hands found a pair of shoulders. As I gasped and coughed, I found myself faced with Rephaite eyes.

"Warden—"

"Hold on to me."

My arms were so weak, but I managed to sling them around his neck. The muscles of his back shifted fluidly as he swam through the Thames, cutting through it as if the current was just a whisper against him.

I must have blacked out for an instant—then I was aware of being lifted from the river, of water cascading from my body. When the night air hit me, it was as if frost was covering my lungs, creeping around my ribs, glazing every inch of skin. His familiar voice said, "Paige, breathe," and I did. Warden pressed me tightly to his chest, against heat, and wrapped his coat around me, sheltering me from the snow. I shivered uncontrollably.

He stayed with me until the others found their way to us. Nick kept me awake on the drive to safety, talking to me, asking me questions. I swung between moments of painful clarity, like seeing Driscoll break down in tears, and darker periods, when all I could do was try to keep warm.

We retreated to a safe house in the central cohort. As soon as we were inside, Nick went into doctor mode. On his orders, I took off what was left of my clothing and washed in tepid water. Once he had checked me for open wounds and ordered me to tell him straight away if I felt sick or feverish, I was swaddled in thick blankets and left to dry. I made myself a warm cocoon and focused on preserving heat.

I dozed for a while. When I lifted my head, there was a Rephaite in an armchair opposite me, gazing into a fire. For a chilling instant, I thought I was in Magdalen—that we were in the penal colony again, in that tower, still uncertain of each other.

"Warden."

His hair was damp. "Paige."

Prickles raced along my skin. I pushed myself up on my elbows.

"Dani," I said, my voice thick.

"She is safe. It will never be traced back to her," he said. "False information about the warehouse was planted across several Scion departments. They have no way of knowing which was the leak."

Vance must have only suspected that I had someone on the inside, then. As I pinched the blankets closer, I noticed that my hands were steady. I wanted them to shake. I wanted to feel myself responding to my voyants' lives being pointlessly lost, but I had seen death on the screens since I was a child: it was drip-fed to us every week, breathed into our homes, our lives steeped in it, until blood was as commonplace a thing as coffee—and after all I had seen in the last few months, it seemed I had stopped being able to react. I hated Scion for it.

"You got me out of the water."

"Yes," Warden said. "Tom told me about your endeavor. The scrying squad had sensed a portent, but the Glym Lord was intercepted by a scanner on his way to stop you. Pleione and I followed you in his stead."

"Is Glym all right?"

"Yes. He escaped."

We had come so close to death. If not for Warden, the river would have swallowed me.

"Thank you," I said quietly. "For coming for me."

With a curt nod, Warden rested his elbows on the arms of the chair and clasped his leather-clad hands in front of him, a posture he had often adopted in the colony. I waited for the axe to fall.

"Terebell is angry that I went without permission," I said, when the silence had gone on for too long. "Isn't she?"

He reached for the table in front of us and held out a steaming mug.

"Drink this," he said. "Dr. Nygård says your core temperature is still lower than it should be."

"I don't care about my temperature."

"Then you are a fool."

The mug stayed where it was. I took it and drank a little of the saloop, if only to make him talk.

"Tell me, Paige," he said, "are you deliberately trying to provoke Terebell?"

A question, not an accusation. "Of course not."

"You chose to go without her permission. You ignored her order to seek her approval before taking any major decision."

"I had a lead," I said, "and a limited amount of time to follow it." Another slight nod.

"While you were sleeping," he said, after another silence, "your commanders received a report. Around an hour after your excursion to the warehouse, a polyglot was detained. According to the witness, her aura activated the large Senshield scanner at Paddington station."

I hadn't thought it was possible to turn any colder. Polyglots were from the fourth order. An order that Senshield shouldn't be able to detect.

"Of course, this could be nothing but hearsay. But if it is true," Warden said, "then the technology has improved dramatically."

A dull flutter started low down in my stomach. I tightened my fingers around the mug.

"It's not hearsay." My voice was hoarse. "Vance told me herself that she . . . trapped me, to use me to recalibrate Senshield." I wet my lips. "I'm seventh-order. How—how could exposure to *me* help it detect the fourth?"

"I do not know enough of the technology to guess."

"She said something about my . . . radiesthesic signature." My breath quickened. "If this *is* my fault, Terebell will—" I could almost feel the color draining from my face. "We can't lose your support. Without it, the Mime Order will fall apart."

"Terebell is very unlikely to withdraw our financial support as a result of this. It is as much in her interest for the Mime Order to continue as it is in yours," he said. It didn't comfort me. "She will reserve judgment until the consequences of your actions become apparent."

"They're already apparent. I fell into a trap. I helped them improve Senshield. And I lost three people. I could have saved at least one of them if my gift had been stronger." I couldn't keep the exhaustion from my voice. "I told you I was out of practice. I called you, before we left."

"I was engaged."

"With what?"

"We were dealing with another Emite. In the suburbs."

The rigor that went through me had nothing to do with my fall through the ice. While I was fixated on Senshield, the Ranthen were trying to stop us being eaten alive. Enemies were closing in on us from all sides.

"War requires risk," Warden said. "This may yet prove to be a strategic error, but you took what precautions you could. No one knew that Hildred Vance had been recalled to the capital, or that she would lay a trap for you. Even Alsafi was unaware."

"Three voyants are still dead for nothing."

"They knew there was a chance of failure." His face was cast into shadow. "I asked Alsafi about Senshield's core. He does not know

71

its location, and as he works in the Archon, we may safely assume that it is not there."

I looked into the fire. "I will find it."

A log collapsed into the hearth.

"You should not have gone to the warehouse yourself," Warden said. "You are Underqueen. If you fall, there will be no Mime Order."

"You could always find another human."

"Not one that the syndicate would accept. There is no time for another scrimmage." He paused. "And there is no other human that I trust as I trust you."

I looked him in the face, trying to find the truth. He was offering me a chance to let him back in. Exposing a vulnerability, a break in all that Rephaite armor. This was a door I needed to open.

"I need to speak to the others about Vance," I said. "I'll . . . report to you with what we've decided. I'm sure you'd like to get back to Terebell."

Warden held my gaze, then said, "As you wish." He stood. "Goodnight, Paige."

5

Back in Time

The image of Vance's face was too fresh for me to get any more sleep. I dressed and left the fire behind, taking a blanket with me. From what I remembered of the escape, most of the voyants in the team had been returned to their cells, but Maria and Nick had stayed, as had Tom and Glym, who had met us on the way to safety. I found them in the next room, where Maria was sitting up, ladling broth into her mouth. Nick got up and crushed me to his chest.

"Paige," he said. "I tried to reach you, sweetheart. I tried. If Warden hadn't been there—"

"But he was." I patted his back. "I'm fine."

"You saved Driscoll's skin, you know," Maria said. "He would have gone under if you hadn't pushed him."

I looked her over. "Are you all right?"

"Bullet graze. I've had worse."

Trepidation stirred in my stomach. I sat down beside Nick, keeping the blanket around my shoulders.

"Warden told me about the report," I said. "That the fourth order can be detected."

"Let's not worry too soon, Underqueen," Glym said. "The mime-lord who reported it is uncertain that the captured voyant *was* a polyglot. More likely she was from one of the lower three orders."

"We need to find out quickly if it's true. If the fourth order can be detected—"

"There's no evidence of that yet," Tom soothed. "It would be . . . bad, I admit—"

"Bad?"

"All right, *very* bad, but it's just like Glym says. It'll be nothing but misinformation. Or scaremongering."

"I disagree," Maria said. I glanced at her. "I know Vance, and trust me, she wouldn't lie unless she had to. She said to Paige that she was using her to change Senshield. That means she was." She paused to draw a breath. "Paige, if this is the case, which we must assume it is, the syndicate must never know."

Silence followed her words. She was right: if they knew that my error had threatened the entire fourth order, the Unnatural Assembly would almost certainly move to depose me.

"Tell me more about Vance," I said eventually.

She interlocked her fingers on her stomach. "I'll tell you what I know of her," she said, "but she already knows everything about you."

From the way that face had looked into my soul, even through a screen, I didn't doubt it.

"Let's have a little history lesson," Maria said. "Hildred Diane Vance joined ScionIDE at the age of sixteen and served in the Highlands for five years. During that time, as Tom will remember, she helped crush several uprisings in what was then called Scotland."

Tom, who had been watching her from beneath the brim of his hat, now came into the lamplight.

"Believe it or not, I'm a wee bit younger than Vance," he said. "I remember how people whispered her name when I was a lad, even in Glasgow. Like they were scared she might be able to hear them."

"Sounds like she was very young to have so much power," I said.

"So are you," Maria pointed out.

The thought of any similarity was unsettling.

"Young Hildred's superiors noticed her appetite for slaughtering unnaturals, and they rewarded her for it. Her rise through the ranks was meteoric. She's now seventy-five, and the longest-serving member of Scion's upper echelon."

I had to wonder how close she was to the Sargas. She sounded like their sort of person.

"When Vance moved against the rebels in the Balkans, she knew the names and backgrounds of all of our leaders. She'd planted double agents among us within days of her feet touching Bulgarian soil." A shadow winged over her face. "She soon learned that my unit's commander, Rozaliya Yudina, was one of our best. She also learned that Rozaliya had once had a younger brother, who had died before the family left Russia. Somehow Vance knew that, amidst all her other suffering, this was Roza's weak spot.

"The surviving insurgents were thin on the ground when Vance set the trap. She knew that Rozaliya's death would devastate the morale of the remaining militants. So Vance's soldiers found a boy. But not just any boy. A boy who looked like Roza's lost brother. During our final stand, this ten-year-old was thrown onto the street and told to scream at Roza for help. And Roza hesitated." Her fist clenched. "The boy had been given a toy bear to hold. Inside was a plastic explosive."

The small amount of warmth in my body disappeared.

How much did Vance already know about me? My official record would give her a decent starting point. Jaxon might have told her things, if he had sunk that low. It was clear she knew at least a little about how my gift worked. And she knew I had a father.

"One reason Vance is lethal is because she doesn't underestimate her foes," Maria said. "I suspect we escaped today because she truly didn't think we'd be mad enough to take the ice."

"So we outfoxed her with our stupidity," I said.

"Exactly. But she'll remember that you took that risk." She tapped her temple. "It goes into her mental database. The more she learns about you, the better she becomes at predicting you."

This was making the other staff in the Archon seem feeble. Vance was a puppet with a brain, and that made her far more dangerous than Weaver, who did not think for himself.

"What we need to work out now," I said, "is if she's brought more than a few paratroopers with her. Are we taking on an army?"

Glym made a skeptical sound.

"No. ScionIDE won't come here," Maria said firmly. "This is the heart of the empire. Martial law has never been, and will never be, declared in London. They have to give an impression of peace in the capital, or the whole idea of empire will collapse from within."

Nick shifted closer to me. "Then why is Vance here at all?"

"To deal with Paige, most likely," Glym said. "The syndicate will go back to its old ways without her. It will no longer be a threat."

It was true. The syndicate could survive if I was captured, but it might never again be the cradle of a revolution.

"We need another lead." I rubbed my arms, which were peppered with goose bumps. "Nick, talk to Dani again. Glym, go to Paddington and establish the truth of the report—whether the fourth order really is detectable. We also need to prepare for whatever Vance is planning next, which means that all of the Unnatural Assembly have to be properly armed, for starters. Tom, I want you to negotiate a better agreement with the arms dealers."

When I got up, Maria said, "And where exactly are you going?"

"To make sure that Jack Hickathrift has evicted the remaining members of the Seven Seals." I buckled my jacket. "Best I prove to Terebell that I'm following some of her orders, if not all."

"Hildred Vance is on your trail, kid. You shouldn't be wandering off."

"If I lie low, she's already won. We might as well go to the Archon and bow to the Rephaim now." I stepped into my boots and laced them. "For the time being, we keep what happened at the warehouse between us. We'll regroup with the others at the Mill tonight."

I hadn't been back to I-4 since the scrimmage. The thought of being close to Seven Dials, at the time, had been too painful.

The commanders wanted me to take bodyguards. I refused, but agreed to have Eliza with me. As we waited beneath a streetlamp for our rickshaw to arrive, hands bunched into our pockets to keep them out of the cold, Nick emerged from the safe house.

"I want to come with you," he said.

"I need you to liaise with Dani. We have to know if she can find out anything more about Senshield, even if it's just—"

"Paige," he said, his voice thick, "please."

When I took a second look, I understood. There were crescents of shadow under his eyes.

"I know why you want to do this," I said, gentler, "but Vance is on to us, Nick. I need you focused."

"You think Zeke will make me lose focus." He shook his head. "Does that mean you're not focused, either?"

It took me a moment to recognize what he was implying. What he had just implied in front of Eliza. When it sank in, my jaw hardened. Even Nick looked shocked at himself, but it was too late: it was clear from Eliza's face that she had caught the scent of a secret.

I drifted to the corner of the street, my arms folded. I heard him say "give me a moment" before he came after me.

"Sweetheart," he said, "I'm sorry."

"No one else can know." I spoke quietly. "Nick, I trusted you when I told you about Warden. I need to be able to trust *you*, of all people. If I can't—"

"You can." He took one of my hands. "I'm sorry. I nearly lost you. I already lost Zeke. I just feel . . . I don't know. Powerless." He sighed. "It's not an excuse."

Powerless was the right word for it. It was how I had felt in the river, and in the warehouse, knowing that Vance had played me right into her hands. I was a queen at the mercy of pawns.

The rickshaw appeared at the end of the street. Nick looked wretched. I had never argued with him, not once, and I didn't want to start today.

"It's okay." I squeezed his hand. "Look, if Zeke's there, I'll be as kind as I can. And you know I'll try my best to persuade him to join us."

He hugged me close. "I know. Take this." He tucked a heat pack into my pocket. "I'll talk to Dani now."

I wrapped my hand around the heat pack as the rickshaw trundled away, but the cold was in my blood. Snow floated around us, catching in my eyelashes and the wispy curls around my temples.

"Paige," Eliza said, "what did Nick mean, when he asked if it meant you weren't focused, either?" When I failed to conjure a suitable lie in time, she nudged me in the ribs. "You'd better not have slept with Hickathrift behind my back."

"I wouldn't dare."

Eliza smiled, but it didn't quite touch her eyes. She knew I was keeping something close to my chest.

A blood-smeared sky greeted us in Covent Garden. Early morning shoppers were out in force, waiting around the stalls and outside shops for the post-Novembertide sales to begin. I smoothed my scarf over my face, watching for any hint of a military presence. I imagined the wind taking my scent right to Vance.

An alarm went off as we crossed a junction. Vigiles were wrestling a weeping augur away from an oxygen bar, cuffing her hands behind her back. We walked as quickly as possible without arousing suspicion, going in the same direction automatically. After all, we both knew where Jack Hickathrift would be. There was only one place the mime-lord of I-4 could reside if he expected to be taken seriously.

Seven Dials had been garlanded with red and white lights for Novembertide, which were being taken down. In mutual, wordless understanding, we walked past the entrance to the den, to the sundial pillar.

I laid a hand on the bone-pale stone. This had been the keystone of our chaotic world, the heart of the syndicate as we had once known it. I had stood before this pillar when Jaxon had made me his mollisher. Eliza circled it in the same way I was, as if to remind herself that it was real. Behind it, on a nearby building, a line of bleached graffiti was just about visible.

BACKSTABBERS NOT WELCOME

Amaurotic workers and shoppers were giving it nervous looks. Our underworld was invisible to the people around us, but it was dangerous to linger. Eliza blew out a breath, reached into her coat, and took out a key. A label hung from it, reading BACK DOOR in Jaxon's elaborate cursive.

We opened the courtyard gate and passed the blossom tree, which had been stripped bare by the winter. In the hallway, we stamped the snow from our boots. As Eliza stepped on to the first-floor landing, her muses flew in and swirled wildly around her aura. Pieter was particularly overjoyed, bouncing around in the æther like a firecracker.

"Guys, it's okay," she said, laughing. "Oh, I can't believe you're here—I thought Jaxon had taken you!"

I left them to get reacquainted. "Hey, Phil," I said, when he did a celebratory twirl around me. Pieter gave me a sullen sort of nudge before he returned to his beloved medium.

They couldn't come back with us. Jaxon had long since bound them to the den, and unless we could find and scour away the blood he had used to tie them here, they were trapped.

On the next floor, I paused outside the door to my old room, feeling as if I had wandered into a museum. When I set foot in it, I found it devoid of everything I had squirrelled away over the three years of my employment. My precious, lovingly curated chest of antiques and curiosities from the black market; the bookshelf full of blacklisted literature and records—all gone. Even the bed was missing. The painted stars on the ceiling were the only evidence that someone had ever lived in here.

An aura brushed against mine. I turned sharply. Jack Hickathrift was standing in the doorway, dressed in a poet shirt that was open to the waist. One hand had been on the knife at his belt, but he let go of it at once.

"Underqueen," he said, with a deep bow. "Your pardon. I thought it might be an intruder."

"I feel like one."

"I'm sure. This must be very strange for you." He opened the door wider. "Please, come through."

He led me into the adjacent room, which had been Jaxon's office. Everything was still in its rightful place. I took a seat on the edge of the chaise longue, while Jack sprawled on the couch, leaving the mime-lord's chair empty. "Do I hear another guest downstairs?" he asked, just as Eliza sidled into the room, pursued by her muses. "Ah, the famous Martyred Muse. I've heard many tales of your talent from the market." He held out a hand for hers and kissed it. "May I offer you both a drink? I found a very fine brandywine at the Garden."

Eliza sat beside him. "Sounds intriguing," she said, smiling at him.

Jack raised his eyebrows at me, but I shook my head. He observed Eliza with interest as he reached for the bottle.

"Now," he said, "what can I do for you, my queen?"

"I'd like an update on what's been happening in the section."

"Of course."

"First—has there been any sign of the White Binder?"

"None," he said. "I highly doubt I'd be alive if he was still anywhere close."

I cleared my throat. "What about two remaining Seals?"

At this, Jack pursed his lips. He poured Eliza a generous amount of brandywine.

"When I came to the section, I found them in this building. I offered them shelter, as you requested, but Nadine refused, and Zeke had no choice but to go along with it. Fortunately, he persuaded her to leave without violence. She said they were going to find the White Binder." He passed Eliza the glass. "It seems Nadine was the one who plotted the destruction of the Juditheon, spurred on by those who see her as Jaxon's rightful heir. They were trying to attract his attention, to let him know that he still had loyalists in the citadel."

That was why Didion and I had been the targets. We were the living symbols that things did not always go Jaxon's way. I thought of the graffiti on the wall outside this den.

"It seems clear now that this last-ditch attempt to summon him failed." Jack motioned to the vacant chair. "According to my sources in the Garden, the small movement has since collapsed. And now there are no more Seals in I-4, you have nothing more to fear, my queen."

Nothing more to fear from Jaxon's supporters. And a little less to fear from Terebell.

"Thank you," I said. "It seems like you have everything—and everyone—under control."

I stood to leave, as did Eliza. Jack kissed her hand again, lingering for a little longer than before. "It was a pleasure to meet you," he said silkily. She left with another winning smile.

Terebell would be pleased to know that there was no more threat from Jaxon's loyalists and that the last of the Seven Seals had gone—I had at least obeyed her on this—but there was nothing else to celebrate. If Nadine and Zeke had gone to Jaxon, they were already in the Rephaim's clutches.

As I made to leave, Jack held up a finger and reached into his pocket. "I almost forgot, my queen. Zeke asked me to get this to the Red Vision," he said, and handed me a scroll. "You need not read it. It's a love letter—a very romantic one, albeit tinged with the heartbreak of separation."

"You know it's considered impolite to read other people's mail."

He smiled. "I consider it my responsibility, as mime-lord, to know exactly what transpires in this section."

I placed the scroll into my inner pocket, making sure it was buttoned in. It might give Nick a little comfort.

"Underqueen," Jack said, and I looked up, "I hope I don't presume too much to make you an offer." He turned his come-hither eyes on me, making me raise an eyebrow. "All syndicate leaders have need of succor. The position of Underqueen is a taxing one." His hand came to rest high up on my waist. "If you ever wished to have a . . . private audience, you know where to find me."

He was so close that I could smell the spice oil on his skin, see every silken detail of his face.

He wasn't who I wanted.

"Jack," I said gently, stepping away, "we hardly know each other. I'm flattered, really, but—"

"I understand," he murmured. "You already have a lover."

"Yes. No. I mean—" For goodness' sake. "Whether or not I do, it doesn't change the fact that I won't be taking you up on that offer. But I do appreciate your loyalty. And I thank you."

He frowned a little as he smiled. "For what, Underqueen?"

I kissed him lightly on the cheek. "For putting your knife through a man's neck for me."

"We call the Swan Knight, mime-queen of IV-4. What matter do you wish to bring before the Underqueen?"

We were only halfway through the audience and requests from the syndicate were coming thick and fast. The voyants parted to let the Swan Knight through. She had been soundly thrashed by a berserker named Redcap during the scrimmage, and used a cane to approach the dais. Her request was for money, for repairs to a damaged building in her section.

I was seated between Glym and Wynn, listening. A film of sweat covered my collarbones. I had promised to grant this audience, but I was desperate to be back on the streets, gathering information. I needed to know if the report was true. And I needed to see Danica. She was still our best and only link to Senshield, and we couldn't stop looking for the core.

A soothsayer came forward and pleaded for food. Wynn promised that the Pearl Queen would help her. Another petitioner asked me if his cell could be relocated, as there was a new scanner in his area and they didn't like having to get so close to it every day.

"I know I'm a sensor, not at risk," he said, making me tense, "but I can't stand walking past it. We all hate it. The lower orders can't even go out."

I said I would consider moving the cell to a neighboring district. Others asked if I could do the same for theirs.

I imagined how much worse it would get if the fourth order really could be detected.

The final person to come forward was Halfpenny, mime-lord of II-5. Like the Swan Knight and Jack Hickathrift, he had been the mollisher of a gray marketeer and had come to power when his superior had died in the Rose Ring. He was heavily tattooed, with eyebrows he dyed marigold. We had exchanged a handful of words in the past.

"Underqueen. The Glym Lord came to one of my cells last night and asked for volunteers for an assignment—an assignment in which you were involved," he said. "One summoner went with him. I wish to know where he is now."

Glym glanced at me.

"I'm afraid he won't be coming back. I'm sorry," I said. "He was killed by paratroopers."

Whispers. *Paratroopers*. A military word, not one that had been heard often in this citadel.

Halfpenny folded his fleshy arms. "What happened?" When I didn't answer immediately, he said with an air of real disappointment, "You said you'd be different from Hector. We shouldn't have secrets here. I want to know exactly what you did."

This was the first time anyone had challenged me in public. He had the right to do it, but I bridled. "I can't reveal the nature of all of our assignments, Halfpenny. We're moving against an empire, a militarized empire. If anyone were to betray our plans—"

"First you let the Jacobite walk free," he continued, to resentful muttering from the audience, "and now you've baited them into attacking us, at a time when we're already under serious threat from Senshield. Why were there paratroopers in the capital, if not because of you?"

"Listen to this. You'd think the Underqueen was on trial," Wynn cut in. "She doesn't have to justify herself to you. You were happy enough to do as Haymarket Hector demanded without question, but now Paige is Underqueen, you whimper and whine. Take your disrespect elsewhere."

At this, several voyants began to murmur agreements. Others, however, were clearly ruffled by the sight of a vile augur speaking with impunity at the side of the Underqueen.

"I did my best to change things under Hector," was all Halfpenny said. "In my section, at least."

Wynn snorted.

"Binder wouldn't have risked our lives," someone called from the corner. "And you betrayed him. Who's to say you won't turn your back on us, too?"

Silence ruled in the basement of the Mill, broken only by a gasp. I waited several moments before rising from my seat.

"This syndicate," I said, "is a monarchy. Its leaders' power is passed not from parents to children, but between Underlords and Underqueens. Ours is an authority based not on the blood of our families, but the blood we spill on the ashes in the Rose Ring. That blood is our promise. It was my promise that with my crown, I would only ever do what I thought was best for my people—and

I promise you now that I would shed blood again for any of you. And I expect to, before this is over." I paused. "This audience is finished."

My nape was burning as I left the basement. Halfpenny had been reasonable enough, considering I'd broken his nose during the scrimmage.

The other high commanders—except for Minty, who was at Grub Street—were waiting for me in the surveillance room. I could tell from their faces that they had news for me. Quietly, I locked the door behind Wynn and took my seat, trying to tamp down the rising consternation.

"Paige," Maria said, "it seems the report was accurate."

Those few words punctured what was left of my confidence.

"How do you know?" I said.

Tom sighed. "A whisperer was taken this morning. I knew him. His aura was yellower than a lemon."

Shock washed over me. I hadn't wanted to accept it, but now I had no choice. The four most populous orders of clairvoyance were visible, their years of walking the streets at an end. That left a fraction of us who could roam London without fear of detection.

And all because I had gone into the warehouse without ensuring that our information was reliable.

"Vance used my aura to improve Senshield." I kept my voice low. "We need to focus on damage control."

They were all silent, watching me.

If I told the syndicate the truth, many of them might blame me for our new vulnerability. If I lied, and they found out anyway, their reaction would be much worse. Either way, I needed them to believe as I did: that revolution was crucial to our survival. If we were to endure with four of the orders in this much danger, that belief would be vital.

"I have to speak to the Unnatural Assembly about this," I said. "To warn them." I hesitated. "I should . . . tell them the truth about how Scion did it. I don't want to rule with lies."

"I wouldna do that, Underqueen," Tom murmured.

"They have to know that they can trust me. If I lie to them—"

"You won't be lying," he stressed. "You'll be leaving something out, for the sake of harmony."

"Perhaps you should take the rest of the night to consider this, Underqueen. It will be difficult to bring the Assembly together during curfew, in any case," Glym said. "It would be prudent to wait until sunrise."

He had a point. I would only put them in more danger if I forced them outside now.

"I want them all at St. Dunstan-in-the-East at five A.M., before Weaver can make any early announcements," I conceded. "I'll tell them myself that the fourth order is in danger, and I'll hold a vote on what we should do next: go into hiding, or stay on the streets. Whatever the outcome of that vote, I'll have to ask the Ranthen to sanction it."

"Never mind a vote. Those of us who are detectable *must* hide," the Pearl Queen said. Maria gritted her teeth. "Well, what else is there to do? Senshield is intruding farther and farther into our lives by the day. Personally, I have no desire to be pounced upon by Vigiles if I stray too close to a letter box. Let us not put pride over sense."

"This is the Mime Order's decision to make. Together." I sounded much calmer than I felt. "I'll see you tomorrow. Be there at five, not a second later."

They murmured their goodnights and went their different ways; Maria patted my arm as she left. I took the stairs to the ground floor, wearing a mask of unconcern, and walked straight into Nick, as I headed for the doors. My muscles felt so spring-loaded with tension that I flinched away from him.

"Paige?"

"Sorry. I didn't see you. I'm just—" I stopped when I saw his face. "What's happened?"

"It's Dani. She's gone."

I shook my head. "Gone?"

"Every trace of her: her clothes, her equipment, everything. No sign of a struggle."

"That means nothing." I gripped his arm. "Nick, she could have been discovered—"

85

"I doubt it. They would have stayed in the hideout to lie in wait for her allies."

If she hadn't been taken, then she had left us of her own accord. My first deserter, and it was Danica, of all people. Danica Panić, the last person on earth to run from a problem.

Surely she hadn't gone to Jaxon.

"Eliza saw her earlier, and she didn't say anything. I think what happened at the warehouse really shook her, Paige."

The words dug out a hollow in my chest. "That's our last link to Senshield gone," I said. His face reflected my disquiet. "Maybe it's time for us to approach the Vigiles. Like Warden said, they want Senshield destroyed as much as we do, and they might have information. We can't give up on finding the core. Destroying it is the only way."

"We'll need to be very careful."

"You don't need to remind me." I drew my coat closer. "They . . . confirmed the report."

"Tom said." He laid a hand on my shoulder. "Are you going to tell them the whole truth?"

"I don't know yet." I glanced behind me and lowered my voice. "I'm announcing the news tomorrow. I want to do it tonight, but—"

"Don't, Paige. If you're doing this, you need to know what you're going to say. It needs planning. And you should get some sleep," he added gently. "You don't look well."

"I'm fine."

"You're not a machine. Just give yourself a few hours to think and rest up."

I wanted to argue with him, but he was right. My muscles ached from the lingering shock of my fall into the river. I hadn't washed or eaten properly in days. My wounds were hurting where I had forgotten to put on salve.

And there was someone I had to see.

Something I needed to repair. Not just for my own sake.

"Tomorrow it is." I reached into my jacket. "Zeke gave this to Jack Hickathrift to pass on to you. I haven't read it." I held out the scroll. "They've left Seven Dials. I'm sorry."

He took it carefully. "Thank you, *sötnos*." It went into his coat, close to his heart, as he squinted at the snow. "Let's hope they don't run into any scanners. And that they've found somewhere warm."

I didn't tell him that they might have gone to Jaxon. He already looked so exhausted.

"They'll know all about it tomorrow morning," I said. "Wherever they are."

He sighed. "I said I would help Wynn polish her medical skills tonight. You just rest, Paige. Doctor's orders."

"Sure."

He walked into the shadows of the Mill. I eased up my hood and headed out into the snow.

6

Hourglass

It was nine by the time I entered the Lambeth hideout, drenched and shivering, my face raw from the cold. I took off my coat and boots and reached for the golden cord.

There was no reply.

I needed to see him. Now, before he left for the Netherworld. It could be weeks before he returned. To distract myself, I lit a fire and made as much of a meal as I could with our limited stores of food, then boiled some water and filled the tin bath. I sat in it until my fingertips creased.

Had Danica gone to Jaxon with our secrets? Had she been a spy all along—had we walked into the trap because of her? I was doubting everything I had once believed about the people closest to me.

On the other hand, she might have just lost her nerve—and I couldn't blame her for running from Vance. She had been a small child when Scion had invaded her country, as I had been. She must have a healthy fear of anything related to the army.

I brushed my teeth and tended to my wounds. I could see why Nick had said I looked ill. My face was almost gray. Still, he had been right: being full and clean made me feel more alert than I had in a few days. Now all I needed was more than two hours' sleep.

I tried the cord again. Nothing. Warden wasn't coming.

In the parlor, I crawled on to the couch with a blanket, too bone-tired to face the stairs. Beneath the pall of fatigue, I had the same feeling I experienced whenever I thought of Jaxon or saw a Vigile, and it wouldn't go away. That fight-or-flight sensation.

When the front door opened, I sat up. I heard him step into the hallway, felt his familiar dreamscape. He crossed the parlor and lowered himself into the armchair.

Neither of us looked at the other for some time. Finally, I said, "Was Terebell happy for you to come here?"

"I did not ask her for permission." Snow was melting in his hair. "What is it you need of me, Paige?"

Even now, I loved hearing him say my name. Loved the way it sounded on his tongue. He imbued it with singularity, as if I were the only person in the world who could ever possess it.

"The report was accurate," I said. "The scanners have been adjusted to identify the fourth order. The majority of our recruits are detectable now." I swallowed. "I'll be announcing it to the Unnatural Assembly tomorrow."

He was silent for some time. "Until Senshield is fully portable, and fully functional in terms of the orders it can detect, the Mime Order can survive," he said. "You must focus on gathering and training recruits, preferably by draining them from the Vigiles' ranks. Then we begin to move against the anchor. With you as its leader, the movement will thrive."

"You really believe that."

"I always have."

There was a half-empty bottle of wine on the table—Nick, again, it must be—and I reached for it.

He was right. Vance had dealt us a terrible blow, but we still had time: it would be a few weeks before there were enough scanners to end free movement.

"Let's just hope the syndicate doesn't find out that Vance used me," I said.

"You have decided not to tell the whole truth, then."

"It will only cause discord."

He made no comment. I rose and took a wine glass from the cabinet before returning to the couch.

"Warden, I owe you an explanation," I said, "and I wanted you to hear it before you leave."

"You owe me nothing."

"I do."

I filled the glass for him and handed it over. His eyes were almost human in their darkness.

It took me a few tries before I began. I wet my lips, looked away, looked back at him.

"When I saw him last," I finally said, "Jaxon claimed that you were . . . bait for me. That you chose me in the colony on Terebell's orders, not of your own volition. And that made me think that everything was a lie, that the Guildhall was—" My cheeks warmed. "That it was just a way to cement my trust in you. That you didn't really mean it."

"Bait," he repeated.

"He's saying that you were ordered to seduce me. For her purposes."

That brought a flare into his irises.

"And you believed it," he said.

"I thought—I started to believe it was all a ruse. To make me think you cared about me so much that you would go behind her back to be with me. So I would do anything for you in return."

The admission hung between us for some time. Warden swirled the dark wine in its glass.

"And are you seduced?"

The heat of the fire was drying his hair. The light brought out notes of darker, chestnut brown I had never noticed before.

"I haven't decided," I said.

We studied each other for some time.

"Look, I'm more than aware of how paranoid it sounds, but I lived with Jaxon for three years without knowing the truth about whose side he was on. He must have been laughing at me, when I told him about the Rephaim. When I tried to get him to help me." I returned the bottle to its place. "Now I just—I don't know who else I've been playing the fool for."

His next words were soft. "You have heard other Rephaim name me flesh-traitor. It is understandable for you to wonder why I would have chosen this path, if not for some ulterior purpose. It is also understandable for you to doubt those closest to you now Jaxon has shown his true colors."

"Why, then?"

"Why did I choose you in the colony," he asked, "or why did I kiss you on the night of the Bicentenary?"

I held his gaze. "Both."

"You will not like the answer to the first."

Rephaim didn't make a habit of disclosing their emotions. Warden had made oblique statements about his feelings toward me, but this was the first time he had volunteered any information.

"At the oration, twenty years ago," he said, "there was a young man with auburn hair and black eyes, full of contempt. While the other humans kept their heads down, he alone stared back."

"Jaxon," I murmured.

"He became Nashira's tenant that year. Her only one."

"Nashira was his keeper?" It didn't surprise me.

"Yes." He paused. "You looked at me in the same way, twenty years later. You looked me in the eye, asserting yourself as my equal."

I remembered that night all too well.

"I suspected, in the years to come, that Nashira's favorite was the traitor. It tested my faith in all of humanity. Yet when I saw that glimpse of him in you, I sensed that you might have the courage to rebel; that only I could be your keeper. Terebell had taken an interest in you, but she did not order me to take you in. Quite the opposite. She thought I was a fool for bringing you into such close quarters." His fingers tapped the arm of the chair. "Of my own accord, I elected to take you into Magdalen and hide your progress from Nashira. She could see your red aura. I knew that she would try to steal your gift."

"So you did it to protect me."

"It was not a wholly altruistic act. If Nashira had mastered dreamwalking, she would have become far more powerful, making it difficult for us to revive the Ranthen."

It was disturbing to hear him talk about Nashira. "But you first chose me because . . . I reminded you of Jaxon."

He didn't answer. I tried not to show how deep the words cut me.

"How close were you to him?" he asked.

I considered. "Mollishers are usually closer to their mime-lords than I was to him. They're lovers, sometimes, but Jaxon doesn't have any interest in sex. I was his protégée. His project."

Warden rarely interjected, like a human might to show continued interest, but neither did he look away from my face.

"Tell me, Paige," he said, "does Jaxon know that you were once in love with Nick?"

"I never told him," I said, "but he might have guessed. Why?"

"What Jaxon said at the Archon plays upon certain aspects of your past and personality. He knows that you cannot abide anyone trying to make a fool of you—and he knows, most likely, that the first person you loved did not love you," he said. "Jaxon has carefully poisoned your impression of me. He knows the way you guard your heart. In your mind, I am now someone who might be making a fool of you, who cares nothing for you, and who only means to use your gift for his own gain—another thing you fear."

He understood so much about me, and I still knew so little about him.

"What he has done is insidious. Nashira must be delighted to have him back at her side." Warden's eyes scorched. "There is no way for me to prove to you that I am not what he claims. Not unless I publicly turn against Terebell, which would cause tension within the Ranthen. Perhaps that is what Jaxon expects me to do. To win back your confidence at the expense of our ability to work together." He looked back at the fire. "With one falsehood, designed to target what he sees as your emotional vulnerabilities, he has demolished the foundation that you and I have laid. Nine months, and your trust in me is fading."

If true, it meant that Jaxon had thought of everything. This was mental warfare. The only way to fight was to refuse to do what he expected. To trust that Warden was my ally.

"I make no apology for refusing your request in front of the Ranthen. Only for the hurt it caused you," Warden said. "I would choose Terebell's orders over yours again—if it meant that we would not be sundered, and if it held the Mime Order together. Hiding what I feel for you, being forced to do nothing to support you in public—this is the price I will pay for change. And we all must pay a price." He settled back into his chair. "Jaxon's foul scheming may have left scars on my body, but I will not allow it to scar the alliance we have built together."

I seemed fated to flee from one set of strings to another, endlessly caught in a web of deceit.

Yet trusting Warden felt . . . *right*, somehow. It was a feeling I couldn't deny, a certainty I could never explain.

"I should have told you sooner," I said finally. "I've let it eat away at me for weeks, but . . . I did tell you, in the end. And I still don't know if this can work—but it will take more than one lie from Jaxon to break my trust in you."

Warden lifted his head. "Do we have a truce, then?"

"Truce."

Weeks of dancing around the truth, and just like that, it was over.

A cool tingling started beneath my ribs. Warden laid down his glass and looked at me, and his look pierced me through. It would only take a step to bring us close enough to touch.

Instinct made me glance toward the door. I had heard him turn the key and draw the chain across when he arrived, as we all did when we came in for the night.

The fire crackled as we moved toward each other, as he gathered me into his arms. As I searched the deep, endless pupils of his eyes, I let him learn my face with his hands. He must have known every inch of it, but he traced my features as if he wanted to decipher them.

"We shouldn't start this again." I rested my head against his chest. "Maybe it's best if we just . . . let it go."

Warden said nothing to contradict me. No words of comfort. No white lie to make things easier. After all, it *would* be best.

"You must think about the risk. The Mime Order would collapse if the Ranthen knew. Everything we've worked for—"

He waited for me to continue, but I couldn't.

"I consider your company worth the risk," he said into my hair, "but the choice is always yours."

I drew back and considered his face for a last time. I couldn't ask any more questions tonight; couldn't keep second-guessing myself. Jaxon was the liar, the snake in the grass. Warden had earned my trust. I had to let myself believe that he was worthy of it—for now, at least.

I sought his lips first. The choice was mine.

We held each other in the firelight. It was some time before I led his hands into my blouse. The kiss broke as he met my gaze, as he parted the silk from waist to throat. A chill spread over my stomach and breasts.

There was a low fire in his eyes as he took me in. I was perfectly still, trying to tell what he was thinking. After a few moments, his gaze flicked to mine again. When I nodded my assent, he brushed the backs of his knuckles over my collarbone, then my shoulder and throat. I linked my arms around his neck. I was cocooned by his aura. His other hand glided over the seam in my side, where the skin was knitting back together.

A truce couldn't last when we were at war. For the time I had him to myself, I wanted as much of him as he would give.

Vance's trap had made me remember my mortality. I was tired of holding back from Warden. Tired of yearning to be close to him. Tired of denying myself. I cupped his face with my hands and kissed him deeply, as I never had before. As if he sensed the need in me, he took me fully into his arms. A soft ache bloomed between my legs. I felt my lips quake, heard the blood throbbing through my veins, as he lowered his head to where the wound tapered off, just shy of my breast, and kissed the delicate new skin. I lifted myself into his hands.

Once he had seen to my side, he worked his way down my body. His lips lingered on my stomach, making me shiver, but he went no farther. Not yet. That was for another night. He laid his head on my chest, and I combed my fingers through his hair.

It might be naïve, but I wanted to believe in this.

"Warden."

"Hm?"

"You never told me why you kissed me, at the Bicentenary," I murmured. "You only answered my first question."

He lay still.

"So I did," was all he said.

I let it go. It was enough that he was here. It was enough to be beside him, to know that he was with me.

The next kiss was softer. We shifted our positions, so my back was against his chest, and stayed like that in the light of the fire. We looked at each other for a long time, not speaking.

The room was an hourglass that hadn't yet turned. My breathing and my heartbeat grew slower, falling into line with his. When I was close to drifting off, Warden drew me deeper into his arms and lowered his head a little, so his cheek lay alongside mine. My skin prickled as he touched his lips to my jaw, where the welt was. I threaded my fingers between his knuckles.

"There is one way that you might see proof that I am on your side. Something that would betray me," he said, his voice a rumble in his throat, "if anyone but you could see."

I was so fire-warmed and drowsy, I couldn't think of what he might be talking about.

"What can I see?"

He only held me closer. I tucked my head beneath his chin and tried to keep my eyes open, so I could savor these fragile hours. In the softened state that comes before oblivion, I imagined that this moment could be safe from time, like he was. I imagined that the dawn would never come.

"Denizens of the citadel, this is . . ."

My eyes opened, furred with sleep. The fire had gone out, leaving a chill on my skin. I couldn't work out what had woken me.

Warden's arm was around my waist, his hand on my back. Sleep had made his body heavy beside mine. I nosed closer to his chest, where it was warmest, and lifted the blanket over my shoulder.

". . . internal security has been compromised . . ."

I snapped upright, muscles tensed. There was no key in the lock; no footstep in the hall. No dreamscapes here but Warden's and mine.

It took me a moment to work out that the disembodied voice was coming from Nick's data pad, muffled by the cushion that had fallen on to it. With slack vision, I lifted it from the floor. Warden stirred beside me.

"*We must not be tempted by change, when change, by its very nature, is an act of destruction*," Frank Weaver was saying. "*Mahoney's group, 'The Mime Order,' is now classified as a terrorist organization under Scion law. It has shed the blood of Scion's denizens and threatened the Inquisitor's peace.*"

I waited, not breathing.

"*However, all is not lost. Thanks to a recent development in Radiesthesic Detection Technology, we were able to use Mahoney's own unnaturalness to recalibrate our Senshield scanners.*" No. No, no, no. "*Four of seven types of unnaturalness are now detectable.*"

"Vance," I whispered.

It was her. Weaver might be the one speaking, but I sensed her face beneath his, her fingers knotted in his strings.

They had made the announcement before I could, and they had laid the blame at my door. If the syndicate believed it, they would never forgive me.

I should have insisted on speaking to the Unnatural Assembly hours ago, curfew or otherwise . . .

"*To ensure that Senshield is used with the greatest possible efficiency, and to support internal security forces at this time*," Weaver continued, "*I have no choice but to execute martial law, our highest level of security.*"

Warden lifted himself onto his elbows.

"*A division of ScionIDE, our loyal army, has been recalled to safeguard this citadel. They are led by Grand Commander Hildred Vance, who is determined to restore our capital to its former state of safety before the new year. Upon the arrival of the First Inquisitorial Division in the capital, martial law will be effective in the Scion Citadel of London until Paige Mahoney is in Inquisitorial custody. All denizens should remain indoors until further notice. There is no safer place than Scion.*"

The broadcast ended, leaving the anchor to spin on the screen.

Martial law. We had guessed it was coming, yet hearing it from Weaver made it truly real.

The short-lived warmth was torn away from me, like rind off fruit. I snatched my blouse from the floor and left the pocket of heat in the room, needing air, needing the cold to shock me back to reality. When I flung open the front door, the night hit my body like a shout hits the ears. I leaned against the door frame, clutching my blouse around me. The wind scalded my legs and cheeks.

Something was straining in my dreamscape. I could hear things I hadn't heard since I was six years old. Gunfire and screaming. Hoofbeats. My cousin's tortured cries.

Warden stood in the doorway to the parlor. I took deep breaths.

"I need to see the commanders, now. The syndicate won't survive martial law for long." I towed the cold into my lungs, as if it could freeze the fear. Ice was spreading through my core, forking out to every limb. "You get the Ranthen. Find me as soon as you can."

I strode past him, back into the parlor. As I searched for my phone, I didn't make eye contact with him. I dug the burner out from behind the couch, where the shapes of our bodies were pressed, and buckled on my coat and boots while Warden prepared for the séance.

Neither of us spoke, even when I left.

In case of emergency, our meeting place was always Battersea Power Station, which was close enough to the safe house for me to go on foot. I didn't allow myself to think as I ran, weaving past squadrons of Vigiles, urging my legs through freshly piled snow. Soon I was squirming under the fence that surrounded the derelict—the skeleton of a massive, coal-fired power station that had long since fallen out of use. Stars glistened above its four pale chimneys.

A few sets of footprints had already spoiled the snow. I found Glym, Eliza and the Pearl Queen waiting inside, all with grave expressions. Behind them, Maria was slumped over a control panel. Her hair flamed against her pallid brow, and she was strangling a bottle with one hand.

Memories gathered like crows in my mind. None of them were clear, but I had the sense of being surrounded. Suffocated.

Tom and Nick arrived. Next was Minty Wolfson, whose dress, hands, and face were spattered with ink. "Where the hell is Wynn?" Maria bit out.

"She's coming," I said.

When Wynn arrived, she stood apart from the others. For the first time since I had met her, she was armed. I could see the leather strap of a holster where her coat fell open.

"Have all the cells been informed that everyone is to stay indoors, as agreed?" I asked. Nods. "We need to act quickly to get our voyants to safety. ScionIDE is coming to crush the Mime Order. With Senshield, they'll root us out in days, and they won't be anywhere near as easy to avoid as the Vigiles."

"We might have a chance if we stay on the move. Or go to ground here as best we can." Maria drank from the bottle again. "The First Inquisitorial Division has spent years stationed on the Isle of Wight. We know these streets. They don't." She wiped her mouth with a shaking hand. "This could be fine."

She didn't sound convinced.

"It won't work. We can't hide in plain sight anymore," I said quietly. Her face crumpled. "Senshield would have pushed us into hiding in the end. This just . . . forces us to take action earlier than we expected."

The silence that followed was almost painful, heavy with shock and grief. Never, in all of syndicate history, had voyants been forced to leave their districts, their sections, the streets that were their homes. What I was proposing—what I was ordering—was an evacuation.

I was suddenly conscious of the æther; my sixth sense swamped the others. Nick touched my arm, jolting me back.

"Paige?"

"Wait," I said, and ran from the control room.

Scaffolding had been left to rot on one side of the power station where property developers had been defeated by its age. I clambered up it, ignoring their calls for me to wait. A mass of dreamscapes was approaching from the south, moving past us at a steady pace. Regimented.

Nick was in pursuit, navigating the vertical labyrinth. When I reached the top, I ran to the base of one of the four chimneys and grasped the rungs of a ladder. Behind me, Nick heaved himself off the scaffolding.

"What are you doing?"

"I need to see." I tested the ladder with my boot. "Something's coming."

"Paige, that thing has to be three hundred feet."

"I know. Can I use your binoculars?"

His lips pressed together, but he handed them over. I slung them around my neck and climbed.

I moved like clockwork past concrete scabbed with paint. When I thought I was high enough, I turned to behold the starfield of blue streetlamps—London in the dead of night. I could see the illuminated skyscrapers of I Cohort in the distance and the bridges closest to the power station, two of many that reached over the river. The nearest was for trains, but the one beyond would normally be weighed down with traffic, even in the small hours. I took one hand off the ladder and lifted the binoculars.

A convoy of black, armored vehicles was thundering across the bridge, coming from a main road close to here. I almost stopped breathing when I saw the tanks among them. Each vehicle was flanked by armed foot-soldiers. I couldn't see the end or the beginning of the convoy; there must have been hundreds, thousands of them on their way into the heart of the capital.

My heart climbed into my throat. I pressed myself against the ladder when a helicopter rushed over. A helicopter emblazoned with SCIONIDE.

I descended as quickly as I could. When he saw my face, Nick didn't need to ask. Wordlessly, we scrambled back down the scaffolding. The others were waiting for us at the bottom.

"They're here," I said. Minty lifted a hand to her mouth. "A massive convoy. We need all of our voyants from the first four orders evacuated now—into every available hideout—maybe some of the abandoned Underground stations—"

"Jaxon knows those places." Eliza was holding her own arms. "We need somewhere he's never been."

"Damn it, *think*," Maria barked. "Where can we go?"

"There's always the Beneath."

It was Wynn who had spoken. She was standing by the window, her hands in the pockets of her coat. As one, we all turned to look at her.

"The underground rivers. The deepest tunnels. The storm drains and the sewers," she said. "The lost parts of London."

"Oh, for heaven's sake, Wynn, don't be an idiot," Maria burst out. Wynn raised her eyebrows. "The Beneath is the mudlarks' and the toshers' territory. We all know the sewer-hunters have no interest in dealing with syndies. They protect their kingdom of shit like it's a river of gold. Any time we've ever tried to push too far underground, they've driven us off with spears."

"Ruffians," the Pearl Queen said.

"Can we not force our way in?" Tom asked.

"Fighting them would end in deaths. I'm not going to slaughter one community to protect another," I said sharply. Yet going deep underground could protect us from Senshield, and from Vance.

Minty raised an unsteady hand. "I'm afraid force isn't an option," she said. "The Beneath is the territory of the mudlarks and the toshers, beyond debate. It was agreed in 1978 that the deep parts of London would be theirs, and theirs alone. Their right to the Beneath is enshrined in syndicate law. And as you say, Maria, they protect it fiercely."

"There *must* be some way to convince them," I snapped. "It's our only way out of this. ScionIDE won't think to look there; even Jaxon will have no inkling. If we stay below the streets, we can move around the citadel without activating the scanners. If the Mime Order can go where Vance's soldiers can't follow—"

Wynn cleared her throat.

"If I might finish speaking," she said, "I happen to know how we can access the Beneath, without force and with the toshers' permission."

Every head turned in her direction. Maria was good enough to look slightly embarrassed.

"Several years ago, the toshers came to us—the vile augurs— with a plea," Wynn went on. "They needed access to a lost river, the Neckinger; I believe there was treasure there. The entrance sat on Jacob's Island, our land. We allowed them access and to plunder the treasure. In return, their king promised each vile augur a favor. It so happens," she said, "that I never claimed mine."

I didn't dare to hope.

"Wynn," Nick said, "are you saying you might be able to get us into the Beneath?"

Wynn stared hard at each of them in turn, then at me.

"Know this, Paige Mahoney," she said. "If you had punished Ivy at all during that trial, if you had even touched a hair on her head, I would have left you all to rot, and done it gladly."

The silence was absolute. When I could speak again, I said, "Send word to the syndicate. We're going underground."

7

The Great Descent

December 1, 2059

We sent out an alert to the Unnatural Assembly: prepare to evacuate. Stand by for instructions. There was to be no discrimination—everyone from mime-lords and mime-queens to buskers and beggars, would be taken. They were to bring with them only what was essential, and enough food for at least a week.

Scarlett Burnish, the Grand Raconteur, had already appeared on the screens to soothe the nation. Despite her telling them to stay indoors, people were out in force on the streets, seeking answers from the Vigiles, who held their guns close and ignored all questions. Burnish was on every screen: her pale, oval face with its perfect features, framed by blood-red hair—the face that brought them news and announcements, that now asked all denizens to remain in their homes and await further instruction. So few were listening. These were Londoners—they had never experienced the ruthlessness of ScionIDE. They had spent their lives under a thin carapace of superficial freedom, with no idea that any protest, violent or otherwise, could be viewed as treason by the soldiers.

While the others were coordinating the evacuation, Wynn brought Nick and me to what had once been known as Blackfriars Bridge. We followed her down the steps, out of sight of the main road.

"Wynn," Nick said, "where are you taking us?"

"To the mouth of the River Fleet."

"The what?"

Wynn clicked her tongue. "A lost river. Buried over the years, as London was piled on top of it." She kept marching. "Scion won't be looking down there for criminals. Not for a while, in any case."

She glanced over a low balustrade, down to where water swashed against an outcrop of ice. "Low tide. Good," she said, and hitched up her skirts. Then she was climbing over, on to a service ladder. "Paige, wait for a whistle. When you hear it, come down and join me."

"Where the hell are you going?"

She grabbed me by the collar and pulled me forward, so I had to fold over the balustrade. "Look."

I looked. Nick switched on his flashlight, but it took my eyes a moment to find the narrow entrance to a tunnel, hidden beneath the bridge. "Wynn," I croaked, "we can't put the voyants in a *river* for months."

"This is only part of the toshers' network. They use the Fleet and its storm drains to cross the citadel—just as we must, if we mean to evade Vance." She began to climb down. "Wait there."

It didn't take her long. We watched her cross the shingle on the riverbank and disappear into the tunnel.

Darkness. That was what the syndicate now faced under my rule. Days, weeks, maybe even months of being buried alive in deep, forgotten places. I had known that something like this would happen one day, ever since Senshield's first prototype was installed; even when I had only been Jaxon's mollisher, I had feared it—but I had never expected it to happen so soon.

"This could work," Nick murmured. "If the mudlarks and toshers can survive down there, so can we."

The wind lashed my face. "It's our only chance."

The transmission screen across the river was static. Vance was a shadowy figure, rarely appearing before cameras; most denizens would have no clear impression of what she looked like. She hid behind Weaver and Burnish—Burnish, especially, would be able to lull people into accepting martial law, with her pleasant tone of voice and gentle smile.

Perhaps that was a tactic, a way to frighten us. If Vance remained faceless, communicating only through her soldiers' brutality, she would be imagined as something more than human.

The whistle came sooner than I expected. I clambered down the ladder, Nick hot on my heels, and we ventured under the bridge, our footsteps splintering ice.

Beyond the archway was utter darkness. Marbled water washed around our boots.

Two dreamscapes were here. One belonged to Wynn, the other to an amaurotic. Nick shone his flashlight, revealing a stock-brick chamber. The far wall was taken up by sealed iron doors. I never failed to marvel at how many parts of London had been left to rot in the vaults of history; how many of them existed beneath its people's feet, unseen and unknown.

Wynn's eyes reflected the flashlight. The amaurotic who stood beside her was unshaven and defiantly filthy. Grime was embedded in the creases of his face. He wore an oilskin coat, a helmet, gloves and hip-high gumboots, winched up by metal clips on his belt. He carried a long pole, which must serve as both walking-stick and spear.

"This is the Fleet's outfall chamber," Wynn said. "And Paige, this is Styx, the toshers' elected king. Styx, I give you Paige Mahoney, Underqueen of the Scion Citadel of London."

We regarded each other. He didn't look much like a king, but then, a nineteen-year-old with a pinched face probably wasn't most people's idea of a queen.

"Wynn tells me that you wish to move the clairvoyant syndicate into the Beneath," he said throatily. "I see no reason why I should grant this request. If not for Wynn, I wouldn't even be considering it."

I glanced toward Wynn. All she did was raise her eyebrows.

"Because there are soldiers in our citadel. And if you don't," I said, "my voyants' blood will be on its streets today."

"I wouldn't mourn. Your syndicate has long been a festering wound on the face of London," he said, "almost since the first Underlord died. And it seems to me that you have brought martial law upon yourselves."

Nick opened his mouth to protest, but I stood on his foot.

"I promised Wynn anything for opening the Neckinger, but I cannot allow you to enter our network if I fear my people may be harmed by yours," Styx said. "Syndies have never been kind to those of my profession, even when we co-existed. Yet the water-folk were here long before your syndicate. Mudlarks combed the Thames in the days of Queen Victoria. Toshers crawled beneath the streets before London knew the word *unnaturalness*. You're the youngest criminals in this citadel, yet you brutalized us."

"And I don't expect you to forgive us for it," I said. "I can only swear to you that it will not happen again on my watch. We'd be indebted to you. We don't know how to navigate the Beneath."

"No. And it is deadly without a guide." Styx leaned on his spear. "I'm inclined to believe you, knowing you released the vile augurs. Our friends. There are many sorts of outcasts in the Beneath . . . but the risks to us are great."

"It wouldn't be a permanent arrangement," I said. "I only need asylum for my voyants for as long as it takes me to damage ScionIDE."

"And you have a plan to do that?" He sounded skeptical, as well he might.

"Yes."

It was almost true. I had the pieces of a plan, even if I had yet to slot them together.

"Styx," I said, wading closer, "I don't have time to argue or bargain with you. Every minute we spend debating brings ScionIDE closer." My voice shook with the effort of staying calm. "I need to get my voyants to safety—not tomorrow, but now. Today. I'm asking you, one outcast to another, to let my people into the Beneath, so they won't have to face what's above. There are good people among them for every one that's done wrong. If money's what you want—"

"I've no use for money. We make enough from the blessings of Old Father Thames."

"What can I offer you, then?"

"A life."

I frowned. Sunken eyes stared back at me.

"A mudlark was slain by syndies in 1977. Cruelly slain, and tortured before. We require a life for the one that was stolen."

"You want to execute one of mine for a crime committed almost a century ago?" Despite my efforts, my voice cracked. "You're not serious."

For the first time, Styx grinned, showing rotten teeth. "Much as I'd be curious to see if you would make that sacrifice," he said, "I'm not as much of a tyrant as some of your leaders. No, we claim one syndie as a resident of the Beneath."

"To do what?"

"That's my business."

Whatever it involved, it would be a life of darkness. A life in the filth of the underground tunnels. One person condemned to that.

One life to save many.

"Agreed," I said, softly. "You have one of mine, and you let all of my voyants into the Beneath, until the streets are safe again."

The toshers' king took a long knife from his pocket and held out a hand. Slowly, I offered mine. He sliced open my palm, then lowered both our hands into the brownish water. The cut stung ferociously. Rough skin pressed mine, squeezing my blood into the Fleet.

"The river witnesses this settlement," Styx said. "This day, after many days, our communities are reunited. Should you go back on your word, or should your people do any injury to mine during their time here, we will drive you out, whether the anchor will hurt you or not."

"Understood."

"Good." We rose, and he let go of my hand. "The Beneath has many doors, doors to which Scion no longer has keys. You will be safe with us, so long as you obey our orders."

"Just tell us what to do," I said.

We met up with Maria and Eliza at the Old Spitalfields Market. Hundreds of amaurotics milled around the stalls, trying to get provisions before ScionIDE could send them all inside. For all they knew, it could be days before they were permitted on the streets again. Eliza was carrying an enormous rucksack, while Maria was handing out waterproof clothes and flashlights to the voyants who would be coming with us, people who worked in her section.

"The toshers' king has allowed our entrance," I said to her. "We're good to go."

"Fabulous." Maria tossed me an oilskin. "Let's get the hell out of here. Where's the entrance?"

"I-4," Wynn said.

A few rickshaws were still offering rides, albeit for sky-high prices. We hailed a pair and clambered into one with half of the group. The PA system was repeating Weaver's announcement on a loop between periods of droning from the sirens, adding that all denizens should clear the roads for military vehicles. The shops that hadn't closed already were full to bursting, their automated doors pried open by those waiting outside. White Scion cabs were thick on the streets, ferrying people to their homes, but our driver wove a path between them.

The soldiers' marching dreamscapes were on my radar now. Too close for comfort. They might not fire at will in the capital, but we couldn't take chances.

The rickshaw dropped us off close to the Holborn Viaduct, a flyover bridge that crossed a main road, where our group would enter the Beneath. Cars were jammed bumper-to-bumper. Pedestrians scampered around them, fleeing from the mourning of the sirens. Wynn gathered us beneath the bridge and took a strange sort of key from her belt.

"The entrance is that manhole over there." She pointed out a stretch of pavement. "We can't let anyone see us go underground. Eliza, you come with me to help lift the cover. When I signal, Paige and Nick, you follow."

"No. Jos and Ivy first," I said.

She paused before saying, "Very well."

I checked for cameras or obvious scanners, but there were none. Wynn and Eliza dashed across the street. Their heads dipped out of sight as they crouched beside the right manhole. When Wynn stood again and beckoned, Maria nudged Ivy and Jos forward.

Jos was swamped by his oilskin and mittens. He put on a brave face as Ivy pulled his hood over his brow and hurried him across the road. Those two had been on Scion's radar for as long as I had. Wynn waited for them to climb into the shaft, then followed.

My sixth sense was trembling. While Wynn vanished into the pavement, cars began to reverse and swing into frantic U-turns, their wheels mounting the kerb. Others veered away from the center of the road, the way they did when an ambulance or fire engine needed to get through. I didn't need to feel their dreamscapes to work out what was coming.

"Go, go, we need to move," Nick barked. I found myself running into the snarl of traffic, just missing a Scion cab as it smashed into the front of a truck. Horns screamed in protest. Our boots pounded. I saw the manhole, its open lid, the ladder inside it. I tried to push Nick in front of me, but somehow my legs were in the shaft, and my shoulders were following. My hands collided with the ladder. My boots slipped, then found purchase. I clambered down, rung after rung, foot after foot, until I hit solid ground.

Eliza was next, panting with the effort of carrying the backpack. A moment later, I heard a grunt as Nick dropped from the ladder.

"Maria," he called, "get down here!"

Her silhouette was above us, boots on the rungs. "Dobrev, hurry." She took one of her voyants' hands and swung him on to the ladder below her. She said something to him in Bulgarian, and he choked an answer. Without hesitating, Maria reached up and closed the manhole cover.

There were six voyants out there, and the key was in here. The darkness was as good as a blindfold, but I could hear their footsteps, sense their dreamscapes clustering above. "Wait. No, wait for us," a voice cried, raw with terror. Another called out, "Underqueen! Maria, please!"

"Just go, damn it," Maria shouted.

I grasped a rung. "Maria, what are you doing?"

"They're too close!"

She was right. The convoy was seconds away, certainly within sight of the manhole.

To do nothing would abandon them to the mercy of the soldiers. To lift the cover would compromise the only chance of survival we had.

"Leave them."

My words rang through the darkness. It took only seconds for the voyants' footsteps to retreat.

The convoy plowed over our heads. The thunderstorm of wheels and armor reverberated through the tunnel, so it seemed as if we stood in the stomach of a chthonic monster. My hands found a damp wall. I was a little girl again, cowering from the soldiers beneath a statue. All around the vehicles, single dreamscapes were moving at a slower rate. Foot-soldiers. One of them stopped a few feet from the manhole. In the shaft, Maria was motionless. I thought about ordering everyone to run, but one splash, one careless footstep, could give us all away. After almost a minute, the soldier gravitated back to the convoy.

It was a long time before anyone moved. Light flared from Nick's flashlight, revealing the drawn faces of the group. Jos was tearful, Ivy looking at me strangely, and Eliza's hands were over her mouth. When the rumble of the convoy had softened, the Bulgarian voyant tripped off the ladder. Maria jumped the last few feet and switched on a flashlight of her own. The two beams revealed a cramped brick passageway. The ripe smell of decay invaded my nose, laced with something more malodorous.

"So," Maria said, "this is the Beneath. Home, sweet home."

You would never have guessed from her face that several of her voyants had been left behind.

"Why didn't you let them in?" Jos said to us. He sounded choked. "There was time."

His confusion made my heart ache. Maria just handed her flashlight to the newcomer, Dobrev, and groped in the pocket of her oilskin.

"I'm sorry, Jos. They weren't fast enough," I said. "The soldiers would have chased us down here."

"You shouldn't leave people behind just because they're not fast enough."

"Well, we had to, kid," Maria bit out. "If we hadn't, the rest of us would have been killed. Including the Underqueen." She took a cigarette out and stuck it between her teeth. Her hands were shaking. "They know I would never have left them unless there was no choice."

I believed it. Maria was one of the few members of the Unnatural Assembly, who had gone out of her way to show her voyants that she cared about their welfare.

Jos's cheeks were tear-stained. Wynn caught Maria's wrist before she could light up.

"Not here," she said. "Sewer gas."

"Oh, lovely." Maria chucked the cigarette away. "They'll find another entrance."

It was possible, if they could meet up with another cell. Jos perked up.

"Here's the river." Maria shone her flashlight on greenish water. "No sign of shit. Yet."

"We're meeting Styx's contact in the storm drain," Wynn said. "Follow me."

We ventured into the darkness, carrying what few possessions we had brought. The River Fleet coursed between the walls, a cryptic cousin of the Thames. Wynn chalked marks on the walls along the way.

This was the beginning of the end. Nashira's reprisal was finally here.

A suspicion that had been bubbling away for days came to the surface. "Senshield wasn't developed in isolation," I said, thinking aloud. "It was always meant to enhance ScionIDE. The soldiers are spirit-blind, so they need mechanical eyes to detect us. The scanners' spread must have always been timed to coincide with their arrival."

"Senshield detects, ScionIDE destroys." Nick caught a wall for support. "Warden was right about the Vigiles, then. They're superfluous, or soon will be."

"Not until the scanners go portable, which I imagine is on the cards." Maria flicked her flashlight toward the wall, revealing the slime Nick had just put his hand in. He grimaced and removed it. "If that happens, though . . . yes, then the voyant Vigiles are doomed. Krigs don't work with unnaturals, and they'll have no further purpose."

Above us, ScionIDE was on the march. How many of the thousands of voyants in the syndicate would get to the Beneath? How many would be killed trying to reach it on my orders?

And it could all be for nothing. If a single entrance was compromised, we would find ourselves smoked out like a plague of rats.

There were plenty of rats down here. They twitched under our flashlight.

We waded upstream against a gentle current. The water wasn't too deep, but with the supplies weighing us down, it wasn't easy work. Jaxon would pop a rib laughing if he ever got wind of this. The Underqueen's glorious descent into the sewers.

Wynn led us down a ladder, into the storm drain, which was just about dry enough to sit in.

"One of the toshers will collect us from here." She sat on the slope of the tunnel, so only her boots were in the water. "They're moving us to one of Scion's old crisis facilities. They were built by Scion in its early days in case of war or invasion, but it seems they were forgotten when better ones were constructed."

We could only hope.

Ivy ran a hand over her bristly hair. "Are they dry?"

Wynn squeezed water from her skirts. "So they say."

Beside me, Nick's brow rested against his clasped hands. It wasn't hard to guess who he was thinking about.

Eliza dug into her rucksack and handed out packets of biscuits. We shared a canteen of water to offset their dryness. Jos had been bright-eyed with distress, but he soon dozed off against Ivy, who curled an arm around him. Dobrev elected to sleep, too, and didn't seem to care how filthy he got doing it. Parts of the tunnel were caked in what looked like used toilet paper, so I rested my head on my knees, which weren't much cleaner, and tried to clear my head. Only hours ago I had been lying with Warden in the light of the fire. It felt like a lifetime had passed since then.

Time moves strangely underground. I had left my watch at the den, but it had to be past sunrise. One of the flashlights flickered out.

"Reminds you of the Rookery, doesn't it?"

Ivy was leaning against the bricks. The others had fallen asleep, leaving the flashlights on top of Eliza's backpack.

"I guess you weren't in there much. I wasn't, either. But we knew about it. The squalor." She was staring at the ceiling. "I'm trying to figure you out, Paige. You were happy to leave those voyants just now, but you didn't kill Binder at the scrimmage. Or in the Archon."

"I wasn't *happy* to leave them." It came out hoarse. "I did it to protect us. I'm trying to protect all the people who are left. Who survived."

She drew in a breath, deepening the hollows over her collarbones. "Yeah," she said. "I know."

Now the adrenaline had worn off, I felt the burn in my hand where Styx's knife had opened it. I didn't sleep, but I pretended. I didn't want to talk if anyone woke up. My mind was too full of thorns. ScionIDE. The bargain with Styx. Terebell, and how she might respond to this disaster. Senshield.

But most of all, Vance. That eerily calm face and the eyes that seemed to stare right through me. In a matter of hours, she had reduced me from an Underqueen to a sewer rat.

The net was closing in around me.

I allowed myself a few deep breaths. Not all of it was my fault. I had to be rational.

Not all of it, but some. And *some* was far too much.

Dobrev turned over in his sleep and knocked the second flashlight into the water, putting it out. The darkness was so thick that it seemed to seep inside me with every inhalation.

Hours must have passed before our rescuer arrived. A slender amaurotic with a lamp on her helmet, clad in the same sort of uniform Styx had worn. Auburn hair was visible in the lamplight, cut haphazardly around her face, which was splashed by a grape-stain birthmark.

Wynn said, "Styx sent you?"

The tosher nodded and beckoned for us to follow.

It was a long walk. Styx had ordered the tosher to guide us to a crisis facility over four miles away from where we had entered the Beneath, where some voyants had already been taken via the

Underground. Our noses quickly forgot the smell. The darkness wasn't so easy to bear. Jos was a trouper, as usual, but he was soon exhausted, so Nick hitched him up on to his back. Every so often, water would rush from a nearby pipe and swell what was already around us, reminding us that there was no way out if it came higher. It rose past our knees, carrying waste I thought it best not to examine too closely. The tosher didn't seem worried by the idea that we could be swept away. She guided us in silence, sometimes stopping to listen to the tunnels or pocket something from the water.

Wynn seemed just as comfortable. This had nothing on the squalor of Jacob's Island.

We cut through a chamber, out of the storm-relief drain, and into the mainline. By the time we had scaled the ladder, we were all drenched to the bone. Maria braced herself against the wall and coughed up bile.

The tosher stopped a few feet ahead of us.

"What now?" Nick said. His cheek was smeared with dirt.

"We can't go any farther upstream," Wynn said.

Maria wiped her mouth on her sleeve. "You're not telling me we have to go back out."

"No." She nodded to an opening in the wall. "We have to go through here. It will take us into the crisis facility."

The tosher handed her a flashlight, which she shone on the passageway. The sight of it made my throat close up. It was barely wide enough for Jos, let alone the rest of us. And we would have to crawl through it, in near-total darkness, for as long as it took to reach the other side.

Wynn crouched beside the opening and followed the tosher. "Take this," she said to me, and passed me the flashlight. Beside me, Nick was still as stone, transfixed by the prospect.

"It's okay," I said. "I'll go first."

8

Counter Play

It felt like years that we were in that final tunnel, a pipe so cramped and black that it plagued me with persistent thoughts of being in a coffin. I could hear Eliza choking back sobs of disgust as we crawled, elbow-deep, through congealed filth, following the bluish light of the headlamp. It was hard to remember, through the aching and the stench and the sense that we were being suffocated, that daylight had ever existed. When the tosher opened a grate, the nine of us were poured into a pit, where murky, leaden water stagnated in a pool. Shaking with exertion, I towed myself on to a set of winding steps and lifted a heavy-eyed Jos out with me. He was dead on his feet.

Another tosher, who carried a signal lantern, met us at the top of the steps and, without a word, led us down a passageway. The walls were gray and nondescript. We passed a door embossed with the word BATHROOM.

"Well," I said, "this is civilized."

"Oh, yes." Maria picked a string of tissue from her hair. "Then again, everything seems civilized when you've just been getting friendly with other people's excrement."

Another bathroom was just around the corner. As far as I could see, everything inside was functional.

"This is incredible," I said. "Why did we never know about this?"

"Not many do," the tosher said.

He stopped and showed me a diagram on the wall, titled II COHORT DEEP-LEVEL CRISIS FACILITY, SCION CITADEL OF LONDON. Two cylindrical tunnels ran parallel to one another, each split into an upper and lower deck to provide extra room, and they were linked at several points by smaller passages. Not only were there bathrooms, but there were also side tunnels for use as medical wings, canteens, storage rooms, and so on.

"Does anything work?" I asked.

"Showers, but don't overdo it. The water collects down below, and it won't go anywhere unless you get the pumps working. I reckon everything else would function if there was power."

"We were told that some of our voyants were already here," Wynn said.

"Yeah. They were choosing their bunks, last I saw."

"Bunks?"

"That's right."

The tosher headed back to the staircase, leaving us to take in our surroundings. After losing half our group in the descent and wading through the dark for hours, good news was a surprise.

I set Jos down and stripped off my stinking oilskin. Alsafi might be able to help us get the power back on if we could get word to him.

"We should set up a meeting room for the commanders," I said.

"And somewhere secure for you to stay, Paige," Nick said gently.

The brief exhilaration flickered out. I didn't need him to spell it out for me; the syndicate would be baying for my blood.

"There's a supervisor's post on the other end of the facility," said Wynn. "That should be secure." She brushed past us. "I'm going to see who else is here."

Still plastered in filth, she hurried up the stairs, holding up her drenched skirts with one hand. For her sake, I hoped Vern and Róisín—her family—had made it down here. Ivy hesitated before following her, and Jos, who tended to go wherever she went, stumbled after them.

"Right," I said to those who remained. "Before we do anything, I suggest we wash."

The suggestion was met with sounds of approval. If I had to face the music, I might as well do it clean.

Stained curtains divided the bathroom into eight shower cubicles, each of which contained an equally stained towel. I would have recoiled on any other day, but I was already coated in all manner of dirt, so I steeled myself and undressed. As promised, the showers just about functioned. I excavated a bar of soap, which looked about a century old, and scrubbed myself raw, scouring under my nails and soaking my hair until the water I wrung from it was clear. I patted myself dry with the corner of a towel and pulled on some spare clothes from Eliza's backpack.

There was a water-spotted mirror by the door. With no greasepaint to hand to mask the shadows under my eyes, I would have to appear before my subjects with a naked face. I turned away from the reflection.

After hours of limbo, it was time to see the syndicate.

We took the stairs to the upper deck. Distorted sounds echoed through the tunnel. Lanterns had been set on the floor, showing me that at least eighty voyants had found their way into the facility so far—more than I had expected.

The relief curdled when I saw what was happening. Wynn was shielding Ivy, who looked lifeless, while Vern was locked in a brutal fight with a sensor, bloody at the mouth.

"Stop it," Róisín was screaming. "Leave him alone!"

They were surrounded. I flung pressure through the æther, scattering the knot of attackers. The sensor let Vern go and clapped a hand to her bleeding nose.

When they found the source of the disturbance, hatred filled their faces. I had almost allowed myself to believe that the discovery of this refuge would soften their fury, but I could see now that I had underestimated it.

Nick placed a hand on my shoulder. "Paige," he said, "let's go to the supervisor's post."

I brushed him off and crouched beside the bunk. Ivy was conscious, just, her fingers pressed into Wynn's shoulder. Her other hand was against her cheek, but I could see the blood flowing from beneath it, leaving runnels down her neck. When I guided it away, I drew in a breath. A rough "T" had been sliced into her face. Jos was hiding behind her, shaking.

"Eliza," I said, too quietly for the crowd to hear, "get them to the medical wing. Bar the door."

I rose and brazened out my subjects. Under those bloodthirsty stares, I wanted nothing more than to leave—but if I walked away now, if I showed them that I was afraid, I would lose all my power.

"Who," I said, keeping my voice soft, "is responsible for this?"

Wynn cradled Ivy closer and wrapped her other arm around Róisín. Eliza coaxed them out.

"I'll ask once more. Who cut Ivy?"

"She's a traitor," a voice said from the back. "Let everyone remember it. Let *her* remember it."

"We don't want her down here. Let the soldiers take her." The sensor spat at Vern and wiped angrily at her nose. "Whose side are you on, Underqueen? First you don't punish the Jacobite when she was helping sell us on the gray market—then you bring the army down on us—*and* it turns out you've helped them change Senshield. You're worse than Hector ever was, and that's saying something!" Shouts of agreement filled the tunnel. "Every sensor who's detained from now on—that's on you, Mahoney. Their blood is all over your dirty Irish hands."

"Traitor," someone bellowed.

"Traitor!"

"You showed them how to sense us," a whisperer shouted. "It's all right for you, dreamwalker! You're seventh-order! So much *higher* than the rest of us, aren't you?"

"You're helping Scion!"

"Vile augur-lover!"

More of them piled in, delighting in my downfall. Somebody hurled a shard of rubble, catching my cheek. I restrained my spirit from flying at the perpetrator. I had to rise above. To be strong. Nick shouted at them to get back, but nobody was listening.

They screamed their wrath straight into my ears, so close that my face was freckled with spit, but I didn't flinch. *Tyrant. Murderer. Warmonger. Brogue. Traitor. Traitor. Traitor.* Their voices became Jaxon's voice; their many-headed rage, his vengeance. I would be damned if I took one step away, if I gave an inch. The syndicate had never bowed to cowardice.

"Nick," I said, "take Jos back to the lower deck."

"If you think I'm leaving you—"

"Do it." Before he could argue, I raised my voice to the mob: "I don't have time for this. The only traitors here are those who threaten the peace. If you'll excuse me, I need to prepare this facility for the rest of the Mime Order. And thanks to this incident, it seems I'll need to cordon off a holding cell. The next person to spill blood in here will spend a month in it."

I strode straight through the sea of bodies. When the first hand grabbed my arm, I threw out my spirit.

Nobody tried to touch me again.

I marched between the bunks with my flashlight, through multiple sleeping areas, past another empty medical room and signs reading KITCHEN and CANTEEN and STORAGE. When I reached the supervisor's post, I crashed through its door and closed it behind me. Inside was a dead transmission screen, a desk without a chair, and a bunk that folded down from the wall. I lowered the bunk and sank on to it, aching from the four-mile trek.

In the tunnel, the shouting continued for a while before dying down. My nails bit into the skin of my palms.

I couldn't be taken by surprise like that again. Law and order would be critical down here. I needed to rally my commanders and work out what to do next, but my confidence was running between my fingers. In a confined, pitch-black space, where nobody could blow off steam, a flicker of resentment could ignite a riot.

They were right to resent me. I had brought down the might of the Archon on our heads. These voyants had lived without many things in their lives, but by trying to fight Scion head-on, as no syndicate leader had before, I had taken away the one thing that had sustained them. I had taken away the streets.

My cheek was throbbing where the rubble had struck me. I had to think, and quickly. We had somewhere to hide, but we couldn't last down here forever.

The only way to free the Mime Order was for a group of us to get back out there and use every available resource to find Senshield's core and destroy it. The soldiers would still be there if we succeeded, but if they had no way to detect us, we could risk a return to the surface.

Where was it? I let my backpack slip on to the floor and wrenched it open, rifling through it for my map of London. Maybe there was a pattern in the scanners' locations, or some abandoned place where they might be keeping the core—something, anything . . .

I stopped when I saw it. An envelope, nestled among my clothes, addressed to me. Danica's handwriting.

Inside it was a note, hastily written.

Paige, as you'll know by now, I've left. I applied for a transfer to Scion Athens after the scrimmage, and they approved it two days ago. I'm not the revolutionary, gung-ho, against-the-government type, and of you and Jaxon, you seemed like the easier person to run away from.

I would, however, like to leave you with a parting gift. It relates to Senshield.

She had never meant to stay with me, but it was clear that she hadn't betrayed me. I read on.

You may have noticed, over our years of cohabitation, that I don't like being outsmarted. Vance fooled you through me, which, in my self-centered mind, means that Vance bested me personally, and that I am partly responsible for the deaths of the people on your assignment. Apparently I have a conscience.

I traced the blur where the side of her hand had smudged the letters. She must have been deeply humiliated to admit to any of this.

So I've spent my last hours in London doing better investigation. I discovered something very interesting, and this time, it's not false information. I made sure.

A while ago, I mentioned Scion's plans for a portable scanner. At the time, I was under the impression that they were still in the early stages of design. I was wrong about that, too. As you read this, handheld scanners are being manufactured for military use in a factory in Manchester, which is owned and controlled by a government department called SciPLO. These scanners will be linked to the core, whatever or wherever it is. My feeling is that you'll want to pay a visit to Manchester, in the absence of better leads.

I could feel sweat forming on my upper lip. Handheld scanners, and sooner than we had thought. I imagined an army, each soldier carrying one. This couldn't be happening.

I appreciate that you need somewhere to start in a citadel that's not familiar to you, so here's one more breadcrumb. SciPLO's records indicate that one of their workhands, Jonathan Cassidy, is wanted for theft. It might be a long shot, but if you can find him, he may be willing to give you more information about the manufacturing process.

I hope this makes up for my error. I'd say goodbye, but unfortunately for both of us, we will meet again.

I scrunched the note into my hand.

Portable scanners. A death sentence.

The door opened. I snatched up the knife in my boot, expecting to see a murderous voyant.

"Warden," I said, lowering it.

He came to sit beside me, and I knew he had followed the cord to my side. He lifted a hand to my face, turning it gently. His thumb touched my cheek and came away bloody.

"What happened?"

"The inevitable." I pressed my fingers over the cut. "This place is a pressure cooker. They won't last a month down here without killing each other. Or me."

"You were right to call for an evacuation," he said, unruffled as ever. "So long as you find a way to replenish your supplies, the Beneath may serve you better than your original network of buildings. Fortunate that you had mercy on Ivy, or the Mime Order would have no haven. Your compassion has repaid you."

"For the time being." I unfolded Danica's letter and handed it to him. "We won't be returning to the surface for a while."

He read it, expressionless.

"If portable scanners haven't already been issued to the soldiers, they will be soon." I took back the paper, pocketed it. "This is on me, all of it. If we'd gone back to our lives after we got out of the colony, none of this would be happening. Everyone would have just continued with mime-crime . . ."

My jaw and throat were aching. Warden shifted off the bunk and crouched in front of me.

"Never allow yourself to believe you should be silent." His voice rumbled from deep in his chest. "If you had been silent in the colony, then both of us might still be there. Even if you had never become Underqueen, Senshield was on the horizon. The scanners might not have come so soon, but they would have come. There is no choice but to fight."

A tear escaped. I blotted it with my sleeve. "I should never have risked going to that warehouse. I helped make Senshield stronger."

"You did. It is done," he said. I lowered my head. "This was the right thing to do, Paige," he said again. "You will be safe here. Alsafi will reconnect the power as soon as he is able."

Alsafi. Slowly, I looked up.

"If I were to put together a team," I said, "could Alsafi get them to Manchester?" When he didn't answer at once, I continued: "It's where the scanners are being made. It's the next step to track down Senshield's core. And I trust the information this time."

Warden seemed to consider this. "I am not able to contact Alsafi directly," he said. "After I requested that he restore the power, he told us to cut off further communication with him, most likely because the risk of receiving our messages has become too high. However, I believe he divulged the identities of certain people in his network to Pleione. She may be able to arrange safe passage. If she is successful, you will have to choose someone you trust as your interim."

"I didn't mean *I* would go. I'd send a team. The leader of the syndicate never leaves London."

"Traditionally. You are not a traditional Underqueen."

"Warden, I can't go. If you think they're pissed off with me now, they'll be murderous if I run away."

"Consider the alternative. The Mime Order blames you for this state of affairs. While you are here, their anger will remain fresh. Many will resist your orders out of resentment." His gloved hands cupped mine. "You broke from convention by turning on your mime-lord, Paige. You can do it again."

He might be right. The time for tradition was gone.

"You'll stay now, and help us," I said. "Won't you?"

"No."

I stared at him. "You must be joking," I said, when he gave no explanation of his own accord. "You're not seriously abandoning us now?"

"We must have Rephaite support, Paige," Warden said. "Now more than ever. Terebell has no intention of changing her plans— and after what she regards as your insubordination, it may be best that the two of you do not see each other for a time."

I could only imagine how enraged she must have been when she realized what Vance had done at the warehouse.

"Fine." I pulled my hands free from his and stood. "I need to speak to my commanders."

"I also wish to speak to your commanders. If I may."

"You don't need to ask permission."

He looked at my face for a long time. I wondered if he could understand the emotions bubbling through me: the bitterness and disappointment, the fear of what the future would bring.

We left the supervisor's post together and took the parallel tunnel back to the other end of the facility, avoiding the voyants in the bunks. I didn't want to get into the habit of hiding from my subjects, but it was safer if I let their tempers simmer down.

As we passed one of the cross-tunnels, the lights on the ceiling flickered, then glowed, and a bluebottle hum filled the facility.

"Alsafi." I switched off my flashlight. "He's quick."

"He knew the need was pressing."

"Is he sure Scion won't notice?"

"They abandoned this facility a century ago. It is forgotten. He will see to it that it remains so."

Our surroundings were a little more welcoming now. None of the bulbs grew too bright—Alsafi must be being cautious with the electricity—but they warmed the concrete and cast-iron.

The others had claimed places on the lower deck. The vile augurs had clearly felt safe enough to emerge, for the time being: Wynn and Vern had occupied one pair of bunks, while Róisín was at the top of the next set, and Ivy at the bottom of the next. Jos was above her, fast asleep beneath two blankets, and Maria had dumped her rucksack opposite Ivy. When she saw Warden's towering figure, Ivy pushed herself farther into her bunk.

"You found bedding?" I said.

"Not much," Nick admitted. "Are you okay?"

"Of course." I spotted a bag on the floor. "Whose is that?"

A hoarse voice came from the doorway. "Mine."

I turned to see Tom and Glym, both a little worse for wear. It was Tom who had spoken, and he was grinning, if grimy. I was so relieved to see them that I embraced them both.

"Minty asked us to deliver a message." Glym looked grave. "She has decided against entering the Beneath. She would prefer to stay in Grub Street and assist us from there."

I wanted to protest, but Minty Wolfson was the soul of Grub Street, and I couldn't imagine her anywhere else. "And the Pearl Queen?"

"We've heard nothing from her."

Four out of six commanders, Warden, and both my mollishers. More than enough to decide on our counter play. I beckoned the others into an empty side tunnel, where someone had set up a table and chairs. Warden barred the door behind us before taking a seat.

"Time for us to plan our next move," I said, "because things are about to get much worse."

"Worse," Maria echoed. "Than this."

I handed her Danica's note. She read it and turned away with a groan, fisting her hands in her hair.

"Portable scanners. For the soldiers," she said. "It's a damn good thing we did move underground."

Tom took it from her, digested it.

"I know it's not good news," I said as they passed the note around, their faces turning grimmer as they read, "but it does give us a new lead on Senshield." I raised my chin. "I'm going to Manchester. If that's where portable scanners are being manufactured, we might be able to find out how and where they're being linked to Senshield, and that, in turn, could lead us to the core. It's a chance, at any rate."

Eliza shook her head. "You want to *leave*? Now?"

"That would be unprecedented," Glym said. "No syndicate leader has ever left the citadel. It may not be a popular move—"

"I didn't become Underqueen to be popular. Tom, Maria, will you come with me?"

Tom beamed. "I'm with you, Underqueen."

"Absolutely," Maria said.

It was risky to take two commanders away, but I sensed their skills would be the most useful. Tom was a powerful voyant and had knowledge of the country beyond London, while Maria had experience as an insurgent, as well as the sort of relentless energy we needed for this journey.

"Good. And Glym," I said, "will you be interim Underlord?"

There was an odd silence. Glym blinked, but dipped his head. "You do me a great honor, Underqueen."

Glym was loyal and well-respected, had years of experience as a leader in the syndicate, and didn't take any nonsense from the Assembly. "Your priority is to preserve life while we're gone," I said. "Get as many voyants into this facility as you can. Get the pumps and ventilation working. Send the higher orders to retrieve food and drink for the lower. Keep the peace. Above all, make sure this place isn't compromised."

Warden had watched our discussion in silence.

"What did you want to say?" I asked him quietly.

He looked between my commanders.

"The Mime Order is an alliance between our two factions," he said. "You have all contributed your skills and knowledge to its continuation. Now, we wish to give something in return."

"Oh, at last," Maria said.

Warden gave her a sidelong glance before continuing. "With Senshield now able to detect four of seven orders, all clairvoyants in this country, whether they yet know it or not, are in an extremely precarious position. If ever the time was ripe to sway them to our cause, it is now. It would be advantageous to alert them to the situation in the capital and urge them to join the revolution."

"And how do you propose we do that," said Maria, "given Scion's famous tolerance for freedom of information?"

Tom snorted.

"I suggest," Warden said, undeterred, "that we send a message through the æther—one that would reach many voyants at once—encouraging them to assist the Mime Order in its fight against Scion." There was silence from us all. "I take it you have all attended a séance at some point in your careers."

Nods. I had been part of a few séances during my time as Jaxon's mollisher. They were group summonings of spirits, requiring the presence of at least three voyants.

"Well-conducted séances can amplify clairvoyant gifts. I propose that we hold one here. First," Warden said, "I would draw memories from any willing ScionIDE survivors, which will illustrate the threat they pose. Paige will enter my dreamscape and experience them with me. Immediately after, she will jump into a willing oracle."

"Okay," Nick said, frowning.

"This stage is theoretical, but I believe that Paige should be able to transfer the memories from my dreamscape to the oracle's, allowing them to be projected into the æther. The longer we can sustain the séance, the farther the message will travel. We will need most, or preferably all, of the Unnatural Assembly for it to travel far and wide."

Maria folded her arms. "Sounds great. Why haven't we been doing this all along?"

"You did not have a Rephaite with you," Warden said. "Now, who here has had dealings with ScionIDE?"

Maria chuckled. "I'll share. My memories are nice and gruesome."

The room's attention shifted toward Nick, who was hunched on a supply crate. He wet his lips. "My experience was . . . personal. I don't know if I want it made public."

"Take mine," I said to Warden. "My memory of the Dublin Incursion."

"You were too young," Warden said. "Those memories may not be clear enough."

Nick circled his temples with his fingers. "Have it," he said. "If it will help the country understand, have it." His knee bounced. "I can't project the emotions in the memory, you realize. Just images."

"The images may be all that is needed. Visions of a violent past—portending a violent future."

Nick nodded, resting his forehead on one hand.

"Let me do the projection," Tom said gently, patting him on the back. "I've a wee bit more experience in the art."

Another nod.

"It is settled, then. If you can persuade the Unnatural Assembly to perform the séance," Warden said, "I will help you strengthen it."

Tom grimaced. "You dinna think the Assembly will all hold hands together, do you?"

"Oh, they will," I said.

"They willna like it, Underqueen."

"I might be wrong," I said, "but I don't think Scion will give a damn whether they like it or not."

9

The Cost

It took sixteen hours to gather enough of the Unnatural Assembly to perform the séance. They were scattered far and wide across the citadel, pinned down in various segments of the Beneath.

While the toshers tried to bring them to the facility, the rest of us got to work on making our new home habitable. We laid bedding on the bunks. A team was set up to work on the pumps and the ventilation system. What food we had carried was stashed in the canteen area, ready to be distributed. Weapons were taken from their owners and locked away.

The work kept me too busy to speak to Warden again. Sometimes we passed each other as we carried boxes of bedding between the sectors, and I would catch a glimpse of his face in the dim light, but I always avoided eye contact.

All the while, more voyants trickled into the facility. Some came through a passage that connected to the Underground, others through the sewers, and others still through a building on the surface.

We cleaned up the medical wing as best we could, pooling our supplies, and Nick and Wynn were handed the keys. Wynn immediately called me in and sat me down on a crate. Her hair was back in its fishtail braid.

"Let's see that hand. And your face," she said. "We can't have you dying of infection before you go."

The cut from Styx had long since stopped bleeding, but knowing me, I would tear it open if it wasn't stitched. Wynn laid my hand in her lap, took a small bottle of alcohol from her skirts and tipped a little stream on to the cut on my palm, then dabbed some more on to my cheek.

"Are you all right, Wynn?"

"We're used to poor treatment by now." My palm smarted. "Paige, you must choose someone for Styx, and do it soon. He won't forget about your bargain."

"What will he do if I don't send anyone?"

"He'll go to Scion. The toshers take vows very seriously," she said. "That's why he cut you. Once the river has witnessed your oath, you're bound to it. If you go back on it, there's no reason for him to protect us."

"Would you be opposed to me sending a vile augur?"

"Not if they were willing."

"And if they weren't?"

She slowed in her work. "That would depend."

I let her clean my wounds in peace for a while. Once she was satisfied, she plucked a needle from her cardigan and washed it in the alcohol.

"Wynn," I said, "you've seen that the voyants still despise Ivy." Her face tightened. "It could cause a lot of trouble while you're down here. They're crying out for blood."

Wynn looked up sharply. "Don't you dare."

"I won't make her go." I lowered my voice. "I want to give her the option. She might be safer with the toshers than she is in here."

"It would be for a lifetime. That was what Styx demanded."

"I will get her out," I said.

"How?"

"However I can. She will not stay there forever."

She returned her attention to my palm, her jaw stiff. The needle shoved into my skin.

"You know how frail she is," Wynn said, with unusual softness. "She doesn't sleep. Her stomach won't take much food. And you ought to see the scars her keeper gave her. She has been punished more than enough for what she did." Her shoulders pulled back. "Ivy is like a daughter to me. All the Jacob girls are. Send her, and I'll go to Scion with our whereabouts myself."

"Wynn." I grasped her wrist. "You wouldn't. You'd kill all the vile augurs in here, as well as the rest of us."

Her lips pursed. She cut the thread and enfolded my hand in a clean bandage.

"I don't know what I'd do. You know I've no love for this syndicate, Paige. My loyalty was only ever to you." She secured the dressing. "Go on, now. I have another patient."

Her face had turned to stone. I left.

The next patient was outside. Ivy. She was standing with Róisín, who seemed to have taken on the role of bodyguard.

"Paige," Ivy said, but I ignored her. My footsteps matched my heartbeat as I walked away. "Paige?"

It would sate their bloodlust to give Ivy to Styx, and it would keep her out of danger. Every minute, I expected to hear that someone had snapped and taken *justice* into their own hands, and I feared it.

Ivy was a survivor. While I was in Manchester, however, I wouldn't be able to protect her. I wanted to see her settled in a safe place, somewhere where she could mend, where she would be surrounded by people who cared about her, and that place wasn't here—but if she was ever going to reach it, she had to last for the next few weeks.

For now, the decision would have to wait. It was time for the séance.

I joined my mollishers in the cross-tunnel, all three of us silent and tense as we waited. Eliza worried a lock of her hair, while Nick, who stood with his arms folded, was statue-still. I knew that the thirty members of the Unnatural Assembly who had arrived had been summoned to an empty stretch of the upper deck, where there was enough room to form a circle. Their voices mingled in the darkened space. They must have come willingly, but even so, I had no idea what sort of reception awaited us.

"Nick," I said, watching his closed face, "you don't have to do this."

His gaze was distant. "It's time I faced it."

A few more mime-lords and mime-queens trailed into the chamber. I watched them out of their sight. No sign of the Pearl Queen.

When the three of us stepped into the tunnel, their voices slammed into me like a wall: shouts for justice for their missing sensors, for explanations, for evidence of a plan to get rid of the army. Some of them bawled that I was a murderer and a turn-coat. I watched as this ostensible Assembly collapsed into a snarl of cavilling, shrieking, and fist-shaking while Eliza and Nick moved in front of me, calling for order. Spirits quavered nearby, ready to attack. When one of the new mime-queens punched Jimmy O'Goblin, I brought them all to heel with my spirit. A wave rolled through the æther and broke against their dreamscapes.

They quietened, their expressions wary. *They need to be afraid of you, or they will never respect you*, Glym had told me. *All you have to do is show them what you can do, if you choose.*

Several of them had souvenirs from the scrimmage: scarred faces, burns, missing fingers. Others had more recent wounds. I spotted Jack Hickathrift, who smiled at me with one side of his mouth.

"The Underqueen," Nick called.

I stepped forward. Eliza and Nick flanked me, both forming spools for my protection.

"Members of the Unnatural Assembly," I said, "as you're all aware, we are facing a crisis on an unprecedented scale. With the call for martial law and the increased presence of Senshield, I have had no choice but to order the syndicate into the Beneath." A few mutters, but I was holding their attention. "After years of threaten-ing us with Senshield, Scion has not only installed hidden scanners across the citadel and recalibrated the technology, but combined the threat of it with the presence of ScionIDE—their army."

"Because of *you*!"

"Go to hell, dreamwalker!"

"We should have never let you have the crown. This wouldn't have happened under Binder!"

Others chimed in with their agreements. My commanders were at the back of the gathering, watching tensely, but I'd told them not to leap to my defense. I needed to handle this on my own.

"Pipe down, the lot of you, and listen to me," I said sharply, speaking over the noise. "We have received reliable intelligence that a Senshield manufacturing hub is in Manchester. I intend to go there myself, along with Tom the Rhymer and Ognena Maria. We are hopeful that we will be able to gain crucial information with regard to the power source of Senshield. And when we find out what that power source is, I vow to you, we will destroy it."

The reaction was immediate and livid.

"How do you expect to do that?"

"Ah, so that's how it is! Scarpering at the first sign of trouble!"

"Craven!"

"Putting other citadels in danger, too, are we, brogue? Going to expose *more* voyants to Scion?"

And so on, until the Glass Duchess snapped, "Shut up and let the woman speak!"

Gradually, the commotion died down.

"This was always going to happen," I said, fighting to keep my voice cool. "Hector denied it, and so did every leader before him, but now we know that the only way out of this is to resist. Scion has just used me as their excuse. They've used *us* as their excuse, because they are *afraid* of us. They've been afraid of the power of the syndicate from the beginning, the potential for voyants to unite against them. That's why Senshield exists. That's why we're here. If ScionIDE is allowed to remain, armed with the new, portable scanners, they will not rest until they have stamped out the voyant way of life. If we are to survive, we *must* fight." I pointed upward. "Up there, Scion is preparing to wage war against us. Let's give them a taste of their own medicine."

Something I'd said had reached them. A smattering of applause went through their ranks.

"You wish to declare *war* on Scion? In this weather?" the Heathen Philosopher blustered, one eye magnified by his monocle. "The Unnatural Assembly is an administrative body that facilitates the felonious activity of worthy clairvoyants. Certainly not one with the capacity to declare *war*."

I was beginning to appreciate Hector's restraint in not killing the whole lot of them.

"They declared war on *us*," I said, my voice growing stronger, "the day they put their first voyant on the gallows. They declared war on *us* the day they spilled the first blood on the Lychgate!" Cheers. "You are the clairvoyants of London, and I will not see you extinguished. We are going to reclaim our streets. We are going to seize our freedom. They made thieves of us—it is time to steal what's ours!"

The words stemmed from a place in me I hadn't known was there. More cheers, louder. Calls of support.

"You've got some cheek, brogue," Slyboots sneered, and they died down. "None of us signed up to be soldiers."

"I did," Jimmy O'Goblin slurred.

"Jimmy, sober up or hush up," I said. Jeers followed. Jimmy jeered along with them, then looked confused. "I know the odds are daunting, but we have the æther. We can fight our way back to the surface, because we have a means to do so. Clairvoyance—our gift. As the Ranthen have shown us, we *can* use it against amaurotics. It's a matter of unlocking our potential. Of trusting the very source of knowledge that binds us together.

"If the White Binder had become Underlord, he would have made you into an army, too, but not one that fights for freedom. You would have been an army of messengers, spreading word of the anchor. You would have survived," I said, "but at what cost?"

"Rubbish," Slyboots shot back. "Binder would have found a way to make it work."

"Mind your tongue, Slyboots," I said curtly. "I know you helped the Silent Bell burn down the Juditheon—and if I remember correctly, your old mime-lord was one of those involved in the gray market. I hope you don't share the same sentiments."

He opened his mouth to argue, but Glym clipped his ear. "Speak to your Underqueen with respect," he said, "or you will not have a tongue to mind."

"You've got no right to give us orders," the Ferryman said. He was a wiry, white-haired augur, someone I knew only by sight.

"You've never known hardship, girl. You're seventh-order; you don't know what it is to be exposed to Senshield. You're the daughter of a Scion doctor. You were chosen by a wealthy mime-lord, who you betrayed for power. Give me one reason I should go to war for you. You're the one who brought this down on us."

Dark muttering followed his statement. I tried to muster the words to counter it, but it was like trying to pour from an empty bottle.

"Leave her be," Tom growled.

"Oh, she talks a good game, but I'd like to see her spend one day in the gutter. And she left Ireland quickly enough when—"

"Stop," I cut in. "I'm not asking you to go to war for me. I'm asking you to *wait* for me. And once I return, I'll be asking you to defend yourselves. To take back what's ours." I paced before them, looking many in the eye. "When I became the ruler of this syndicate, I expected some backbone. I expected to see that unquenchable desire for *more*—the desire that drives this under-world. It's what I've seen in all our eyes—the eyes of gutterlings, pickpockets, mollishers, mime-lords—since I first took to these streets. Years of oppression never crushed it, that flame that has led each of us to resist an empire that strives to destroy our way of life. Even if we've acted on it in the shadows, everything we've done, in the century the syndicate has existed, has been a small act of rebellion, whether daring to sell our gifts for coin or merely continuing to exist, and to profit." I stopped. "Where is that desire now?"

Silence answered me.

"You've always known your worth. You've always known that the world owes you something, and you meant to take it, no matter the risk. Take it now. Take more." Applause. Jimmy punched the air. "I will not allow this to be our extinction. Today, we descend. Tomorrow, we rise!"

This time, there were roars of approval. Halfpenny, I noticed, was one of those who clapped, even if he didn't speak. In the midst of it all, unheard by most of them, the Ferryman spat on the concrete floor.

"I'll not follow a brogue to my death," he said.

He offered a mocking bow before he left. My stomach flurried, but only his mollisher followed him. I pressed on.

"It's time to tell other voyants in this country about the Mime Order's cause. Here and now, we are going to conduct a séance and send a message to the voyants of Britain. It's going to multiply and spread through the æther like the branches of a tree, as far as we can send it. At the end, they will see . . . *this*."

I motioned to a section of wall, where Eliza had painted our call to arms.

THEY CAN DETECT FOUR ORDERS NOW.

HOW LONG BEFORE THEY SEE US ALL?

WE NEED EVERYONE, OR EVERYONE LOSES.

NO SAFE PLACE. NO SURRENDER.

The black moth flew beneath it.

At that moment, Warden emerged from the shadows and came to stand beside me, towering above them all. Spring-heel'd Jack let out a nervous snicker.

"Form a circle," Warden said, "and join hands."

Spluttered protests and hoots of laughter followed this command. "I'm not holding *her* hand," somebody said, making the nearest mime-queen look wounded.

"By all means," he said, "stand beside a person whose hands offend you less."

Maria took a candle from her pocket. I attached my oxygen mask. Painfully, like children cajoled into playing together, the Unnatural Assembly shambled into what could arguably be described as a circle. Some grasped each other's hands with casual ease; others were almost hysterical at the thought of touching their neighbor. As Nick and Eliza joined the ring, Warden reached for my hand.

Our fingers interlocked. My pulse flickered through my hands, in my neck, at the crease of my elbow. Worn leather pressed against my palm, soft between my knuckles and beside my inner wrist. Nick took my other hand, while Tom took Warden's. The ring was closed.

The Unnatural Assembly stood in silence together, waiting for the æther to open around them.

I had never thought to see this in my lifetime.

Warden murmured in Gloss. The candle grew brighter. Spirits were drawn into the ring, where they basked in an unbroken chain of auras. Nick and Maria had already dosed themselves with salvia; both were swaying on their feet.

"Tom," Warden said, "the message. Hold it in your mind."

Tom squinted at the graffiti, mouthing the words. Close by, Maria's head rolled forward, but she kept hold of the hands on either side of her. Warden's aura shifted.

"Now, Paige."

My spirit jumped, into his dreamscape.

I had been here before. The path was familiar, through the red velvet drapes and over the ashes to his sunlit zone, where I joined his dream-form beside the amaranth in the bell jar. He was already gazing at the smoke that was gathering, storm-like, in his mind.

I had never been inside him while he was using his gift. His hand took mine, echoing our position outside the dreamscape. And now that no one else could hear, I gave him a message.

"Meet me at midnight, on the lower deck."

His dream-form nodded.

The golden cord vibrated with a force that was almost violent, pulled like a tightrope by our proximity in a single dreamscape. Gradually, the smoke began to twist and form shapes. Memories.

He is searching for her in the forest, buried to his ankles in snow, holding up a lantern from their father's storehouse. This was Nick's memory. I couldn't explain how I knew. I was seeing through his eyes, feeling as he must have felt, but still an observer. *Eight sets of footprints snake between the trees, veering away from the path. The sound of his heart fills his ears like a drum.*

A new memory, someone else's. *The gun must have been heavy at first, but now it is as much a part of her arm as a muscle. She releases it only to ransack the other woman's pockets. Blood cascades down her chin and soaks the neckline of her shirt. Her hands never shake when she searches a corpse, but this one is different. This one is Roza.*

"Stoyan!"

Her hands sift through wet tissue and fabric and bone, picking out two precious, blood-slick bullets. One she must save for herself, one for Hristo.

Survival first. Pain later.

"It's over," Hristo says. "All they need is a formal surrender. We'll go to the border, to Turkey—"

"You can try."

The district is ablaze around them. All she can hear is the rattle of gunfire. The English soldiers are almost upon them. "Sit with me, Hristo," she says. "Let's go to hell with a little dignity."

"Stoyan—"

"Yoana." She lights her last cigarette, her hands gloved in blood. "If we're dying now, please, for once, call me by my name."

Hristo kneels in front of her. "If you won't try, I must. My family—" He squeezes her wrists. "I'll pray for you. Good luck, Yoana."

She hardly notices him leave, knowing she will never see him again. Her gaze falls to the gun.

Back to Nick. I was rooted in place, unable to stop watching.

Now there are more footprints than eight people could make. He runs. A patrol has come through this part of the forest.

In the clearing, the tents have been torn down. A sign gives notice of their execution.

She is curled on her side by the ashes of their campfire. Håkan is nearby, prostrate, his coat drenched in rust. Their hands reach across snow. Between them, the bottle is undamaged, the bottle they must have bought in secret, the bottle of wine with a Danish label. He gathers her body into his arms and screams like a dying thing.

Warden's dream-form released me, and the cord rang again. "Go, Paige," he said.

My spirit fled.

I woke gasping for air. Nick was on his knees, his hand crushing mine. I jumped again, tearing from my body.

I glimpsed enough of Tom's dreamscape to tell that it took the shape of a factory. Dust fell all around me as I launched myself into his sunlit zone, where his dream-form's hand reached for mine.

Contact between two dream-forms was deeply intimate, but there was no time for embarrassment. The moment we connected, I knew Warden had been right. The memories arced between us like lightning.

Now all we had to do was hold on.

As soon as I landed back in my body, Tom gritted his teeth and projected the memories as oracular images. They hit us first; then the rest of the Assembly drew in their breath as they succumbed. Instead of the dream-like way in which Warden experienced memory, I saw them like pages in a flick book. The forest and the burning street smothered my vision.

"Hold the circle," Warden commanded. The memories repeated over and over, faster and faster, lifted away from us by the spirits, until all I could see was the moth and the message.

It held for a while, long enough to be remembered. Then we all fell down.

Night and day didn't exist in the Beneath, but the séance had exhausted the Unnatural Assembly. The lights turned off, allowing them to sleep. I had already noticed the division in our ranks. Most of my supporters had clustered on the lower deck, while those who spoke against me were on the upper. All I could do was hope that Glym would be able to unite them.

I sat on the vacant bunk beside Eliza's, gazing into the blackness. The thought of leaving now, when I was just about holding on to their loyalty, was hard to stomach. Even harder to stomach was the knowledge that Nick, who was asleep or pretending to be, had spent the last few hours in his bunk, ignoring anyone who spoke to him.

His private memory had been used as fuel. As propaganda. His little sister's murder.

"You're going to give me to Styx."

The voice was hoarse. Light flickered from the end of a flashlight.

"I overheard you talking to Wynn." Ivy was sitting cross-legged on her bunk. "I want to do it."

Wynn had covered the "T" on her cheek with a square dressing. I didn't say anything.

137

"She doesn't want to see it, but you know I won't last long down here. Someone will cut my throat when I'm looking the wrong way. The only reason they haven't killed me already is because you've been here," she said. "So it has to be me. For all our sakes."

I breathed in through my nose.

"If you stay with us," I said, "then you'll be killed. But if I send you, Wynn will betray us to Scion."

"There is another way."

The new voice had an Irish accent. Ivy aimed the flashlight. Róisín Jacob was awake, watching us from her bunk. Her lip had puffed up since the attack.

"I know the toshers. Used to help them scavenge in our section of the Neckinger," she said. "I like Styx. And I'm in better shape than Ivy. Send me."

"Ro," Ivy started.

"You're in no fit state to be crawling through tunnels. You'll give me to Styx," she said to me, "and Wynn will accept it without question, because I'll tell her I'm going of my own free will."

"They won't let you. This is my responsibility. It was *my* crime." Ivy's voice cracked. "Besides, Paige needs to punish me, or someone else will."

There was a pause before Róisín said slowly, "They *will* see you punished. You'll be officially chosen, and then I'll offer to go in your stead. But, Ivy, the one person here that Wynn won't stand to lose again is you. She suffered enough the first time."

Ivy buried her head in her arms. "I don't know," she said, her voice muffled.

"You need to decide by tomorrow," I said. "The Glym Lord will announce that he's stepping in as interim Underlord in my absence. He'll also announce that Ivy Jacob has been sentenced to a life in the Beneath for her crimes against the syndicate. Róisín, if you're going, you'll need to come forward and insist that you take her punishment. And, Ivy, you will act as if seeing Róisín sent in your place is a far higher price to pay than going yourself."

I had never heard myself sound so callous. Ivy stared at Róisín, then flung me a bitter look.

"I won't have to act," she said, and turned over.

I dropped my gaze, clenched my jaw. Róisín watched the lump beneath the blanket for a while.

"She'll understand," she said to me. "Wynn, I mean. All she's ever wanted is for us vile augurs to be able to make our own choices. I've made mine."

She laid her head back on the pillow. I rose from the bunk and walked into the darkness, holding my jacket around myself.

Relief warred against self-disgust. I had been ready to send Ivy. Barely a month of being Underqueen, and I was already becoming someone I didn't recognize. Someone who would punish a person who was already broken. Someone who would do anything to achieve her aims.

Only a tissue of morality now set me apart from Haymarket Hector.

Warden was waiting for me in a deserted sleeping area. I sat on the opposite bunk and set my flashlight down on the mattress.

"You leave for Manchester in four hours," he said.

My fingers ran over the bandage on my hand.

"Lucida will be here by morning. She will ensure the Glym Lord is accepted as your interim, and that no further violence occurs." He paused. "I make the crossing to the Netherworld at dawn."

I only nodded in response. The two bunks were so close that our knees almost touched.

Sweat coated my nape. I had thought about these words all day, but couldn't let them out. I couldn't even look at him. I would only lose the will to do this.

"The other night, I made a mistake," I said eventually. "I should have called the Unnatural Assembly right away, to tell them about Senshield being able to detect the fourth order. So they could hear it from me first. So I could frame it to our advantage."

My words were too clear in the silence of this place, a silence untouched by the music of the citadel.

"I could have got there before Weaver. But I let myself be persuaded to wait until morning, because I wanted to see you. I wanted to be with you—to be selfish, just for a few hours. Those hours put Weaver ahead of me."

His gaze burned on my face.

"I'm Underqueen, and you're . . . a distraction I can't afford."
It took effort to say this, to believe this. "I swore to myself that I would sacrifice everything if it meant I could take down Scion. If it meant that voyants could be free. We can't let the Mime Order fail, Warden, not after what we've been through to get here. We can't put it in jeopardy."

It was some time before he said, "Say it."

My face had been hidden behind my hair. Now I lifted it.

"You said change had a personal cost for all of us." I looked him in the eye. "You are what change will cost me."

We sat there for a long time. I wanted to take it back; with difficulty, I stopped myself. It seemed like a lifetime before he spoke again.

"You need not justify your choices."

"I wouldn't choose it. Not if it wasn't necessary. If it were different—" I looked away. "But . . . it isn't."

He didn't deny it.

Jaxon had been right about words. They could grant wings, or they could tear them away.

Words were useless now. No matter what I said, how hard I tried to articulate it in a way that he could understand, I would never be able to express to this Rephaite what it would do to me when I surrendered him to the war we had started, or how much I had wanted our stolen hours to continue. I had thought those hours would be my candles, as our days grew darker. Points of light, of fleeting warmth.

"Perhaps this is for the best," Warden said. "You already dwell too deep in shadows."

"I would have gone into the shadows for you," I said. "But . . . I can't allow myself to care about you this much, not when I'm Underqueen. I can't afford to feel the way I do when I'm with you. We can fight on the same side, but you can't be my secret. And I can't be yours."

When he moved, I thought he was going to leave without saying anything. Then, gently, his hands clasped mine.

If I ever touched him again, he would be wearing gloves. It would be in passing. By mistake.

"When I return," he said, "we will be allies. Nothing more. It will be . . . as if the Guildhall never was."

It should have been a weight off my shoulders. My life was already too dangerous. Instead, I felt hollow, as if he had taken something from me that I had never known was there. I went to him and buried my face in his neck.

We sat with our arms around each other, holding too tightly and not tightly enough. Once we left this place, there would be no more talks beside the fire. No more nights spent in his company, when I could forget the war and suffering that loomed on the horizon. No more dances in derelict halls. No more music.

"Goodbye, little dreamer," he said.

I almost voiced my answer. Instead, I pressed my forehead against his, and deep in his eyes, a flame was kindled. As his thumb grazed my jaw, I committed the way his hands felt on my skin to a hidden vault in my memory. I wasn't sure which of us brought our lips to the other's first.

It lasted far too long for a farewell. A moment. A choice. A mirror of the first time we had touched this way, behind the red drapes in the nest of the enemy—when danger had been everywhere, but a song had still been rising in us both. A song I wasn't sure that anything could silence.

Our lips parted. I breathed him in, one more time.

I stood up, turned my back, and walked away.

PART II

Engine of Empire

10

Manchester

December 3, 2059

The train glided across the snowbound English countryside. Not that we could see any of it—the four of us were hidden in a small baggage compartment—but Alsafi's contact had given us a satellite tracker, a requirement for safe passage, allowing us to watch the progress of our journey.

We had met the contact outside Euston Arch station, and she had sneaked us on to a non-stop service after pressing the tracker into my hand. Another member of Alsafi's network would take us to a safe location in Manchester.

I had decided, in the end, to take Eliza with us, too. She and Tom had long since fallen asleep, but Maria and I were alert.

"So," Maria said, "the plan—such as it stands—is to locate this person Danica thinks can help us—"

"Jonathan Cassidy," I said.

"—locate the factory where the portable scanners are being made, and infiltrate Senshield's manufacturing process. Find out how they build the scanners. That's it? That's the famous plan?"

"Well, it's a start. If you want to dismantle something, you should know how it's put together. There must be a point at which an ordinary piece of machinery is converted to an active Senshield scanner." I sighed. "Look, we don't have any other leads. And you never know: we might unearth some information about Senshield's core, and how it's powered—and where it is."

"Hm." She peered at the tracker. "Let's hope Danica got her facts straight this time, or we could find ourselves walking into another trap." The light from the screen tinged her face with blue. "There's some information in here about 'enclaves,' but I don't understand it."

I took it from her and tapped a tiny symbol of a house on the screen. ENCLAVE, the tracker read. LOOK FOR BLACK HELLEBORE.

"What's black hellebore?" Maria said.

"He's using the language of flowers," I realized, after a moment. "Black hellebore points to the relief of anxiety. We must be able to find shelter and supplies where it grows."

Alsafi must have been preparing for an emergency like this for a long time. Interesting that he spoke the language of flowers, the code the syndicate had used in its scrimmages for years. I had never liked him in the colony, but his work was turning out to be vital to our survival.

While Maria dozed, I occupied myself by studying Scion Britain on the tracker. The territory covered the places that had once been called Scotland and Wales, which were no longer recognized as separate countries; *England* and *Britain* were used almost inter-changeably by Scion. The island was divided into eight regions, each of which had one citadel, which acted as its regional "capital"— though all bowed to the will of London. The surrounding areas were peppered with towns, villages and conurbations, all under the yoke of Scion outposts. We were headed into the North West region, to its citadel—Manchester, center of industry.

It had been ten years since I had last left London. It had kept hold of me for so long.

I nodded off against the side of the compartment for a while, my hand still curled around the tracker. Everything that had happened over the last few days had left me hungry for sleep.

At just past one in the morning, the train came to a halt, jolting me awake. Maria took the tracker from my unresisting hand. When she saw our location, she stiffened.

"Something's wrong. We're still forty miles away."

"*Ladies and gentlemen, we apologize for the delay in your journey to Manchester. This is Stoke-on-Trent.*" I pressed my ear to the wall, straining to hear the muffled voice. "*Under new regulations imposed by the Grand Commander, all Sciorail trains from London are now subject to regular checks by Underguards. Please accommodate their needs as they move through the train.*"

My heart pounded. Had Vance snared us again already? She was always one step ahead—always waiting for us, somehow.

Maria shook the others awake. We gathered our belongings and crept toward a sliding door, which would allow us to steal away without the Underguards seeing. I reached for a lever marked EMERGENCY DOOR RELEASE. As it pushed outward and glided aside, letting in an icy gust of wind, I glanced out of the compartment, searching for oncoming trains. Mercifully, there was no one on the other platform.

"Now," I whispered.

The Underguards were getting close—I sensed them. Eliza carefully turned and swung her legs on to a short ladder, which took her down to the ballast between the tracks.

Footsteps slapped along the platform, and I caught a snatch of voices. ". . . why Vance thinks they're going to be here . . ."

"Waste of time."

I went next, followed by Tom. As Maria got out, she grabbed at the door for support, causing it to slide shut.

"As soon as they leave," I breathed, "we get back on."

We edged a little farther down the track, shivering in the frigid air. When the Underguards entered the baggage compartment, we all pressed ourselves against the train and grew still, waiting for one of them to look out and see us. Finding nothing of interest, they soon retreated, muttering about paranoid krigs and pointless work. I motioned to Maria, who reached up to grasp the door—only to find that there was no handle. The only thing there was a fingerprint scanner. We were shut out of the train.

As the Underguards left the platform, a whistle sounded in the station.

Too late. The train was moving. We didn't have long before we were exposed on both sides. I beckoned frantically to the others; Tom pulled Maria away from the door. We sprinted back the same way the train had come, into billows of snow, while our ride left Stoke-on-Trent without us.

We kept running, our boots crunching through ballast. Only when we were a fair distance from the station did we slow down to catch our breath. We helped each other over the fence, on to the street, and clustered beneath a bus shelter, heads bent to see the tracker. I brought up a map of our location, which offered up morsels of data about Stoke-on-Trent. Status: conurbation. Region: Midlands. Nearest citadel: Scion Citadel of Birmingham.

"We can't stay here for long," I said. "Outlying communities are too dangerous. They're much more observant than people in the citadels."

Maria nodded. "We'll have to walk."

Eliza was already shivering. "In this snow?"

"I walked across countries to get to Britain, sweet. We can make it. And let's face it: it wouldn't be the most insane thing we've done this week." Maria peered over my shoulder at the tracker. "Looks like twelve hours on foot to the center of Manchester. Probably a little longer, in this weather."

I clenched my jaw. Every hour left the Mime Order in more danger. "There's an enclave farther north." I tapped the tracker. "We'll walk from now until sunrise, stop there, and press on when it gets dark again. The contact we're due to meet will guess that something went wrong."

Maria patted Tom on the back. "Can you make it that far?"

Tom had a slight limp from an old injury to his knee. "There's no other choice," he said, "unless we mean to stay here and wait for the Gillies to find us in the morning."

I adjusted my winter hood so only my eyes were uncovered. "Then let's stretch our legs."

Although Stoke-on-Trent was quiet in the small hours, it put me on edge. Even a notorious outlaw could be anonymous in the capital of all Scion, but not in settlements like these. It reminded me of Arthyen, the village where I had first met Nick. Its residents had been on a permanent quest to see unnaturalness in their neighbors.

We stole through the streets, passing darkened shops, small transmission screens, and houses with the occasional lit window. Maria went ahead to scout for cameras and guide us out of their way. I only managed to relax a little when the streetlamps were far behind us and we were out in the countryside. It wasn't long before we crossed the regional boundary, which was marked by a billboard reading WELCOME TO THE NORTH WEST.

For a while, we risked the road, which had been recently cleared of snow. Ruined churches dotted our way. Tom found a sturdy branch to use as a staff. To distract myself from the blistering wind, I started counting stars. The sky was clearer here, and the stars burned far brighter than they did in London, where the blue haze of the streetlamps watered down their light. As I picked apart the broken necklaces of diamond, trying to find the constellations, I wondered why the Rephaim had taken the stars' names as their own. I wondered why he had chosen *Arcturus*.

After a truck gunned past us and blared its horn, we ducked under a barbed-wire fence into the fields, where snowdrifts were piled like whipped cream. More of it was falling, catching in my lashes. We had the tracker, but it was so disorienting, with the black sky above us and white as far as the eye could see below, that we finally risked switching on our flashlights. The world around us was drained of color, flickering with snowflakes.

"I can't wait to advertise the Mime Order to the n-northerners. 'Join Paige Mahoney for unexpected rambles through snow and shit,'" Maria bit out through chattering teeth.

I chased white powder from the tracker again. "Nobody s-said the revolution would be glamorous."

"Oh, I don't know. I like to think that in the great uprisings of history, they had beautiful d-dresses and decadence to go with the misery."

Tom managed a chuckle.

"If my Scion History class on the French had it right," I said, through numb lips, "the dresses and decadence were p-part of what caused those uprisings."

"Stop spoiling my fun."

We passed a row of pylons, steel goliaths in the frozen sea. The power lines above us were so laden with ice that some of them almost touched the ground. I reached into my jacket, where I had stashed some of the precious heat packs Nick had given me, and handed them out to the others. When I cracked one, warmth bled into my torso.

The conditions had one advantage: they stopped me thinking about anything but keeping warm. They stopped me thinking about Warden, about whether I had made the right choice in telling him that it was over. Thoughts like those would lead me down a darker path than the one I walked on now. Instead, I envisioned a glorious bonfire and promised it would be waiting for me at the end of every field we crossed, over every wall and fence we encountered. By the time the sun climbed over the horizon, turning the sky a moody red, my muscles were on fire, I could no longer feel my toes, and I was so caked in snow that the black of my coat and trousers had been engulfed by white.

The first we saw of the enclave was a lodging-house with a thatched roof, so covered in snow that it looked like an ornament for a cake. I could just see the clusters of white flowers on its windowsills.

"There," I said. It was the first time I had spoken in hours. "Black hellebore."

Maria squinted. "Where?"

Eliza pulled down her scarf. "You know black hellebore is white, don't you?"

"Of course. N-nothing makes sense." Maria stomped ahead. "These people had better have hot chocolate."

We walked faster through the last stretch of field, coaxing our legs into carrying us just a little farther. It must have been too early for anyone to have cleared the snow from the village: the few parked cars were buried, and there was no evidence of roads or paths beneath it.

Something pricked at my sixth sense, stopping me in my tracks as Eliza circled around to the front of the lodging-house. I had the sudden notion that I had been somewhere like this before, though I was certain I had never set foot in the North West. There were no spirits. Not one. A warning beat in the pit of my stomach: *stay away, stay away.*

That was when Eliza let out a blood-stewing scream. It jolted adrenaline through my veins, giving me the strength to pull my knife from my boot and run over with Maria. We found Eliza beside a fence, one hand clamped over her mouth. The snow before her was marbled with crimson.

A bird croaked at us and fluttered off the wreckage of a human being. The ribcage was torn open, bone laid bare beneath drapes of flesh, and most of the left arm was missing, but the face, the face of a woman—untouched. Dark hair was strewn across the snow.

Shock made my ears ring. Human remains littered the village. The victims had been decapitated, dismembered, thrown, and mauled in the rage of an eternal hunger. A shroud of snow glistened over the bodies. A head had been tossed into another garden of hellebore, bruising the white blooms with blood. The weather had kept flies at bay, but they must have been lying here for a day, at least.

"What did this?" Maria muttered.

"Emim." I turned my back on the slaughter.

"Let's bury them." Tom swallowed. "Poor bastards."

"We don't have time to *bury* them, Tom," Eliza said, her voice cracking. "It could come back."

Tom traded a look with Maria, whose pistol was in her hands. It wouldn't help her. They might have learned a little about the Emim from *The Rephaite Revelation*, and now they knew what they did to flesh, but they had no idea what it was like to be in their presence.

My boots sank to the ankle as I followed my instinct to the edge of another field. When I found the source of my unrest, it took all my nerve not to run at once. I dug through the snow with gloved fingers, revealing a perfect circle of ice—too perfect to be naturally occurring.

This was where the monster had come through. The Ranthen knew how to close the doorways to the other side, but it was an art they had never shared with their human associates.

"We have to leave," I said. "Now."

Even as I said it, an eldritch scream echoed over the snowdrifts. A sound exactly like the cries that must have risen from this village when the creature came, a sound that grated along my spine and raised every hair on my nape. Eliza grabbed my arm.

"Is it close?"

"I can't sense it." All that meant was that it was slightly more than a mile away. "It will come back here, though, to its cold spot. Come on. Come *on*," I barked at Maria, who seemed rooted in place.

So we pressed on through the fields, away from the village of the dead.

Nashira had told us that Sheol I had been there for a reason: to draw the Emim away from the rest of the population. They were attracted to ethereal activity like sharks to blood. "*No matter what the costs of that colony, it served well as a beacon,*" Warden had told me. "*Now they will be tempted by the great hive of spirits in London.*" London and elsewhere, it seemed. The voyants gathered in the enclave must have tempted the Emite from its lair.

I had never wanted to believe that Nashira was right: that by rendering the colony useless, I had put lives at risk. That Warden and I might be responsible for the deaths of everyone in that village.

An hour later, we were crossing yet another field, our heads bowed against the roar of the wind, leaden with exhaustion. It felt as if splinters of glass were slashing me across the eyes. It was only fear of the Emite that kept us moving, but it stayed off my radar. It hadn't caught wind of us.

We heard the car coming from a long way off. The engine sounded like a death rattle of a rusty tractor, so it was unlikely to be a Scion vehicle, but we couldn't take any chances. Wordlessly, we made for the hedgerow that ran alongside the main road and hunkered down behind it. Minutes later, our faces were dappled by the glow of headlights.

The car pulled over close by. Too close. It was a small, urban runaround, coated in soot. I told myself it was just turning—until the door opened, and a silhouetted figure emerged.

"Paige Mahoney!"

We stared at each other.

"Hello?" A muttered curse. The newcomer tramped across the road and peered over the hedgerow. "Look, if you don't come with me now, you'll be on your own out here."

Despite the urgency, his voice was somehow mellow, with a rolling accent I had occasionally heard at the black market. At first, I stayed put. Vance was laying traps for me, and I had no intention of running into her net again. But there was only one dreamscape in the car—no Vigiles lying in wait, no paratroopers above.

I rose, ignoring Maria's hiss for me to get down. A flashlight glared in my direction.

"Ah, good. Found you," the voice said. "Get in, quick. We don't want to run into a night patrol."

The words *night patrol* got the others moving. I squeezed into the back of the car with Tom and Eliza while Maria swung herself into the front. The man behind the wheel was probably in his mid-twenties, tangle-haired and bespectacled. His dark skin was smattered with freckles and small moles, and a good few days of stubble coated his jaw.

"Underqueen?" When I raised a hand, he glanced at me in the rear-view mirror. "I'm Hari Maxwell. Welcome to the North West."

"Paige," I said. "These are my commanders, Tom and Maria, and Muse, one of my mollishers."

"Your what?"

I searched for a suitable alternative. "Second-in-command. Deputy."

"Ah, right. I can call you Paige, can I? You don't expect 'Your Majesty?'"

He said this without a trace of sarcasm.

"Just Paige," I said.

A fine layer of coal dust surrounded his eyes. He had the aura of a cottabomancer, a rare type of seer that dealt with wine. "Sorry, what was your name, again?" he asked Eliza.

It took her a moment to notice who he was talking to. "Me?" She tilted her head. "Muse."

"Doesn't sound like a real name."

"I only tell my friends my real name."

Hari grinned and turned the car, yanking the gearstick. The engine retorted with a coughing fit.

"I waited for you at the station, then thought I'd head out to find you," he said, once we were on our way. "Anyway, sorry to leave you stranded for so long. What happened?"

"There was a spot check at Stoke-on-Trent," I said. "Underguards."

"How did you get here, then?"

"We walked," Maria said, "hence the 'dejected snowman' look we're all modeling."

Hari let out a breath. "I'm dead impressed you walked all this way. 'Specially in this weather."

"Not much choice." I peeled off my gloves. "What have you been told?"

"Just to assist you however I can."

It was a forty-minute journey into the heart of Manchester. Hari put on some music. It was good, which meant it had to be blacklisted.

The Underguards had set us back by a day. Another day that the others were stranded in the crisis facility. Another day of ScionIDE hunting those who hadn't made it into the Beneath. Sooner or later, Vance would begin to wonder why the scanners weren't detecting as many voyants as she had anticipated, and she would make it her mission to root them out.

"Hari," I said, "does 'SciPLO' mean anything to you?"

It was a while before he answered. "Yeah," he said, and cleared his throat. "Means something to everyone here. They're factories. Stands for Scion: Processing Line for Ordnance."

"Ordnance," Maria repeated. "Weaponry?"

"Right. Anything that can kill you, SciPLO makes it. Guns, ammo, grenades, military vehicles—anything that isn't nuclear. Don't know where they handle that."

Maria raised an eyebrow at me.

This was promising. It fitted with what Danica had said. Senshield was a military project, after all.

"What about a Jonathan Cassidy, an ex-employee of SciPLO, wanted for theft?"

"Sorry," Hari said. "Doesn't mean anything to me, but I can do some digging for you. Anything else you want to know?"

"Are you aware of a link between SciPLO and Senshield?"

"No, but I've never worked for SciPLO, so I might not be the best person to ask."

"Do you know anyone who does?"

"Not personally. Funny you should come here asking about it now, though: they've just introduced quotas in the SciPLO factories. The workers used to be able to sneak out the odd weapon, but the whole black market's dried up in the space of two weeks . . . I never wanted a gun myself, but a lot of the Scuttlers carry them in case they run into Gillies."

The handle of a knife protruded from his boot. Maria put her feet up on the dashboard. "Scuttlers?"

"The local voyants."

"Who leads them?" I asked.

"We don't have a big syndicate like yours. We just have the Scuttlers, and the Scuttling Queen." He glanced at me with full-sighted eyes, taking in my red aura. "By the way, was it you who sent those images?"

So they *had* reached Manchester.

"Not me," I said. "Tom."

Hari shook his head in awe, smiling. "You must be the best oracle in Britain, mate."

Tom chuckled. "I had some help."

For the rest of the journey, I questioned Hari relentlessly about SciPLO. Fortunately, he was happy enough to talk. He told us that the arms industry had been based in Manchester for decades, and that SciPLO manufactured weapons for both the Vigiles and ScionIDE. It had always been a secretive division of the government, but particularly so in the last year, when production had increased exponentially. The workhands were now forced to do eighteen-hour shifts or risk losing their jobs, and they could face execution without trial for attempted theft or "industrial espionage," which included talking to your own family about your work. Hari knew very little about what went on inside, but reassured me that somebody might be willing to share the information I needed.

The crystalline fields soon gave way to the austere buildings of the Scion Citadel of Manchester. High-rise apartment blocks were dotted far apart, like blunted gray digits, stern and monolithic, each a hundred stories high. The lower rungs of the citadel were suffocating under smog—you could hardly see the dingy blue of the streetlamps through it. Jerry-built houses cowered in the shadow of gargantuan factories, which vomited black smoke.

An industrial chimney had fallen on to a dwelling in a slum, crushing it. Every surface I could see was wallpapered with layer upon layer of soot. Most denizens wore a mask or respirator, as did the Vigiles, who had them built into their visors. That would work to our advantage.

"Do you have Senshield scanners in this citadel?"

"Not yet," Hari said. "You have the prototypes in the capital, don't you? Are they as bad as they sound?"

"Worse," I said. "And they're not prototypes now." I glanced at him. "You don't seem worried."

"Ah, I doubt they'll bring them north for a while. It's people in the capital who matter. Scion wants them to feel safe."

A humorless smile touched my lips. "People don't feel safe up here?"

"Well, let's see how you feel. If you end up believing there's 'no safer place' than Manchester."

He stopped the car on a street of red-brick buildings, most of which housed shabby establishments selling food: hot-water-crust pies, bone broth and fresh bread, pickled tripe. The snow had been swept on to the pavement and trampled into slush. I could just make out a rusted sign reading ESSEX STREET. When I opened the car door, a thick miasma scratched the back of my throat and spread a foul taste over my tongue. With my sleeve over my mouth, I followed Hari into a cookshop on the corner, the Red Rose, which promised traditional food from Lancashire. He led us through a warm interior, up a flight of stairs in the back, and through an unmarked door to the apartment above.

We gathered in a dimly lit hallway. "Welcome to the safe house." Hari drew several chains across the door. "Don't go back outside without a respirator. I've got a few spare."

He showed us all to our rooms. While the others were placed on the second floor, with Maria and Eliza sharing the larger room, I was led up a flight of cramped stairs to the attic.

"And here's yours," he said. The floor creaked under our feet. "It's not much, but it's cozy. Bathroom's down the hall if you want a wash. I'll contact the Scuttling Queen for you."

"No need for that." I dropped my backpack onto the floor. "We might want local help at some point, but we should start searching for—"

"You can't do anything here without being introduced to her."

"What if I do?"

Hari blinked. "You can't." When I raised my eyebrows, he shook his head, looking uneasy. "You just can't. She needs to know what's going on in her citadel. If she finds out a voyant leader from London is on her turf without her permission, there'll be trouble."

I supposed I would expect the same, were our situations reversed. "How quickly will she get back to you?"

"When she chooses to."

"I can't wait long, Hari."

"You can't rush her." He grimaced at my barely concealed frustration. "I'll get her to see you soon, don't worry."

He closed the door. The attic was small, furnished with nothing but a bed, a clock, and a lamp. I left my snow-encrusted outerwear to dry over the radiator and sat beside it, warming my fingers. Every joint in my body felt stiff and rusted.

We needed to be out searching for Jonathan Cassidy, or sizing up the factories, trying to locate the one that made scanners. Anything might be happening in London while I waited for this Scuttling Queen to contemplate her schedule. This felt like trying to get an audience with Haymarket Hector again. I had grown too accustomed to the Underqueen's power, to being able to walk where

I chose without announcing myself. Here in Manchester, I had no such privilege.

Something made me focus on the golden cord. For the first time in months, I couldn't feel Warden at all—not even his silence. Usually, I was aware of him in the same way I was aware of my own breathing, not noticing it unless something was wrong. Now he was gone.

Eliza appeared in a loose-fitting sweater with two mugs of tea, steering my thoughts away from him.

"Mind if I join you?"

I patted the floor in invitation. In our more carefree days in Seven Dials, I had always liked to sit and talk with Eliza in the evening.

We huddled up to the radiator, sipping the tea. "Paige," she said, "the village—the Emim . . . is that going to keep happening now?"

"Unless the Ranthen know a way to stop it. Or unless Scion builds another colony." I blew lightly on the tea. "We're caught between being torn apart by monsters, or being ruled by them."

"The Ranthen will have a solution. They know more about the æther than we do." She pressed her sock-clad feet to the radiator. "I was thinking about the séance the whole way here. You never told me you saw ScionIDE, too."

"When I was six, in Dublin. I don't remember much of it."

"I'm sorry."

"I'd have shown you, in the séance," I said, "but you heard Warden. I was too young for the memory to be useful."

"I guess he knows what he's talking about. Jax never wrote that much about oneiromancy."

It occurred to me for the first time that Jaxon might have learned about oneiromancy *from* Warden, by observing him. It wasn't mentioned in the original edition of *On the Merits of Unnaturalness*—but it had appeared in later ones. He must have done plenty of research on the new kinds of clairvoyance he encountered in the colony. Never a man to waste an opportunity.

"Warden's . . . interesting, isn't he?"

"That's one word for him," I said.

"You must have ended up getting quite close to him. Living with him for six months."

I shrugged. "He's a Rephaite. There's only so close you can get."

She was watching my face intently. When I didn't elaborate, she said, "Paige, why did you choose Glym to be interim Underlord?"

"I thought he was the right person for it."

"Okay, but shouldn't it have been Nick? He's mollisher supreme. Or . . . me, if not him."

I had broken with another syndicate tradition, and I hadn't even thought about it. Of course, the mollisher supreme always took over from the leader. Now I understood why Glym had been surprised. It must have seemed as if I didn't trust the competence of my own mollishers.

"I didn't mean to snub you," I said. "Glym will be fair, but hard. It's what they'll need in the Beneath."

"You don't know what my approach would have been. I started off in the pits of the syndicate; I know how hard it can be, how tough you have to be. Don't underestimate me, Paige—and don't underestimate my loyalty to you." I looked away. "You don't know what it took me to leave Jaxon at the scrimmage. You and Nick were always together, from the moment you arrived. Jax was all I had.

"I still left him. You made me see that he was just like the dealers who used me as their runner. I saw that you wanted justice for everyone with an aura, not just those you considered superior. So I chose you." Her eyes were full. "Don't you dare take that for granted."

She must have had to muster a lot of courage to say this. I tried to think of something, anything to say.

"Eliza," I said, "I am sorry. I've just—"

"It's okay. Look, I know how much you have on your shoulders. I just want you to know that you can trust me. With anything."

I could see from her face that she needed me to understand this, to acknowledge it, but I did trust her; I always had—I had just never thought of telling her so. Maybe I had spent too much time around Rephaim, forgotten how to show what I was feeling. Before I could say anything in answer, Hari appeared in the doorway.

"The Scuttling Queen will see you tonight," he said. "Seems like she might just move at your pace, Underqueen."

I needed to look presentable. Not polished, but presentable. I brushed past an automatiste as I made my way to the shower, but he didn't seem to be interested in small talk, which suited me just fine.

The bathroom was an icebox. I washed in a hurry, stepping in dirty water, then dressed in gray trousers, a rib-knitted black jersey with a roll neck, and a body-warmer. My hair was a lost cause, a knotted brier after hours in the wind, and I knew from experience that brushing it would cause mayhem. As I reached the bottom of the stairs, Hari elbowed his way through the door with a paper bag in hand.

"Ah, good." He shut the door with his heel. "Here's something to eat. You must be starving after that walk."

I followed him into the kitchen, which was small and dim, like all the rooms.

"Sorry it's so cramped. I've got one guy staying—you probably saw him—he's wanted for painting a caricature of Weaver on the Guildhall." Hari snorted with laughter as he set down several cartons. "Rag pudding." He slid one across the table. "It's not pretty, but it's good."

Inside was a gravy-soaked meat parcel, a spoonful of mushy peas, and thick-cut chips, cooked in beef dripping. It was only when I smelled it that I realized I was famished. As we ate, I noticed a pamphlet under his elbow.

"*The Rephaite Revelation.*" I brought it across the table, tracing the illustration on the front. The pamphlet I had written to warn the syndicate about the Rephaim and Emim, which the Rag and Bone Man had edited to work to the Sargas's advantage. "I didn't know it had made it up here."

Hari gulped down his mouthful. "The voyant publishers in Withy Grove got hold of a copy and printed their own. People loved it. Then they reviewed it in the *Querent*, and since then—"

"The what?"

He swept aside some unopened mail and presented me with a saddle-stitched booklet with a coffee ring on the cover. "It's a voyant newsletter. Scion is trying to stop it spreading, but it keeps coming back."

The headline was printed in the old black-letter script. SECOND VIGILE REVOLT ON THE HORIZON AFTER SHOCKING ORACULAR IMAGES FROM THE MIME ORDER, it blared. In smaller print: THE QUERENT SAYS NO TO KRIGS IN MANCHESTER! NO TO SENSHIELD IN OUR CITADEL!

"*Second* Vigile revolt," I read out. My pulse sharpened. "There was a first one?"

"It was only small, to be honest. A handful of our night Vigiles turned on the factory overseers a few days ago. Didn't last long—they were easily brought down. But there are rumblings that there will be more."

"Why?"

"They heard about the Senshield expansion in London and thought they were going to lose their jobs. They won't be needed if Senshield spreads. And if they aren't needed . . ."

He drew a line across his neck. I handed back the newsletter. Warden had been right; the Vigiles *were* ripe for revolution. Regardless of how long such a tense alliance would last, we might be able to call upon them while we were here without fear of betrayal—especially if we told them that Senshield was about to become portable. That would be the true death knell for their employment. And for them.

Tom came into the kitchen with Maria, who drew up a chair. Her hair was back in its usual pompadour style, and she had painted a ribbon of aquamarine across each eyelid.

"Interesting." She gave the rag pudding a poke. "Hari, do tell us. Who is this mysterious Scuttling Queen?"

"Aye. Last I heard, it was a Scuttling King." Tom cracked open a pudding box. In the gray light of morning, he looked his age, his face gaunt and speckled with liver spots. "Attard, wasn't it?"

"Yeah—Nerio Attard. It's an old family," Hari said. "They've ruled the voyant community here for four generations. They tried to set up a Council of the North about thirty years ago, to bring more of us voyants together, but it didn't last. Nerio got beheaded by Scion a couple of years back, but he had two daughters. Roberta is the one their father chose to take over in the event of his death—she gives me a bit of money to keep this place up and running. She's the Scuttling Queen. Then there's Catrin, the younger one, who's sort of her muscle. She was detained a few days ago."

"For what?" I said.

"She helped the Vigiles stage their uprising."

That meant that if she wasn't already dead, she would be soon. "If I needed Roberta's help," I said, "do you think she would be open to co-operating with me, even if it's just by sharing information?"

Hari rubbed the back of his neck. "Really depends how you present yourself when you see her. She's not keen on competition, but as long as you don't show signs of wanting to take over as leader of the Scuttlers or anything, it's a possibility." He eyed his watch before shoveling in a few more mouthfuls of food. "We'll go to the Old Meadow now. Better to be early than late."

I looked to Maria. "Where's Eliza?"

She pulled a face. "I think something possessed her. I heard noises. No answer when I called her, and the door's locked."

Eliza wouldn't want to miss this meeting, but she would be confined to bed for a good few hours after a trance. "Let me check on her," I said. "Do you have any cola, Hari? And the key to her door?"

"Ah, yeah."

He passed me a glass bottle from the fridge. I took it up to the first floor and unlocked the room. Eliza was lying unconscious where the rogue spirit had dropped her, her lips tinged with the blue of spiritual contact. Finding no ink or paints to hand, the muse had made her scratch the beginning of a face into the wall with her nails, leaving them ragged and her fingertips bloody. I lifted her chin and checked her airways, as Nick had taught me to do if she experienced an unsolicited possession, before I cleaned up her hand and covered her with blankets. She murmured incoherently.

The æther takes as often as it gives, people said in the syndicate. It was true. My nosebleeds and bouts of fatigue; Nick's migraines; Eliza's loss of control over her body. We all paid a price for our connection to the spirit world.

"She all right?" Hari said when I returned.

"She's fine. Your wall, not so much."

He frowned slightly before handing me a full-face respirator.

I saw the world through glass eyeholes. The mask was uncomfortable, but it would keep me anonymous. I laced my feet into snow boots and zipped myself into a hooded puffer jacket with a thick fleece lining.

We followed Hari from the cookshop at a distance. Not one star could be seen through the smog. When we reached a main road, we squeezed into an elevator labeled MONORAIL OF SCION MANCHESTER, which winched us up to a station platform.

It took less than a minute for a train to arrive. It must have been sleek once, but now it was worn and soiled, and it rattled on the track. I stepped over the gap and took a seat in the deserted carriage. Maria sat beside me and picked up a copy of the *Daily Descendant*.

The others removed their respirators. Taking advantage of the invisibility afforded by mine, I took a good look at the people around us. Despite the late hour, none wore everyday clothing. One man was clad in the crisp red of those who worked in essential services, but he stood out—most were in slate-gray or black boiler suits. Black was for skilled personnel, but I didn't know what gray signified. Only two of the passengers wore the white shirts and red ties that filled the Underground every morning in London. Hari nudged me and tapped the window.

"There."

It took me a moment to see it in the darkness. Its walls were as black as the sky.

A factory.

It dwarfed the monorail track. Even in the train, the clangor from inside made my teeth vibrate. SCIPLO was painted in towering vertical letters down one side of the building, with a white anchor beside it. Its employees, whose gray uniforms almost blended with the smog, filed in and out through titanic gates. Each pressed their finger to a scanner before entering or leaving. There were at least ten armed Vigiles at the gates, another six patrolling the street outside, and I had no doubt there would be more within those walls.

"Terrible life they have in there." Hari shook his head. "The work kills you. They handle dangerous materials for long hours and not much money—plus, they get fined for the slightest thing. Most have to shave off their hair so it won't get caught in the machinery."

Tom's brow was deeply furrowed. I remembered the factory in his dreamscape, the gloom and the dust.

"They've started beatings since the quotas were introduced. If you don't meet your target, you'll know about it in the morning." Hari nodded to where a squadron of Vigiles was escorting several gray-clad workers. "Even the kids don't escape it."

I tensed. "They have children working in there?"

"Kids are cheaper. And small enough to clean under the machines."

Child labor. It wouldn't be tolerated in London, though enough unwanted children washed up on the streets there and ended up working for kidsmen for no money.

"Since you want to find out more about SciPLO, you could try and get one of the workhands to talk—if the Scuttling Queen gives you permission to do your investigating, that is—but it won't be easy." Hari pushed his glasses up his nose. "Might be an idea to visit Ancoats. A lot of factory workhands live in that district. Mostly Irish settlers."

I watched the factory until it was out of sight.

We crossed a bridge over the River Irwell. Below us, dead fish rolled like balloons on the water.

After a while, the factories and foundries gave way to warehouses. Soon enough, we were stepping off the train and down a stairway to the street below. As my boot hit a manhole, I thought again of the Mime Order, and the people who were relying on me. I needed to persuade Roberta Attard that we presented no threat to her; that she should let us conduct our investigations in peace; that she should help us, even. Didion Waite had once described me as an "ill-mannered, jumped-up little tongue-pad" when I tried to sweet-talk him, which didn't seem to bode well for our meeting, but Attard and I were both leaders of our respective communities. That had to count for something.

In the shadow of the track, letters on an archway declared this district to be the Old Meadow. The "meadow" in question was little more than a scuff of grass, encircled by a wrought-iron fence. In the feeble glow of a streetlamp, a group of children kicked a ball to one another, watched by a greyhound. One of them whistled as we came closer.

"You here to see the lady?"

Hari pocketed his hands. "Tell her I'm here, will you?"

She threw the ball and took off across the grass. "Give us a fiver, Hari," one of the boys wheedled. He was missing his front teeth and a chunk of fire-red hair. "Just for some grub."

Hari opened his wallet with a long-suffering sigh. "You ought to be at the factory, you. You'll starve."

"Ah, sod the factory. I've done enough scavenging." The boy held out a hand. Half of his index finger was missing. "Do us a favor, mate. I don't want to be crawling under those machines again." When Hari threw a coin, he caught it with a laugh. "You're a good bloke, Hari."

"Get that dog some grub, too. Where'd you even find him?"

"The McKays' house, where the chimney fell. He didn't have anywhere else to go."

As the boy knelt to pet the greyhound, Tom shook his head. "Poor weans," he muttered. "Just look at them."

"Yeah," Hari said sourly. "Just look at how much of my hard-earned money I give them."

"Are they all orphans?"

"Yep."

I watched the scene through my respirator. In London, I had never seen a child with missing fingers. Dockland workers and syndies, but never children.

Soon enough, the girl was back. "Come on, then," she said to us. "The lady will see you now."

11

A Tale of Two Sisters

Our guide led us into the pits of the district. I had walked in the worst slums of London, but they always hit me hard. This one was devoid of all but silent life. A nightwalker lolled like an abandoned doll on a step, his mouth a ruddy smear, while two elderly women swept ash from the pavement—a Sisyphean task if ever there was one. Tom's face grew tighter with every step.

"She's never in one place," Hari told us. "She has a few retreats, and you never know which one she'll choose."

She was sane, then. That was a decent start.

We passed under a great plane tree, which had somehow endured the pollution for long enough to grow to a remarkable size. It still wore a few brown seed-balls, but the flaking bark was blackening, losing its hard-fought battle with the air. In the next street, ramshackle houses were jammed together like teeth on a jaw. The girl pointed at a door with a tarnished keyhole, which was opened by a sensor when Hari knocked. Sunshine-yellow cloth covered his nose and mouth. We followed him into a tiny parlor, where a fire burned low, illuminating a mattress and the woman staring into the hearth.

Six feet tall and broad-shouldered, Roberta Attard, the Scuttling Queen, was a formidable presence. Her aura marked her as a capnomancer. Must be useful to have smoke as your numen in these conditions.

"Hello, Hari." Her voice made me think of sawdust. Without looking at me, she added, "You must be the Underqueen."

She garnished the title with a hint of contempt. When she turned to face me, I saw that her skin was the sepia of shadows in old photographs, her lips mulberry red. A bevy of tight black curls erupted from beneath a cap, which was angled to allow her bangs to cover most of her left eye. At first glance, I would have said she was in her early thirties. I removed my respirator.

"And you must be the Scuttling Queen," I said.

"Two queens of thieves in one citadel. Scion must be petrified."

There was a moment of sizing each other up. She studied my face, lingering on my jaw. Her cheeks were a patchwork of thin scars. She was only a little taller than me, but she was taking full advantage of the three-inch difference and looking down her nose as she addressed me.

"Who are your friends?" she said.

"These are two of my high commanders. Tom the Rhymer and Ognena Maria."

Tom took off his hat. "I've heard a tale or two of your father, Scuttling Queen," he said warmly. "It's an honor."

"Cheers," she said.

There was nowhere for us to sit, so we all remained standing. Attard pushed herself away from the mantelpiece. Her muscular legs were covered by soot-smeared white trousers. The boots beneath were brass-capped, with wooden soles. She wore a sea-blue neckerchief, and several belts hung about her hips, each with a polished buckle and sheaths for her many knives.

"I hope you'll forgive me for demanding a meeting," she said. "I had a feeling you'd be on the move after that . . . vision." She closed her eyes briefly, as if the pictures were still unfolding in front of her. "Didn't realize you'd come to humble Manchester, though. Let's cut to the chase—what do you aim to do while you're in this citadel?"

"We're here to investigate Senshield," I said. "With the view to destroying it."

Attard huffed a laugh. "You're not serious."

"I didn't travel two hundred miles to tell jokes."

"You're still a fool," she said.

"We could use allies while we're here," I said calmly. "I'd be grateful if you could ask your people to accommodate us as best they can, and to provide assistance if we need it."

"You sent the vision to scare us into helping you, then?" Without letting me reply, she said, "Well, you're out of luck. ScionIDE *might* come here, but from what I can tell, they're in Britain for the sole reason of snuffing out the movement you started. They'd only move into this region if they found any trace of that movement here. If *you* were spotted here. By helping you, we'd be signing our own death warrants."

"No," I said. "They're cracking down on voyants and any voyant activity, and that's going to be a nationwide problem before long. Scion wants to eliminate organized clairvoyance, and here, in its heartland, we might be able to stop it succeeding. The first thing I want to do is stop Senshield."

"Good for you."

"Oh, come on. You'll have it on your streets within a year," Maria cut in. "It detects four orders now. It's expanding. Are you just going to wait for it to catch you? You and I are both augurs. We know the risk."

Attard stiffened. It was clear she wasn't accustomed to people speaking to her as equals. "There's no sign that they're going to build them here," she said. "*If* they do, we plan to map their locations and avoid them. That's how my father always did it. Stay out of Scion's way."

"How do you plan to stay out of the way of the portable scanners they're making?" I asked. "The ones they're making in this citadel?"

Her lips parted, then pursed. For some time, she stared at the fire with a tensed jaw.

"I don't know what you're on about," she said.

"I have evidence that they're building a handheld version of Senshield in the SciPLO factories," I said. "I need to see them for myself; to work out how they're being powered, if possible. If we can locate and neutralize the core—"

"Where is this *evidence* you have?" she asked. "I've not heard of portable scanners being built."

"I have an insider in my employ."

"Unless I see evidence, I'm not buying it," was the brisk reply. I had the feeling she wouldn't accept Danica's crumpled note as proof. "Either way, my voyants aren't going near those factories. SciPLO has round-the-clock security. Nobody in this citadel would be stupid enough to try a break-in, not even with your visions scaring them. These people already know fear. They live and breathe it every day at work."

"The factory bosses," Tom murmured.

Attard nodded. "The overseers. Most of all, Emlyn Price, head of said overseers. The Ironmaster, we call him. He became Minister for Industry last year," she said. "He usually lives in London in his fancy townhouse, but he's been up here for months now. Even brought his spouse and kids with him. They stay in a gated community in Altrincham."

"And the people working under him don't want to fight back?" Maria demanded. "They don't want to stop living in this hell?"

I had always liked Maria for her willingness to give anyone a tongue-lashing, but I could sense she was riling Attard.

"I wouldn't know," the Scuttling Queen said, staring her out. Maria folded her arms. "None of my Scuttlers work in the factories. That's exactly why my family created the network: so voyants could stay out of them. So they wouldn't get so desperate for money that they were forced to be workhands. We steal our money. We earn it with our gifts."

"I understand, Scuttling Queen," Tom said gently. "I used to work in a cotton mill myself, in Glasgow. I ken what it's like."

"It's worse than you remember."

"I'm sure it is," he said. "But surely we should at least investigate what the Underqueen suspects. If it's true, it has implications for us all."

"I disagree. And I'm not letting you to do this." She thumbed the buckle of one of her belts. "You're not going to break into a factory, potentially bringing hell on us all, on the off-chance that you might be able to find out how Senshield works. I won't have my people die for a pipe-dream."

"People like your sister?" I said.

"Do not talk to me about my sister."

Her tone was razor-edged. I glanced toward Hari, who shook his head.

"Are you saying you won't allow us to stay?" I said.

"Oh, you can stay, Underqueen." She laughed a little. "Stay as long as you like. Just don't try getting into one of those factories, or I'll send my Scuttlers after you. And you won't much like that."

I tried to think of how someone else would handle this situation. Nick would ask her questions, try to get to the root of her reluctance to fight, but I didn't have time for that. Wynn would demand to know why she was refusing her duty of care to her people, but that would get her back up. Warden was both soft-spoken and forthright in a confrontation, which, coupled with a pair of chilling eyes I didn't have, tended to get people to listen to him.

In the end, I could only do things my way.

"Freedom of movement in your citadel will eventually be crushed if we don't act. Sooner or later, the Scuttlers will be forced into hiding." I stepped forward. "Help us. Let us do what we need to do here. Just one soldier, with *one* portable Senshield device, could devastate your community." I was about to snap. "My syndicate has been forced underground, unable to move for fear of detection. It will get worse, and soon, if we don't fight back now. We never thought it would happen to us. We ignored it for months, and now we're paying for it."

Attard drew in a breath.

"You're a leader. It's your responsibility to protect the Scuttlers," I said softer. "Do you want to see them buried alive?"

Her head turned sharply. "Don't you swan up here and question my ability to lead, Londoner." She fixed a hard stare on me. "I mean to protect them. I mean to protect them as my father did, by keeping them out of harm's way. If we don't get involved, Vance won't come."

Maria sighed. "Try to stop lying to yourself."

"You're the one lying to yourself if you think provoking Vance is going to bring you peace." She cast a scathing glance over Maria. "You sound Bulgarian. How did rebelling turn out for you?"

Maria shut her mouth, but the look she gave Attard was murderous.

Was everyone in the world in denial? Everything we knew was changing, washing away the safety of tradition, and her solution was to stand and wait for it to pass. She would be waiting her whole life.

"Cause any trouble on my turf, and you'll live to regret it," Attard finished, turning away. "And don't contact my sister, either. She can't help you."

I inclined my head and made for the stairs. "Then I guess we're done here." No point wasting any more time at a dead end.

Roberta Attard said nothing as we left.

"She's just like Hector," I seethed. "Does she really think the trouble's going to stay in London?"

Maria blew cigarette smoke out of the train window. "There were hundreds like her in Bulgaria. Some people believe that if they keep their heads down and stick to their safe routine and trust that nothing bad will befall them, then it won't. They see things happening to others, but they think they're different; they're special; it could never happen to them. They believe that nothing can get better, but also that nothing can get worse. They're cowards, in one way, because they won't fight, but they're also brave, because they're willing to accept their lot in life. *Glupava smelost*, we called it. Foolish courage."

My boot tapped out a furious rhythm. Part of me didn't blame Attard for wanting to avoid Vance, but I couldn't listen to it.

"Hari," I said, "there must be someone else who can help us get into a SciPLO factory."

"She's right about the security, you know. You'd be mad to try and get into one of those places."

"I am mad." I sought his gaze. "You work for Roberta. Would you help me if I kept trying?"

Hari sank deeper into his jacket. "I do work for her," he admitted, "but not exclusively. She just gives me the odd bit of money to run the safe house, like I said."

"Is that a 'yes'?"

It was a while before he said, "I was told to help you however I could." Another pause. "I guess what she doesn't know won't hurt her."

Maria patted his shoulder. "Good man."

The Red Rose was thick with customers by the time we got back to Hari's district. The place had a homely smell of gravy and nutmeg and coffee, tinged with the pervasive stench of factory smoke, which clung to the patrons' clothes as they entered. A whisperer with braided hair was serving the food, calling out orders in a musical voice. Sensing her aura stiffened my resolve. If she were in London, she would be at risk of detection.

We found a peaky Eliza sipping cola in the safe house. "How was it?" she croaked.

"Useless," I said.

She frowned. Without another word, I went up to the attic and sat on the windowsill.

Sallow gray mist swirled past the glass. I stared into it, allowing my mind to wander.

When you dream of change, it shines bright, like fire, and burns away all the rot that came before it. It's swift and inexorable. You cry for justice, and justice is done. The world stands with you in your fight. But if there was one thing I had learned in these last few weeks, it was that change had never been that simple. That kind of revolution existed only in daydreams.

Someone knocked on the door. Tom the Rhymer's grizzled head appeared a moment later.

"Everything all right, Underqueen?"

"I'm fine."

"Don't blame yourself, lass. She's a fool." He stepped inside, his weight listing on to his good leg. "Hari's got some business in the citadel, somewhere where the less savory folk of Manchester gather. Thought we could go along. Try asking after this Jonathan Cassidy that Danica mentioned."

"Okay." I got up. "Are *you* all right?"

"Still a wee bit tired after the séance. It took a lot out of me." He hesitated. "I—I still don't understand how it was possible. I felt—well, forgive me, Underqueen, but I felt like there was more to it than Warden was telling us."

I sighed. "Tom, if there's one thing I can tell you about Rephaim, it's that there's always more to it than they see fit to tell you."

Hari's den of criminals turned out to be a supper room called Quincey's. It was a slender building on a street corner, with a dirty terracotta façade and windows that fluttered with candlelight. It must have been close to dawn, but if the silhouettes were anything to go by, the place was packed. A gaunt costermonger was selling bread rolls and soup from a cart nearby.

Inside, the walls were dark and tiled, and an amaurotic was playing "The Lost Chord," a blacklisted parlor song I had always liked, on a piano. Each note strained to be heard above the chatter. Somebody threw a handful of nails at the performer—tough crowd— but he sang on.

It was warm enough to make the windows sweat. Hari took us up a floor, shepherded us into a booth, and held out a wad of cash.

"Courtesy of the Scuttling Queen. A token of her gratitude for your, uh, co-operation." I was about to decline, but Maria snatched it. "Now, I've got to speak to one of my suppliers—keep your heads down."

The others unmasked, but I kept my respirator on. I wasn't fool enough to bare my features here, criminal retreat or not.

Maria stood. "I'm starving. I'll get us something to eat." I caught her wrist.

"See if you can find anything out about Cassidy," I said. "Just be subtle about it."

"As if I'm ever anything but."

She elbowed her way to the bar while I sat with Eliza and Tom, considering our surroundings. A transmission screen above us was broadcasting a local game of icecrosse, Scion's national winter sport. Jaxon had never allowed us to have the games on in the den, due to their "frivolity," but Nadine would often sneak out to the nearest oxygen bar to watch them. Icecrosse was an amaurotic obsession in London; many of those watching here, however, were voyant. When the Manchester Anchors scored a point, half the spectators slumped over the bar while the others shouted in triumph and pounded each other's backs.

"Paige," Maria said, when she returned (I could barely hear her over the commotion), "the guy at the bar said Cassidy was known for stealing weapons and selling them to black-market traders. His employers at SciPLO eventually caught him red-handed. He escaped on the way to the gallows and is rumored to be in hiding, but no one knows where."

"Naturally," I said. "Any useful information about him?"

"He's bald, amaurotic, and always wore a rag over his face. That's all. Helpful, I know." She squeezed into the booth next to Eliza. "I asked about the SciPLO factories. Apparently there are seventeen of them altogether, of varying sizes, all focused on munitions. And there's no reason Scion should have spent the last year mass-producing munitions, not unless they're planning another incursion."

"Or they're trying to arm all their soldiers with the scanners," I pointed out.

"I highly doubt you need *seventeen* factories to do that. Either way, we should stay here and take them out."

"The factories?" Tom said. "All seventeen?"

"Yes, the factories. All seventeen. Get rid of them."

"Right," I said, deadpan. "And how do we do that?"

Maria flicked on her lighter. "I'm a pyromancer, Paige." She beckoned a spirit, and it carried the flame to the end of her cigarette. "I promise you, I can manage a little arson."

Eliza yanked down her hand. "Maria, there are *rotties* in here," she hissed. "What are you doing?"

"Nobody cares, sweet. Look."

She motioned to a nearby table, where a seer was sitting with a crystal ball beneath her hand. GENUINE UNNATURAL, a sign proclaimed. OUTCOMES OF ALL ICECROSSE GAMES REVEALED. The unnatural in question was surrounded by eager amaurotics, none of whom appeared to be reporting her.

The conversation paused while a waitron laid out our food and glasses of hot chocolate. "What I'm saying," Maria continued, when he left, "is that if we can't get into the factories—"

"We're not burning anything down," I said. "If we destroy the factories, we destroy the trail that could lead us to the core."

"You have any better ideas, kid?"

I surveyed the room again. "We have to track down this Cassidy. Dani wouldn't have given me his name if she didn't think he could help."

"We could also contact Catrin Attard," Maria said.

Eliza tilted her head, and I explained: "Roberta's sister, condemned to hang. If she helped the Vigiles revolt, she's clearly willing to resist Scion."

"The Scuttling Queen warned us against communicating with her sister." Tom looked over his shoulder. "We shouldn't disrespect her wishes on that front. This is her turf."

"We can't quibble over *turf* anymore, Tom," I said tersely, and he grunted.

"She could drive us out if she finds out we're poking around. Besides, by all accounts, Catrin is under Scion's lock and key."

I massaged my temple. If we were going to enter SciPLO without dying in the attempt, it would have to be carefully planned.

"I have an idea about where we can find Cassidy," I said. "It's a long shot, though."

"This whole revolution is a long shot," Maria reminded me.

"Hari mentioned a district called Ancoats. He said a lot of Irish workers live there."

Eliza frowned. "So?"

"*Cassidy* is the anglicized form of an Irish surname."

Her expression cleared. "Like yours."

"Exactly." *Mahoney* was the one part of our heritage my father had clung on to. "If he's hiding in Ancoats, the people there might reveal his location to one of their own."

"Good thinking," Maria said.

I finished my drink. "While I'm gone, we need to pursue other angles. Tom: I want you to try speaking to some of the factory workhands. Ask what they do in there, see if anyone's likely to talk. Maria, Eliza: find out if Catrin Attard is still alive and where she's being held. And make sure you don't attract attention from Roberta or the Scuttlers."

Between all these lines of investigation, we had to find something that could nudge us a little closer to unlocking the secret of Senshield. If we didn't, and I returned to London empty-handed, I doubted I would be Underqueen for long.

12

Fortress

I allowed myself to be persuaded to go back to Hari's for an hour's sleep, a decision I soon bitterly regretted. Shortly after our return, a friend of Hari's called to say an inspection of the nearest SciPLO factory was under way, meaning increased government activity for the next few hours. Hari categorically refused to let any of us leave until they were gone.

I found myself pacing around the attic as the morning wore on, consumed by frustration. The clock became a source of mockery. Every second was another second the Mime Order was trapped, and so far our mission had gone nowhere. I couldn't imagine how Nick was holding up.

At noon, I lost patience and knocked on the door to Hari's room. "Hang on a mo," he called, but I was already through.

"Hari, we really have to—"

I trailed off, and my eyebrows shot up.

The curtains in the room were closed. Hari was sitting up in bed with his arm around Eliza, whose head rested on his shoulder. Both were disheveled and heavy-eyed. When she saw me, Eliza let out a yelp of "bloody *hell*, Paige" and clawed the sheets around her bare shoulders. I cleared my throat.

"Underqueen." Hari fumbled for his glasses. "Sorry. Uh. Is everything all right?"

"Spiffing. If you're . . . finished," I said, "would you mind checking to see if we can leave?"

"Yeah, course."

I retreated sharpish. Behind me, Eliza let out a mangled groan that sounded like "never live this down."

I should have learned years ago not to barge through closed doors. That habit had landed me in hot water plenty of times while I was collecting money for Jaxon.

Jaxon . . . I envisioned him smoking a cigar in the Archon, chuckling as the army brought London back to heel.

In the kitchen, I piled on layers of clothing while I waited for the others to emerge. Hari hurried in after a couple of minutes, wearing a fresh shirt and a sheepish expression.

"The inspection just ended," he said. "You can go now, if you like."

"Good." I fastened my jacket. "We should be back in a few hours."

"I'll be working. Come to the counter when you get back and I'll give you the key."

Maria and Eliza joined me in the hallway—the latter with pink cheeks—and we left for the monorail station together, walking through a drizzle. While we waited for our respective trains, Eliza whispered, "Sorry, Paige."

"You don't need to apologize. I'm not the sex patrol."

She bit down a grin. "No. But I shouldn't get distracted." Water dripped from her hairline. "It's just . . . been a while."

"Mm-hm." I blew on to my hands.

"Don't do anything reckless while you're out of our sight." She elbowed me as my train appeared. "You have a bad habit of not coming back when you get on a train."

"When do I *ever* do anything reckless?"

She gave me a skeptical look. I stepped on to the train before she could answer.

The sky must never be blue above Manchester. I watched the citadel through the window, taking in the flickers of activity beneath the monorail track. When the train rounded a corner and jounced past another SciPLO factory, I leaned forward until my breath misted the glass. A small group of workers were gesturing angrily at the Vigiles beyond the gate.

This place was on a knife-edge.

As the train pulled away again, my thoughts inevitably drifted to Warden. I hadn't felt the cord since just before we had left London. I had thought at first that he had broken it somehow, but it was there—just still. I must not be able to feel him while he was in the Netherworld, working his way through the ruin of that realm beyond the veil.

It was strange to remember the distant, shadowy dealings of She'ol, embroiled as I was in human affairs. They would be searching for Adhara Sarin, to persuade her that I was capable of leading the Mime Order against the Sargas. Perhaps they had already found her. But when she asked for evidence of my skill as a leader, Warden would have nothing to give her. Not yet. He believed in me so utterly, and I had given him so little in return.

Thinking of him made a sharp pain flare behind my ribs. The silence on his side of the cord was unsettling, as if I'd lost one of my senses.

The district of Ancoats slumped in the shadow of the largest SciPLO factory in the citadel. I descended from the monorail and trekked through the snow, my head stooped against the wind, grateful for the protection of the respirator. As I wandered past back-to-back dwellings—infested with dry rot, so small that I could have reached up and touched their roofs—I passed a scrawl of orange writing on the stonework: MAITH DÚINN, A ÉIRE. Seeing the Irish language in Scion jarred my nerves, then filled me to the brim with homesickness for the place I hadn't seen since I was eight.

The people here moved like sleepwalkers. Most wore threadbare factory uniforms and blank expressions. Others sat in doorways, wrapped in filthy blankets, their hands outstretched for money. A young woman was among them, her arms wound around two small boys. Her cheeks were blotched with tearstains.

I asked for Jonathan Cassidy at several small businesses in the district: a coal merchant, a shoe-shop, a tiny haberdashery. I was met with averted eyes and mumbles of "not here." Almost as soon as I had left the haberdashery, a sign reading CLOSED appeared in its window. It was tempting to take off my respirator and prove I wasn't trying to track him down for Scion, but there was no guarantee that I would be safe here.

My search soon brought me to a cookshop Hari had mentioned, which was perched on the corner of Blossom Street. Its narrow door had no window or handle. Shrivelled paint named it *Teach na gCladhairí*—House of Cowards. A yellow-bellied eel twisted on its sign.

A wilted bouquet of must and cigarettes awaited me inside. Paintings of tempestuous landscapes cluttered the walls, which were covered by peeling floral paper. I drew my hood down and sat at a round table in a corner. A bony, sour-faced amaurotic barked at me from the bar.

"You want something?"

I cleared my throat. "Coffee. Thanks."

She stormed off. I replaced my respirator with my red cravat. Within a minute, the waitron had banged down a cup in front of me, along with a dish of soda bread. The coffee looked and smelled like vinegar.

"There you go, now," she said.

"Thank you." I lowered my voice. "I wonder if you could help me. Do you have a patron by the name of Jonathan Cassidy?"

She gave me a dirty look and stalked back to the bar. Next time I should show my wallet.

There were several other patrons nearby, all sitting on their own at small tables. Somebody must know where this guy was hiding. For appearances' sake, I picked up the greasy menu and scanned it.

"You should try the stew."

I glanced at the bearded amaurotic who had spoken. He had come in after me, and had just been served. "Sorry?"

"The stew."

I eyed it. "Is it good?"

He shrugged. "It's grand."

It was tempting, but I couldn't linger. "Not sure I trust the cook, to be honest," I said. "The coffee smells like it should be on chips."

The man chuckled. Most of his face was obscured by a peaked hat. "You from Scion Belfast?"

"Tipperary."

"That's quite an accent you've got. You must have left a long time ago."

"Eleven years." I could hear my lilt thickening just talking to him. "You from Galway?"

"I am. Been here two years."

"And I suppose you don't know anyone called Jonathan Cassidy, either."

"Not anymore," he said. "I've left him behind."

I looked away, then back, as I realized what he was implying. He extended his free hand.

"Glaisne Ó Casaide." After a moment, I shook it. The palm was thickly callused. "Changed the first name completely when I came here, but I couldn't bring myself to cut all ties. I'm sure you know the feeling, Paige Mahoney."

I sat very still, as if even the slightest flinch could make him reveal my identity to the rest of the district. This man might be a fellow fugitive, but there wasn't always honor among thieves. "How did you know?"

"A Tipperary woman with a scarf over her face, seeking out someone wanted by Scion. Doesn't take a genius. But I won't tell." He turned to look out of the window. "We all have our secrets, don't we?"

When I saw the other side of his face, I only just kept my expression in check. The cheek around his jaw had rotted away, showing blackened, toothless gums and absent teeth.

"Phossy jaw. You get it working with white phosphorus," he said. "Can't go to a hospital. One of the many downsides of not having the correct Scion settlement paperwork, along with the poor wages. And they wonder why I started a little business on the side."

As he spoke, more of the inside of his mouth showed. I glimpsed the pink flesh of his tongue.

"I heard a young woman was asking about me. Supposed you must have good reason," he said. "When my friend the haberdasher pointed you out, I followed you in here. So, what do you want?"

This was my chance. With a quick glance around the room, I joined him at his table.

"I know you worked for SciPLO. That you stole from them. I was told that portable Senshield scanners are being manufactured in one of those factories," I said under my breath. "Is it true?"

It was a long time before he gave me a single nod.

"That's correct. In the one called SciPLO Establishment B. That's the only place they make them," he said. "Unfortunately, you won't get an eye-witness account, if that's what you're after. When you're assigned to that place, it's a life sentence. The workhands eat, sleep, and die behind its walls."

"They *never* come out?"

"Not since a year ago. It's a fortress. Few are fool enough to apply to work there, so the workhands have to be forcibly drafted from other factories, usually without warning." He spooned stew into his mouth. "No one goes in or out. Even the venerable Emlyn Price rarely emerges, though I've no doubt he's free to come and go. He's based in there."

The Minister for Industry himself. This reeked of military secrecy. Now we were on to something. "If nobody comes out, how do you *know* that's where they handle Senshield?"

"We just do. All of us."

"Have you ever heard anything about how the machines work— or how Senshield itself works? How it's powered, for example . . ."

He laughed hoarsely. "If I had that information, I would have sold it already. Thanks to Price, that secret is locked inside Establishment B. Even the Scuttlers can't claim to know exactly what goes on in there, and they know most things that occur in Manchester."

I frowned. "How do you know about the Scuttlers? You're—"

"Can't avoid knowing them. Roberta doesn't cause trouble with us, but she doesn't care much for those who aren't unnatural. She minds her own. Her sister, on the other hand . . ."

Disgust oozed into every crease of his face.

"I take it you're not fond of Catrin," I said.

Ó Casaide used the soda bread to mop up the last of his stew. "She's a nasty piece of work. They say it didn't sit well with her when she wasn't chosen by their late father to rule, so she makes up for it by terrorizing those she considers weak."

She would have fitted in well in the age of Haymarket Hector.

"We're one of the districts she preys on. If I had a penny for every time she turns up to demand money for 'protection' from the same thugs she employs to torment us . . ."

"Does she pick on people randomly?"

"Usually, but she has a particular grudge against us. She had a long rivalry with a Scuttler from Dublin. Catrin won the final confrontation, but he got in a good swing before she stabbed him in the gut. Scuttlers use their belts to fight, you know." He made a snapping motion with his hands. "Since then, she's punished us for the man who scarred her face." His brow darkened. "She'll be hanged at Spinningfields tomorrow, and good riddance."

What disturbed me most was that, in spite of this new knowledge, I wasn't ruling out this woman's help.

The waitron thundered past with a bowl of gruel. "I saw some workhands protesting earlier outside one of the factories," I said. "Do you know who leads them? Are there any other key players here but the Attards?"

He shook his head. "Those are just random outbreaks. They've been happening more often since that bastard Price introduced the quotas."

"Price sounds like the root of the misery here."

"He is. Things were bad before him, but not this bad."

Emlyn Price. I thought hard. Roberta Attard had said that he had become Minister for Industry a year ago, which coincided with increased munitions production and the acceleration of Senshield. If he was responsible for making sure Manchester's production was on schedule, he was key to Vance's success.

"Thank you," I said. "You've been very helpful."

I had got what I had come for. I was almost on my feet, ready to return to the others and tell them that Establishment B was our target, when I found myself sinking back into my chair.

"You left Ireland two years ago." I kept my voice low. "What has Scion done there since I left?"

Ó Casaide pulled the peak of his cap slightly lower. "You got out a long time ago. I'm thinking you remember it as it used to be. The Emerald Isle." He barked out a laugh. "What a load of shite."

"I saw the Molly Riots. I was in Dublin."

He was silent for some time.

"You left around 2048, I take it," he finally said.

I nodded slowly.

"Just in time. After they hanged the last of the riots' leaders, the remaining rebels went to one of four massive labor camps, one in each of the provinces of Ireland. Then they were joined by anyone with a strong back—anyone who wasn't necessary to keep the country running in other ways. I was in the Connacht camp for four years, cutting down trees for nothing but bread."

The words were going in, but I couldn't make sense of them. I had known that most of the country was under Scion rule, except for pockets of rebel-held land, but I hadn't thought it would be much different from how it was here. Anti-unnatural propaganda. *No safer place.*

"Took me far too long to escape. I reached the coast and stowed on board a ship carrying lumber to Liverpool. Then I made a living for myself here. For a time."

He kept eating. The room was tilting on its head. They were using forced labor in Ireland, my homeland—bleeding it dry to fuel Nashira's vision of a world ruled by Scion.

"I don't understand," I managed. "On ScionEye, they've always talked about 'the Pale.' I thought—"

"You thought that was the only area Scion had full control over. It's a nice lie they tell their denizens, so they can convince everyone that we brogues are violent. There is no Pale. Scion controls Ireland."

The next question was one I shouldn't ask. He was right; I shouldn't taint my memories. I shouldn't know. I should keep my childhood in a glass box, where nothing could stain it.

"Did you—" I stopped, then: "Did you ever hear of Feirm na mBeach Meala?"

"I didn't."

Of course he hadn't. "It was a dairy farm in Tipperary. Family-owned," I said, already knowing that he would shake his head. "The owners' names were Éamonn Ó Mathúna and Gráinne Uí Mhathúna."

"They would have lost it. Most family farms were merged into larger ones. Factory farms."

My grandfather had always been opposed to factory farming. His animals had been treated gently. *Quality over quantity*, he'd told me once while he bottled milk. *Rush the cow, spoil the cream.* That farm had been their life; all they had worked for since they married in their teens.

"Thank you," I said. "For telling me."

"Not a bother." The man patted my hand. "I wish you all the best of luck with what you're trying to do, Paige Ní Mhathúna, but it's best you don't think about Ireland anymore. There's a reason this cookshop is called by the name it is." He turned away. "All of us left loved ones in the shadow."

Manchester spun past the window, a mural of gray shapes against the sky. I sat in silence on the monorail.

The birthplace of my memory was gone. I should have known that Scion, traders in human flesh, would have no mercy on the children of Ireland. I pictured soldiers marching through the Glen of Aherlow, setting fire to everything they touched.

The wind scourged my face as I got off the train. My ribs felt broken, as if they could no longer hold my shape. I had left, and my grandparents had stayed. And it couldn't be undone. Even if they weren't dead, losing the farm would have killed them inside. I forced myself not to think of them dying in a camp, or trying desperately to live off the land.

I would become stone. For the people here, for my grandparents, for myself. I would shatter Scion, as they had shattered the country I loved, even if it took me every day of the rest of my life.

And I *would* begin here. No matter what the cost.

Darkness had fallen by the time I got back to Essex Street. The Red Rose was stifling and crammed with people, most of whom were engrossed in another icecrosse game and sporting waistcoats stamped with MANCHESTER ANCHORS or MANCHESTER CONQUER-ORS. When I'd forged a path through the elbows and backs, Hari beckoned me to the counter. I took the polystyrene cup of tea he handed me, along with the key to the safe house, and trudged up the stairs, leaving flecks of snow in my wake. Tom was waiting for me in the living room.

"Any luck, Underqueen?"

"Yes." I took off my respirator. Beneath it, my hair was pasted to my forehead and nape. "Looks like we need to get into SciPLO Establishment B."

I relayed to him what I had learned. He stroked his beard, eyes slightly narrowed.

"They're going to great lengths to keep what happens in there a secret," he said when I finished. "Why?"

"Senshield is Vance's key weapon. She has to protect it," I said. "A *portable* Senshield, especially, has to be kept secret—if the Vigiles had more than a suspicion that they were about to become obsolete, then Scion would be dealing with more than a few small-scale revolts. I think she wants to arm all the soldiers with the scanners, then axe the Vigiles."

"Maybe you're right. Well, nice work. I didna have any luck on my end," he said. "I dressed like a beggar and waited outside Establishment D. I couldna get many of the workhands to talk, but those that did said nothing out of the ordinary happened in there. Gillies drove me off after a while, so I went to Establishment A. Same result."

"That's because there's nothing to know," I said, "unless you work in Establishment B."

He smiled grimly. "And nobody comes out of there to tell the tale."

Eliza and Maria returned as he spoke. They had visited the voyant publishing house in Withy Grove, trying to find out what they could about Catrin, to no avail. While the *Querent*'s writers were sympathetic to the Mime Order's cause, they had the same ethos as Grub Street: strictly revolution through words. I updated them on what I had uncovered, then told them to get warm and have something to eat. I needed space to think.

In the attic, I sat alone and marked two locations on a map. The first was that of SciPLO Establishment B, which was in the adjacent section of the citadel. The second was that of Spinningfields Prison, quarter of a mile from here, the current abode of Catrin Attard.

For a long time, I sat in the dark, considering my options.

Leaving aside the botched raid on the warehouse, this would be the Mime Order's first heist. There was information in that factory, and I meant to steal it.

First, I needed to get inside. I was a dreamwalker, capable of moving through walls and locked doors, but my weakness—my need for oxygen—put me on a time limit. My life-support masks weren't designed to sustain me for more than a few minutes; I needed longer to investigate the factory, and if it was there, to destroy the core—and I didn't yet have the mastery of my spirit to stay in someone else's body for that long without causing damage to my own.

I would have to go to the factory in person. And to do that, especially without alerting Roberta, I would need help.

Catrin Attard was eager to oppose Scion, if her short-lived union with the Vigiles was anything to go by. She would have the level of local knowledge and support, as an Attard, to get me into SciPLO Establishment B. There were a lot of good reasons to approach her. She was about to get acquainted with the end of a rope.

Catrin and Roberta Attard. These sisters were like two halves of Hector: one with his bloodlust, the other with his unwillingness to change.

Terebell would want me to do whatever it took to find Senshield's core. Something in that factory would lead us there. I felt it.

I got up and restlessly paced the room. As I passed the window, a glint of color caught my attention. A Scuttler was opposite the safe house, watching. Her lavender neckerchief was vivid even in the smog.

Roberta. She had sent her people to keep an eye on me, and she didn't care if I knew it.

A burst of resolve had me tipping the contents of my backpack on to the floor, searching out my oxygen mask. Despite the injury it had suffered during the scrimmage, my gift had sharpened over the past few months. I might be stronger than I thought. There was one way to find out.

I had learned a hard lesson at the warehouse, going in without any evidence but what Danica had overheard. This time, I would make certain that we weren't walking into a trap.

I knew the physical location of Establishment B, but it took a while to find it in the æther. When I was sure I had the right place—crammed with weakly flickering dreamscapes, enfeebled by fatigue—I took hold of the first person I encountered.

A warren of machinery surrounded me. Everything was washed in the inimical glow of a furnace. The smell was beyond atrocious: a hot, iron stench, as strong as if the walls were bleeding. And the *noise*: a deafening cacophony of gears and mechanisms, a soulless heartbeat that vibrated through my teeth. I was a morsel in the mouth of hell. My host, who I had managed to keep on her feet, was soaked in sweat and hunched over a tray of metal sheets. Hands moved on either side of her, combing through them with quick fingers.

This was a real, working factory, at least—not another dummy facility set up by Vance. I cast my eyes around for any hint of Senshield, any trace of ethereal technology. It always took a while for my vision to clear after a jump, but I could just see an armed Vigile standing guard in the doorway.

"Password."

I flinched at the rough voice. A second Vigile, with a face concealed by a respirator, moved in front of the workstation. I was so taken aback, I could think of no more eloquent response than: "What?"

"Password, now."

The other workhands cowered. When I only stared, mute with shock, he said, "Come with me." The other Vigile's head turned sharply. "Commandant, suspected unnatural infiltrator."

"I'm sorry," I said faintly. "I just—I've forgotten it."

He grasped my host body by the shoulder and shoved her away from her workstation. Panic had me scrambling for the æther—I threw off my borrowed flesh and soared back into my own body.

My fingers clawed at the oxygen mask and I rolled on to my side, gasping.

Scion had found a way to stop me accessing their buildings. I should have expected this, after I had walked straight into the Archon in a stolen body, bold as brass, and threatened the Grand Inquisitor. Now they had patched that weakness in their armor. All they had to do was be vigilant. If anyone behaved strangely, they could ask for a password, which would have been agreed upon earlier. If the person couldn't give it, they were identified as a possible victim of possession.

I felt naked. My gift was the one weapon I had known I could use to hurt them.

This had to be Vance, with Jaxon as her adviser. He knew I couldn't access memories—that I wouldn't know a password. He knew the signs to watch for: the vacant eyes, the nosebleeds, the jerky movements. I hadn't yet learned how to act natural in a host.

I pulled off my sweater and breathed, letting the sweat cool on my skin. The workhand would have fainted when I left her; they might not guess it had been me. Her forgetting the password might be put down to the heat or exhaustion.

It still meant we had to act quickly, tonight.

I joined the others in the kitchen, where they were sitting around the table, making short work of one of Hari's homemade butter pies. As soon as Eliza clapped eyes on me, she was by my side.

"You've been dreamwalking."

I nodded and took a seat, setting off a throb in my temple.

"I want to release Catrin Attard. Hear me out," I added, when Tom grimaced. "We need help getting into Establishment B, and I've just discovered that I can't dreamwalk inside."

Eliza frowned. "Why?"

"They almost caught me doing it just now."

Maria hissed in a breath. "Shit."

"I don't think they realized it was me," I said, "but they'll be suspicious. We need to go ourselves, and fast."

"Right. I take it you have a plan."

"Establishment B is guarded by Vigiles. We know that Catrin Attard has friends among them. This is our moment to try for their support—if ever they were going to rebel or offer us assistance, now is the time. I'm going to make Catrin an offer: if she helps us get into the factory, I'll let her out of prison."

"You're lucky Glym's not here," Tom muttered.

"I never ruled out working with the Vigiles. I said that if we needed them, we'd reconsider. And we need them now." I sat back. "If anyone has any other ideas, let's hear them."

Tom and Eliza both stayed quiet, as I'd known they would. This was the only lead we had.

"Burn it down?" Maria said hopefully.

This was what I got for trying to build an army out of criminals.

Spinningfields Prison, like all places where death was common, was easy enough to find. While my spirit was still supple, I jumped into the guard in the watchtower, who was midway through his cup of tea when I occupied his dreamscape. The hot drink spilled over his thighs.

The interior of the prison was designed to resemble a clock, with the watchtower at its heart, surrounded on all sides by five stories of cells. I heaved my new body from its chair, panting with the effort of doing this for a second time today, and descended from the watchtower, careful to avoid the guards on patrol.

The stairs to the gangways quaked as I stepped on to them. I walked past voyants and amaurotics: malnourished and silent, like the harlies in the Rookery, many with visible symptoms of flux poisoning. A whisperer was rocking on his haunches in the corner of one cell with his hands over his ears.

As I searched, I tried to make my stride more fluid, my expression more alive, but I could see just from my shadow that I was moving about as naturally as a reanimated corpse. Something to work on.

I stopped when I sensed a capnomancer. A woman lay on the floor with her feet up on the bed.

"I thought I got a last meal," she rasped.

When there was no reply, the prisoner rolled her head to the side. Her skin was tinged with gray, and she had flux lips.

"Ah, you're probably right." Her laugh was sharp. "Wouldn't want to throw it up on the gallows."

A down of dark brown hair covered her scalp, short enough to expose a small tattoo of an eye on her nape. When she pushed herself on to her elbow, the light from the corridor reached her face. That face was all I needed to confirm her identity. A tress of scar tissue stretched from her hairline almost to her jaw, obliterating her left eye and hardening what I imagined had once been delicate features. The remaining eye narrowed.

"What's the matter with you, you daft 'apeth?" She cocked her head. "Ah, I see. Come to stare at the mutilated wonder."

"You know that ScionIDE is coming. No matter what." My host's tongue felt thick in his mouth. "I hear you're the best chance of getting Manchester to do something about it."

"What is this?"

"An opportunity."

She gave a shout of laughter. Someone bawled from another cell: "Keep your mouth shut, Attard. Some of us want to sleep."

"You'll have plenty of time for that when you're dead," she sang back, making laughter echo through the prison. The smile faded, and she lowered her voice. "An opportunity, you say."

"I want you to help me break into one of the factories and steal information," I said. "As a condition of your release, I also want you to stop intimidating the people of this citadel. In return, I'll walk you out of this place. You can kiss goodbye to the gallows."

Catrin pushed herself against the wall, looking as relaxed as anything, but her good eye was like an iron rivet. Somewhere beneath the scarring and the sneer, she must fear the noose.

"I'd heard Paige Mahoney was a dreamwalker," she said. "And I doubt there's more than one."

"There isn't."

"Hm. You must really need a hand if you've come to me, and not my big, bad sister," she said. "On second thoughts, I bet you did ask for her help, and she turfed you out on your arse." She inspected her nails. "Even if I agree to your demands, you've no guarantee I'll keep my word. You don't know what I'll do when I get out of this hellhole. Must be terrifying for you, dreamwalker. Not being able to control everyone, everywhere."

"You don't know what I can control," I said. "You don't know where or when I could reach you."

Her chuckle sent a chill through me. She picked at the laces of her prison-issue boots.

"This offer has a time limit, Attard," I said.

She lay on her back again. "Does it?"

"Yes. So does your life."

That gave her pause. All that awaited her here was the gallows.

"I'll help you get into a factory," she said finally. "And, seeing as you'll be sparing me the noose, I might find it in my heart to cut my little protection tax and leave those brogues alone. But if there's one thing we Scuttlers must have," she purred, "it's vengeance. I warn you that if you release me, there will be some trouble between me and Roberta."

"Why?"

"I saw her standing there when I was arrested, *watching*. I shouted for help and she turned her back, knowing what I'd get for treason. Maybe it's time I showed this citadel that Daddy made the wrong choice."

"You have issues, Attard."

"And you don't?"

I had to smile at that.

Catrin Attard stood. "So," she said silkily, "if I promise to be very, very good, how do you plan to get me out of here?"

"Just do exactly what I say."

13

The Ironmaster

Spinningfields Prison may have been cleverly designed, but it didn't have half the staff it needed. I escorted Catrin out while the other guards' backs were turned, delivering her into the custody of Maria and Tom, who were waiting near the entrance. They would ensure she didn't seize her freedom without carrying out her side of the bargain. Catrin put on the coat Maria handed her and told them to take her to somewhere called the Barton Arcade. Eliza and I would follow in a different car.

I dropped my host outside the prison and returned to my own body.

I was getting better at this.

The Barton Arcade was a nineteenth-century structure on a main road, elegantly made from cast iron, white stone and glass, like an old-fashioned conservatory. At least, the stone might once have been white, and the glass might once have shone, had their beauty not been buried under decades of industrial filth. Several of the panes were cracked or defaced with graffiti, while dead wisteria climbed up one of its two domes, strangling its metal skeleton.

Catrin Attard was waiting for us beside the door, watched by Maria.

"The famous Paige Mahoney." She sounded winded. "Not quite as menacing as you seem on the screens, are you?"

"I'm on a tight schedule here, Attard," I said. "I'd appreciate it if we cut the bullshit."

Most of her face was covered by a mask, but I heard the smirk when she said, "And who's this?"

Eliza's face was hard. "Her second-in-command."

"Ooh, fancy."

She cocked her head, beckoning us into the hideout. The interior told me that this had once been a small retail gallery, presumably built for the overseers and anyone else with more than a few pennies in their pockets. Faded shopfronts promised fine perfumes and jewelery.

And a stranger was waiting, silhouetted against the moonlight that shone in through the roof.

"Your friends told me you're interested in Vigile help, so I thought I'd call a friend of my own." Catrin laid a hand on his back. "This is Major Arcana, my contact in the Night Vigilance Division."

It was exactly what I'd wanted from her, but I found myself stiffening as he came closer. His mouth and nose, like mine, were hidden in a respirator.

"Paige Mahoney." It distorted his voice. "An honor, truly."

He extended a hand, which I cautiously shook. I could bear the idea of working with Vigiles if it moved us closer to Senshield, but old instincts weren't easily quelled.

"Tell me, Major," I said, "do you still hunt your own kind?"

"Not anymore. Cat persuaded me to desert," he said. His creased brow softened when their eyes met, reminding me uncomfortably of the way Cutmouth had looked at Hector. "And I had my reasons for joining the NVD. One was Roberta Attard. Under her, the Scuttlers won't adapt to change. And we all know change is coming now."

"I wonder if you'd still be on the other side if machines weren't coming for your job."

"Maybe I would. It gave me a full stomach and somewhere to sleep," he said evenly, ignoring Tom's dark look. "Many voyants feel their only option is to remain in the ranks. If I can help you destroy Senshield for the sake of their livelihoods, I will."

They must have a close bond, these people who had traded honor for borrowed years from Scion. Catrin touched his arm lightly before she paced across the floor.

"You let me out, Mahoney, so you must want to raise some sort of hell in this citadel," she said. "The question is . . . what sort of hell?"

"I told you. I need to get into a factory."

"Which one?"

"SciPLO Establishment B."

She looked from face to face, as if one of us was going to crack a smile and admit to the joke. "Brogue's got ambition," she said. "What do you think you're going to find in that place?"

"Portable Senshield scanners."

She snorted, but Major Arcana breathed in, making his respirator whirr.

"We're trying to find Senshield's core," Eliza said to him, "so we can destroy it. Paige thinks if we see how the scanners are being manufactured, we might be able to pinpoint the location of what powers them. It might even be inside Establishment B, if we're lucky."

I doubted that, but we could hope. We were overdue some luck.

"Portable scanners. We saw this. In the cards." Major Arcana was muttering to himself. "Ace of Swords. The exposure of truth. You are the one who comes with the blade . . . to cut away the shadows Scion wove around us." He stared at me for a long moment before turning away abruptly, as if breaking from a trance. "All the years of loyalty we gave them . . ."

I was reminded painfully of the tarot reading Liss had given me before her death in the colony. Catrin placed a hand on Arcana's waist and drew him toward her.

"I'm sure the Major would love to help you," she said to me, pressing him close, "but I have one condition."

"There are no conditions, Attard," I said. "I released you in exchange for your help."

"And now I'm negotiating, like any good daughter of Nerio Attard." Catrin had a wolfish look on her face. "I want to come in with you. That's my condition. I'd like to help liberate voyant-kind from Senshield." Seeing my jaw tighten, she paused. "Of course, if you say no, I could just go to Roberta and tell her what you're doing. I'm sure that will go down well."

I should have known that our bargain couldn't be so easy. I couldn't have Catrin Attard joining us; she would be a liability.

"Major," I said, turning to him, "you don't need Catrin's permission to help us. If you think the Ace of Swords pointed to me—"

"I'd do most anything to get rid of Senshield," he admitted, "but I won't go against Cat."

I distinctly saw the corner of her mouth flinch. It had me wondering how these two had met, far less found solace in each other: the conflicted Vigile and the firebrand Attard sister, who now stood together, firmly allied. As much as I disliked the idea of her coming with us, I had no choice but to accept.

"Fine," I said. That smile crept back to her lips. "Attard, you follow my orders to the letter in there."

"Oh, but of course, Underqueen."

We planned the raid by moonlight in that derelict arcade.

Major Arcana had a contact who had been stationed at Establishment B for several weeks. At 6 A.M., when the shifts changed, she would let our team through the gate and smuggle us into the factory via the kitchen.

"The next step will be locating the portable scanners," I said. "There must be some sort of storage room, if we could find that."

"Or the loading bay," Tom said. "That would be our best bet— find out where they're kept before being shipped."

I nodded. "Stealth will be crucial. We need to be particularly careful that we don't run into Emlyn Price."

"Paige," Maria said suddenly, "you dreamwalked inside. Were the workhands wearing respirators?"

"Not that I saw."

"Then you can't come in with us. A uniform isn't going to hide your face."

It was true. My presence would blow the whole operation. It was for selfish reasons that I wanted to go in: so I could feel like I was making a difference. I had led the charge into the warehouse for the same reason, which had given Scion their deadliest advantage in years. A leader worth her salt would learn from her mistakes.

"Fine," I conceded. "We'll compromise. I'll come into the complex with you, but I won't go into the factory itself. I'll stay hidden near the door while you search for the scanners. In case you need support."

"I'll stay with you, Underqueen," Tom said.

"I have to meet my associate," Major Arcana cut in. "Meet me outside Establishment B at quarter to six."

"Let's hope my sweet sister doesn't find out about this," Catrin said, "or she'll ruin our chances."

"Let's hope you don't do that, either," I said.

"We might disagree on how to run a citadel, Mahoney, but we agree on one thing." She made for the door. "Senshield can do one."

We spent our last, precious minutes making the infiltration team look as much like workhands as possible. Catrin and Maria already had short hair; we briefly debated shaving Eliza's for authenticity—she blanched at the suggestion, but didn't complain—eventually deciding against the razor. Plenty of workhands did risk keeping their hair, and it was unlikely to arouse suspicion. Instead, we dirtied it with grease and bound it at the base of her skull.

As we concealed our weapons, I told the team what little I knew about ethereal technology: that it could be identified by a strip of white light; that they might be able to sense it in the æther. Other than finding evidence of the core, their priority was to steal a portable scanner so we could examine it elsewhere.

Just before six, we met Major Arcana outside the massive brick wall that surrounded SciPLO Establishment B. Through the gate at the front—the only way in—I could see that the building was of the same design as others of its sort: black metal, hard angles, a few square windows on the second floor, and a door that had to be ten feet high. It was a bleak design, brutally utilitarian, constructed with no thought for beauty.

"My contact will be along shortly. She's persuaded some other Vigiles who are supportive of our movement to leave their posts for a few minutes," Arcana said. "They won't come out on our side, but they'll look the other way. I'll be waiting in the van for when you need your getaway. Good luck."

Catrin pulled him in for a rough kiss before he left. His form was swallowed by the smog.

We waited with our backs against the wall, out of sight of anyone inside. I tried to ignore the moil in my stomach. This time, I was certain we had come to the right place. Every whisper in this citadel had pointed me here.

Moments passed. I thought no one would come for us, that the contact had been apprehended—until someone pressed their finger to the scanner on the other side of the gate.

Our abetter was a slight, dark-skinned woman. Silently, she ushered us inside. Unlike street Vigiles, she wore no body armor and carried no firearm, though she did have the standard-issue helmet with a visor. Her only visible weapon was a truncheon. She led us out of sight of the main entrance and past a corrugated-metal door, keeping us close to the factory wall. At any moment, I expected to hear a shout or be blinded by a searchlight, but it was still dark enough to obscure our movements, and no one challenged us.

When we reached the entrance to the kitchen, the Vigile used her fingerprint again, unlocking it.

"Night shift is just ending," she said, speaking for the first time. "Join the group that's leaving the sleeping quarters for the day and blend in. I can give you twenty minutes before I'll have to let you out again—after that I have to clock in to the sleeping quarters. Anyone who doesn't get back on time will be trapped inside."

Twenty minutes. That wasn't nearly enough time for the team to search the whole place. It was frustrating that I had to stay hidden, but Maria was right. My face was too famous.

"Do you know where the portable scanners are stored?" I asked the Vigile.

"Afraid not. You're on your own there."

Eliza stepped into the darkness first, touching a nervous hand to her hair. Catrin followed. As Maria went after them, I grasped her arm.

"Don't take your eyes off her," I said against her ear, nodding at Catrin.

"Naturally."

"Tom and I will wait for you here. Remember—anything you can find out is a bonus at this stage."

She patted my arm and disappeared inside. The Vigile closed the door. "I have to return to my rounds," she said to me and Tom. "Stay out of sight. You won't find every Vigile sympathetic to your cause."

"Thank you," I said.

She marched away. Tom and I hunkered down to wait behind a nearby industrial waste receptacle. It would be a long twenty minutes.

"I trust that Catrin about as far as I could throw her," Tom muttered.

The wind howled against the cheap fabric of my boiler suit, chilling my ribcage. "I trust most people about as far as I can throw them," I said, "but if we're going to win this war, we need most people."

We stayed near to each other for warmth, keeping an eye on his wristwatch. A lifetime seemed to pass between each click of the second hand.

I wasn't made to stay behind.

After five minutes, two more Vigiles passed, but neither of them checked behind the waste receptacle. Eight minutes. Ten. Fifteen. Sixteen. By eighteen, I was getting nervous.

"If they don't come in time—" Tom murmured.

"We are *not* leaving here without one of those scanners."

I had hardly finished speaking when three chimes rang out from inside the factory, each note climbing higher than the last.

"*SciPLO Establishment B, this is the Minister for Industry. Be aware that an intruder has been detected. Security protocol is now in effect. All doors to the factory floor and loading bay will close in thirty seconds.*" The Ironmaster's voice resounded through the building. "*All personnel, remain at your stations and report any unauthorized activity or individuals immediately to a Vigile or overseer. Failure to do so constitutes high treason. Remember, the safety of your assigned machine is paramount.*"

We stared at each other. At any other time, Tom would be advocating caution, but not where Maria was concerned. My attention snapped to the æther; I found them almost at once, not far from us. "Follow me," I said, and we rushed toward our entrance, through the empty kitchen, ending up in a long, wide passageway with an immensely high ceiling. Fluorescent lighting illuminated its concrete floor from one end to the other. Letters on the wall indicated that this was the passage that led to the sleeping quarters.

A low-pitched grinding came to my attention. A massive internal door was closing on our left, sliding downward on its rails—the way to the factory floor, our only way to reach the others. Beyond it was the furnace I had seen when I had dreamwalked in that room; I could feel its heat on my face already, infernal and suffocating. We broke into a dead run, our footfalls drowned by the roar and hammer of machinery. My palms slammed into the door just as it closed.

"Damn it." I stepped back, staring up. "There has to be a way to release the doors."

"There will be." Tom was panting. "In the overseers' office. On the upper floor."

Footsteps were approaching. Vigiles.

We separated. I turned right, into an offshoot of the central passageway. It was a dead end, but the double doors to a freight lift presented me with a way out. I rattled the button to call it, certain that at any moment a squadron of Vigiles would round the corner and riddle me with bullets. When it arrived, I threw myself inside and groped for the controls. Three floors. I hit UPPER and buckled against the side of the lift.

The lift trundled upward, jolting my stomach. Every heartbeat was a punch, each reminding me that it could be the last. I was in a Scion building, breathing the same air as a high-ranking Archon official, and all the doors were closed. It took all my willpower to keep the panic restrained.

When the lift opened, I sidestepped into a corridor. Off-white walls and a vinyl floor, like you'd find in any office block. A sign reading ADMINISTRATION. Minimal lighting. Pressing myself into a corner, I nudged my focus to the æther. Tom was still, and slightly farther from me than anyone else—he must be hiding in the basement. Maria and Eliza were together, and if their proximity to the other workhands was anything to go by, they remained on the factory floor, presumably undetected.

It was Catrin who had given the game away. I should have known she would be the one to put the assignment in jeopardy.

She was close to me. Very close. On this floor. Three unfamiliar dreamscapes clustered around her. I reached into my boiler suit and closed my hand around the handle of my knife.

Price would be up here.

At the end of another corridor, I was faced with a door marked OVERSEER, which was flanked by wall-length windows. When I looked through one of them, the first person I saw was Catrin Attard, bleeding from a fresh wound to her temple. Her wrists were strapped to the arms of a chair. Two Vigiles stood on either side, each grasping one of her shoulders.

Someone was standing in front of her, hands flat on the table that separated them. Catrin's gaze darted to me. I made to duck out of sight, but seeing Catrin look, her interrogator turned. I found myself facing a man who could only be in his twenties, not much older than me, wearing the uniform of a Scion official.

Price.

It was too late to hide. The Ironmaster took me in with piercing gray eyes, lighter than mine. His hair was dark, his skin smooth and pale, and he wore gold cufflinks.

"Paige Mahoney." He sounded almost friendly. "I never expected someone so . . . exciting."

14

No Safer Place

"Let me in, Price."

"Now, why would I possibly do that?" His bodyguards had their guns trained on my chest. His voice was muffled by the glass, but I could hear him well enough. "I appear to be very secure in here. Let's keep a door between us, shall we?"

Several knives lay on the table in front of him, no doubt taken from Catrin's boiler suit.

"I'm a hands-on kind of person," I said.

Price laughed. "Yes." He lowered himself into a padded chair. "I know you tried to enter the factory earlier today. I commend you for your bravery, coming here in your own skin."

Without warning, I possessed the man beside him. Through the glass—and my new eyes—I saw my own body reel before collapsing like a house of cards. The other bodyguard quickly took aim at my host, but I already had the gun against Price's head. Vance would be livid if they let her Minister for Industry die at such a crucial time for Senshield.

"Now we can talk—face-to-face, as it were," I said, my voice steely. I hadn't intended to be interrogating anyone tonight, but now that I was, I had to find out all that I could. And if he was going to talk, Price had to believe I was capable of murder. "I know you're manufacturing the portable scanners here. You're going to tell me where they are." I paused. "You're going to tell me how they're connected to Senshield's core. And then you'll tell me how to disable it."

It was a shot in the dark; I didn't expect the reaction. Price gave me an incredulous look, then let out a peal of boyish laughter. I stared at him, unnerved.

"Wait. You don't think they're connected *here*, do you?" He shook his head. "Oh, dear. Somebody really has got her facts muddled. You didn't honestly believe that by sneaking into this factory, you *had* Senshield, did you? The . . . *portable scanners*, as you call them, that we manufacture here—they are deadly, yes, but not yet equipped with ethereal technology." Every syllable was savored. "I'm afraid they're connected to the core . . . elsewhere."

If he wasn't telling the truth, then he was very convincing. Still, a little more persuasion couldn't hurt. I shoved the gun against his head.

"Liar."

"And to think, the Grand Commander genuinely believed you were a threat. I've always admired Vance for respecting the intelligence of her enemies, but this will disappoint her." He smiled. "She suspected you might come here, you know."

That was how they had been ready for me. The intuition of the Grand Commander. Vance had warned them that Paige Mahoney was sniffing around Senshield and that this facility was one of her potential targets. She had taught them what to expect from the enemy.

"I'm disappointed in her, too," I said lightly. "If she'd prepared you better, I wouldn't be holding a gun to your head."

Catrin was observing the conversation with her head tilted back and her shoulders relaxed, as if she were watching a play. Aside from the cut head, she was no worse for wear.

"Release her," I said to the other Vigile. He didn't move. "Open her restraints, or I'll put a bullet through his head."

"She will," Catrin said to him. "She's brutal, this one."

I didn't take my eyes off her as the Vigile obeyed. She stood and rubbed her wrists before reclaiming one of her knives from the table. As she turned to face Price, I spied a glint in her eye.

"Well, here he is. Emlyn Price, the Ironmaster. The man who turns blood into gold. You're quite the legendary figure around here, you know," she said. "One might say you're the king of this citadel." She lifted his chin with one finger. "Well, we all know what happens to kings here in Scion."

Price, to his credit, didn't appear to be afraid. His mild smile stayed exactly where it was.

A vision suddenly entered my dreamscape, blinding me. An oracular image. Tom had sent me a crystal-clear picture of a keypad, followed by a glimpse of stenciled letters spelling LOADING BAY.

The scanners. He had found them. And we must need a code to get to them.

"You see this scar on my face?" Catrin said to Price. The vision dwindled. "Hard to miss, I know. Now, my friend Paige here would like to know where Senshield's core is. If you don't start talking, I'll give you a matching one. What do you say to that, Price?"

"You can torture me for as long as you like," was the calm reply, "but I promise you, all you're going to draw from my lips will be falsehoods." He looked back at me. "We prepared for all eventualities."

What happened next cleaned the smile off his face. Lightning-quick, Catrin brought up her arm and rammed her knife straight through the back of his hand. I flinched inside. Price stared at it, at the blade embedded between his knuckles, before he let out a roar of agony.

"Where is the core?" I asked.

"Liverpool," he managed. "It's in Liverpool."

"Is it?"

I forced myself to keep my eyes on him. He was just another puppet, another piece in Vance's machine. When Catrin wormed the blade deeper, he made a sound that twisted my gut.

"Cardiff," he bit out. "Belfast."

"Enough," I said sharply. "We have no way of knowing if he's telling the truth."

"Oh, I know." She let go of the knife. "I'm just having fun."

Price stared at his hand, panting. The blade affixed him to the table.

He had been prepared for this, too. Someone like Vance would expect her employees to be willing to suffer, even lose their lives, to protect her military secrets from insurgents. That didn't mean the Ironmaster had no weaknesses. And not all secrets needed to be drawn out with a knife.

I unlocked the door and occupied my own body. When I returned, stepping over the crumpled form of the bodyguard I had used to get in, I pulled up a chair and sat down opposite the Minister for Industry. Red burbled from one of his nostrils as my spirit probed the edge of his dreamscape.

"First, let's go back to the scanners. I know they're in the loading bay, but we need you to give us the code to get in," I said. "Don't make me ask twice, Minister."

"I'm afraid Hildred is a step ahead of you on that front." Sweat varnished his forehead. "There is only one code to open the loading bay. Entering it incorrectly will destroy its contents."

The first response this stirred in me was fear, but it faded as quickly as it came.

"I don't believe you," I said.

"Why?" He sounded genuinely curious.

"Because Vance wouldn't just destroy huge quantities of her own equipment. We all know how urgently she wants these scanners operational. There's also the matter of *how* the contents would be destroyed. I doubt you'd have a procedure which involved blowing up the loading bay, risking the entire facility. Vance isn't that wasteful."

"You're shrewder than I gave you credit for. Already a little less naïve than you were. You and Hildred are similar, you know. She also learns from the enemy, and from past mistakes." Blood was slithering from his hand. "If you were on our side, perhaps she would have been your mentor."

"I'm done with mentors."

"Now, now, don't slide into arrogance. Even Hildred has mentors." If his watering eyes were anything to go by, the pain was swelling.

"I'd like to talk less about mentors and more about the code, Price," I said. "If you think you won't tell me, I assure you, you will. It's hidden in your mind, where Vance thinks it's safe. Fortunately for me, I know all about minds. We voyants call them *dreamscapes*."

"You can't access my memories."

"No, but I can see things." I clasped my fingers and leaned across the table. "Let me demonstrate." I pushed my spirit against him again, dipping into his dreamscape. A vein bulged between his eyebrows. "You feel safest in a garden, where you can escape from the pollution. There are foxgloves and roses, and a winding path, and at the center of it all is a marble bird-bath, sheltered by oak trees. You often see it in your dreams. Is that your home in Altrincham?"

His breathing was shallower. "Impressive," he said, "but we all know what you can do, dreamwalker." He dropped his voice to the softest whisper. "The Suzerain has told us all in detail."

"Your family feels safe there, too, I imagine," I said, hoping he hadn't seen my shiver. "You must miss them when you're here. Are they waiting for you to come home?"

The tiniest flicker of apprehension crossed his face. His pupils were constricted.

"I want the code. If you don't give it to me, I promise you this: when I leave here, I will go straight to that beautiful garden in your mind, and I will kill your wife and children. You will come home and find them dead, and you'll wonder why you didn't just hand over the code. A few little numbers. Vance will never even have to know."

Somehow, I kept my voice under control. Price's attention twitched to his unconscious bodyguards.

"I don't think you would, Mahoney," he said. "You're not a born killer."

"Killers can be made."

All the amusement fled from him. Slowly, Price extended his uninjured hand toward a control panel. His spousal ring glinted as he pressed one finger into a button.

"That was the door release. The code to the internal door of the loading bay is 18010102."

"And the external?" He gave it. "Thank you. Catrin, with me."

"You're just going to leave him?" she said. "He'll alert Vance."

"She already knows." I stood.

Price's silence was all I needed to confirm it. I took a pistol from the nearest bodyguard and checked it for bullets before turning my back on the Minister for Industry.

I didn't breathe again until I had rounded the corner. Price had believed me, looked at me and seen someone who could murder innocents. Darker still was the realization that I had almost believed my own words, believed in my ability to carry them out if he denied me what I wanted. I could not allow myself to become a monster. I could not allow anyone else to look at me and see Hildred Vance in nascent form.

I was halfway back to the freight lift when his dreamscape guttered and vanished from my radar.

By the time I reached the overseers' office, Price was dead.

Blood was everywhere, sprayed across the table and the carpet, pooling darkly around the Ironmaster's neck. Catrin Attard stood over him, holding the knife that had opened his throat.

"You—" I gripped the door frame, white-knuckled. "You fool. What the hell have you done?"

"He had nothing else to offer."

Her calm demeanor was unsettling. This wasn't a hot-blooded killing.

"This was your aim all along," I realized, cold all over.

Catrin nodded. "Killing Price? That has always been my goal—mine and Arcana's. But this was the first time we saw an opportunity—and a scapegoat if it all went wrong." She smiled, and I knew who that scapegoat would be. "Big risk, assassinating an Archon official." She wiped her knife on her uniform. "If the response on the streets is fear and anger, I can blame you. No one has to know I was even here. But if it's deemed heroic, I'll make sure everyone knows that I'm the Attard sister who ridded Manchester of the Ironmaster at last. Finished him with her own knife."

She smiled again at my stunned face.

"You wait and see, Mahoney. The Scuttlers will rally behind me. I'm the true heir. I'm the one who's willing to do what's necessary for this citadel. In a few days' time, I'll be Scuttling Queen."

"You've lost your mind," I said. "Vance will have revenge on this entire citadel for what you've done."

"She would have come here in the end. And the good thing is that the Scuttlers will be ready." Her smile widened, showing teeth. "Who did you kill to get your crown, Mahoney?"

I shook my head, disgusted with myself for not seeing this, and left her with the corpse. As I broke into a run, I tried to smooth out my breathing. Price had been wrong about me. I was still naïve, still the woman who had walked into that trap in the warehouse. I should have trusted my gut, used Attard to get us into the factory and then forced her to wait outside.

I had to make this worth it. We didn't have long now until someone found the body and reinstated the security protocol.

The freight lift took me back to the lower floor. When I emerged, I could see there would be enough confusion to cover our escape. I slipped through the moving line of workhands and into another passageway, the one Tom had taken when we'd separated.

I found the others hiding near the vast door to the loading bay. Without pausing for breath, I tapped in the eight-digit code.

"Where's Catrin?" Eliza said.

I ducked beneath the door as soon as it began to open. "Leave her. We don't have much time."

On the other side, I keyed in the same code. The others just got under before we were sealed in.

Maria threw a switch. A flicker crossed the length and breadth of the ceiling before stark lights thrummed to life. The loading bay, which was large enough to accommodate several heavy goods vehicles, was piled with crates, stacked in units so high they almost touched the ceiling. Several amaurotic workers lifted their hands when I pointed my stolen gun at them.

"Underqueen," Maria said.

She sounded strange. Handing the pistol to Eliza, I joined her beside a crate, the lid of which was slightly ajar. We hefted it aside and made our way through layers of packaging before we got to the final container.

Inside it was a rifle.

For a heartbeat, I just stared at it, uncomprehending.

"Guns." My mouth was sandpaper-dry. "But the scanners must be here, they *must*—"

"They are." Maria passed me a sheet of laminated paper. "You're looking at one."

I took it with icy fingers.

She had handed me a diagram of a weapon called the SL-59. Each of its components was sparsely labeled, as if the designer had been reluctant to go into too much detail. It clearly showed a compartment under the scope of the rifle, which ought to have some kind of capsule inside it. A capsule labeled RDT SENSHIELD CONNECTOR.

It took me a while to understand, then to accept, what I was seeing.

Maria lifted the rifle carefully. "It seems like a normal gun," she said, "except for this." She tapped the empty compartment. "Once the connector is in place, you have an inbuilt Senshield scanner." Her brow creased. "I just . . . don't understand this."

"You do," I said. "You just don't want to believe it."

Scion's motto had always been "no safer place." They strove to create an impression of peace; they had relied on it for two centuries, to prove to their denizens that the system worked, that they were safer than anyone else in the world. It was a silent bargain they made: let us remove unnaturals, no questions asked, and in return you will be protected.

A gun-mounted Senshield scanner heralded a new age. Martial law had never been intended to be a temporary measure while they dealt with the Mime Order; Scion wanted to turn Britain into a truly military state. They were ready to declare open war on unnaturals, if need be, and they now had a way to fight us without risk of collateral damage.

"Paige," Eliza said, "look at this."

She indicated a label on the lid of a crate. Above the Senshield symbol and the data, there was a destination. I ran my finger over the precious letters, the reason we had infiltrated this factory.

ATTN: H. COMM. FIRST INQ. DIVISION
PRIORITY: URGENT
PROJECT REF: OPERATION ALBION
SHIP FROM: SCIPLO ESTABLISHMENT B, SCION CITADEL OF
                  MANCHESTER, NORTH WEST REGION
SHIP TO: CENTRAL DEPOT, SCION CITADEL OF
                  EDINBURGH, LOWLANDS REGION

"Edinburgh. They're being sent to Edinburgh. That must be where they're connected to the core." Eliza loosed a breath. "That's it, Paige."

The feeling in my heart wasn't quite hope. It was hard to feel hope in a room filled with war machines, with danger closing in. I looked again at all the towers of crates, at the level of organization and preparation that Scion had attained over the years, while we had occupied ourselves with mime-crime and ignored the growing shadow.

There was only one way to stop it now.

Maria reached into the crate. "Quickly," she said. "Grab one each."

We fumbled with the weapons, wrapping them in our coats. Suddenly the alarm sounded again, making us all flinch. Bands of red light arced through the loading bay.

"Now might be a good time to mention that Catrin killed Price," I said. "I imagine we're about to feel the consequence of that."

"Come on!" Tom was by the exit, punching in the release code as the sound of a door opening grated through the loading bay. "Underqueen, hurry!"

He didn't need to ask twice. We crossed the loading bay at speed, weighed down by our plunder, and reached the outer door.

Maria ducked through. Tom was on the other side, holding the colossal door open with nothing but his own strength. Sweat poured down his face as he forced his shoulder against it. Eliza scrambled under next, almost losing the rifle as it slipped from the crook of her arm. As the Vigiles opened fire, Tom let go of the door. I threw the rifle ahead of me and slid through the gap, into the snow, just before a teeth-rattling crash of metal against concrete made me throw my arms over my head. I gathered up the rifle as Tom hefted me to my feet.

The factory gate was ajar; Major Arcana's contact had left us one more chance for escape. We ran, our boots sliding on fresh snow. When a Vigile sprang out on our left, Maria threw a knife into his thigh. Tom slowed, panting heavily, as we closed in on our exit.

"Tom—" I pulled his arm around my shoulder. "Come on. You can make it. Just a bit farther . . ."

"Leave me, Underqueen," he rasped.

"No. Not this time."

More gunfire from behind us, and the ever-growing peal of the alarm. Maria flung open the gate. A few more desperate, staggering steps, and we were through it, into the van that awaited us on the corner. It was only when Major Arcana slammed his foot on the accelerator that I realized who was in the front seat, still smothered in the blood of Emlyn Price.

Catrin Attard caught my eye in the rear-view mirror.

"Pleasure working with you, Underqueen," she said softly, taking in the scanner-gun I was hugging to my chest. "I'm glad we both got what we wanted."

15

The Grand Smoke

December 6, 2059

Another night, another journey.

This time, we were on our way to the Lowlands.

Hari had helped us escape the citadel. It was best that he didn't know exactly what we had done, or Roberta might think he had been involved, but he knew something had happened. He had wished us the best of luck, kissed Eliza on the cheek, and passed us into the care of another member of Alsafi's network, who had stowed us into the back of an armored Bank of Scion England vehicle bound for Edinburgh. I stayed close to the stolen scanner-guns, like an animal guarding its young.

Sweat pearled on my neck and forehead. Catrin might work to protect her people if Vance retaliated, or she might just continue the cycle of violence that had left her with that scar. I had no way of knowing. I might never see what I had done to that citadel.

We had to keep moving—following the next clue in our seemingly endless pursuit of Senshield's core. Following crumbs cast into the wood.

"Tom," I said into the darkness of the moving vehicle, "does the Lowlands have an organized voyant community?"

Tom had been quiet since our escape. I heard him take a deep breath before he spoke.

"I'm not sure. There was a group in Edinburgh that sheltered people during Vance's reign. They were mostly osteomancers, led by a person called the Spaewife. If they're still there, they might help us."

His voice was slower than usual. "Tom, are you all right?" Maria asked.

"I'm fine. Just need some sleep."

I couldn't imagine ever sleeping again. My head was heavy, my thoughts mired in fatigue, but Vance's face was engraved on my vision. It floated in the darkness, disembodied and all-seeing, like something a dose of flux would summon. I felt too watched to close my eyes.

Vance would know where we were heading, I was sure of it. She knew I was on Senshield's trail. She would discover that the rifles had been taken—rifles marked for shipment to Edinburgh. That was more than enough to send her after us, but I saw no other choice but to chase the next lead.

Eliza drifted off first, followed by Tom, whose sleep was restless. I lay on my side with my head pillowed on my arm, trying not to think about how many crates had been in that loading bay. How many guns.

A rustle of movement came on my left, accompanied by the glare of a flashlight. Maria was unwrapping one of the scanner-guns.

"I didn't get a chance to examine this properly in the loading bay," she said, by way of explanation. Her fingers skimmed over the barrel. "SL-59. The 'S' stands for *Scion*. As for the second letter, that's usually the designer's initial." She inspected different parts of the gun. "Ah, there it is . . . Lévesque."

"Someone you know?"

"Only by reputation. Corentin Lévesque, a French engineer."

"And aside from the space for a Senshield . . . connector, there's nothing unusual about the gun?"

"Not that I can see."

The next step had to solve the puzzle. It had to show us how the scanners were linked to the core. I lowered my head back on to my arm and, despite the fact that Vance's face still hovered before mine like a portent, drifted into a fitful sleep.

The Scion Citadel of Edinburgh, regional capital of the Lowlands, was cloaked in coastal fog. After the effluvia of Manchester, the air tasted almost sweet—but it was also much colder, lashed by wind from the North Sea. The driver who had brought us here presented me with a key and told us where to find the safe house.

The streets were quiet in the small hours, which was fortunate, given what we were carrying. There were no skyscrapers here. It was an opium-dream of a time long past; a city of bridges and crumbling kirks. Mist laced around the old stone buildings, which had rooftops crowned with snow. Edinburgh was sometimes called the Grand Smoke, and now I knew why: there were chimneys everywhere, and it seemed as if we were walking through a cloud. The citadel was carved into the unruly Old Town, where the laborers and service workers dwelled, and the more modern and expensive New Town.

On a ledge of volcanic rock, a decaying fortress knelt on the skyline of the citadel.

"Edinburgh Castle," Eliza said. "They say it's haunted by the spirits of the Scottish monarchs."

"You read Jaxon's history books, too?"

"Every one. Jax taught me to read with those."

Jaxon still eluded me. It was all too easy to think of him as the enemy, the traitor. Yet this was a man who had taught an orphaned artist to read. She hadn't needed to know her letters to earn him money.

Our little party traversed the lantern-lit stairways that squeezed between the houses.

"It's good to see Scotland," Tom said hoarsely. His face was losing color. "Just need . . . a lie-down."

Maria rubbed his back. "You're getting too old for this."

His laugh was more of a wheeze.

We pressed on through the citadel: past a train station, across a bridge, and up a narrow street. Chandleries and apothecaries, cutlers and wigmakers, bakeries and bookshops nestled together on the stony incline.

The safe house was in an alleyway halfway up, blocked off by an iron gate. When she read the gold letters above it, Eliza tilted her head.

"Anchor Close? Is this a joke?"

"Best place for a safe house," Maria said. "Who'd dare put rebels in Anchor Close?"

The gate let out an agonized creak. The safe house was up the flight of steps beyond. Its windows were shrouded by curtains, their sills capped with moss, and a lantern sputtered beside the door. It took my shoulder to open it. The smell of mold snaked out from inside.

The décor was as melancholy as the exterior. Claret walls patterned with floriated designs, coated with decades of grime. Furniture that looked as if a pennyweight could break it. Some dusty numa were piled on a table, guarded by a ghost, which drifted sullenly away from us as we shuffled into the hallway. As we shucked our coats, Tom began to wheeze. I reached for his hand. Cold as marble.

"Tom," I said, "what's wrong? Is it your leg?"

"Aye, it's . . . giving me trouble. I'll live, Underqueen."

The words winded him. I squeezed his arm.

"I'm taking him upstairs," Maria said, her tone clipped. "Eliza, get the painkillers. In my pack."

As Tom mounted the stairs, leaning heavily on the banister, I caught Maria by the sleeve and said quietly, "It's not his leg. Something else is wrong."

"How do you know?"

"He's not getting enough oxygen. I know the signs."

She stiffened. "Do you have your mask?" I handed it over, and she followed him up the stairs.

Eliza brushed past with a warming pan. As I reached for the handle of another oak door, my sixth sense tingled. Three dreamscapes: one human, two Rephaite. How had I not noticed? Breathless, I pushed it open and found Nick and Lucida sitting on faded armchairs beside a fire—and in the corner, watching the flames dance in the hearth, was Warden.

Nick got to his feet and offered a weak smile. I wrapped my arms around him. "You're freezing, *sötnos*," he said, holding me close.

"I'm so happy to see you, but—" I let go of him, realizing what the presence of the Rephaim meant. "You and Lucida should be in the Beneath."

"It's okay," Nick said. "Terebell sent some reinforcements. Pleione and Taygeta are there."

I relaxed a little. Taygeta Chertan was Pleione's mate—one of the Ranthen who had arrived to support me at the scrimmage. She was just as intimidating as Terebell, with a penetrating stare and a sharp tongue, which made her perfect for keeping the syndicate in line.

"How do things stand in the Beneath?" I wasn't sure I wanted to know the answer.

What little gladness had come into Nick's face when he saw me disappeared. "It's . . . bad," he said. "We need to get them out of there. For all our sakes."

If he didn't want to give me specifics, it must be hell in the crisis facility.

"Where's Ivy?" I said. "Did she go into the Fleet?"

Nick returned to his armchair. "Glym announced that you'd sentenced her to join the toshers to protect the syndicate, which renewed a certain degree of support for your rule. Not that they've forgiven you entirely," he added, "but they feel slightly warmer toward you now than they did a few days ago."

They had been ready to eviscerate me a few days ago, so that wasn't saying much.

"Róisín came forward to take Ivy's place out of concern for her health, which most of them grudgingly accepted. She was due to leave when we realized Ivy was gone." I raised my eyebrows. "One of the toshers said she'd asked him where she could find their king, then gone back into the sewers with food enough for a few days. She left this on her bunk."

He passed me a rolled-up scrap of cigarette paper. The note was written in a spiky, quaking hand.

You can't save us all, Paige.

"It's not a pleasant thought," Nick said, "but I don't think there was another way."

Unwillingly, I remembered those dark, oppressive tunnels, the silence broken only by the drip of water.

"There wasn't. Not if Ivy was going to live." I pocketed the note. "I'm going to get her out of there."

"Róisín went after her. For now, they have each other. Once you're back and Senshield's gone, you'll have enough power to bargain for their lives."

"And hopefully a few more supporters." I glanced at the two Rephaim. "I take it you found Adhara Sarin, and that's why you've been allowed to return?"

"Yes," Warden said. "Terebell is attempting to forge an alliance with her, assisted by Mira and Errai. She elected to send the rest of us back across the veil to support you."

I looked at him for a beat too long, searching his face for injuries. He looked just the same as before he had left.

"Which leaves us free to help you," Nick said. "So fill us in. What did you find in Manchester?"

I almost didn't want to burden him with this, but I couldn't lie to him. "Well," I said, "Dani was right. They are manufacturing portable scanners." I retrieved one of our prizes from the hallway and laid it on the table. "Only . . . I don't think she realized how *multi-purpose* they're intended to be."

Nick slowly rose to his feet.

"This is—" He swallowed. "But this is a gun. You're saying *this* is equipped with Senshield?"

"It will be, once it's activated."

"Nashira is preparing for war," Warden said.

I looked up at the sound of his voice. Nick turned to face him. "War with who, exactly?"

"Clairvoyants." Warden cast a detached look over the rifle. "This version of the scanner gives Scion a means of slaying unnaturals without risk of collateral damage. If it came to physical combat with the Mime Order, they would be able to fight back without injury to amaurotics. It means they can safely carry out martial law with no danger to 'natural' denizens."

"So they can keep saying 'no safer place' to amaurotics," I said, "while leaving no safe place for us."

"Yes."

Nick closed his eyes. "Do I want to know how you got this, Paige?"

I told them about our search for Senshield in Manchester: my attempt to negotiate with Roberta; my visit to Ancoats; the uneasy agreement with Catrin and Major Arcana; the break-in, and the murder of Emlyn Price. By the time I was finished, my throat hurt from talking.

"I keep thinking you can't do anything more dangerous." Nick pinched the bridge of his nose. "How you got out of that factory alive . . ."

"Vance will turn her attention to Manchester now," Warden said.

"No. She'll punish Manchester, but she'll come here in person," I said. "She'll know by now where we've gone." I held my hands close to the fire. "Here's what I suggest. We seek out the local voyant community, if it still exists, and ask them if they know the location of the depot where these rifles are activated. Even if they don't, I think it's a good idea for us to connect with them, so we have people to call on if we need help. Hopefully the séance reached them." Nick nodded. "Once we've found—"

"Nick."

Maria was in the doorway. There was none of the usual good humor in her expression.

"A word," she said.

With a slight frown, he followed her. When I heard their footsteps upstairs, I faced the two Rephaim.

"Be honest," I said. "Do you think Adhara is likely to join us?"

"If she sees a reason to," Warden said.

His tone implied that she didn't see one yet. That she wasn't willing to throw her lot in with mine. I couldn't really blame her; apart from leading the revolt in the colony, all I had done so far was take control of the syndicate and start its transformation into an army of disgruntled criminals. I could claim no significant victories against Scion. My shoulders dropping, I turned and went to find a room.

Upstairs, I deposited the scanner-guns on a bed. Their weight sent up a cloud of dust. Two burner phones and a charger waited on the windowsill, presumably donated by whoever owned the safe house.

"Paige."

Nick stepped into the doorway, wiping his hands on a cloth. As soon as I saw his face, I knew something was very wrong.

"Tom," I said.

"He's dying, sweetheart."

The cloth was bloody.

"He can't be," I murmured. "How?"

"You couldn't have known. Tom made sure of it," he said. "He took a bullet when you left the loading bay. He's been bleeding internally for hours . . . I'm amazed he's lasted this long."

"He was holding the door open for us. That must be when—" I released an unsteady breath. "Can I see him?"

"He asked for you."

He led me across the landing to another door. The æther was gaping open beyond.

Inside the little room, Maria was hunched in a chair, her head cradled in her hands. Tom lay in a bed that was far too small for him, his hat on the nightstand, his shirt peeled open. He already had a corpse's pallor. His broad chest was stained by plum-colored bruising, the blood bundled beneath his left pectoral. His eyelids cracked open.

"Underqueen."

"Tom." I sat on the edge of the bed. "Why didn't you say anything?"

"Because he's a stubborn old fool," Maria said thickly.

"Aye, and proud." His words tripped into a wheezing breath. Maria almost bowled over the jug as she rushed to pour him water. "I didna want to slow you down, Paige . . . and I wanted to see Scotland again, one last time."

I stroked the back of his hand with my thumb. Perhaps I would have stayed quiet, too, if I'd thought I might see Ireland.

"I worked as a mule scavenger in Glasgow in my younger days, before I went south. I saw what Scion would do for their metal." His chest rose and fell unevenly. "I just . . . couldna bear to see it still happening, all these decades later. It had to end. It all has to end."

Maria tipped the water to his lips. Tom took a little and leaned back into the pillows.

"Paige, I dinna want you to watch me snuff it, but I have a last favor to ask of you," he said. His face creased into something like a smile. "Just a small one. Bring Scion down."

"I will," I said quietly. "I won't stop. One day, they'll call this country by its name again."

He managed to lift a big hand to my cheek. "That's brave talk, but I can see in your eyes that you're doubting yourself. There's a reason we accepted you as Underqueen, and there's a reason the anchor's been trying so hard to find you. They know they canna control someone with a flame like yours. Don't ever let them put it out."

I pressed his hand.

"Never," I said.

With Tom's death, I lost one of my most faithful commanders. One of the few truly honest people in the syndicate.

We had no time to mourn for him. No hours left to absorb his passing. I stood with Maria outside the safe house while she lit her first roll of aster in days. A ten-minute smoke was the only grace period I could allow her before we had to get back to the streets, to our task.

"He was a good man. A gentle soul." Rain seeped down her face. "So it begins again. I lost so many friends during the Balkan Risings. At least Tom knew what we were really fighting. The Rephaim."

I still knew so little of that invasion. Maria tilted her head into the rain.

"In 2039," she said, "they marched through Greece. Then, in 2040, they came for us."

"How old were you?"

"Fifteen. Along with my friend Hristo, I left my home town of Buhovo and joined the youth army in Sofia. That was where I met Rozaliya Yudina, the woman in the memory. She was . . . charismatic, free-thinking, single-minded in her search for justice—rather like you. Roza convinced us that we had to fight, even if we weren't unnatural. She was adamant that any organization that labeled one group of people as evil would eventually do the same to others. That to treat any one person as less than human was to cheapen the very substance of humanity." Sorrow tensed her features. "Training was rigorous, and we knew our chances were small, but for the first time in my life, I was free of my father, free to be who I truly was. Yoana Hazurova—not Stoyan Hazurov, the son he had never loved.

"When ScionIDE approached, we made our own cannon. We stole the guns of dead police. We defended Sofia." She inhaled deeply. "We lasted ten days before our country issued a surrender. Hristo fled to the Turkish border . . . I highly doubt he got there."

"You picked up a gun in your memory." A drop of water iced my nose. "You weren't going to use it on the soldiers."

"Ah, you noticed. Unfortunately, it jammed. The soldiers beat me almost to death, then threw me into prison." Her face twisted with bitterness. "Several years later, the new Grand Inquisitor of Bulgaria forced prisoners into heavy labor. I fled on a boat to Sevastopol and spent months traveling west, determined to find a large community of voyants. London's underworld embraced me." Lilac smoke plumed from her roll. "We didn't last long, I know. But with every friend lost and home burned, we fought harder."

"What kept you going?"

"Rage. Rage is the fuel. And people need to see suffering, the blood of innocents shed. But they also need to see people standing, Paige."

"Who chooses who suffers and who stands?"

"You have to stand. We *must* get rid of Senshield now, no matter what. If you return to the capital with a dead commander and no evidence that you've damaged the core—"

"I know."

Nothing would protect me then, Underqueen or not. Loyalty would sour to hatred. Even my allies among the Unnatural Assembly would abandon me. ScionIDE would steamroll us all.

Time was of the essence, now more than ever.

"Did he—before he—did Tom say where the voyants were based?" I asked.

"Yes. The Edinburgh Vaults."

"Where are they?"

"Off a street called the Cowgate, which lies beneath South Bridge," she said, "but the entrance is hidden, and he wasn't sure where."

"I'll go now. You . . . finish your aster."

"No. I'll take Eliza and start scouting for information about the depot elsewhere." She dropped the roll and ground it out underfoot. "Vance will already be ahead of us, but let's not let her get too far."

Back in the house, I unearthed a map of Edinburgh and spread it out on a table. The Rephaim had gone out—presumably to find some unsuspecting voyants to feed on. I could feel fear building underneath my exhaustion. Eight hours had passed since we had left the factory. For all I knew, Vance was already here.

Nick came down the stairs, looking as tired as I felt.

"Where are you going, *sötnos*?"

"To find the Edinburgh Vaults. Tom thinks—thought—they were a hideout for a group of voyants who have been active in this citadel for decades." My finger skated across the map, over the latticework of closes and wynds that branched off the Grand Mile and then south a little, until I found the Cowgate. It wasn't far. "He said they were somewhere around here. Coming?"

"Of course." He reached for his coat. "Vance could be here by now. Dare I ask if the depot is on the map, so we can avoid having to ask the local voyants for help finding it?"

"That would be too easy."

I zipped up my puffer jacket and buckled my boots. A clock was ticking somewhere in the house. There was no time—but there was something I had to say to him.

"Nick," I said, "we . . . never spoke about the séance. What happened to your sister."

He turned away from the firelight as he shrugged on his coat, obscuring his expression.

"There's not much to say." He saw my face and sighed. "The soldiers were on patrol in the forest in Småland, close to where we lived at the time. Lina had gone there without permission to camp with some of her friends for her birthday. They had bought some bottles of Danish wine on the black market. Our father sent me after them. Hours too late." He drew in a long breath. "Later, Tjäder justified it by saying they'd bought the wine to induce unnaturalness in themselves. Håkan, Lina's boyfriend, was the eldest. He was fifteen."

I lowered my gaze. Birgitta Tjäder's reign of terror in Stockholm was common knowledge—she saw any infringement of Scion law as high treason—but I couldn't imagine what sort of mind would perceive a group of children drinking wine as deserving of the death penalty.

"I'm so sorry, Nick," I said softly.

"I'm glad it was in the séance. It means that Lina is in everyone's memories now," he said, his tone stiff. "Tjäder was under Vance's command. Whatever we do to hurt her is worth the risk."

I felt the golden cord and glanced up. Warden was in the doorway, his irises hot from a feed.

"Do you know Edinburgh, Warden?" I said, straightening.

"Not as well as I know London," he said, "but I had cause to visit during my time as blood-consort."

"Have you heard of the Edinburgh Vaults?"

"Yes." He looked between us. "Would you like me to take you there?"

16

The Vaults

Even in the situation we found ourselves in, I could appreciate the beauty of the Old Town. Its buildings were beautiful and motley, with spires and rooftops that clambered skyward—as if they longed to reach the same heights as the nearby hills, or to touch the sky the sun had warmed to a finger-painting of amber and coral. Warden led us up the flight of steps outside the safe house, past a smear of white graffiti. ALBA GU BRÀTH. A cry for a lost country.

"Paige," Nick said, "what's going on between you and Warden?"

Warden was a fair way ahead of us, too far to hear if we kept our voices down (unless Rephaim had uncannily good hearing, which had proven far from impossible). "Nothing."

Nick looked like he wanted to ask more, but, seeing that his long strides had taken him too far from the humans, Warden had stopped to let us catch up.

I had thought I was acting as I always had around him in public, but something had betrayed me to Nick. As I walked at Warden's side, I was conscious of my expression, my body language, my heartbeat.

"When were you here last?" I said to him.

"Eight years ago."

The steps led us up to the Grand Mile, where cast-iron streetlamps burned from the fog—clean, pale fog, the breath of the sea. Beneath our feet were broad, piebald cobblestones, sheened by rain. Restaurants and coffee houses were filling up with evening trade, their patrons gathered near outdoor heaters, hands clasped around steaming glasses, and close by, a young man played an air on a *cláirseach*. Farther down the street, a squadron of day Vigiles was on patrol. Warden could just about pass as human in fog as thick as this, although he was taller than everyone else on the street.

We shadowed him down an incline, into a slum that sprawled beneath a bridge, darkened by a canopy of laundry, where the smells of cooking and sewage basted the smoke-thickened air. Tattered Irish flags—green, white, and orange—were draped across the bridge; accents like mine flitted between windows. It was forbidden to display the old Irish tricolor under any circumstances—Vigiles must never come through this district. Families huddled around outdoor fires, warming their hands, while a wizened man lifted clothes from a barrel and wrung them through a hand-operated mangle. A sign above his head read COWGATE.

Another corner of hell for the brogues. Scion had let a handful of them flee from the terror of the occupation, only to watch them drain into the gutters and leave them there to rot.

My father must have known that it was only the mercy of Scion, and his ability to hold on to a job in their ranks, that kept us from a life like this one. Even before we had left Tipperary, he had drummed it into me that I should never speak my mother tongue, not even in private; nor should I remember the stories my grandmother had told me, nor sing Irish melodies. I should be an English rose. I should forget.

In his own way, he had been trying to protect me. I might learn to forgive him, one day, but it didn't mean I agreed with what he had done. There was no reason we couldn't have remembered our past, and our dead, in the privacy of our home.

Nick touched my shoulder, lifting me from the churn of thoughts.

Warden awaited us in a street that splintered off the Cowgate. I felt his eyes on my face, but I made myself a mask.

"The South Bridge Vaults," he said. "Sometimes known as the Edinburgh Vaults."

The entrance was a slender archway. Unmarked. It looked just like the entrance to an alleyway; no one would think it was anything else—but I suspected we would never have found it on the map. The mingled stench of fish and smoke came rushing out. We reeled back, coughing.

"Fish oil. The tenants burn it for light," Warden said.

The passageway was so dark; it was as if a hole had been cut out of my vision. "Here goes, then." I bent my head a little and stepped in.

Inside, it was worse than I could have imagined. No daylight pierced these corridors of stone.

The ceiling was curved and low. I kept one hand on the wall, my boots scrunching through oyster shells and rat droppings. Stale drafts raised gooseflesh on my arms, but they weren't what made this place so oppressive. Every pore of the æther here was choked with old, vindictive spirits.

Water dripped from the ceiling, forming pools in the corners. Every so often, a fish-oil lamp would bring a sickly light to the gloom, giving us a glimpse of the dwellers of the Vaults. The amaurotic homeless, asleep inside cramped alcoves in the wall, curled around their few possessions. Children huddled around a tallow candle, playing games with bottle tops and making cat's cradles with string.

The ceiling squatted lower with every step. Nick's breathing was uneven.

"I don't see any auras," he said.

The last lamp had long since disappeared. I felt the brick outline of another archway and eased my hand into the blackness. A draft scuttled up my arm, lifting every fine hair.

"Wait." I moved into it. "There are dreamscapes somewhere below. I think there's—"

The wall gave way beneath my hand, and my boot plunged into nothing.

Some merciful reflex made me twist instead of toppling forward, sparing my head as I crashed on to a slope. I was slithering into an abyss, heels and hands tearing at smooth walls, gasping the air that rushed up to meet me. Rough stone nicked my cheek. More grazed my hip and thigh before my left side smashed through wooden boards. I fell with them, slammed into a rock-hard floor, and rolled to a painful halt among the fragments.

For a long time, I didn't move for fear that I had broken something—then the golden cord vibrated, shocking me enough to make me breathe again. I gritted my teeth and pushed myself on to my elbows.

"Dreamer!"

Nick's voice was somewhere above me, echoing in the pitch-black. Dust shot into my nostrils, and I sneezed. As soon as I got to my feet, my head cracked against stone, buckling me again.

"*Bloody* shitting fuck—"

"It sounds as if she is alive," Warden said.

I directed a dark look toward the ceiling. "I'm fine," I called. My hand scraped against a wall. "But I can't see a thing."

A shard of light flashed past, giving me a glimpse of the boards I had come through. A sign reading TYPE E RESTRICTED SECTOR lay among them.

"Perfect." I leaned against the wall. "I always wanted to die alone in a Type E Restricted Sector."

"What?" Nick shouted.

"It's a Type E—"

"Paige, you know that means the structure is unstable! Why aren't you panicking?"

"You're panicking enough for both of us," I sang.

"Stay there. Don't move a muscle."

Silence descended as they retreated. The utter lack of light was disorienting. Like a tomb.

Well, I wasn't just going to sit here, whatever Nick said. I rose with caution, navigating with my hands.

From what I could tell by touch, I was in a tunnel about five feet wide. A short distance from where I had fallen through, what felt like wooden barrels formed a line along one wall. I might be able to scramble back up the slope, but it was steep and damp, and the darkness deep enough to drown in.

As I searched blindly for another way out, my sixth sense demanded my attention. I felt the voyants' dreamscapes before I heard their footsteps. There was just enough time for me to conceal my features with my scarf before they came into the tunnel.

The walls ran wild with tongues of firelight, deepening the shadows. When the torch swung toward my face, I shielded my eyes against the heat.

"*Dè tha sibh a' dèanamh an seo?*" Finding myself at knifepoint, I stood and raised my hands. The man was a vile augur, skinny and bare-faced. There must be little need to hide your identity down here. I listened carefully to what he said next: "*A bheil Gàidhlig agaibh?*"

I lowered my hands slightly. The language sounded very much like Irish, but the words weren't quite what they should be. I thought he was asking me what I was doing here, and whether or not I spoke . . . wait, of course—it was Gàidhlig, the old language of Scotland, long since banned by Scion. It had the same roots as Irish, but that didn't make me fluent.

"*Táim anseo chun teacht ar dhuine éigin,*" I said, speaking slowly. *I'm here to find someone.*

The knife lowered by degrees. "Spaewife," the man called, "we've found a brogue. Think she might be wanting to join us."

Spaewife—Tom had mentioned that title. The leader of Edinburgh's voyant community.

At the other end of the passageway, five hooded voyants stood in silence, each carrying an iron lantern. The woman at the front, who was wrapped in a twilled shawl, had the aura of a cartomancer. Her salted black hair was hewn into a bob, and her dark, close-set eyes were narrowed.

"How did you get in here?" she said to me in English. "Who told you about the false wall?"

"No one. I just . . . found it."

She eyed the shattered planks. "A painful discovery, no doubt."

"I need to speak to the leader of the Edinburgh voyants," I said. "Are you the Spaewife?"

She looked me up and down without comment, then spoke softly to one of her companions and walked into the gloom. Two other voyants grasped my arms and escorted me through the passageways.

When a hand came to the back of my head and pressed, I ducked under another archway. Oil lamps sputtered in every nook and cranny in the small chamber beyond. A group of vile augurs sat, hand-in-hand, around a rough triangle of bone; spirits danced between them. Other voyants were sitting or lying in deep alcoves— laid with minimal bedding—or eating from cans. Most of them were deep in conversation, their voices raised to fever pitch. I caught the name "Attard" and stopped dead.

"What's that about Attard?"

The nearest voyants stopped talking. The Spaewife placed a hand on my back.

"We've just had news from Manchester," she said. "I suppose you haven't heard."

"Roberta Attard, the Scuttling Queen, is dead," a medium told me. "And you'll never guess how."

"Dinna make her guess." One of the osteomancers chuckled.

"She was murdered," the medium finished. "By her sister."

I must have been taken into another vault, but I didn't remember moving my feet. Next thing I knew I was sitting down, and someone was offering me a hot ochre drink that smelled faintly of honey and clove.

"You're all right, now."

My hands were like ice. I wrapped them, finger by finger, around the glass.

"You're very pale all of a sudden. I hope Roberta wasn't a friend of yours," the black-haired cartomancer said.

"Catrin—" I cleared my throat. "How do you know that Catrin killed her?"

She let go of my shoulder and sat on a cushion opposite me. Her hooded attendants stayed close.

"The news came to us this morning, by way of Glasgow," she said. "Catrin Attard had joined a Mime Order raid on a factory and killed the Minister for Industry, the man they call the Ironmaster. Roberta confronted her and the two of them ended up fighting for leadership of the Scuttlers." She shook her head. "Terrible thing to happen. Roberta was a good woman, by all accounts. She wanted the best for her people."

I sat quietly.

An Underqueen should consider this purely in tactical terms. And maybe in those terms, this was good; this was progress. Catrin was a warmonger. With her sister gone, she could prepare the voyant community to take action against Scion. This was war, and war was ugly.

Yet the knowledge that my actions had resulted in Roberta's death, even if it hadn't been my intention, was stomach-turning. Catrin would have killed her brutally, publicly, to prove that she was the one their father should have chosen, the one who would do anything for the Scuttlers. She had warned me. She had said there would be trouble between them.

I had turned the Manchester underworld upside-down, and I had no idea what would happen to it now.

"On you go." The Spaewife nodded to the glass in my hands. "Hot toddy. Always makes me feel better."

I had to put Manchester behind me. Now was the time to reveal what I was really here for. When I raised my head to address the Spaewife, I caught sight of faces behind her.

Photographs clung to one wall of the vault, yellowed and faded by age. In one of them, a family of three stood in the mist, with verdant hills in the background. One was a thin woman with a wistful expression; the other, a man in an oilskin, smiling in a way that didn't reach his eyes. They each held the hand of a small girl with the same black hair, coiled into ringlets and bound with ribbons on either side of her head. Even though I'd met her many years after this photograph had been taken, I knew her.

"You knew Liss Rymore?" I said.

"Aye." The Spaewife studied me. "And who might you be?"

I hesitated before unwinding my scarf, revealing my face. The hooded voyants exchanged glances before looking back at me.

"Goodness me," the Spaewife muttered. She clasped her shawl around her shoulders. "Paige Mahoney."

I nodded.

"You were in Manchester? You led the raid on the factory?"

"I did. I wanted to steal a military secret from Scion. What I found there led me here, to Edinburgh," I said. "I'm close to uncovering the information I need—so close—but I need allies here, people who know we have no choice but to fight. If you want to help the Mime Order, then help me find what I'm searching for."

She raised her eyebrows. "You sent the visions?"

"A friend of mine did that. An oracle."

"And you let Catrin kill the Minister for Industry."

My lips pressed together. "Catrin Attard made her own choice," I said after a moment. "What she did to Price, and to Roberta— that was not on my orders."

One of the other voyants grasped her arm suddenly. "Wait, Spaewife," he said.

He spoke to her too quickly for me to properly follow, but one word got my back up: *fealltóir*, an Irish word, used during the Molly Riots to refer to the handful of Irish people who had assisted Scion.

"I'm no traitor," I said curtly.

The Spaewife's eyebrows crept higher. "You have Gàidhlig, do you, Underqueen?"

"Gàidhlig or no, she ought to prove her claim," the bearded man beside her said, looking askance at me. "You might be one of Vance's spies, for all we know. Someone who only *looks* a great deal like Paige Mahoney, and who wants us all on the gallows for treason."

"Don't be a fool. The Underqueen is a dreamwalker," the Spaewife said. "Have you ever seen that sort of red aura?" Apparently the whole of Britain knew about my gift. "Besides," she went on, "she knows Liss."

She went to stand beside the wall of photographs and gently touched the one that Liss was in. For the first time, I saw the resemblance.

"Are you—" my mouth was dry. "Are you Liss's mother?"

"Close enough. Her aunt. Elspeth Lin is my name." She returned to the cushion and poured herself a drink. "You ken my niece, then?"

The truth would hurt her, but I had to tell it. It wasn't fair to leave her with false hope. "I'm sorry you have to hear this from a stranger, Elspeth," I said. "Liss is . . . in the æther."

Elspeth's smile receded.

"I feared she was lost," she murmured. "I read my own cards a few weeks ago. Four of Swords. I saw Liss in a pool of colors, drifting far away." She took a deck of tarot cards from inside her shirt. "I saw you, too, Paige. A great wave washed around your feet, and dark wings lifted you away. This card represents both a beginning and an end. Answering a call."

She shuffled through her deck and passed me a card titled JUDGMENT. It showed a fair-haired angel sounding a trumpet, surrounded by billows of smoke. The gray dead rose from their graves, lifting their hands, while high waves reared against a pale blue sky.

"A powerful card," she said. "You're going to make an important decision, Paige. Very soon."

I held it for a long while. Readings always troubled me, but perhaps it was time I faced my future.

"You must tell me what happened to Liss." The muscles in her neck stood out. "Tell me it was swift, at least."

My throat seemed to grow smaller. "She died in September, in a prison camp just north of London, after ten years of imprisonment. I was with her." Each word strained. "I said the threnody."

Elspeth bowed her head a little. I took a slug of the honeyed drink. It still hurt that Liss, who had given me the strength to bite my tongue and play the game when all I'd wanted was to kick and scream, had never set foot outside her prison. She should have been here.

"I see." A heavy sigh lifted her chest. "We canna grieve for those who've gone. Not before we've fought to change the world that took them. If you were a friend to someone as sweet and good-hearted as Liss, that gives us all the more reason to help you."

I handed back the Judgment card.

"Liss did an ellipse reading for me before she died," I said. "Perhaps you can help me understand it."

Elspeth presented me with her deck, and I took her numen from her hand with care. It was a sign of great trust and respect for a soothsayer to allow another voyant to handle the very thing that connected them to the æther. Delicately, I shuffled through the deck and laid out the six cards in order: Five of Cups, King of Wands inverted, the Devil, the Lovers, Death inverted, and Eight of Swords.

"An ellipse spread uses seven cards," Elspeth said.

"The last one was lost."

"Hm. Liss was always far better at the art than any of the other Lin women. She could see visions. No one else in the family had that power." She tapped her finger on each of the cards. "Do you know what any of them mean?"

"The first two, I think."

Five of Cups was my father in mourning, presumably for my mother. The King of Wands, I was sure, was Jaxon, and referred to the hold he had once had over my life.

"That makes sense. Your past and your present. The third card would have indicated your future at the time of the reading." Elspeth plucked it from the deck. "The Devil."

"Liss said it represented hopelessness and fear, but that I'd chosen that path willingly," I said. "That it's something I can escape, even if I don't know it."

Elspeth held the card up to the light.

"You're moving against Hildred Vance. She's certainly a force of hopelessness and fear, and it seems she was in all our futures," she said darkly, "but nobody gives in to her willingly—certainly not the Underqueen of the Mime Order. So it can't refer to her." She studied the card as if, by the sheer force of her will, the Devil would peel off its face and reveal its true identity. "Notice the other figures in the image. The Devil looms over a man and a woman."

She flipped it to face me. The painted, horned head was as sinister as its name insinuated, with its downturned mouth and staring white eyes. Two naked figures were on either side of the pedestal, bound to it, and by extension, to each other, by a silver chain.

"The two figures in the Devil card closely resemble the couple in the Lovers card, which comes next. They could almost *be* the Lovers. Look closely. The Devil controls them. Manipulates them."

The words left a fine sweat on my brow.

Controls them. Manipulates them. The Devil could be Terebell. Both Warden and I were chained to her: Warden by his loyalty, me by my need for her money. And we were also bound to each other by a chain, albeit a chain of gold.

"Someone stands over the pair in the Lovers card, too, though there's no chain." Elspeth pointed to a winged figure above the man and woman. "I'm not certain what this figure represents in this instance, but . . . someone is always watching this couple."

Liss had given little detail on the Lovers, except that it would show me what to do. *There's tension between spirit and flesh*, she had told me. *Too much.* I hadn't understood her at the time, but I had since collided with a lover—or someone who might have become one, at least.

As a Rephaite, Warden was the pivot between spirit and flesh. We had always felt watched, knowing the consequences of discovery. If he represented the path I should be taking, then by trying to distance myself from him, by telling him we had to part, I had gone astray; I had turned my back on the counsel of the cards.

And yet . . . he could so easily be the Devil himself . . . or a puppet-master in its service, keeping me chained to it, to Terebell.

Was he meant to be my lover or my downfall?

"The way I see it," Elspeth said, "you must follow the path of the Lovers. Stay close to the person you think the card might represent, and make sure you've identified that person correctly. If you stray from whoever it is, I suspect you'll be vulnerable to the Devil." She gathered the deck back together. "I hope the answers soon become clear to you, Paige."

My brow was knitted. I had more questions now than I'd had before.

I shook myself. I couldn't dwell on this, not when I was getting so close to solving the mystery of what might power Senshield.

And not when another devil could be watching us, preparing to cast another net around me—a devil named Hildred Vance.

"There's a reason I came to find you," I said. I looked between the voyants. "I need to know exactly where the Edinburgh Central Depot is."

Elspeth's expression was guarded. "Why?"

"I—I can't explain now. But it's important."

She pursed her lips. "You'll not find the depot on any map," she said, "but those of us who have lived here for years know fine well where it is. It's in Leith—a military district beside the port, off-limits to denizens. Don't try to get in. You'll wind up dead or captured."

Just going outside put me at risk of winding up dead or captured. If I let that daunt me, I'd never do anything.

17

Blood and Steel

Nick and Warden eventually found me, after making their way through a convoluted network of tunnels. We emerged from the Vaults into the light of a low sun, which had banished much of the fog and now glared off the snow. I was armed with a military-grade pistol from Elspeth, whose people had been able to build up a cache of weapons over the years, stolen from vehicles bound for the depot. She had promised that if we needed assistance, supplies, or somewhere to hide during our time in Edinburgh, we were welcome to come back.

As we made the return journey to the safe house, I pictured the faces of those who were suffering under Scion. The Mime Order, entombed in the Beneath. The factory hands, shorn and beaten. The Irish, ostracized. The night Vigiles, threatened by a technology that might destroy us all.

Yet now I thought of others, too: the living, the defiant. Elspeth Lin, the last of a family that Scion had torn apart, resolved to fight back. My commanders in London. The Ranthen. The people who were here with me now. I didn't know if we could stop the machine, but a fire had started deep within it. Even the smallest flame could raze the strongest house.

Some had to suffer. And some had to stand.

Eliza and Maria were waiting for us in the parlor. From their frustrated expressions, their investigations in the citadel had been fruitless. When we entered, Eliza stood.

"Did you find the voyants?"

"Yes," I said. "And they'll help us."

Relief crossed her face. "And the depot?"

"It's in Leith, on the coast. We go now."

Maria was already entering the district's name into the tracker. "Ah," she breathed. "Yes. Look at what happens when you try to zoom in on Leith." She showed me the screen. The district was a nebulous smear on the coast, not too far from the center of Edinburgh. Blurred. "Scion doesn't want any satellites to see what's going on there."

"All the more reason for us to go. Eliza, you stay here," I said. "We need someone on the outside if we get into trouble."

"Be careful," she said.

We set off for Leith as soon as it was dark. Instead of an Underground or a monorail, Edinburgh had a system of automated trams that ran round the clock. While the Rephaim went their own way, preferring to move quickly through the shadows, the rest of us found a tram toward Leith and took seats at the back, away from the other passengers. We got off at the terminus, where Lucida and Warden were waiting.

A fence stood between us and Leith, covered with red signs. All I could see beyond it was more buildings. I spied a camera jutting from a wall and backed into the shelter of a doorway.

WARNING

SCIONIDE MILITARY INSTALLATION

ACCESS TO THIS ZONE IS RESTRICTED BY THE
GRAND COMMANDER IN ACCORDANCE WITH
SCION LAW. USE OF DEADLY FORCE IS AUTHORIZED.

"We're going in," I said.

"How?" Maria asked, looking mystified.

I lifted an eyebrow.

"Ah," she said, with a smirk. "Of course."

The guard behind the fence was alone. It took me more time than I wanted to worm into his dreamscape, and he made a hell of a fuss as I overcame his defenses, but I managed to keep my claws in him for long enough to walk him to the gate and open it. As soon as she could fit through, Maria charged forward and knocked him out with the butt of his own gun. I returned to my body as Nick was carrying me into the facility. The gate closed with a hiss behind us, sealing itself with a throb of red light.

Nick set me on my feet. We were into the military district, edging through the darkened streets that must lead to the depot. Warden and Lucida stayed ahead of us, ready to silence any soldiers that appeared, while Nick kept an eye out for cameras and scanners. With every step, a feeling that we were being watched crept up on me. Had Vance predicted our arrival? Was she here already?

Despite the cold, my nape was damp. A wrong move here could get us all killed. I sensed people in the buildings, but no one was outside on the streets. This section of the military district must be solely administrative, a smokescreen hiding the real secret.

I was proven right when we came to a ten-foot concrete wall. A fence towered at the top, crowned with a corolla of metal spikes, adding another nine or ten feet to the height of the barrier. Yet more signs warned that deadly force was authorized.

We weren't getting inside this place in a hurry.

"Somebody give me a boost," I said.

"Wait. I'll go first." Maria tied her coat around her waist. "Warden, you're the tallest. Mind giving a lady a leg-up?"

Warden glanced at Lucida, who was visibly scandalized by the idea. Maria, blissfully unaware of the Rephaite aversion to touching humans, gave him an expectant look.

"I will," Nick said, and cupped his hands.

Nick was strong, but he couldn't raise Maria quite high enough. She made one grab for the wall that almost unbalanced them both, causing Nick to swear through his teeth and lower her.

"Sorry." When she was back on the ground, Maria grinned at Warden. "Has to be you, big man."

A hysterical urge to laugh seized me. Lucida didn't seem thrilled by this state of affairs, but we weren't in a position to debate it. Warden lifted Maria easily, letting her stand on his shoulder. She caught the lip of the wall and scrambled up.

In the moments she was out of sight, I didn't breathe. I half-expected to hear a gunshot, but her head soon popped over the edge.

"Come on," she whispered.

Avoiding Warden's gaze, I stepped on to his hand, then climbed on to his shoulder. He held my calf to steady me, sending a shiver right the way up to my back, as I stretched to grasp Maria's hand and let her take some of my weight. My boots scraped on the smooth wall, seeking traction. When I was up, Maria patted me on the back.

"Take a look down there, Underqueen," she said, a little hoarsely. "Just . . . try not to scream."

I hunkered down on my stomach and crawled to the fence.

What I saw beyond it, I knew I would never forget.

Tanks. Hundreds of tanks. They formed perfect columns on the concrete in front of a jet-black warehouse. Heavily armed soldiers swarmed around them in gunmetal armor. Even in my darkest moments, I could never have imagined that a force of this magnitude really existed. Locked out of the district, the people of Edinburgh must have no idea that they shared their citadel with so many machines of war.

This was what the factories were generating in Manchester, what human blood had been shed to create.

Warden appeared on my right. His eyes torched as he took it in. Nick joined us and dug out his binoculars. I let him absorb it all for a minute before I reached for them and focused on the nearest unit. The soldiers' armored backs were stamped with SECOND INQUISI-TORIAL DIVISION, and I could see now that the rifles they carried had a thin strip of white light along the barrel.

Active. The scanner-guns had been brought here from Manchester as ordinary firearms; now they were pieces of ethereal technology.

Just visible in the darkness beyond the floodlights were the iron hulls of warships. Some spilled even more soldiers down a gangway, while others drank them back in.

"Second Inquisitorial Division," I said quietly, reading the soldiers' armor again. "That's the overseas invasion force, not homeland security."

Images knifed their way to the front of my mind. Sunlight on the river. Placards held against blue sky. A blaze of copper hair as my cousin turned to meet his doom.

"Scion's last incursion was in 2046," Maria said. "They're overdue another." Her face was bloodless. "This is how Vance means to commemorate the New Year. Some free-world country has fallen into the shadow of the anchor, and now they mean to crush it."

I looked to Warden. "Did the Sargas ever talk about any more invasions?"

"Their aim is the total domination of the human world," he said. "They mentioned no specific targets in my presence, but no place is safe from their ambition."

We stayed there for a long time, taking in the immensity of our enemy. The tanks, the artillery, and the soldiers moving around it all, like clockwork.

"Wait." Nick was peering through the binoculars again, at two figures in the distance. When he lowered them, I watched the emotions wrestle on his features. "*Helvete*. It's Tjäder."

Maria snatched the binoculars before I could. A moment later, she lowered them.

"And someone else." She glanced at me. "Someone you'll be delighted to see."

I took the binoculars from her unresisting hands.

They were walking away from one of the warships, flanked by soldiers. I remembered Birgitta Tjäder's face from the colony; pale and with high cheekbones. Her thick hair was braided and wound at the back of her head, and she was garbed in light armor, carrying a helmet under her arm. Tjäder was best-known as Chief of Vigilance in Stockholm, but she was also the commandant of the Second Inquisitorial Division—the one whose orders had murdered Nick's sister.

The feeling evaporated from my limbs when the lights threw the second person into sharp relief. The Scion official beside Tjäder was an arrow of a woman, who barely came up to her shoulder. Even from a distance, I knew her. That high, pallid hair; the Rephaite-like lack of expression; those abyssal black eyes, almost devoid of whites, framed by fine-cut brows—eyes that swallowed information, letting nothing escape. The last time I had seen this face, it had been on the screen in the warehouse, and I had been helpless in a net.

Hildred Vance, the woman destined to conquer the world for the Rephaim. Finally, I was seeing her in the flesh.

This time, she wasn't just going to trap me from afar. This time, I knew, she had come to collect me herself.

She was clad in a tailored suit and a high-collared cape, the sort with crimson lining that all of Scion's most senior officials wore. As I watched her, her eyes flicked upward, and it seemed for all the world as if she was looking straight at me. Nausea unfurled in the pit of my stomach.

"We have to go," I murmured.

Nick tensed. "What's wrong?"

Vance had already looked away, but I was shaken. "She knows we're up here." I swallowed, hard. "She was looking right at me."

Maria chuckled softly. "Everyone thinks that when they look at her."

"Well, this has made our decision for us," Nick said. "We're not going in now."

"Senshield's core could be in there," I said, thinking aloud. "The scanners might be activated in that warehouse. Right under our noses." Now that Vance had given her attention back to Tjäder, I returned to the fence. "I'll be damned if all this was for nothing. I have to go in."

"No. I will go," Warden said.

The rest of us stared at him incredulously.

"Don't be insane," I said. "Even if you could get through the barrier—" He took hold of two of the bars that made up the fence and strained them apart, creating a breach just large enough for him to get through. The rest of that sentence died on my tongue, but my mouth turned dry as stone. He was serious. "Warden, you are not going in there. As Underqueen, I order you not to go in there."

He didn't take his eyes off the depot. "Permission to disregard your orders, Underqueen."

"Permission not granted. Permission categorically denied."

"Paige, we don't have a choice," Maria cut in. "If we leave now, we lose our chance of finding out what powers Senshield. It's what you've wanted to do from the beginning. The only way to help the Mime Order." She grasped my arm. "We're all in this with you. We're all willing to stand."

Warden stayed where he was, waiting.

It made the most sense for him to go. If he was shot, he would survive. He was strong enough to escape capture by humans. He had the element of surprise if someone saw him, giving him enough time to react, and he could move swiftly and silently through a heavily guarded building. In short, he was a Rephaite, and that made him better for this mission than any of the humans.

"Permission granted."

He didn't hesitate. Almost in one movement, he was through the fence and over the edge of the wall. Maria crawled through the gap and looked down, holding her hood in place.

For the time he was gone, I stayed prone on the concrete, keeping close to Maria and Nick. Here on the coast, the wind was callous. I watched Tjäder and Vance disappear into the vast warehouse, watched the soldiers stop to salute the Grand Commander.

I didn't want Warden in there. The thought of him near Vance was sickening. I cleaned the mist from my watch and saw the seconds click away, imagining the soldiers emptying their bullets into him, dragging him off.

He would come back. He must come back.

I would not consider what would happen if he didn't.

A leather-clad hand appeared on the wall, making us all flinch. A moment later, Warden came into view, holding something in the crook of one arm.

I let out my breath. He joined us on the other side of the fence. "Did anyone see you?"

"If they had," he said, "I presume that we would know of it."

"And the core?" My breaths still wavered. "Is it there?"

His gaze met mine. "Not the core," he said, "but there is this."

He presented me with a scanner-gun, like the ones we had stolen from the factory, but with one, crucial difference: the white stripe. This one was active.

Warden watched my face, as if measuring my reaction. "Perhaps this is best explained at the safe house."

"You saw something in there," I conjectured.

"Yes."

He handed me a holster. I removed my coat for long enough to buckle it on, shuddering when the cold hit my torso. Maria secured the scanner-gun inside it.

"Come on." My coat was just about bulky enough to hide its shape. "Let's take a look at this thing."

The guard was still unconscious when we passed him. Getting out of the district was even easier than it had been to get in, but we broke into a run as soon as we were past the fence. Suddenly, the sheer stupidity and danger of what we had done was catching up with us. We parted ways with the Rephaim and took another tram back to the center of the citadel, disembarking close to Waverley Bridge—one of the two bridges crossing the valley that ran through the middle of Edinburgh, dividing the Old Town from the New Town. Rain drenched us as we returned to Anchor Close.

Eliza was bolt upright on the couch. When she saw us, she let out a low groan of relief.

"There you are."

Nick leaned down and wrapped an arm around her. "We're okay."

"Did you see the depot?"

"Yes. Be glad you didn't," Maria said. "Are the Rephs back?"

"Upstairs. They said they were doing a séance."

Maria cleared the table. "Right," she said. "Let's see what a fully activated portable Senshield scanner looks like."

I carefully set the scanner-gun down. Maria was the first to lay hands on it.

"An activated SL-59," she said. "Our new worst enemy."

She dragged a finger along the thread of light. Once she had detached the magazine and scrutinized the bullets, she handled the weapon with practiced ease. Even knowing that it was empty, Eliza tensed when it pointed at her.

"Sorry, sweet," Maria said. "I just want to know what we're dealing with. The gun itself still seems unremarkable, so I assume it's the scope that's—" She peered through it. "Ah. There."

She let me look. Through the scope of the SL-59, the world lost all its color. Eliza's body was surrounded by a faint glow that had to be her aura. Nick, however, was dark.

"May I?"

Warden had appeared in the doorway with Lucida, who always seemed to be just behind him now. Maria shrugged and handed him the scanner-gun, which he examined. I had never seen a Rephaite hold a firearm; the effect was unsettling. After a few moments of silent contemplation, he removed the scope and took a capsule from beneath it, snapping a tress of wire. The white light ebbed, and the gun was just a gun again.

"I found no evidence of a single core inside," he said, "but these were being added to the guns inside the warehouse."

He held the capsule out in the palm of his hand. It was silver and almond-shaped, about the size of your average painkiller.

"What is it?" I asked. "Is it an ethereal battery?"

"No," Warden said. "There is no spirit inside it."

"Let's see."

Warden handed me the capsule. Its surface gave way just a little when squeezed. I pressed it between my finger and thumb until it ruptured, releasing a tiny amount of liquid—glowing yellow-green liquid, with an oily consistency. Lucida let out a hiss of Gloss.

"What is that stuff?" Eliza said.

"Ectoplasm." I ran it between my fingers. "Rephaite blood."

Handling it drank the warmth from my skin. The æther glittered around me, making me light-headed.

Warden's face was taut in a way I had never seen it before. I felt the barest shadow of his reaction through the cord: disgust.

"No ethereal battery makes use of Rephaite blood. This is a different sort of device. Notice that the ectoplasm is luminous," he said. "Usually, a certain amount of time outside a Rephaite's body will darken and crystalize it, extinguishing its properties. This has been kept active."

"How?" I asked.

"I cannot say."

Warden paced slowly around the gun. His eyes flamed brighter with every step.

I watched him. "What are you thinking?"

"There are only two Rephaim who would have had the necessary security clearance, and sufficient knowledge of the æther, to help create this technology. Nashira and Gomeisa Sargas," he said.

He kept pacing. Nobody else spoke while he considered.

"As I told you in the colony, Paige, Nashira's gift is similar to that of a binder—though far more dangerous, as she can not only control a spirit, but steal the gift it had in life," he finally said. "Let us suppose that she found a spirit with a gift that allowed for particularly good detection of the æther. She could bind it to every Senshield scanner, and every gun, through this." He nodded to my fingers. "Through her own blood. By placing a drop into each scanner, she has been able to link every one to this spirit and imbue them with its gift. The spirit *is* the core. It powers all of Senshield and every scanner—all through the conduit of Nashira's blood. That is my supposition."

"That's . . . quite a supposition," Maria said.

I wiped the liquid off on my jacket, disturbed by the thought that it might have once flowed through Nashira.

"A binder's blood is like ethereal glue," Eliza murmured. "That's what Jaxon used to say. He could smear a bit of his blood onto an object to compel a spirit to stay beside it."

"He couldn't attach one spirit to *many* places," Nick said.

"But Nashira isn't a normal binder, is she? She must be a sort of . . . super-binder."

Lucida, I noticed, had stiffened at the sound of Jaxon's name.

"Would Nashira ever do that?" I wasn't sure I believed it of her. "Would she really let humans take pints of her blood and put it into hundreds, thousands of scanners?"

Warden was still looking at the gun.

"Perhaps," he said.

"Does that mean—" I couldn't face this possibility. "Does that mean there is no physical 'core'—that it's just a spirit? One of her fallen angels?"

"Where would it be kept?" Maria said. "Here in Edinburgh?"

"Not necessarily," Warden said. "The spirit could be anywhere." He paused. "But . . . it is most likely with Nashira. Wherever she is."

My legs could no longer take my weight. I sank into a chair.

"Are you saying we have to destroy Nashira?" I said very softly. "That's the answer?"

"Or banish the spirit."

"Can it be banished? We don't know its name."

"Perhaps. This is conjecture."

"We need more than fucking conjecture!" I snapped. "Whatever the hell powers Senshield, it isn't here. We thought we'd find the core in the depot, and we didn't. All we have is guesswork and another fucking gun. I nearly killed us all in Manchester to get here— I *did* kill Tom—and for what? For this?" I showed them the blood on my fingers. "For *conjecture*?"

Nobody answered. I turned away from their eyes, feeling my own fill with heat.

"Paige," Maria said, "this journey was always a shot in the dark, right from the start, but that doesn't mean—"

"Wait." Eliza held up a hand. "Do you hear that?"

We listened. A message was coming through the PA system. I pulled my hood up and went back outside.

Snow brushed my face. It was the middle of the night, not the usual time for Scion to be making public announcements. When we reached the top of the steps, we found ourselves at the edge of a small crowd of people. The vast transmission screen on the Grand Mile was full of Hildred Vance.

"*. . . Grand Inquisitor has heard your calls for fair and equal treatment of all criminals who pledge allegiance to the Mime Order,*" she

246

was saying. "*Tonight, as Grand Commander, I hope to demonstrate to you the benefits of martial law.*"

Vance stared into the citadel, her voice made manifold by the speakers across Edinburgh. Usually she spoke with a white background behind her, like other Scion officials did when they addressed the public, but this time she seemed to be outside somewhere. I recognized the place at once; she was in front of the ruined Gothic monument on Inquisitors Street, just across Waverley Bridge. I had seen it on our way to and from the depot.

She was letting me know she was here, in the citadel.

"*Two days ago, we received intelligence that Paige Mahoney, leader of the Mime Order, had escaped the capital and traveled to the North West to spread her violent message of contempt for the anchor. I have a message for Paige Mahoney. She cannot insult the anchor with impunity.*"

The crescendo of voices around us drowned out her next words. The next thing I heard: "*. . . execution will be carried out immediately, in accordance with martial law. So perish all the anchor's enemies.*"

Her face disappeared, replaced by a white screen. When the broadcast returned, the feeling drained from my face.

It wasn't the sight of the executioner. It wasn't the golden sword in his hands, poised high for the kill. It was the man whose neck was cradled by the block. No cloth over his face. Hands shackled behind his back. A man who seemed so much older than he had when I had last seen him, with his bloodshot eyes and unshaven jaw and threads of silver in his hair.

LIVE: EXECUTION OF COLIN MAHONEY, the screen informed the country. UNNATURAL PROGENITOR AND TRAITOR.

Don't scream.

It came out of the ringing in my head—the survival instinct. Screaming would let everybody know that I was here. Nobody else cared about Cóilín Ó Mathúna. Nobody was left. Nick was speaking to me, grasping my shoulders, but I couldn't tear my gaze from the taut, lined face on the screen. Every bead of sweat, every quiver of his lips, was so crystal-clear that I almost believed I was there with him on the Lychgate, waiting for the blow.

My most recent memories were of times when I had needed him and he had looked away. When I had held out my arms and he had turned his back. But now, in his final moments, I felt more like his daughter than I ever had. I remembered the night before he told me we were leaving our home—eleven years ago, a world away. He had carried me out into the fields and pointed to the sky, where meteors were weeping over Ireland. And his words came from a memory long buried, words I had forgotten until now.

Look, seillean. *Look*. He had sounded lost in a way I hadn't understood. *The sky is falling down on us.*

When the sword came down, I didn't close my eyes.

I owed him that much. To see what I had done.

I don't remember how I got back to the safe house. I have a dim memory of my tongue prickling, and a sense that I was floating. As I drifted in and out of consciousness, my thoughts became a shattering of ruby and gold, a labyrinth of thorns with no escape. Somewhere in the twisting darkness, I heard my grandmother singing a lullaby in Irish. I tried to call to her, but my words stumbled out of my mouth and broke, their wings useless. When my eyes opened, I was underneath a blanket on the couch and the hearth was full of embers. I watched them glimmer for a long time, allowing them to entrance me.

I was an orphan now. My father and I hadn't spoken properly in a long time, since before I was taken to the colony, but I realized now that he had always been at the back of my mind. He was the embodiment of a simpler world; someone I might have reconciled with after all this was over, when he understood that I had only ever been fighting to make life better. Whatever happened, I had always known I had a family to return to at the end.

I was dimly aware of Lucida's glassy voice in the hallway: "We do not have time to delay. I do not understand why she has not moved."

"Grief." Nick. "He was her family. Don't you have parents?"

"Rephaim are not offspring."

He sighed. "If we're going to do this, someone needs to make sure she doesn't follow us. I know Paige. She won't let us put ourselves in danger if she's not doing the same."

"I'm coming with you this time," Eliza said. "I want to prove to her that I can hack this."

They shushed each other as I shifted, making the couch rock on its brittle legs. My head was throbbing. I had almost drifted away again when a cool hand touched my forehead.

"Paige?"

Nick was crouched beside me, his brow furrowed. With a heavy-eyed nod, I pushed myself on to my elbows and into a sitting position. I drank from the mug of tea he handed me.

"I'm so sorry, sweetheart."

"It was always going to happen. He was dead the moment I left the colony." My throat was raw, softening my voice. "I should feel worse than this."

"You're in shock."

That must be why my hands were steady. That must be why I felt burned through.

Maria and Eliza sidled into the parlor. Eliza sat beside me and squeezed my hand, while Maria dropped into the armchair. At first, I wanted to shrink away from their sympathetic expressions; I couldn't stand them. I was the one who had killed my father, not Vance. I was his murderer, the reason he was dead, not worthy of compassion.

My eyes closed. I couldn't allow myself to think like this. Scion had started to demolish my family long before they had known my name, starting with Finn in Dublin. There might have been things I could have done better—I could have tried harder to reach my father, to rescue him from their clutches—but it wasn't my hand that had wielded the blade.

"I'm going to kill her," I murmured. "Vance."

"No. That's exactly what you *mustn't* try and do." Maria held down my arm. "This is another move in Vance's psychological war against you, the war that started when she used you to change Senshield. You've come too close to her secret. Now she wants you gone."

I tried to make myself listen. All I could see was the blood on the sword.

"You've impressed her. She wasn't expecting a nineteen-year-old woman without any military training to evade capture for as long as you have. Now she's going to try and draw you out for the last time."

Nick placed a hand on my shoulder. "How?"

"That broadcast was clearly pre-recorded," Maria said. "You can tell—the sky was lighter than it is now. She was standing right next to a landmark. That was intentional. She wants Paige to go straight there, hungry for vengeance. That's where she'll have set up the next trap."

It took effort to hold my body still.

"Why kill him?" My eyes felt parched. "Why not keep him alive to blackmail me?"

"One: because she deemed that he was less useful to her alive than dead. Two: because there's a next move to come. This is just what she did to Rozaliya," she said. "First, she clouds your judgment. Then, knowing you're vulnerable, she'll strike. You need to stay calm, Paige. You need to defy what she expects of you."

My fist closed, blanching my knuckles.

"We're not going back to London with nothing to show for it," I said. "I want to destroy those scanners."

"That's exactly what we were thinking. We can set fire to the warehouse," Maria said hungrily.

I shot her a weary look. "Are you a pyromancer or a pyromaniac?"

"Come on, this isn't central Manchester we're talking about," she wheedled. "Fire is efficient and leaves no evidence. Fire is our friend."

It would certainly send Vance a message, even if it failed; even if it was an insane, desperate plan, one I would never have sanctioned under ordinary circumstances.

"Fine," I said, after a moment. I wasn't in the frame of mind to argue. "Burn it down."

Maria gave a little crow of triumph.

"How will we get close enough to the warehouse to cause this great inferno?" asked Nick, who had been listening, amused. "It's guarded, if you remember correctly."

"We'll manage," Maria said, looking positively optimistic.

"We can call on Elspeth's voyant community for backup," I said. When I made to get up, Maria's face changed; she reached out and grasped my shoulder firmly.

"You can't come, Paige. Not this time."

"I'm Underqueen," I said, my voice cracking. "If this is our last stand—"

"Paige," Nick said, "you just lost your father. You're the most wanted person in this country, let alone this citadel."

"And you're too susceptible to Vance's manipulation," Maria said gently. "We're all in agreement, sweet. You need to be as far away as possible from all of this."

I could tell from the others' faces that they would brook no argument. My gaze shifted to Warden.

"Fine," I said hoarsely. "I'll go to the hills, stay out of the way. I won't even be able to see or hear the transmission screens from there. Warden, will you come with me?"

"Good idea," Nick said, visibly relieved. "You shouldn't go by yourself."

I could tell that Warden was trying to work out what I was up to, what reason I could have for choosing him over one of the others. It would be our first time alone since our agreement. Finally, he answered.

"Very well."

"Excellent." Maria slotted her guns into their holsters. "Come on, then, team. Let's give Scion a night to remember."

18

Vigil

Warden and I set out on foot through the rain, taking enough provisions to last me until dawn. We were making for the hills behind Haliruid House—once a royal palace, now the official residence of the Grand Inquisitor in the Lowlands, which I doubted he visited often. The others had left for the warehouse in a state of feverish excitement. After days of whispers and machinations, they were finally going to destroy a Scion building—or try, in any case.

Neither of us said a word as we walked. The park in the grounds of Haliruid House was thick with pine trees. We hiked around them and up the rough-hewn hills, belted by a bitter wind. The higher we ascended, the thicker my breath clouded, and by the time we reached a good vantage point, my hair glistened with drops of moisture. The thermals I wore under my clothes sealed in some body heat, but I couldn't stop shivering.

We made camp below an overhang. The space beneath was sheltered from the rain and afforded us a clear view of the citadel. I took out some canned heat and placed it between us.

"Do you have a lighter?" I said, finally breaking the silence.

He reached into his coat and handed one to me. I lit the alcohol inside the can, setting a blue flame.

Our vigil began. I was supposed to be safe from Vance up here, but she was waiting for me in the citadel, preparing to spring her trap. I couldn't imagine what it would be this time. All I knew was that it would be designed to result in my capture, and in turn, my eventual death. She had no intention of letting me escape this place.

Above us, the sky was a chasm, a mouth that threatened to swallow the earth. Up here, I could almost pretend that only we existed.

There was a tight weight in my stomach. My failure and my father, knotted together.

"My condolences for your loss, Paige."

I shifted, if only to stop myself freezing in place. "I don't know if *loss* covers it. He was taken."

He glanced at me, then away. "Forgive me. Some . . . subtleties of English still elude me."

"People do say it. It just doesn't make sense."

We were associates now, nothing more. I was Black Moth, Underqueen of the Mime Order, preternatural fugitive, failure. And he was Arcturus, Warden of the Mesarthim, Ranthen commander, renegade and blood-traitor, committed only to the cause.

The last thing I should be doing was pouring out my heart to him.

"The clearest memory I have of my father is from when I was five. He'd been away on a business trip to Dublin," I said, "and I'd been counting down the days until he came back to Tipperary. Every morning, I would ask my grandmother how long it was until he was home. I would sit at the kitchen table with her and draw pictures for him." I traced the criss-cross of my bootlaces. "Eventually, he came back. I sensed him. Even when I was very young, I could feel dreamscapes. Not for as far as I can now, but far enough.

"I knew he was coming. Felt his dreamscape. I waited for him at the boundary of my grandparents' land, until I saw the car in the distance. I ran to him. I thought he'd pick me up, but he pushed me away. He said, 'Get back, Paige, for pity's sake.' I was so little;

I didn't understand why he wasn't happy to see me . . . I still loved him, for years. I tried. And then, at some point, I just . . . stopped trying."

Warden watched my face.

"I don't think I reminded him too much of my mother, or that he blamed me for her death. Nothing like that. I think he knew I was unnatural, and it . . . disturbed him. My cousin knew." I held my fingers over the flame. "Sorry. You don't have to be my grief counselor."

"Our agreement did not make me indifferent to you."

The wind dried my eyes.

"I know how your mother died," Warden said, "but not her name. That does not seem right."

I hadn't spoken it aloud in years, for fear of hurting my father. "Cora," I said. "Cora Spencer."

The only dead member of my family who hadn't been killed by Scion.

"You feel that you are not as angry about your father's death as you should be."

"He was family," I said. "I should be grief-stricken. Or consumed by the need for revenge, like Vance wants me to be."

"I cannot advise you. I am nobody's son. What I will tell you is that you cannot force yourself to mourn. Sometimes, the best way to honor the dead is to simply keep living. In war, it is the only way."

Silence fell. It was a tense silence, but his words did ease the strain.

I thought of the cards. The Devil, the Lovers. He could be either of them, or both, or neither.

"You knew what I was feeling," I said. "Do you always know?"

"No. On rare occasions, I have some sense of your feelings. A glimpse into your mindset. It soon fades," Warden said. "Whatever the cord is, it remains an enigma. As do you."

"You can talk. I've never met someone so wilfully cryptic."

"Hm."

I looked in the direction of the sea, where Vance's warships floated. Wind rushed through our shelter, chilling my neck. The conversation had distracted me from what I had to do.

"You are welcome to my coat."

Even my knees were shaking. "Don't you need it?"

"Not for warmth. It would invite unwanted attention," he said, "were I to be without a coat in this weather."

He showed no sign of being cold, so I nodded. When he handed it over, I draped it over my jacket, trying not to be too aware of the faint scent of him that clung to its lining.

"Thank you." I held it around me. "I'd heard Scotland was freezing, but this is something else."

"The temperature has been lowered by new cold spots. The veils between our worlds continue to erode."

The silence closed in again, inevitable as the tide. Tension spread through my back and shoulders.

"This is it." I wet my chapped lips. "How long did we last against the anchor? Three months?"

"This is not the end."

The wind tossed my hair across my face. I huddled deeper into his coat.

"Warden, there's . . . a reason I asked you to come up here with me." I looked him in the eye. "First, I wanted to say that—I'm sorry."

His expressions had never been easy to read, but the shadows made it impossible.

"Sorry for what, Paige?"

I drew a deep breath. "The Sarin have made it clear that they'll only support the Mime Order if it has strong leadership. I wanted to prove that I was the leader you needed—that I could change things. I failed."

My thumb circled the old scars on my palm. I couldn't bring myself to watch the fire die in his eyes again.

"You believed in me. Right from the start, you believed I was the one who could lead the Mime Order, the one who could lead the voyants out of the colony. Even I ended up believing it. But I failed. I failed them, and I failed you. So when we get back—" I made myself say it: "I'm going to give up my crown. And I want you to choose someone else to be your human associate."

Warden said nothing. I held my head up.

"I won't leave you in the lurch. I'm not going to abandon the Mime Order, but I've proven that I'm not the person you need to lead it. You need someone who can win the voyants' support after this, someone who can achieve a strong enough victory against Scion to persuade Adhara of their worth. Maria is probably your best bet. She understands war, and she gets on well with most of the Unnatural Assembly. She's reckless, though. If not her—"

"Paige."

"—Eliza would do well. She knows London, and she's stronger than she realizes. There's Glym, too, if he wants to continue. And Nick. He survived for years in Tjäder's Stockholm. He'd make you proud. Any of them would."

Warden didn't move. I chanced a look at him, trying to see something, *anything* in his expression.

"Paige Mahoney," he said, "I never thought that you, of all people, would prove worthy of your yellow tunic."

I was too drained to be hurt.

"You're right," I said. The cold made it harder to speak. "I am a coward. I—I left them in the shadow . . ."

"Who?"

"My family. Did you know about Ireland, Warden? Do you know what the anchor did to Tipperary?"

His face didn't change. "I thought you knew."

"No," I said, with a weak laugh. "No. But it doesn't matter. I know what I have to do. If the Mime Order's going to have a chance, I have to abdicate."

The shadows set his eyes on fire.

"Fool," he said softly. "Do you think so little of yourself?"

"Call me a fool again," I said, just as softly.

"Fool. You have swallowed the same poison that Vance is pouring into her denizens' wine."

Warden moved the tin of fire from between us and sat beside me, I looked up at him, taking him in.

"I did not let you give up your memory of ScionIDE for the séance," he said. "I want you to find it now."

"Why?"

"Because it is time you remembered."

The golden cord was taut as a violin's string, quavering with our proximity. He was the bow, and I was the music.

"Tell me how," I said.

"Only you know."

His aura intertwined with mine. So did his arms. He reached into my memory.

Golden light filled my vision, and the taste of copper sickened me. The ground fell away. A bitter taste flooded my mouth before a dam ruptured, and I was swan-diving through time and space—my body ripping itself to shreds, fracturing and re-forming again and again and again—

And then—

Kayley Ní Dhornáin on the street in Dublin, auburn hair on fire under the sun. Finn, my cousin, vanishing from sight, roaring incoherent anguish. Kay's shirt is black, but the blood shines through. She never saw the gun that killed her.

Hands, small hands, shaking her. My hands. *Kay.* A sob in my ears, a child's sob. *Kay, wake up, wake up.*

The flags of Ireland all around her. A man, one of Finn's friends, raising his hands above his head.

Stop, he pleads. *She wasn't armed.*

He, too, is unarmed. They shoot him dead. The man who knows his freedom is a threat.

Panic. At this age, she hardly understands it. It crashes, breaks, and surges into the crowd, a living, monstrous thing. The grown-ups are scared, as scared as the children. An airless crush of bodies, pressing in on her from all sides. Mouths that scream, hands that shove. *Mercy.* Pushing. Falling over her own feet. Bronze statue that glints under the sun. Climbing, clinging to Molly Malone. *Don't let them see.* Crawling underneath her wheelbarrow. *One, two, three.* Tears soaking her cheeks. *We're coming to get you, Paige.*

Beyond, a giant watches. Lanterns in its eyes. It sees her.

Finn, help me, please.

My eyes flickered beneath their lids. Petrified inside my mind. Warden knelt with me in the dirt, in the damp, his hands grasping my arms.

A toy left in the blood, never to be reclaimed. Wandering through streets of death, past the bridge. Faceless soldier. Running. Nothing. When Aunt Sandra found her, she was a doll. Not a girl.

Flowers at the lovers' funeral, bouquets of wildflowers on the coffins. One stands empty. They wanted to be buried by the tree. Only fair to respect their memories, despite the absence of his body, despite her father's fury that he took a child into the carnage. That she was brought back dripping red, mute, and drawing monsters in her schoolbooks. Her family singing the song from that day, the song of Molly Malone and her ghost. First time that she's spoken at the grave.

Finn, she says, *I'm going to make them pay.*

Warden framed my face between his hands. The sleep-dealer was deep within the dark vaults of remembrance.

Listen to me, Paige. We have to change our names. His features blurring, distorting. *Paige, it's not enough. At school, you say your name differently. Mar-nee. Like an English name.*

A Dhaid, scanraíonn an áit seo mé.

We don't speak Irish anymore. Not anymore.

Spinning. I was falling into a whirlpool of memory. Down, down into the depths of decades.

Molly Mahoney! Molly Mahoney! Hands twisting her hair. *She smells like death. They killed our soldiers.* Jeering faces. *Dirty boglander. Go back to your swamp, brogue.* Never heard the word before now. Sounds so cruel, like a sentence, like a curse. An older girl shoving her, girl with parents in the army. Girl whose mother was in Dublin that day. *Where's your red hair, Molly Mahoney? Wash my mother's blood out, did you, did you? Don't want dirt like you in this school. My dad says you'll kill us all.*

Sounding out those syllables. *Mar-nee. Mar-nee.* Broken record. Don't recognize this word. Not her name. Not a name. One day she will show them all this fire that lies inside her, fire that burns the inside of her skull and fills her to the brim with rage. One day she will haunt them to the grave.

One day I will show them what it means to be afraid.
Stop.

Reels of recollections, tapestries of colors. Somewhere in the vortex, I recalled myself. No more of this. With my last drop of conscious thought, I struggled against Warden's influence, kicking free of the current. The golden cord burst into flame, and—

—darkness—

Water pearling over stones, mirror-still and crystal-clear. No reflection; only a steep drop to the deep below, and a bed of stainless pearls.

Nothing lives. Everything is.

Cloud forest. Emerging-place. Instinct guides him here. Above, twilight—blue hour, time of Netherworld. Time without time.

Silhouettes of trees in the mist, taller than any Earth-tree. Amaranth. Before the conflict. Veils between this world and theirs. Nothing living here, and nothing dead.

Stranger. Dancing. Not his kin, but kith to his spirit. Dark hair stream-fast on sarx. Lilt of their bodies. Collision of dreamscapes. Feel of her, scent of her in the water. Her name is a song on his lips, a name not tamed by a fell tongue. *Terebell* and *Arcturus*, names they will bear when war has begun.

Beyond the veil, mortals sleep. When their lives end, Rephaim are waiting. Free of pain, free of sickness. Dislocated half-things. Wandering. They pine for a place where a falling sun puts them to sleep, where hunger never ends, where the ground waits to be fed with flesh—

I wrenched free of the memory and lurched to my feet, backing away from him until our auras ripped apart. Sweat and tears bathed my cheeks. Voices echoed through my ears; I tasted fear and smelled the blood and smoke again. The nightmare was over, but all of it was real.

"How—how did you do that without salvia?"

"I do not need salvia. It is an aid," he said. "No more."

"It's not really your numen."

"No."

My throat was a clenched fist. Everything in my body felt contracted with terror.

"Paige."

"I remember everything. I saw—" A single tear ran to my jaw. "A Rephaite. In Dublin."

"Gomeisa Sargas was there to bear witness to the Incursion, and was pleased with what he saw. Since then, Hildred Vance's mind has been his most reliable weapon."

My young mind must have closed down, locking the memories deep into my hadal zone. The streams of death, so great in number that the gutters had run red. The soldiers marching across the bridge; the vanguard riding stallions; hot breath steaming in the morning air. Babies and children, men and women—all of them dead. From under the statue of Molly Malone, I had watched the soldiers drag the bodies away to be dumped into the river, knowing that if I moved an inch, if I let out one sound, I would be among them. Butchery orchestrated by Hildred Vance, with Gomeisa Sargas pulling every string.

And it would happen again. Any day now, it would happen again.

The tears kept coming. I breathed as evenly as I could, dabbing my eyes with my sleeve.

"I saw you in the Netherworld."

The light in his eyes flickered. "The golden cord must have allowed you to mirror my gift."

"You were dancing with Terebell."

"She was my mate," he said, "long ago."

I was too numb to absorb it, but part of me had known. There was no other reason for her to be so protective of him, to be so intimate with him. She wasn't like that with any of the other Ranthen.

"Why isn't she your mate anymore?"

Warden looked back at the citadel.

"It is not wholly my tale to tell."

There was a tender pressure at my temples. "I didn't realize that you thought in Gloss," I said. "I know I couldn't have understood your voice, or your thoughts, in my body—but with the golden cord, my spirit could make some sense of the language. Like a mental translation. It was like—like hearing a song I used to know—"

I buckled against him. Warden caught my arms, steadying me, and we knelt again.

"All of this has already happened." My voice splintered in a way I couldn't stand. "We—I can't let Vance do it again, I can't—"

"You are still here. So is the Mime Order."

I found myself leaning into him heavily, seeking out his heartbeat. His embrace was tight enough to warm me, but not so tight that I couldn't pull away, as I should. As I must.

"Why did you show me all of that?"

His hand came to the back of my head.

"Because you needed to remember. To remember why you must be Underqueen." His voice rumbled through both of us. "You have known what it is to be a citizen of the free world and a denizen of Scion. A Londoner and a daughter of Ireland. A prisoner of Sheol I. A mollisher of I-4. You understand all that is at stake in the war to come, and why it is necessary. You know what it is like to live beyond Scion as well as within it. You know what the world could become if they are allowed to expand their domain."

"Other people have—"

"No one else in the syndicate has your history with Jaxon Hall, who could now be the Sargas's right hand. Only you watched Nashira kill a child because you refused to be her weapon." His gaze was inescapable. "You *burn* to destroy Scion. To avenge all that has been done to you. To undo the world they fashioned and reshape it. The Ranthen chose you. I chose you. Most importantly, you chose yourself. On the night of the scrimmage, you decided that you, not Jaxon, were the one to lead the syndicate."

I had no argument to offer. The dive into my darkest memories had taken all my strength.

Warden hitched his coat back over my shoulders. I pressed myself against him, letting him stroke my damp curls. Neither of us stopped the other. We stayed like that until the little flame in the tin went out, lashed by wind and shards of rain.

"Whether or not I decided that," I said quietly, "it doesn't change the fact that we've failed."

"You have risen from the ashes before. The only way to survive," he said, "is to believe you always will."

The motion of his gloved hand on my hair steadied my breathing. I held him close to me, letting his warmth take away the pain of the past, just for one fragile moment. I wanted him all over again, wanted him with an intensity I had never known, but I couldn't act on it. Nothing had changed. So I slid myself from his arms, feeling as if I was tearing a seam. I picked up the lighter and tried to ignite the alcohol a second time, but it stayed cold.

The silence between us was fraught with unspoken words. When I looked at him again, his eyes were afire.

"Paige."

"Yes?" I said softly.

A quake in the æther made me tense. I turned sharply to face Leith.

The disturbance was far away, too far for my spirit to fly, but stealing closer by the moment. The æther filled itself with the softest, fluttering tremors—like the ripples from a footstep near water, or birds unsettled by a gunshot.

Warden noticed my tension. "What is it?"

My heartbeat marched to a new drum. I could hear nothing but that call to arms behind my ribs.

Something was coming.

19

Offering

My burner phone rang in my pocket. I scrambled to pick it up, forcing my numb fingers into action.

"*They're marching,*" Maria said. "*The army. They're marching on the citadel.*"

"What?" I stood. "Did they see you?"

"*It had nothing to do with us—we never even made it to the depot—*" Her voice faded, then returned: "*. . . get out of here.*"

I clutched the phone tighter. "Where are you?"

"*We'll meet you on Waverley Bridge.*"

She hung up.

"Shit." I shoved the phone into my pocket. "The army—it's coming here, now. Marching on Edinburgh. What the hell is Vance doing? Why would she send soldiers to catch a few rebels?"

Warden touched my cheek, met my gaze. "Remember what Maria said. You must assume that whatever she is planning, however large the scale, however grand the aim—everything she does will be aimed at you."

I stared back at him, swallowing my dread. For a decade I had buried ScionIDE and the Incursion beneath the flowers, locked them in a strongbox where I could never truly see. I had been a child, suffocated by fear. Every memory I thought I'd had was a mockery of the true violence I'd seen—violence that would never sleep if Senshield remained active.

We might yet stop it.

And I thought I might know how.

"Warden," I said, "if I entered Vance's dreamscape, and you used me as a conduit, would you be able to see her memories?"

"You should not enter Vance's dreamscape."

I drew myself up. "If you want me to be a leader, I suggest you follow my orders, Arcturus."

His face was still a mask, but a light came back into his eyes. I searched their burning depths.

"We do not go any closer than we must," he said.

I should have known he would help me. I pressed his hand in mine, full of words I knew I wouldn't say.

We made our way back down the hill and ran between the pine trees. Half a moon smiled down at us. As I sprinted beneath the branches, adrenaline crashed from crown to toe, erasing all the pain from my old wounds. I came to life in the arms of fear. Some would suffer. Some would stand. Either way, Hildred Vance would surrender information we could use against her, the information I had chased across the country. Hildred Vance, who had killed my father. Hildred Vance, who had overseen the fall of Ireland.

At the edge of the park, I skidded to a stop, unable to believe what I was seeing. A multitude of people had amassed before the gates of Haliruid House—hundreds of them, gathered around a fountain on the enormous driveway, all of them shouting at the Vigiles and brandishing signs: KEEP THE WAR MACHINES IN LONDON, NOT THE LOWLANDS. VICIOUS VANCE. DITCH THE DEPOT. NO MORE BOMBS IN BONNY SCOTLAND. Among them were black moths, splashed on to placards and held up high.

A protest.

Where the hell had this come from?

The roar of the crowd was extraordinary. Warden stayed close to me. I ducked my head, lifting my scarf over my features, and backed into the shadows beneath the pine trees. I had sensed

Vance's dreamscape at the depot; I could find it again. I dislocated and searched for her.

"She's close," I said.

"Close enough?"

I opened my eyes. "Yes."

NVD vehicles were screaming to a standstill outside Haliruid House. When a commandant got out, one of the protestors hurled a swollen balloon at him. It exploded like a blister, and the offal inside oozed down his riot shield.

"Butchers," someone screamed.

A driver emerged. Without a word, she shot the offender in the abdomen. He doubled over like a jackknife, and the Vigiles raised their guns to fire—but now another throng was pouring around the side of the building. I had to focus, to tune out the noise. I leaned against Warden, pressed my oxygen mask to my face, and tore free of my body, vaulting first into the æther, then, like a stone skipping across water, into Vance's dreamscape.

A chamber of white marble, with a high ceiling and a grand staircase. Clean, elegant lines. Monochrome.

Vance's spirit stood at the very top of the stairs. She saw herself, it seemed, exactly as she appeared in the mirror, down to the last line on her face. No evidence of any self-hatred for her crimes, any hint of a conscience. Like any amaurotic, she had no way of seeing her own dreamscape, or consciously taking control of her dream-form. Her spirit was a gray, machine-like thing, programmed to respond to an invading threat as best it could without direction. I ran to meet it and wrestled it to the floor. Its hands gripped my arms.

"You," it hissed.

Its jaw moved as if on a hinge. Horror almost made me let go. An amaurotic shouldn't be able to make their dream-form speak.

"Me," I whispered.

I was too far away from her physically to unseat her spirit from the center of her dreamscape. All I could do was grasp it.

Vance's dream-form trembled violently, setting off an earthquake in her dreamscape. Someone must have trained her to be able to defend herself, but I was used to overcoming voyant dream-forms.

An amaurotic's, even that of Hildred Vance, was easy to suppress. I took hold of its head, only to see that my dream-form's hands were coated to the wrist in blood.

The golden cord drew tight, connecting Vance to Warden. I felt myself straining under the pressure as he used me to bridge the physical distance between himself and the Grand Commander. The ancient power of his gift surged through me, like electricity through a conductor, so strong that my dream-form began to shake. When it stopped, I shoved myself off her, sick to the depths of my spirit. I had touched the purest essence of the woman whose orders had slaughtered thousands.

My silver cord was lifting me away when Vance seized me. Black eyes gaped at me, glossy brooches in the dream-form's head.

"I will kill them all," it warned. "Give yourself up . . ."

I twisted away from her. As I fled, the threat resounded in my ears. She was capable of anything.

I darted into Warden's dreamscape, just in time to see the memory for myself. And there it was, frozen in his mind: the power source, the core of Senshield, my own personal grail—the end of the road. Mechanical, yet beautiful. A light sealed beneath a pyramid of glass. A spirit, trammeled and harnessed. Ethereal technology in its most powerful form.

And I knew where it was being kept.

I tore off the oxygen mask. "Did you feel it?"

His eyes scorched. "Yes."

A gasping laugh escaped me. "Warden, that was the core. It's real."

I had never quite believed that this hare-brained quest would be successful; that I would really discover where the core was. Now I had seen.

Now I knew.

The core was locked out of our reach in the most high-security building in the Republic of Scion. It was inside the Westminster Archon, the cradle of the empire and workplace to hundreds of its officials, back in the Scion Citadel of London. I had come all the way here, only to have to return to where we had started. I didn't care. It had been worth it.

Because I knew something else, too. Something Vance's memory had betrayed, like a fracture in her armor. It was a fear she couldn't shake, and that no amount of money could repair.

Senshield was not indestructible. There was a vulnerability. I could feel that anxiety eating away at her, like rust through iron.

It was all I needed to know.

We had to meet the others. Pushing our way past bewildered denizens and protestors, we moved at speed through the streets of the Old Town. A few hours ago, the streets had been calm—now a protest had started in the middle of the night, seemingly at the drop of a hat. A creeping sense of déjà vu was coming over me. When we reached the bridge, I stopped.

"What *is* this?" I whispered.

The Edinburgh Guildhall was burning from inside. Tongues of flame whipped from its windows. Its clock face was red, indicating the highest level of civil unrest, and a vast banner had been draped over its façade. Letters taller than a Rephaite declared NO SAFE PLACE. NO SURRENDER. In front of it, Inquisitors Street was a bottleneck. Hundreds of people were caught between the Vigiles in front of the inferno and the weight of other human beings. They were being herded from all sides, like animals in a pen. Others were climbing on to the Gothic monument on the street to get out of the crush, or trying to reach the bridge so they could flee into the honeycomb of Old Town. The night was full of cries and shouts for help.

I stared at the tableau unfolding before my eyes.

The others were waiting for us on the bridge. Nick was supporting Eliza. Lucida, whose face was hidden by a hood, went straight to Warden and spoke to him in Gloss.

"Eliza." I stopped beside her. "What's wrong?"

"She's been shot," Maria said.

"I'm okay." Sweat glazed her brow and throat. "It's just a scratch."

I knew from Nick's face that it wasn't. "One of the soldiers saw us. We ran straight into them on our way to the depot." His pupils were full stops. "I need to treat her."

"We did our best," Maria said, grim-faced, "but this is it, Paige. We can't take on the soldiers."

Eliza made a strangled noise and pressed a hand over her side. "We're going," I said. "Are the stations open?"

"They're open, but . . ." Maria motioned to the crowd. "We don't have any choice. Let's go."

Nick grasped one of Eliza's arms. I took hold of the other and checked that the Rephaim were with us before we slipped into the horde.

The Underqueen's great descent, followed by her great retreat. Underqueen or not, in this throng I was as powerless as I had been in Dublin as a child.

"Dreamer," Nick shouted against my ear, "can you—"

His lips kept moving, but the roar drowned him out. "What?" I shouted back.

"Are ScionIDE close?"

The æther was so disarrayed, it was almost impossible to concentrate on my sixth sense. I dislocated. With my hearing subdued, I drifted to the edge of my hadal zone. My spirit could sense activity in the æther for up to a mile, but I didn't need to go half that far to feel the legion of dreamscapes converging from the other side of the buildings.

Soldiers.

I snapped back, gasping. My white breath mingled with Nick's as he said, "What is it?"

"They're here. They're already here."

Rain drummed on the streets around us, plastering strands of hair to my face. Nick wrapped one arm around Eliza, tucking her close to his chest, and used his free hand to clasp mine. Maria shoehorned her way between two men and reached for Eliza. Behind us, the transmission screens changed from public safety announcements to images of the street, as if to show us the folly of our actions. The PA system activated with three chimes, and Scarlett Burnish's voice boomed through the citadel.

"*Martial law is now in force in the Scion Citadel of Edinburgh. ScionIDE soldiers will neutralize any denizen deemed to be resisting the imposition of the Inquisitor's justice. The powers of both the Sunlight and Night Vigilance Divisions are now vested in the commandants of ScionIDE. All denizens should cease seditious activity and return to their homes immediately."*

Panic. I remembered the taste of it, the smell of it, like it was yesterday. The crowd jostled and heaved. A wave of movement undulated from one end of the street to the other, passing from person to person, knocking them back like dominoes in a line. Someone bellowed, *"Alba gu bràth!"* I was flattened against a stranger, and Nick's weight pressed on me until my lungs ached. He braced his shoulder against the nearest protestor, growling with the effort of holding a breathing space open for both of us. I felt for Warden, reaching through the rain. I thought he was gone—that he had left me—until a gloved hand took mine.

Shouts rose up, calling for people to get out of the way, to go home, to do what Burnish ordered. Scarlet light jetted from a flare; projectiles cartwheeled overhead. Somewhere in the confusion, a child was crying.

Then I heard it.

Footsteps. Perfectly, regimentally synchronized. Over hundreds of heads, I beheld the vanguard. They were riding on horseback, like before. Birgitta Tjäder was at the front, leading the mounted soldiers.

"Martial law is now in force in the Scion Citadel of Edinburgh. Defiance will be viewed as sympathy with the preternatural entity, the Mime Order. Substance SX will be deployed to disperse sympathizers."

Substance SX. I knew exactly what that was. It had left a scar on everyone it had ever greeted, if it hadn't choked them where they stood. "It's the blue hand!" Voices screamed its name. "Let us out!"

Ahead of me, I could just make out Maria climbing over the ticket barrier. Eliza looked over her shoulder at me as she followed.

"Paige, come on," she gasped. "Stay with us." Nick clung to my hand so tightly it hurt as the knot of warm bodies tightened around us. Shoulders closed together; heads banged; backs clapped against chests. More Vigiles were moving toward us—and black stallions, each bearing the weight of a military commandant. Their body armor, combat helmets, and heavy weapons made the Vigiles seem like toys. Even their horses wore armor, as they had in Dublin.

In Dublin . . .

A thought pierced the panic.

All of this has already happened.

I saw the ruined Gothic monument. The bitter-sweet, chemical smell of the blue hand had already spiked the air, making my head spin—but it was already spinning, like a lathe, turning over the realization, fashioning it into an idea. Above the street, two ScionIDE helicopters were circling us all like birds of prey. White light beamed down, blinding me for an instant. If they saw me, they would take me to Nashira—to the Archon . . .

Martial law will be effective in the Scion Citadel of London until Paige Mahoney is in Inquisitorial custody.

All of this has already happened.

An airless crush of bodies, pressing in on me from all sides.

Mouths that scream, hands that shove.

Mercy.

Everything she does will be aimed at you.

In that moment of not seeing, I saw it all as if from a great distance. I knew what I had to do. It was the only way to save us all. The only way I could rise from the ashes.

Nick still held my hand, but he wasn't prepared for what I did next.

I broke his grip with one brutal tug, cut through a line of people, and ran. He roared my name, but I didn't stop.

Sweat and rain dropped melting crystals on my skin. The people nearest to the conflagration would boil in their own body heat before the soldiers reached them. I was near the thickest part of the crowd when I sensed Warden in pursuit. He was too fast—the only one, apart from Nick, who could certainly outrun me. I dislocated my spirit with violent force, throwing pressure through the æther.

The golden cord sent harsh vibrations through my bones, my flesh, through the whole of my being. My nose leaked blood.

"Get back, Warden," I called.

He didn't. I turned fully to face him, grasped my revolver, and took aim at his chest, stopping him. The tang of metal seeped down my throat.

"Don't try to stop me. I mean it—I will put a bullet in your heart." My voice shook. "And I don't care if it doesn't kill you. It will give me enough time."

"You cannot stop this, Paige," Warden said. "No matter what you do."

I jerked the gun higher. "One more step."

"Nashira will not let you go once you are in her clutches." As he spoke, I could have sworn I heard . . . some echo of emotion, of fear, in the very depths of his voice—I might have thought it was on the verge of breaking, if he hadn't been a Rephaite. If he had been human. "She will chain you in the darkness, and she will drain the life and hope from you. Your screams will be her music." He held out a hand, his eyes blazing. "Paige."

Something in the way he said my name almost disarmed me.

"Please," he said.

I stepped away from him. "I have to."

"If you expect me to stand and watch you hand yourself to the Sargas, you will have to empty that gun into me," he said softer. "Do it."

Blood ribboned from my chin to the hollow of my throat. Slowly, I drew back the hammer.

"Shoot, Paige."

My lips trembled. I steeled myself. A bullet would only slow him down; it wouldn't kill him.

It didn't matter.

I lowered the gun, and Warden nodded, just slightly—but I didn't go to him. Instead, I pulled off the necklace he had given me, the one that had protected me from the poltergeist at the scrimmage—a Ranthen heirloom—and threw it toward him.

Then I ran.

The golden cord throbbed as I sprinted away from him, moving faster than I ever had, a stitch gnawing into one side of my waist. Warden came straight after me. Just as his footsteps caught up, I threw myself headlong into the welter, ducking under arms, shoving past shoulders and hips with all my strength, crawling between legs when there was no other way through. I was more agile than any Rephaite, and even with his talent for blending in, it would take him time to whittle a path through this nightmare without creating another swell of panic.

He didn't understand. He couldn't see what I was going to do.

There were too many people around me. Gasping for breath, I wrenched up my revolver and fired.

Although the soldiers were close, mine was the first gunfire this street had heard tonight. Screams and pleas were offered up like prayers. My palms pushed against sweat-soaked backs. I forced my way through, suffocated by the heat, crying "move" into the storm of human voices. When I fired again, the weight of bodies tilted. Suddenly there was a path to the front—and just like that, I found myself on the transmission screens.

The cameras were tracking me: the woman with the gun, the violent protestor. Flashes blinded me, stripping people to nothing but silhouettes, searing rings of white on to my eyelids. Faces were contorted, monstrous in their fear.

"I'M PAIGE MAHONEY! DO YOU HEAR ME?" I shouted. "I AM PAIGE MAHONEY! I'M THE ONE YOU WANT!"

The golden cord rang like a bell. The first gas shell soared toward us and ruptured.

"STOP!"

Cobalt mist swirled from the cracked egg of metal. Howls of agony ripped through the din as the blue hand clawed toward us. It bruised the night air, stinking of peroxide and decaying blossoms, a smell that made bile well in my gorge. I tore the cravat from my face, letting it flutter to the ground, and threw down my hood.

My hair flew around my face as I broke through the front of the crowd and thrust up my arms before the burning Guildhall, clenching my hands into fists.

"I AM PAIGE MAHONEY!"

This time, I heard myself. Rain drenched my clothes, dripped from my hair.

Smoke drifted, dream-like, between the people and the soldiers, and everything grew still; all screaming ceased, all cries ebbed away. The chemical reek poisoned my senses. Dull pain pounded at the base of my skull as silence descended. The commandants kept their weapons pointed at us.

And there was Vance astride her horse, leading them. Her eyes locked on to mine. Beside her, Tjäder raised a hand, and one soldier dismounted.

This had to work.

It had to, or everything would end.

The commandant was little more than a silhouette. A helmet gleamed in the light of the inferno. There was burning red where eyes should be, and a gas mask covering the rest. I was shaking uncontrollably, but I didn't lower my arms. I was small and I was endless. I was hope and I was fading.

I would not show fear.

The soldier lifted his rifle against his shoulder. In the crowd, someone cried "no."

It was too late to go back. My heartbeat slowed. I stared down the barrel. I would not show fear.

I thought of my father and my grandparents. My cousin.

I would not show fear.

I thought of Jaxon Hall, wherever he was. Perhaps he'd raise a glass to his Pale Dreamer.

I thought of Nick and Eliza, Maria and Warden. There was no way for them not to see.

I would not show fear.

The soldier leveled his rifle at my heart. My arms dropped to my sides, and my palms turned outward. One last breath blanched the air.

A great wave washed around your feet, and dark wings lifted you away.

Interlude

*The Moth and the Madman;
or, the Sad Calamities of War*

by Mister Didion Waite, Esq.

O, Readers of Scion, you may well have heard
of a legend'ry Figure of good Written Word—
his Title, *White Binder*, his Name, Jaxon Hall—
who answers no Summons and suffers no Fool.
Ah! the Mime-Lord almighty of old MONMOUTH STREET
was the Picture of Poise from his Hair to his Feet!
Observe his good Humor, behold his long Stride,
so spotless a Man must be all LONDON's Pride!
But would it surprise you to learn, faithful Reader,
why just such a Fellow could not be our Leader?

One ruinous Year, this Wordsmith decided
that all Voyant-kind should be cruelly divided.
Some called him a Genius! Some called him mad,
some whispered his Writing was terribly bad
(and verily, *Didion Waite*'s was far better,
superior down to each amorous Letter)—

but all seemed to love him, and after those Trials,
he ruled, drenched in Absinthe, from sweet SEVEN DIALS.
O, and even as Binder sought seven great *Seals*,
he grew deaf to his Gutterlings' wretched appeals!

When cruel, od'rous *Hector* was found with no Head,
this good Mime-Lord fin'lly sprang up from his Bed.
He danced in the ROSE RING and fought for the Crown
and his Enemies great and small were cut down.
But close to the End, with a Victory certain,
a daring young Challenger swept through the Curtain!
And lo, who was she, but *Black Moth* arising,
and O, but her Face was most dev'lish surprising!
The famous *Pale Dreamer*, the *White Binder*'s heir,
the Dreamwalker Traitor, a scand'lous Affair!

She struck down her Master with Spirit and Blade,
but to spare us from Bloodshed, her own Hand she stayed.
And to wondering Ears, this Brogue told a Tale
of the Anchor's Façade and what lies 'yond Death's Veil.
Monsters stood at her side! Voyants cried *Underqueen!*
and they called her the Thaumaturge never yet seen.
'Twas on that fair Evening, with Freedom our Lust,
that the Might of THE MIME ORDER rose from the Dust.
The *Binder*, incensed, to the ARCHON set forth,
and the *Dreamwalker Queen* took her Voice to the North.

And O, what a Spectacle! O what a Show!
Alas for the Unnaturals! Where now shall we go?
For two hundred Years we have fumbled like Fools—
we have feathered our Nests and woven our Spools!
Shall we hide in the Night, where Dread will soon find us
or stand against Doom with the ÆTHER behind us?
Alas, when the *Dreamwalker* gave up her Throne,
her Subjects were stranded in Darkness alone,
and whispered that *Weaver* should bring them her head—
but now, when we need her, our young Queen is dead.

PART III

Death and the Maiden

20

Tomb

If this was the æther, it was different from how I remembered it. Pain radiated from a damaged place. I was a child in a red, red field. Nick called to me across a sea of flowers, but the poppies were too tall and I couldn't find my way to him.

There was the spirit among the petals, reaching for my arm, whispering a message I couldn't understand. When I held out my hand to her, it was Warden who took it. I was a woman, the pale rider, the shadow that brought death. The night showered my hair with starlight. He danced with me as he had once before, his skin too hot on mine. I wanted him beside me, around me, within me. So I reached for him, but his teeth tore out my heart.

He ebbed away. The amaranth had grown in my mind, too. As I bled, Eliza Renton spun in a green dress beneath a tower. Lightning lashed its highest turret, and a golden crown fell to the earth and shattered.

The tower loomed in a not-too-distant future, obscuring the sun. And somewhere, Jaxon Hall was laughing.

Each exhalation echoed through my skull, into the emptiness. I had thought this was the æther, but I felt the millstone of my body, smelled the sweat on living skin. There was sand on my teeth, paper on my lips.

Blood thundered in my ears. I had no memory of where I was, what I was doing here, what I had been doing before.

Just below my breastbone was a second heartbeat—thick, gray, deep within my body. It sharpened as I tried to sit up, only to find that I couldn't. The only sound I could produce was a rasp. In a panic, I arched my back and pulled my arms forward, grinding my wrists against bracelets of metal. I was . . . chained. My hands were chained . . .

She will chain you in the darkness, and she will drain the life and hope from you. I shivered as I remembered his voice, his hand outstretched, offering me safety. *Your screams will be her music.*

White light scorched the backs of my eyes. I sensed the ancient dreamscape before I heard the footsteps.

"XX-59-40." The æther quaked around me. I knew that voice; it dripped with an arrogance no mortal could attain. "The blood-sovereign welcomes you to the Westminster Archon."

The Archon.

When my eyes adjusted to the light, I recognized the Rephaite—a male with the pale hair of the Chertan family. At once, my spirit leaped from my fragile dreamscape and slammed against the layers of armor on his mind, but I didn't last long before I stopped trying. Red lightning flashed between my temples, drawing a weak groan from my throat.

"I would not advise that. You have only just emerged from a coma."

"Suhail," I croaked.

"Yes, 40. We meet again. And this time," he said, "you have no concubine to protect you."

A drop of water fell on to my nose, making me blink. I wore a black shift, cut off just above the knee. My wrists and ankles were chained to a smooth board. Another bead of water splashed on to my forehead, dripping from the metal pail suspended above me.

Waterboard. My chest began to heave.

"The Grand Commander has asked me to inform you that your pathetic rebellion amounted to nothing," Suhail Chertan said, speaking over my gasps. "And to tell you this, also: your friends are all dead. If you had surrendered earlier, they would be alive."

I couldn't listen. It wasn't true. It could *not* be true. I lifted my head as much as I could.

"Don't think you've won, Rephaite scum," I whispered. "While we speak, your home is rotting. And so will you, when you have to slink back to the hell you belong in."

"Your prejudice against Rephaim surprises me, given your lust for the concubine. Or should I say," Suhail purred, "*flesh-traitor*." Water trickled into my hair. "The blood-sovereign has forbidden me from causing any enduring damage to your body or aura, but . . . there are ways to inflict pain."

He paced around me. I writhed against my chains, but the first round of struggling had already exhausted me.

"No need to be frightened, Underqueen. After all, you are the ruler of this citadel. Nothing can touch you."

I hated myself for shaking so violently.

"Let us begin with an easy question," Suhail said. "Where *is* my old friend, the flesh-traitor?"

We like to think we're brave, but in the end, we're only human. My hands became fists. *People break bones trying to get off the waterboard.*

"I will ask you once more. Where is Arcturus Mesarthim?"

"Try your best," I said.

His gloved hand reached for a lever. "You sound thirsty." Suhail loomed over me, blocking out the light. "Perhaps the Underqueen would care for a drink. To celebrate her short-lived reign."

The board tipped backward. Gently, almost reverently, he covered my face with a cloth.

Suhail extinguished the lights as he left. I was limp on the board, drenched and shuddering and covered in vomit, unable to so much as lift a finger. My shift and hair were soaked with freezing water. As soon as his footsteps could no longer be heard, I dissolved into rasping sobs.

He had asked me many questions. About the Ranthen and their plans. About what I'd been doing in the Lowlands. Who had helped me get to Manchester. Where the Mime Order had hidden. What I knew of Senshield. He asked if someone in the Archon was helping me. He asked how many of the other Bone Season survivors were alive, and where they were. Endless questions.

I had said nothing, betrayed nothing. But he would be back tomorrow, and the next day. And the next. I had expected torture, and I had expected to be able to withstand it, but I hadn't expected to be so weak that I couldn't use my gift at all, not even to give myself a moment of relief from the pain in my body. The coma must have corroded it—it had certainly left my dreamscape paper-thin.

Sleep called to me. I kept my eyes open, telling myself to focus, to concentrate. I couldn't have much time before they executed me. A few days, at most.

Step one: survive the torture.

Suhail soon came back with his questions. Even after the first time, I wasn't prepared for the ice-cold liquid to flood my mouth and knife its way into my stomach. For the fear that made me fight my chains until my wrists were raw. For the gargling screams I couldn't control, even when Suhail told me I was a yellow-jacket, even when I knew that screaming would crack open the sluice-gates in my throat. For my body to retort with bouts of vomit. I had drowned on dry land over and over, a dying fish flopping on a slab.

Suhail became nothing but the hand that poured. He told me to forget my name. I was not Paige here. I was 40. Why had I not learned the first time? Sometimes he would touch my forehead with a sublimed baton, which had the same effect on my spirit as a cattle prod. As I cried out, the deluge came again. He whispered to me that this interrogation would do no harm, that there would be no physical destruction to my body, but I didn't believe it. All my ribs felt splintered; my stomach was bloated with water; my throat seared from the acid in it. Whenever he left, I fought to keep my eyes open.

Staying alive was physically strenuous. Breathing was no longer a reflex, but an effort.

But I had to live. If I didn't live for just a little longer, everything I had done to get here—all of it would be for nothing.

Day and night were now water and silence. There was no food. Just water. When my bladder was full, I had no choice but to let the warmth seep out of me. I was a vessel of water, nothing more. When he returned, Suhail reminded me of what a sordid animal I was.

I hoped, every minute, that the others wouldn't try to save me. Nick might be foolish enough. They had faced odds almost as daunting when they had got me out of the colony, but there was no way they could infiltrate a maximum-security fortress like the Archon. Whenever Suhail tired of tormenting me, I visualized how they might attempt a rescue. The scenarios I envisioned always ended in a spray of blood. I pictured Nick dead on the marble floor, a bullet through his temple, never smiling again. Warden chained and brutalized in a room like this one, held in a permanent state of torture, denied even the mercy of death to escape it. Eliza on the Lychgate, like my father.

The next night, or day, Suhail fed on my aura as he worked. A Rephaite hadn't fed on me in a long time. Blind panic made me haul against my fetters until the muscles of my neck and shoulders burst into flame. The double blow to my system left me so weak that once it was over, I could hardly cough out what had worked its way into my lungs. When Suhail took the cloth off my face, his eyes were the red of a moribund fire.

"Do you truly have nothing to say, 40?" he said. "You were rather more vocal in the penal colony."

I used the last of the water in my mouth to spit at him. His hand strapped my cheek. Pain staggered up my face, and my head seemed to vibrate with the force of the impact.

"What a great pity," he said, "that the blood-sovereign wants you unspoiled."

A second blow knocked me out.

When I woke, I was face down in a cell. Concrete floor, blank walls, and no light.

Suhail had really done a number on me this time. I could feel that I was badly bruised around my left eye, and my cheek was hot and swollen.

A cup of water sat beside the cot. It took me a long time to drag myself across the concrete and pick it up, and longer still to lift it to my lips. The first sip made me gag. I tried again. And again. Dipping my upper lip into the glass, I let the water soften the broken skin. Then more. Just the tip of my tongue. I retched into my arm. My throat closed in anticipation of the flood.

No. The water could be spiked. I crawled away from it and lay on my back, holding my aching stomach. They would not turn me into a mindless automaton.

When I didn't drink, they sent in a Vigile with a needle. Something that gave me temporary amnesia; I suspected, in lucid moments, that it was a potent mix of white aster and a tranquilizer.

Step two: resist the drugs.

After that needle punched into my muscle, I couldn't remember how to dreamwalk; couldn't even remember that I was able to do it. As if the drug had washed my knowledge of my gift away. When it was in my blood, all sense of identity and purpose collapsed, leaving my mind void. When the dose wore off, another Vigile arrived to top it up.

And so a pattern began—a cycle of sedation.

A near-constant thirst vied with my new fear of water. I would be taunted by thoughts of plunging, ice-cold pools, of crystal depths, of that stream I had glimpsed in Warden's memory. I wasn't sure if it was the drugs, or if I was hallucinating out of dehydration.

The next day, they took me into another room and allowed a squadron of Vigiles to beat me in lieu of the waterboard. With each blow, they asked, "Where are your allies?" "Who's been helping you?" "Who the fuck do you think you are, unnatural?" If I didn't answer, another kick came, along with a mouthful of spit and foul words. They wrenched my hair and broke my lip. One of them tried to make me lick his boots; I fought back viciously, and in the fray, another of them grabbed my weak wrist too hard. From the way the commandant hauled me away at once, the sprain hadn't been intentional.

No one used my name. I was only 40.

After the beating, I lay for hours in my stupor, cradling my wrist. When I finally surfaced, a narrow face was hovering above me. I shrunk away from the flashlight and sheltered my eyes.

"You've been asleep for a while, 40."

That voice, slightly nasal, with a note of self-satisfaction.

"Carl," I rasped.

"Not Carl. 1." Footsteps. "Do you know where you are, 40?" Without waiting for my reply, the person I'd known as Carl Dempsey-Brown faced me boldly. "They keep political traitors in this room before they go to the Lychgate. The last person in it was your father."

I couldn't think about my quiet, weary father being locked in here, kept in his own filth.

Carl smiled at me. I took him in, the boy I'd last seen in the penal colony. Still in his tunic of raw red silk. He had the early flecks of a goatee, and his hair was longer, combed behind his ears. A few loaded syringes of blue and green flux were tucked into a pouch on his belt.

"You're lucky they haven't killed you yet," he said. "It won't be long."

I directed a blank look at the ceiling, hardly able to open my puffy eyes. "Did you get promoted?"

"Rewarded, really. You know they caught the concubine, don't you?" he added. I grew very still. "A few days ago, while you were in the basement. Handed himself over, apparently, so you could live."

His presence had stopped the Vigile from injecting me. My spirit stirred.

"He's an idiot, of course. The blood-sovereign won't let you get away a second time." Carl laughed. "You know, 40, you really ought to have stayed in the colony. It's better in here than it is outside." He sniffed. "And it's only going to get worse out there."

He dabbed his nose on his sleeve. When he found blood on the silk, he uttered a terrified little shriek.

"No! Stop!" His body jolted against the wall. "You're not allowed to do that; it's *forbidden* for you to—"

In seconds I had him pinned, with a needle half an inch from his bare eye. His pupils gaped as he recognized it as his own syringe, plucked like a boiled sweet off his belt.

"Commandant," he screeched.

A set of keys clinked near his waist. I grasped them with a shaking hand.

A Vigile came bursting through the door. I attacked her with my spirit, or tried to, setting off an explosion of pain behind my eyes. No effect. Knowing I had lost this round, I rammed the syringe deep into Carl's arm, making him squeal, before a dart bit my neck. The floor slammed into me.

They had Warden. I rocked on my haunches in the corner, damp with sweat, my fingers flexing in my greasy hair. How could he be so stupid? He couldn't have thought that Nashira would agree to an exchange. She wanted both of us. Always had. Or was this another lie?

I reached for the cord, but there was no answer. I couldn't feel him anywhere.

Rephaim couldn't die, but they could be destroyed. Perhaps Nashira had no more use for him. Had given him a slow end.

No. They didn't have him, couldn't have him—Carl was lying. This was Vance again, trying to derange me. She was going to use every weapon in her arsenal to ensure I was a shell.

She must think Warden was my true weakness, then. Not Nick or Eliza.

I clawed my way to the door and tried to see through the bars. My cell looked out on to a junction in the tunnels, where the Vigiles would sometimes stop to talk during their rounds. A transmission screen ran on the wall, showing my photograph above a scrolling ribbon of news. PAIGE MAHONEY SLAIN IN EDINBURGH. There was no more threat to security.

Slowly, I sat back and leaned against the wall. With my eyes closed, I recalled the heart-pounding moments before the gunshot. The smell of the blue hand.

And I wondered if Vance believed I was beaten. If she thought her strategy had worked.

It had come to me in a flash: the horses, the smoke, the soldiers. People screaming. The cries of the innocent. All this had happened before. It was a stage set, all that chaos; a psychological trap, just like the one she had used against Rozaliya—only this time on a far grander scale.

There, on the streets of Edinburgh, Vance had recreated the Dublin Incursion, just for me. All the elements had been there: an ordinary street thrown into disarray, the army, the protestors, a demonstration that became a massacre. All arranged by the Grand Commander.

She had built a real-life flashback, with Edinburgh as the stage and many of its people as the unwilling actors, people who had been swept up in the deception. But one thing was necessary before she could guarantee my breakdown and surrender. She needed me to be unstable; in a state of rage and grief. That was why she had murdered my father on-screen.

I was to be a child again, lost on the streets in a stampede.

I was to believe that by sacrificing myself, I could prevent that day in my childhood from repeating itself.

Clever. And extraordinarily cruel. She was willing to use innocents in her mind game, to let buildings burn, to endanger hundreds just to catch one. It might even have worked, had Warden not shown me that memory of Dublin. By doing so, he had unintentionally left it fresh in my mind. The cues which should have tipped me over the edge were too obvious; I had recognized Vance's tableau for what it was. Props on a stage. An imitation.

That was when I had realized.

If Vance captured me, she would take me to the Archon and bring me before Nashira—Nashira, who, if Warden had been right, controlled the spirit that powered Senshield.

All I had to do was stay alive for long enough to get to it.

21

Skins of Men

The Westminster Archon wasn't designed for sleep. Every hour, the five bells in the clock tower would ring across London, and the clash of their tongues would tremble through the walls.

Days I had been entombed in my cell, with only a bucket to relieve myself in.

A cloud now lived inside my brain, thickened every so often by a Vigile with a syringe. They were keeping me as little more than a corpse. There was a period of clarity when the dose wore off, during which I received my meal. I was expected to use that time to eat and drink before another needle made me lose the use of my fingers.

They had to bring me before Nashira. She would want to see me before my execution, to rub salt into the wound.

While I was with her, I doubted I would be sedated. In the absence of other options, I would have to try and end her with my spirit. It would be madness, but if I couldn't find the place the spirit was kept and release it, all that was left to do was to destroy its master.

Sweat trickled down my face. Nashira feared my gift; that was why she wanted it so much. I could do it.

I must do it.

". . . just keeps going up. Martial law's here to stay." Two Vigiles were passing my cell on their rounds. "Where are you tonight?"

"Lord Alsafi has asked me to stand guard in the Inquisitorial Gallery. I'll be with them this evening."

I raised my head.

Alsafi.

I hadn't counted on him being here. I might not need to face Nashira at all. If I could get my message to him—the knowledge I had of Senshield, gleaned from Vance's memory— he might be able to act on it sooner than I could. He might be able to find and release the spirit.

Easier said than done when I didn't even have a scrap of paper.

My meal clattered into the cell. I crawled to it and scooped up the slop with my fingers.

An attempt on Nashira's life had to be a last resort. While I could still think, I tried to decode the image of Senshield that Warden had stolen from Vance: a clear globe with a light beneath it. A white light. It did have some kind of physical casing—something that must contain the spirit that powered every scanner. Destroying it, surely, would release that spirit.

I thought harder. Above the globe had been a second glass structure: a pyramid, reflecting the glow—and that pyramid led out to open sky, so it had to be somewhere high up. All I had seen, apart from that, were pale walls. I didn't know what it was, and I didn't know enough about the internal layout of the Archon to find it by sight.

Alsafi could be my eyes.

Except there was no time, and no way to get to him. At any moment, I could be taken to my execution. If I'd been stronger, I would have tried to speak to him in his dreamscape, but I was at my lowest ebb; Vance must have meant to weaken me so badly that I couldn't use my gift. In a sense, she had succeeded: I couldn't dreamwalk. Not even a foot out of my body.

But she had forgotten, or didn't know, that I could use my gift in other ways. She didn't know that I could return to my rawest form: a mind radar, able to detect ethereal activity without lifting a finger. And now, for the first time in days, I did.

Even shifting my focus to my sixth sense was agony. This should be second nature . . . I had survived physical weakness in the colony. I could do it here. Finally, I submerged myself, letting my other senses wind down.

My range had been damaged, but I could feel the æther. And it didn't take long for me to pick up on the turbulence in the Westminster Archon.

The core *was* here. I had been right.

As I lay in the black hole of my cell, I kept track of the dreamscapes in the Archon. Vance's often weaved from one side of the building to the other. Sometimes I fixated on her for hours, trying to work out where she stopped most. She spent a good portion of her day in one place; an office of some sort, most likely.

Footsteps sounded outside. The Vigiles were back from their rounds. I had absorbed as much information as I could about the shifts; these two were my most regular guards.

". . . going to be a long one on New Year's Eve."

"Can't say I mind. Extra pay. Speaking of which, I might put in a request for nights next year."

"Nights? You not telling me something?"

Their shadows moved beneath the door. Hushed tones.

"These new scanners. As soon as they're operational, the rumor is the unnatural lot will be obsolete. All Okonma has to do is sign the execution warrants, and they'll swing."

A rubber sole tapped on concrete. "I was thinking of handing in my notice," the man said. "Martial law's going to be hell for us. Extra hours, seven-day weeks. In the barracks they're saying they're going to dock our pay so they can give more to the krigs. We'll be drudges."

"Keep it down."

They were silent for a long time. The drug was clouding my thoughts again, a siren song to oblivion. I pinched the delicate skin of my wrist, forcing my eyes open.

"You seen all these foreigners in the building? Spaniards, I heard. Ambassadors from their king."

"Mm. They were with Weaver in his office all day." A light rap on the door. "Who do you reckon they're keeping in there?"

"Nobody told you? It's Paige Mahoney."

"Right, nice try. She's dead."

"You saw what they wanted you to see." I heard the view-slot open. "There."

"The unnatural who took on an empire," the woman said, after a pause. "Doesn't look like much to me."

Time passed. Meals came. Drugs came. And then, one unexpected day—if it was day, if day existed any longer—I was woken with a splash of water, dragged up from the subterranean vault by two Vigiles, and pushed into a cubicle.

"Go on," one guard said.

I stumbled away from the shower. The taller Vigile slammed me into the tiles.

"Clean yourself. Filth."

After a moment, I did as I was told.

I was thinner. My skin had a gray undertone that could only have come from flux. Bruises, blue and purple and pear-green, marked the injection sites on my arms, and my legs were badly discolored from the Vigiles' boots and fists. A blackberry stain fanned out below my breasts, where a ring-shaped wound sat just under my sternum.

A rubber bullet. It must have been. I stood there like a mannequin, my legs shaking under my weight.

Moments after I had stepped into the shower, the Vigiles slotted my arms into a clean shift and took me out of the cubicle. Soon concrete gave way to bloodshot marble, painful on the soles of my feet. My head spun like a carousel as they steered me through the Archon, along sun-drenched corridors that hurt my tender eyes.

Slowly, I became more alert. My feet slewed on the floor. This was it. The last walk.

"No," a Vigile said. "You're not dying yet."

Not yet. I still had time.

Somewhere in the Archon, music was booming. It grew louder as the Vigiles manhandled me up flights of stairs. Franz Schubert— "Death and the Maiden."

A plaque on a heavy door read RIVER ROOM. One of the Vigiles knocked and pushed it open. Inside, honeyed light poured through windows overlooking the Thames, slicing between blood-red damask curtains. It gleamed on marble busts and a glass vase of nasturtium.

I stopped in my tracks. He wore a waistcoat the same red as those curtains, sewn with complex foliate patterns. He didn't look up from his book when he spoke.

"Hello, darling."

My legs wouldn't move. The Vigiles took hold of my arms and bundled me into the opposite seat.

"Would you like her restrained, Grand Overseer?"

"Oh, no need for that sort of tomfoolery. My erstwhile moll-isher would never be so foolish as to run." Jaxon still didn't look up. "If you wished to be even modestly useful, however, you can remind your underlings to bring the breakfast I ordered twenty-six minutes ago."

The Vigiles' visors concealed most of their faces, but I heard one of them mutter something about "bloody unnaturals" as they exited the room.

An unruly stack of paper sat on the table to my left. Between us was a silver teapot on a lace tablecloth. A surveillance camera was reflected in its side.

Jaxon finally laid his book aside. *Prometheus and Pandora* was printed down the spine.

"Well," he said. "Here we are, Paige. How things have changed since our last meeting. How far you have wandered."

I took a good look at him. His face was ashen and slightly pinched, and a hint of gray had crept into the roots of his hair. He had lost at least a stone since I had last seen him.

"So," I said, "am I here so you can twist the knife? One last laugh before the end?"

"I would never be so crass."

"Yes, you would."

Even his smirk was somewhat diminished. Whatever his title, he was a human among Rephaim. Even if he was their ally, he would never be their equal. And if there was one thing Jaxon despised, one thing that would eat away at him, it was being anyone's inferior. This must be slowly killing him.

"Before we have our heart-to-heart," he said, "I want to ask you something. Where did you move my syndicate?"

Well, at least he had got straight to the point.

"ScionIDE has noticed a conspicuous absence of voyants on the street. This give rise to the assumption that they have been relocated—but where?" He reclined in his chair. "I confess to frustration. London is my obsession, a place I believed I knew in exhaustive detail—yet somehow, you have found them a way to elude the anchor. Enlighten me, Underqueen."

"You don't really think I'd tell you."

I sounded calm, but tremors were shooting through my body. His gaze dipped back to me, taking in my wretched appearance.

"Very well. If you mean to play coy," he said, "we will have to find another topic of conversation. Your turn." When I didn't speak, he smiled in a way that jolted me back to Seven Dials. "Come, now, Paige. You were always insatiably curious. You must have questions . . . questions that are burning up your mind as you lie there in confinement."

"I don't know where to begin." I paused. "Where are Nadine and Zeke?"

It wasn't my most burning question, but it was important.

"Safe. They came to find me after you cast them out on to the streets."

"If they're in Sheol II—"

"Sheol II does not quite exist yet." He scratched his forearm idly. "You did sink your claws into the others, though, didn't you? Danica, usually so pragmatic—although I hear she's fled the citadel. Clever woman. Nick and Eliza—they proved themselves to be great *admirers* of yours."

I lifted an eyebrow. "Jealous?"

"Not particularly. If the footage I saw from Edinburgh is anything to go by, they have received their just deserts."

They had to be alive. They had to be.

Jaxon leaned toward me and touched the coil of black at the front of my hair. It was all I had left of the dye he had given me to disguise myself when I had returned from the colony.

"A memento, darling?"

"A reminder." I pulled my head back. "That I once let you control me."

He chuckled. "Oh, you flatter me."

A soft knock came, and a line of personnel entered, carrying in the Grand Overseer's breakfast. Ever the epicure. French toast with berry compote; teacakes and whipped butter; then a silver tureen of cream, a pot of coffee, a dish of curried hard-boiled eggs and fresh, thick-cut bread. Jaxon waved the personnel away.

"*Every revolution begins with breakfast*," I quoted as they left. "Is this your revolution, Jaxon?"

"I was under the impression it was yours. A failed revolution," he said, "but you tried."

"I expected to see more of you. You were full of fighting talk when I saw you in the Archon."

"I came to the conclusion that there was little point in starting a war-game with you. I knew the syndicate would tear you to pieces of its own accord, if Vance didn't destroy you first." He assessed me with those pale-blue eyes. "Did you really think you could oust Scion with nothing more than a band of criminals, in their own heartland? This is real life, darling, not a pipe-dream." He poured cream into a cup. "Eat. Let me tell you a story."

"About what?"

"Me."

"Jax, I don't have long left on this earth. I really don't want to spend my last days hearing about you."

"Would you rather lie about in a cell, lamenting your doomed love for Arcturus Mesarthim?"

"Don't be ridiculous."

"Paige, Paige. I *know* you. Nashira told me all about your *embrace*," he said. Heat crept up my nape. "You may not care to admit it, but your heart is as soft as your façade is ruthless."

"Let's not make rash judgments, Jaxon. You of all people know how hard my heart is."

"True. I imagine he's been useful to you. I would probably choose a cold-blooded Rephaite myself, had I the time or inclination to pursue a star-crossed love affair." He added coffee to the cream.

"Now, let us begin. The tale of a humble young man, stolen from the streets, who you no doubt heard many whispers of when you were in the colony."

I didn't argue anymore.

"When I was not much younger than you, I began writing the pamphlet that would one day change my life. *On the Merits of Unnaturalness*, the first document to carefully divide the orders of clairvoyance and rank their superiority. I hope you haven't been insulting me by thinking that the Rephaim dictated it," he added. "The work, the research, the hours of pondering and agonizing, the *genius*, are mine. It was how they discovered me."

The record player switched to a soprano rendition of "Drink to Me Only with Thine Eyes."

"It soon attracted the attention of the Rephaim, most likely because so much of it was correct. I was arrested for the creation and distribution of seditious literature. After a brief detainment in the Tower, I was transported to Sheol I, where I became a pink-jacket almost immediately. My number was 7. I suppose the Ranthen still call me by it."

"No," I said. "They call you the arch-traitor."

He clicked his tongue. "I never thought Rephaim were capable of such histrionics."

I thought of the scars I had felt on Warden, the ones that still burned him, and I loathed the man before me all the more.

"Show me," I said. "Show me your brand."

His eyebrows lifted. "Why?"

"So I know this whole sorry affair isn't just another one of Hildred Vance's mind games."

"Oh, even Vance couldn't concoct something so wonderful and coincidental. Still, you're right to demand proof."

Jaxon Hall never passed up a chance to grandstand. With a slight smile, he sat forward, removed his waistcoat, and opened his shirt, giving me a glimpse of a pallid chest. He rolled his shoulders free of it and turned his back toward me.

And there it was. The rawness had long since disappeared, but the numbers on the back of his shoulder were all too legible. XVIII-39-7.

"Are you satisfied?"

I forced myself to nod. I had never really doubted it, but the brand was the final, irrefutable evidence.

"The discomforts of the colony were tolerable, in exchange for the fruits of knowledge." He set about buttoning his shirt. "Nashira, who took me under her wing, confirmed many of my observations about the Seven Orders. She taught me more. About Rephaite gifts. About *my* gift. My twenty-eight-year-old self fell wildly in love with this creature's mind; her deep understanding of the æther, and her hunger to understand it entirely. I confess to being easily seduced by knowledge."

"You make a lovely couple."

He smirked. "In mind only. I was promoted to red-jacket without ever having to lift a finger against the Emim," he said, sipping his coffee. "A week later, I became the colony's internal Overseer. Life was altogether rather pleasant."

"So you betrayed the Ranthen to make sure it stayed that way."

"I betrayed the Ranthen in order to survive," he said, with the slightest sneer. "I soon heard whispers of revolt in the colony. I had two options: help Arcturus Mesarthim or betray his plans to the blood-sovereign. The only one of those two that guaranteed my survival was the latter." He returned his cup to its saucer. "Naïveté is a deficiency in immortals, and Arcturus was abysmally naïve about human nature."

"He wasn't by the time I got there."

"Yet you charmed him into trusting you. I repeat: naïve. He must have been terribly disappointed when he discovered who you were. The heir," he said, "of his nemesis."

"Don't flatter yourself, Jax. A nemesis is an equal."

"You must think very highly of him. It seems my warning about his true nature fell upon stubbornly deaf ears." He pressed his fingertips together. "I reported my findings. You know what happened next. A little . . . *lesson* was taught." His tongue caressed the word. "The Ranthen traitors were left alone for days with the spirit of the Ripper."

I must have misheard him.

"The Ripper," I repeated.

"Delectable, I know. One of the poltergeists Nashira keeps, the same one you faced at the scrimmage, is the very poltergeist we voyants have hunted for a century." He looked back at the window, so the light fell on his face. "I am almost tempted to write and tell Didion, but no. Far more amusing for him to search in vain for the rest of his days."

No wonder Warden and the Ranthen hadn't trusted me. No wonder if they still didn't.

"You monster," was all I could say.

He held up a finger. "Survivor. Traitor. Marionette, yes. But not monster. This is what humans *are*, Paige. Only the Sargas can regulate our insanity." His hand returned to the arm of his chair. "Do you remember what Nashira said about me the arm of his chair in November—how long it had been since she had last seen me?"

I thought back. "She said . . . that you had been estranged from her for twenty years." I served myself a coffee of my own. Might as well die with caffeine in my veins. "Trouble in paradise?"

"She wanted me to be her Grand Overseer, given my talent for spotting powerful voyants. Someone to guide the red-jackets. I was allowed to leave the penal colony, but as a Scion employee. I was to make a regular payment of at least one higher-order clairvoyant every two months."

"A regular payment." I paused. "The gray market."

"Very good. I was its architect."

"The Rag and Bone Man—"

"—is an associate," he said calmly. "I let Nashira believe I would obey her. Then, one night, I escaped. Shed my old form. A skilled backstreet surgeon created this face." He pressed a finger to one cheek. "I needed wealth to achieve my dream of taking I-4. I kept in touch with the Sargas through calls to the Residence of Balliol, promising to continue my work, but refused to meet again in person."

"How did you get your hands on I-4?"

"I reported its mime-queen and her mollisher, who were detained within a day. Then I announced myself to the Unnatural Assembly," he said. "I found a place to live in Seven Dials. Seven for my number. Seven for my name. I employed the Rag and Bone Man to assist me with my payments. He extended our network somewhat, as you learned in the weeks preceding the scrimmage."

"Then why build the Seals?" I asked. "You had your gray market. Were you planning to send us all to Sheol for extra money?"

"Every mime-lord needs a gang."

"You're no ordinary mime-lord."

He fell silent, gazing out of the window, the remnant of a smile on his lips. It wasn't difficult to piece it together.

"You *did* plan to send us there. Some of us, at least. You arranged my arrest." I could hardly get the words out. "You kept Nick busy so he couldn't take me home, so I'd have to get the train on my own. You arranged for there to be a spot check on that line. When I got away, you told me to stay at my father's apartment. Then you tipped them off."

"Imaginative, Paige, but incorrect. Why would I want you taken? Remember"—he lit a cigar—"it was I who rescued you."

He was still looking away. My hand moved to the table and delicately liberated a piece of paper from the stack.

"Who, then?"

"Hector," Jaxon said. My fingers worked quickly, rolling the page up small. "He met you on the platform, if you recall—to alert Scion when you stepped onto the train. I understand that it was out of spite toward me. Our Underlord was asking for more than his fair share of profits from the gray market, you see, and I denied his request. So he took my prized mollisher and pocketed the money he received from Scion for you. The Rag and Bone Man later, at my behest, arranged for him to be slain by the Abbess. I was originally going to have him removed by cleaner means—a nice gunshot, perhaps—but for his greed, I ensured his death was . . . rather bloodier."

Hector.

All that blood in his parlor, the decapitated bodies—all because Jaxon had wanted vengeance for the theft of his most cherished possession.

Me.

"And that cleared the way for you to be Underlord," I said.

He inclined his head.

"At the time of your arrest, I was no longer working for the Sargas; they had finally grown vexed with my refusal to play the game by their rules. They cut off my considerable salary, which hurt—I had grown used to finery, and to power. And yet, I did not betray you. I saved your life. I put myself in considerable danger to do so. It was when *you* betrayed *me* at the scrimmage—only then that I decided to return to my makers. Not only to continue my lifestyle, before you accuse me of avarice, but to continue my education." Smoke pirouetted from between his lips. "We can learn from the Rephaim."

He finally looked back at me. The roll of paper was already up my sleeve.

I had no guarantee that anything he said was the truth, but his story held together.

He might have saved my life, but that didn't mean he cared about me. He cared about his own pride. He knew he had been the envy of other mime-lords and mime-queens for having a mollisher of my rarity. I had been worth money, money Hector had taken.

"If all I'll learn from them is how to be like you," I said, "forget it."

"It is too late, Paige. You are already like me," he said, "and dyeing your hair will never change that."

"If you'll excuse me, Grand Overseer, I'd like to go back to my cell," I said tightly. "I find myself missing the quiet." I had no time to waste on his games.

As I stood, he snapped upright and hooked a finger under my chin, freezing me. He coaxed me close, so I could smell the cigars and sweetness on him.

"In that case, I will come to my reason for bringing you here. There was a reason, beyond stories," he said very softly. "Nashira is about to present you with your execution warrant."

I had expected it, but I still turned numb.

"I suppose this is goodbye, then," I said. The slightest quake crept into my voice, in spite of myself.

"Not necessarily. There is a chance that I can secure a stay of execution."

"How?"

"You could be very useful to the Sargas, Paige. I have told them that you might be persuaded to join this side of the conflict, under my instruction. I will be Grand Overseer in Sheol II, personally selecting voyants for the new colony." He didn't break his hold on my face. "Come with me to Paris. I will offer myself as your mentor. You can become my protégée and retrain as a red-jacket."

Another Sheol. A return to hell.

"And Nashira would agree to this," I said.

"She doesn't want to kill you. Not until your spirit has . . . matured a little more." His grip tightened. "Think of it, Paige. Mime-lord and mollisher, together again. There is so much more I can teach you about clairvoyance, so much for us to learn together. And think of the alternative. Your gift—your beautiful, singular gift—in Nashira's clutches."

"She'll have it in the end," I said. "Dead or alive, I'll be used as a weapon. Better that I face it now."

"You must stop being so *noble*, Paige. It will not save you." I couldn't escape his eyes. "You can convince yourself that you are nothing like me. Tell yourself that you are the black to my white, the queen that stood on the right side of the board. But one day, you will be faced with a choice, as we all are. One day you will have to choose between your own desires, your own darkest impulses, and what you know to be right . . . and it will harden you. You will understand that all of us are devils in the skins of men. You will become the monster that lives inside us all."

I started away from him. This wasn't the first time that his words had sounded like a prediction.

The Devil.

Had it been me all along?

Was it the devil in myself—the devil deep beneath my skin— that I was meant to resist?

On the surface I was composed, but my insides were a jigsaw of conflicting thoughts. Like a moth, I was drawn to the light that he offered. I was afraid of the humiliation and pain that Nashira would put me through. I was afraid of losing myself to that pain, of losing my mind to it.

I could say yes, with a view to escape. I had played Jaxon's games for four years; I could play for a while longer. But Nashira would have considered this. She would have devised some way to keep me under control.

And I knew Jaxon too well.

"I find it hard to believe that Nashira agreed to this without the promise of something in return," I said.

He smiled. "Tell me where the Mime Order is."

This time, I would listen to the cards. If I agreed, I would be making a deal with that devil inside.

"Not a chance in hell," I said. "Not if you offered me anything in the world."

"You disappoint me."

"The feeling's mutual. You once said, in *On the Merits*, that we had to fight fire with fire to survive," I said. "Did you lose your nerve, Obscure Writer?"

His face closed, and he released me. "All I lost was my naïveté. I have always had the best interests of our kind at heart."

"How is it in our interest to work for the Rephaim?"

"They need us. We need them. You were going to start a fruitless war with them—and war will not improve conditions for clairvoyants, Paige. What we need now is a time of stability and co-operation."

"Have you said as much to your employers?"

"The Republic of Scion is not at war."

"I saw the depot, the factories," I said. "The Second Inquisitorial Division *is* preparing for war, and I won't flatter myself by thinking it was all for me. Who are they invading?"

For some time, he gazed out at the sparkling Thames.

"Scion has long had a tenuous understanding with the free world," he said. "Scion tolerates them, and in return, they tolerate Scion, in spite of occasional incursions." He paused. "You may have noticed ambassadors from two European free-world countries in the Archon. Weaver has invited them here to demonstrate to them the advantages of Senshield, to persuade them that it will identify unnaturals in their countries with infallible accuracy, in the hope that those countries will peacefully convert to Scion. If they do not . . . well. Let us say that my hopes for peace may be scotched in the short term."

As I realized what he was implying, the muscles in my abdomen clenched.

Someone was knocking at the door. Jaxon turned back to me.

"Our time is up. Nashira will make you a final offer," he said. "If you wish to live, take it. Think of yourself."

Another knock. "Grand Overseer," a voice called.

Suddenly I was full of pity, of sorrow, of grief for the man he might have been. I went to him and touched his face with one finger, imagining what it had been like once, before the knife had given it a new shape.

"I am sorry," I said, "to see the White Binder reduced to nothing but a boundling, a pawn on someone else's board . . . I really am disappointed."

"Oh, you may think me the pawn on this particular board, but I am playing on many others. And mark my words, we are nowhere close to endgame." The sun gilded his eyes. "Even so, it seems that, in my brief time as a pawn, I have taught you one very valuable lesson, O my lovely. Humans will *always* disappoint."

22

Ultimatum

Jaxon had confirmed it. Scion was ready to expand its empire again, just as we'd thought.

The Vigile outside my cell had mentioned Spaniards.

Spain was their target. Spain, and possibly Portugal, if there were ambassadors from two countries here.

I didn't know much about the free world, but I knew Scion had promoted the virtues of its system globally in the hope that other territories would join the fold of their own free will. It had worked on Sweden. *Join us*, they would say, *and rid your country of the plague of unnaturalness. Join us, and you can keep your people safe.* Some countries, like Ireland, had been taken forcibly—but it would be easier, and cleaner, if they could avoid costly invasions altogether.

Of course, Scion had many hurdles to overcome if it meant to convince the rest of the world to embrace the anchor. Every free-world government with sense would be wary of a rising, militarized empire. Some would have moral concerns about Scion's methods, although they had always taken care to conceal the beheadings and hangings from the outside. Others might not believe clairvoyance existed, and even if they did, they might fear that innocent people would be mistakenly identified as unnaturals. Nadine and Zeke had mentioned that being one of many concerns about Scion in the free world.

Now, however, Scion had the perfect answer to it. They had Senshield, an accurate means of isolating criminals. Why shouldn't they take control, they would ask, if they had a foolproof method for winnowing the unnaturals from the innocents—a way of removing dangerous individuals from society?

Senshield.

It always came back to that.

The ambassadors being here must be a final test of the water. The scanner-guns would be kept secret, but if they showed an ordinary Senshield scanner to the Spanish—if they proved to them how efficient Scion was about to become, and if they still refused to see the sense in being part of Scion's empire . . . then, and only then, did they mean to invade.

The Vigiles herded me back to my cell and administered my drugs. In the precious seconds before clarity left me, I hid the roll of paper under the mattress of my cot.

If Nashira meant to see me today—and my meeting with Jaxon implied that she did—there was a good chance Alsafi could be with her. He had seldom been far from her side in the colony. And it might be my chance to tell him—somehow—what I knew.

When the drug wore off and my food arrived, I retrieved the paper and huddled close to the door, so I couldn't be seen through the view-slot. When I was certain no Vigiles were about to come through, I turned my palm upward and tore the stitches from Styx's cut with my teeth, then used the blood to scratch three words on to the paper.

COLCHICUM RHUBARB CHICKWEED

By the time the Vigile returned, the note was hidden. I was waterboarded for ignoring my meal.

Alsafi was fluent in the language of flowers.

Colchicum: *my best days are gone.*

Rhubarb: *advice.*
Chickweed: *rendezvous.*

It was evening by the time I was dragged out of the basement again.

Now it was dark, there was more activity in the Archon. We passed personalities I recognized from the news. Ministers in black suits, their crisp white shirts buttoned up high. Vigiles and their commandants. Soldiers. Scarlett Burnish's little raconteurs in their red coats, tapping notes into their data pads, preparing to report their lies. Members of the Inquisitorial courts, gliding across the marble in steel-buckled shoes and hooded cloaks lined with white fur. Some stopped to stare and whisper.

Scarlett Burnish herself was at the end of one corridor, immaculately groomed as ever, holding a sheaf of documents. She wore a sculpted velvet dress with a complicated lace collar, and her hair rippled down to the small of her back, with the top layer braided like a net.

With her was a woman I vaguely remembered seeing on ScionEye. She was petite and sloe-eyed, possessed of a small, upturned nose and skin so pale it almost glowed. Deepest-brown hair was piled up on her head and threaded with rubies. Her gown, made of burgundy silk and ivory lace, fell in a series of tiers to the floor, leaving her collar bare for a necklace of rose gold and pear-shaped diamonds. The layers of the dress didn't quite conceal the swell beneath.

"You look very well, Luce. How many months is it now?" Burnish was saying.

"It will be four soon."

The accent nudged my memory. Luce Ménard Frère, spouse and adviser to the Grand Inquisitor of France.

"Oh, how lovely," Burnish said, all smiles. "Are your other children looking forward to it?"

"The younger two are excited," Frère said, laughing, "but Onésime is very unhappy. He always thinks a new baby will take his *maman* away from him. Of course, when Mylène was born, he was the first person to be cooing over her like a little bird . . ."

They stopped talking as my guards marched me past. Frère placed a hand on her abdomen and spoke in French to her bodyguards,

305

who formed a barrier in front of her. Burnish raked me up and down with her eyes, bid farewell to Frère, and strode from the corridor.

I was led into a final passageway. Above two double doors at the end was a plaque spelling out INQUISITORIAL GALLERY. Just before we went through it, I sneaked the roll of paper from my shift to my hand.

The sheer size of the place was what hit me first. The floor was red marble, as it was in most of the building. An ornate ceiling stretched high above my head, where three vast chandeliers were laden with white candles.

The walls at either end of the hall were hung with official portraits of Grand Inquisitors from decades past, while the side walls were covered by frescoes. To my left was a giant, Renaissance-style depiction of the establishment of Scion, with James Ramsay MacDonald holding up the flag on the banks of the river and shouting to a euphoric audience; to my right, the first day of the Molly Riots. I stared up at the images of the gape-mouthed Irish, with their blood-dusted flags, and Scion's soldiers, painted in lighter tones, who held out their hands as friends. ERIN TURNS FROM THE ANCHOR read a plaque underneath.

A rosewood banqueting table was the centerpiece of this magnificent hall, and a grand piano stood in one corner. Nashira Sargas sat at one end of the table. Gomeisa, the other blood-sovereign, was on her right, in a high-collared black robe, staring at me with his sunken eyes. On her left was an empty chair, and beside that sat Alsafi Sualocin.

Jaxon sat opposite him, smiling, like we were having breakfast again. He couldn't just leave me in peace.

Vigiles were stationed on both ends of the hall, armed with flux guns. I recognized a few of their faces from the penal colony. One of my guards lifted her staff and rapped it on the floor.

"Blood-sovereign, I present to you the prisoner, XX-59-40," she said, "by order of the Commandant-at-Arms."

"Seat her," Nashira said.

I was taken past the other guests and deposited in a high-backed chair between her and Alsafi, with Gomeisa opposite.

Another guard reached for his handcuffs. "Should we restrain the prisoner, Suzerain?"

"No need. 40 is aware that poor behavior here will result in additional time on the waterboard."

"Yes, Suzerain."

The close call stole my breath. If I had been cuffed, they would have seen the note.

I placed my hands in my lap, out of sight of the rest of the table. As the guards bowed and retreated, Nashira took a good look at me, as if she had forgotten what my face was like. Her corrupted aura was a smoking fire, suffocating mine. Her five spirits were all here, including the poltergeist I recognized from the scrimmage—the poltergeist that had tortured Warden.

She had never had just five. The sixth—the most powerful—was elsewhere in this building.

I dropped my gaze to the gold-rimmed plate in front of me. Every muscle was rigid. I dared not even glance at Alsafi, who was close enough to touch.

Once I left this hall, I might never get near Nashira again. Perhaps I should just carry out my original plan, and try my best to push her spirit out—yet I already sensed that I had been mad to think I could. My gift was stronger than it had been the last time I faced her, but that dreamscape was wrapped in the chainmail of centuries. In my weakened state, barely out of my stupor, I would never do it.

"Well," I said finally, when the silence had outlasted my nerves, "this is an unexpected reunion."

"You will not speak without the consent of the Suzerain, scum," Alsafi said.

His voice was so close that I almost flinched. "You have had quite a journey since we last met, 40," Nashira said. "The raid of a well-protected factory in Manchester, an Archon official murdered, and the infiltration of a depot kept secret and secure for decades. You must have thought you had come very close to unlocking the secret of Senshield."

I tried to keep my face blank. One wrong glance, one uneasy shiver, and she might guess that I was still trying.

From behind my hair, I risked a glance at Warden's one-time betrothed, the creator of Scion. She wore all black, slashed with gold at the sleeves and stitched with chips of topaz that glistered in the gloom, as if she was wrapped in a bodice of starlight. Her long hair was bound at the side of her neck, each lock like a coil of fine brass wires.

"I understand why it became your target. Of course . . . it was always a doomed endeavor. The core is indestructible." *Liar*, I thought, remembering Vance's dreamscape and that flicker of fear.

Across the table, the second blood-sovereign—Liss's murderer—didn't say a word.

Gomeisa, Warden of the Sargas, was unquestionably the most disturbing of the Rephaim. None of them looked old—they were ageless creatures—but Gomeisa had a bone structure that lent gravitas to his features, haunting them with cruel insight. Deep hollows lay beneath his prominent cheekbones. His eyes were pressed deep into his head, where they glowed in their sockets.

He had watched the massacre in Dublin. It had been Vance's strategy, but his desire.

"You were wise to give yourself up," Nashira said. "Now, the war and bloodshed the Mime Order wanted to bring to these isles will be avoided."

Under the table, I moved my hand until it brushed against Alsafi's thigh. His own hands had been clasped on the table, but now he sat back just slightly.

"22," Nashira said, "won't you perform for us?"

I turned to look behind me. 22, one of the red-jackets from the colony, was in the corner, dressed impeccably in Scion colors. It took me a moment to focus on his face—and to see that his lips were sewn closed.

"You may remember 22," Nashira said to me, expressionless. "His duty was to secure the Residence of the Suzerain after your rabble fled. Sadly, he allowed a Ranthen assassin to breach the walls."

I did remember him. He had been at the feast she had held for the red-jackets. He bowed and sat dutifully at the grand piano.

Out of sight, a gloved hand touched my wrist. I pushed the note from between my fingers, into his grasp.

"Perhaps," Jaxon said, lighting a cigar, "we should tell Paige about Sheol II, blood-sovereign."

My heart quickened. Nashira gave Jaxon the smallest nod; he offered a gracious smile in return.

"You should know, darling," Jaxon said, "that despite your rebellion, the Rephaim still mean to protect us, as they promised they would in 1859." His cigar glowed. "To that end, they are building a new Sheol in France, to deal with the threat of the Emim. So you see, the Suzerain has mended the mess you made in September. And now that you have been removed from the situation, the Mime Order will not interfere."

Across the room, 22 had been playing a parlor song. Gradually, almost imperceptibly, the notes took a different form.

Just two verses, heavily embellished, disguised so you might miss it if you didn't know it well.

It was "Molly Malone," but not the original version of the song that most people around the table would be familiar with. It was the melody the rebels had used in mourning, which was slower and darker—I would know it anywhere. We had sung it in memory of Finn and Kayley. For a fleeting instant, I was reminded of home, the home Scion had destroyed. And it strengthened me.

"Enough of this charade," Gomeisa said, cutting off the music. "It is time to inform 40 of her fate."

Ice crept into my fingertips.

"Yes." Nashira's eyes were like uncut emerald in the gloom. "The time for . . . persuasion is over."

My body became too aware of its blood.

"XX-59-40, we have given you numerous opportunities to save yourself. It is clear to us that you are beyond reform; that you will not recant your support for the ideology of the Ranthen; that you remain wilfully ignorant of the threat posed by the Emim. Keeping you alive would be a mockery of Scion's laws." She beckoned one of the Vigiles, who unraveled a handwritten document and set it down in front of me. "In ten days' time, on the first of January, you will be executed. Here in the Archon."

The document was a death warrant, signed by the Grand Judge. My gaze skimmed over it, picking out words like *condemnation* and *abomination*. Jaxon's hand tightened on the top of his cane.

"Your spirit will remain with me," Nashira said, "as my fallen angel. Perhaps you will learn, then, to obey."

My ears were ringing now. Somehow, after months of defying Scion, I had never really expected to see this document. My father must have been presented with the same.

"Shall I escort the prisoner to her cell, blood-sovereign?" Alsafi said. I tensed.

"Soon. I would speak to her alone."

There was a pause before the other three stood and left, along with 22, who was marched out by Vigiles. His small defiance, unnoticed by everyone but me, was over. As he followed them, Jaxon gave me a pointed stare that urged me to reconsider.

When the doors closed, and it was just the two of us, there was silence for a long time.

"Do you think human beings are good?"

The question rang, cool and clear, in the vastness of the gallery.

This had to be a trap. Nashira Sargas would never ask for a human's opinion without an ulterior motive.

"Answer me," she said.

"Are Rephaim good, Nashira?"

Outside, the moon was waning. Her stance was almost placid, fingers interlocked.

"You were reared, from the age of eight, in the empire I created," she said, as if I hadn't spoken. "You see it as captivity—internment—but it has sheltered you from crueler truths."

My flesh flinched from that cut-glass voice, the poisonous spill of her aura in the æther.

She went on: "I wonder if you have ever heard of a witch trial. In the past they were common; a matter of English law. Anyone could be accused of being a witch, and put on trial for sorcery. The guilty would be burned alive or drowned, and their accusers would consider themselves morally and spiritually cleansed. That justice had been done.

"During those same times, executions were particularly . . . imaginative. For the crime of high treason, such as yours, a criminal would be hanged until almost dead, then taken down. His abdomen would be laid open, his entrails torn out, his privy parts cut off before his eyes. His body would then be quartered, and his head set upon a spike to rot. The spectators would cheer."

I had thought myself inured to violence.

"No Rephaite," she said, "has ever committed such a brutal act against another. And never would—not even now."

I swallowed. "I seem to recall you threatening to skin another Rephaite."

"Words," she said dismissively. "I have hurt Arcturus for his own good, but I would never be so grotesque."

"Just grotesque enough to mutilate him."

She didn't seem to think this worthy of comment. His scars, his pain, meant nothing to her.

"Before I was blood-sovereign, I dwelled in the great observatory in the swathe of the Sargas. As centuries passed in your world, I learned everything about the human race," she said. "I learned that humans have a mechanism inside them: a mechanism called *hatred*, which can be activated with the lightest pull of a string. I saw war and cruelty. I saw slaughter and slavery. I learned how humans control one another.

"When we arrived in your realm, I used the stores of knowledge I had saved from the observatory—specifically, knowledge of how intensely humans can hate. It was easy to turn the tide of public odium toward 'unnaturals,' and to promise control. That was how Scion was born." She looked through a window, into the citadel. "An empire founded on human hatred."

There was so little feeling left in my body that I was almost unaware of it.

"I have done nothing to you that you have not done to yourselves. I have only used humankind's own methods to bring it to heel. And I mean to continue." Nashira rose elegantly and walked past the windows, toward the other end of the room. "You may think I am your enemy. The Ranthen may have told you so. They are blind."

Her shadow moved across the floor. I couldn't take my eyes from her silhouette.

"When he endeavored to help humans before, Arcturus was betrayed by your mentor. He should have learned then. I punished him, with the spirit of a certain human, to remind him of your true nature."

Hearing his name gave me strength. "He doesn't seem to have learned his lesson," I said.

"He remains in thrall to Terebell Sheratan, unable to see the true nature of the humans he believes he can save."

Something about her tone when she said that name—*Terebell Sheratan*—sent a trickle of unease through me.

"Humans have conducted their own affairs for too long. You have failed to govern yourselves," she said. "If we did not rule, this opportunity to save you would be lost forever."

"I've seen your disregard for life," I said. "You expect me to believe you want to *save* us?"

"Killing you all would destabilize the ethereal threshold beyond repair. Some will live," she said, "to serve the empire. To maintain the natural order. The natural order does not place human beings at the top of the hierarchy; you only think it does. Now is the age of the Rephaim."

I had been naïve. I had thought of Nashira Sargas as purely evil, purely sadistic—but she knew more about us than we did. We had given her the tools to bring us to our knees.

But if we also gave her our freedom, there would be no getting it back.

"This building we stand in," I said, "was designed by human minds and created by human hands. Through nothing but our ambition, and the freedom to create, we can turn a thought into a masterwork. We can make the intangible real."

She was quiet. I had listened to her, and she was returning the courtesy.

"That's what humans do. We make. We remake. We build, and we rebuild. And yes, sometimes we paint with blood, and we tear down our own civilizations, and it might never stop. But if we're ever to unlearn our darker instincts, we have to be free to learn better ones. Take away the chance for us to change, and I promise you, we never will." I looked her in the eye. "I'm willing to fight for that chance."

Nashira appeared to digest this. She stood facing London, a metropolis created by centuries of humanity. London, with its secret, folded layers of history and beauty, as perfectly formed as the petals of a rose. The deeper you ventured into its heart, the more there was to peel away.

"The Grand Overseer has petitioned me to stay your execution," the blood-sovereign said. "For a human, he is . . . insightful. He believes that if I do not allow your gift to continue burgeoning over the years, I may not inherit it at its fullest. I told the Archon's staff to assess you. They agree that your talents have not matured—or that you are simply weak."

The pain had been a test, then, and I had failed.

"For now, you are all I have. Until I find another dreamwalker, I may consider this proposal. I may consider sending you to France, under a new identity, to live out the rest of your natural life in Sheol II."

"What do I have to do?"

Not even her eyes moved.

"Tell me," she said, "where I can find the Mime Order."

Two words now stood between me and my execution. All I needed to say was *crisis facility*.

I could lie my way to borrowed time. I could give her the name of a random street or an abandoned building.

"If you deceive me," Nashira said, "you will find that I am less merciful in the manner of your execution."

There was no way out of this. It was the truth or nothing.

I chose nothing.

"I am Underqueen of the Scion Citadel of London." I raised my head. "I will be that until I go to the æther, and if there's one thing I can do, it's give them a chance. If I give you any part of the Mime Order, I give you hope. And I can't take that away from them."

She was silent for what seemed like hours. Before either of us could speak again, Alsafi came back through the doors.

"Are you finished with the prisoner, blood-sovereign?"

Nashira's nod was hardly visible. She didn't even look angry; just blank. My legs shook, but I slapped on a mask of defiance before I followed Alsafi out of the Inquisitorial Gallery.

I risked a glance as we walked down the corridors. I had no idea what the surveillance was like; better to wait for him to speak. He wore what he had in the colony: that old-fashioned, uniformly black attire, with a cloak over it all. His face was more readable—more *alive*, somehow—than those of other Rephaim, with eyes of a lamp-bright green. This was a Rephaite who took his fill of aura whenever he pleased.

"We do not have long," he muttered. "Your cell is under close surveillance. What *advice* do you have for me?"

"Senshield is here—in the Archon. The core is beneath a glass pyramid," I said, "in a room with pale walls. I think it's somewhere high up—in a tower, maybe—somewhere the Archon's personnel wouldn't be able to stumble upon it by chance, or sense it. There's a white light, too. Bright enough that you might be able to glimpse it from outside."

His face didn't betray whether he recognized the image.

"It can be destroyed, but not by me," I said. "They're keeping me sedated; I can't dreamwalk. It will have to be you."

"It is here, then." His tone was musing. This must be an unwelcome surprise—the realization that it had been right under his nose without his knowledge. It was only my gift that had allowed me to find it, and Alsafi was no dreamwalker. "I assume you know how to deactivate it." When I didn't answer, he said, "I cannot risk my position in the Archon for anything less than certainty. Sacrifice without gain is folly."

"I can't be certain," I admitted, "but—we did find evidence."

His jaw tensed.

"The core is likely powered by one of Nashira's spirits, which is bound—probably by her blood—to some kind of glass sphere." I spoke as softly as I could. "If you destroy the casing it's contained in, it should release the spirit."

"And you believe this will stop all of the scanners."

"Yes."

I couldn't be certain of it; and yet I was, in my gut. To make that many scanners work, surely they must need to contain the spirit in one place, keeping its scores of connections stable.

Alsafi kept walking.

"There is precedent to your reasoning," he concluded. "If a spirit is released from an ethereal battery, the energy generated by its presence is dispersed, and the battery ceases to function. Even if the core is a different form of ethereal technology . . . dislodging the spirit might impair it, if nothing else." He slowed down, buying us a few moments. "The executioner will be summoned soon. I cannot help you escape."

"I know."

His gaze slid to my face. "*Colchicum.*" Pause. "You did not intend to escape."

I gave him no answer.

We were approaching the door to the basement now, and in sight of the Vigiles who now guarded it. They saluted Alsafi before they marched me back into the tomb below.

23

A Priori

Ten days until my execution. It must be meant as a cruel
delay, giving me time to wonder what kind of agony
awaited me. The sword would be too good for the human
who had dared to stand against the blood-sovereign. Perhaps she
meant for me to die in one of the ways she had told me about, to
prove that my faith in humanity was misplaced. They must expect
me to crack under the pressure, to beg Jaxon to spare my life and
take me with him to France.

I didn't. I waited quietly for death—but before I joined the
æther, I wanted to know that Alsafi had destroyed Senshield.

When the drugs came, I was grateful. I submitted willingly to
the Vigiles' hands, to the needles I no longer felt—they took away
the fear that my death would be in vain. With every hour that Alsafi
was unwilling or unable to take action, the Mime Order remained
in the Beneath.

One night, the Vigiles got me out of bed and put me on the
waterboard again, seemingly for their own amusement. When they
dumped me back in my cell, soaked and exhausted, there was a
supper tray waiting. I inched toward it and choked down as much
of the mush as I could.

That was when I found the tiny strip of paper, buried in the food. It was stained, but legible.

DOCK

I breathed easier. Dock. *Patience.* He must be biding his time, waiting for an opportunity to reach the core without compromising his position. The thought was comforting for a while.

But more days passed, and I heard nothing. And no more notes came with my food.

December 31, 2059

New Year's Eve

I was woken one morning by a Vigile aiming the beam of his flashlight into my eyes.

"Rise and shine, Underqueen." I was lifted to my feet. "Time to die."

I was too tired to fight.

First I was transferred to another cell, on one of the Archon's main upper corridors. The door was made up of bars.

The New Year Jubilee was set to be the biggest event in years. It would take place in the Grand Stadium, which was only ever used for ceremonies. There was a screen at the end of the corridor, and I could just make out the broadcast.

Murmurs echoed between the walls as dignitaries and ministers from the Archon filed past my cell on their way to watch the show. Several of them stopped to scrutinize me. Among them were the Minister for Surveillance; the portly Minister for Arts; the sallow-faced Minister for Transport, whose nose betrayed her illegal drinking habit. Luce Ménard Frère and the French emissaries spent a considerable amount of time observing what a frightening creature I was. All the while, I fixed them with a dead-eyed stare. When the French party got bored, Frère stayed behind, one hand on her rounded abdomen.

"I am pleased," she said, "that my children will grow up in a world without you in it."

317

She walked away before I could think of a reply.

Now I understood why I was in this cell. For my last hours, I was to be displayed as a war trophy.

Jaxon came to the door for one last look. I thought I could see authentic sorrow on his features.

"So this is the end," he said. Somehow he sounded both angry and solemn. "I present you with an opportunity to live, to keep your gift from fading into nothing, and you spit at it."

"That's my choice," I said. "It's called 'freedom,' Jax. It's what I fought for."

"And how hard you fought," he said gently. He turned away. "Goodbye for now, O my lovely. I will remember you fondly, in your absence, as my unfinished masterpiece; my lost treasure. But bear this in mind: I do not like to leave things unfinished. Not masterpieces, and certainly not games. And perhaps our game is only just beginning."

I raised one eyebrow. He really was a madman.

With the softest of smiles, he was gone.

Unfortunately, Jaxon was not my last visitor. The next was Bernard Hock, the High Chief of Vigilance—one of the few people in the Archon who was permitted to be voyant, whom I had seen once before in the penal colony. He looked less than pleased to be in a suit as he entered my cell.

"Don't cry now, bitch." He grasped my arm and stabbed a needle into it. "Just lie there nice and quiet. The executioner will be here after the Jubilee . . . then you'll cry."

I shoved him off me. "How does it feel to hate yourself as much as you do, Hock?"

In answer, he backhanded me and left the cell. Soon, the sounds of conversation waned from the corridors.

I shivered on the floor, cold to my bones. It was a short while before the Sargas finally passed, accompanied by Frank Weaver and several other high-ranking officials, including Patricia Okonma, the Deputy Grand Commander. They must be going separately from the rest.

Alsafi brought up the rear. The sight of him made the hairs on my nape stand on end.

None of them so much as glanced at me, but as Alsafi walked by, I saw—as if in slow motion—a tiny scroll fall from his cloak and land within my reach. I waited until they were out of sight before I snatched it.

EUPATORIUM   ICE PLANT   CLEMATIS   GROUND LAUREL

Eupatorium: *delay*. Ice plant: *your looks freeze me*. Clematis: that could either mean *mental clarity* or *artifice*, if I remembered correctly. Ground laurel: *perseverance*.

I read it several times.

Delay—it hadn't happened.

Frozen by a look—he was being watched.

I leaned against the wall of my cell and grasped my own arms, as if that could hold me together. I didn't know what *mental clarity* or *perseverance* were supposed to mean to me now, but one thing was clear.

He hadn't done it.

And I couldn't do it. I had already been drugged—rendering my gift useless—and in a few hours, I would be dead.

With a mewl of frustration, I buried my face in my knees.

They had broken me; Nashira and Hildred Vance had succeeded in breaking me. I was a malfunctioning mind radar. I shook with silent, rib-racking sobs, loathing myself for being so stupid as to hand myself to the anchor; so *arrogant* as to think I could survive for long enough to carry out the mission.

Trembling, I read the note again, trying to control my breathing. Ground laurel. *Perseverance*. What the hell did that mean? How could he persevere if he was being watched?

Clematis. *Mental clarity. Artifice*. Which of the two meanings did he intend me to take from it, and why?

I crumpled the note into my hand.

Nashira will not let you go once you are in her clutches. She will chain you in the darkness, and she will drain the life and hope from you.

When music sounded in the corridor, I raised my head. The transmission screen outside my cell was now fixed on the live broadcast of the Jubilee. The walls inside the stadium were covered by black drapes, each bearing an immense white circle with a golden anchor inside it.

Hundreds of tiered seats provided the best views. The groundlings, with cheaper tickets, had gathered at the edges of the vast, ring-shaped orchestra pit, and were craning their necks to see the top of the stage.

"*Esteemed denizens of the Scion Citadel of London,*" Burnish said, and her voice resounded through the space, "*welcome, on this very special night, to the Grand Stadium!*"

The roar was deafening. I made myself listen.

That was the sound of Scion's victory.

"*Tonight,*" Burnish said, "*we welcome a new year for Scion, and a new dawn for the anchor, the symbol of hope in a chaotic modern world.*" Applause answered her. "*And now, before the stroke of midnight, it is time for us to reflect upon two centuries of our rich history, brought to you by some of Scion's most talented denizens. Tonight, we celebrate our place in the world, and embrace our bright future. Let us set our bounds ever wider, and grow ever stronger—together. The Minister for Arts is proud to present—the Jubilee!*"

The ovation rumbled on for almost a minute before mechanisms began to move in the stadium. A performance, then. Or a message from Vance. *Look at our imperial might. Look at what you failed to thwart.*

A platform rose, and the light ebbed to a twilight ambience. On the platform, a line of children sang a soulful rendition of "Anchored to Thee, O Scion." When the audience gave them a standing ovation, they took a bow, and a new stage was drawn up, this one decked with the old symbols of the monarchy. A man, dressed as Edward VII, performed a lively dance to a violinist's music, accompanied by actors in lavish Victorian gowns. Once the séance table was brought on, the dance became more tormented, and I understood that this was the story of Scion's origin—heavily edited, of course, to remove the Rephaim from the equation. The lighting enflamed, and more performers swept on to the stage, executing acrobatic dances around the principal actor, clawing away his regalia. He was the king who had dabbled in evil, and they were the unnaturals he released into the world. Just like the play at the Bicentenary, all those months ago.

The scenery began to change. Now it was a shadow theater, and new actors were forming the shapes of skyscrapers and towers, rising ever higher until their figures loomed over the stage, where the dancers had all fallen to their knees. This was the remaking of London, the rising from the ashes of the monarchy. The music swelled. Scion had triumphed.

The stage cleared of actors. The lights went out. When they returned, they were cool and muted.

A woman in an embroidered bodice with a black skirt, her fair hair coiled at the crown of her head, was poised on her toes in the middle of the stage. I recognized her at once: Marilena Brașoveanu, Scion Bucharest's most beloved dancer. She often performed at official ceremonies.

Brașoveanu was as still as a porcelain doll. When the camera focused on her, close enough for every viewer to see the finest details of her costume, I realized the skirt of her dress was made up of hundreds of tiny silk moths.

She was the Black Moth.

She was me.

The stadium fell silent. Brașoveanu sailed around the stage to the tune of a piano, fluid yet erratic. Then another dancer ran out—the Bloody King—and snatched her hand, spinning her into his arms. I watched, mesmerized, as the Black Moth danced a *pas de deux* with him. She was the Bloody King's heir; the herald of unnaturalness, of sin.

The dance became faster. Brașoveanu whirled her leg out in front of her and tucked it behind her other knee, over and over, while the lights raced red around her and the music became ferocious, like a storm. The Bloody King lifted her above his head, then swung her into his arms again. She was seduced by evil. Actors held signs marking them as FREEDOM and JUSTICE and THE NATURAL ORDER. Then an army, who had been waiting in the shadows, stepped forward, and all of the actors fell down with their signs, murdered where they stood, while the Bloody King brought the

Black Moth gently to a stop. She walked into the blaze of a spot-light, her arms raised high. This was the moment of my death in Edinburgh.

It was beautiful.

They had made my murder beautiful.

Slowly, Brașoveanu took center stage. A hush had fallen. When she spoke, she raised her head high, and I was sure I saw the dark fire of hatred in her eyes.

"We need everyone," she said, and her microphone sent it all around the stadium, into the home of every viewer in the country, "or everyone loses."

I froze. My own words, a call to revolution, spoken on a Scion stage—that couldn't be right. The camera, which had just panned to the Grand Box, caught the complacent smiles of the ministers stiffening before it cut back to the stage. There was an apprehensive silence.

This had not been part of their plan for tonight.

Brașoveanu took her bow; then she slipped a silver pin from her bun and peeled open her throat.

Screams erupted from the groundlings, the only ones close enough to see the red sheeting down her neck. I stared, thunder-struck, as she dropped the pin. That blood was as real as mine.

Brașoveanu collapsed on the stage, as elegantly as she had moved in life. The orchestra played on. The male dancer, who was wearing an earpiece, lifted her wilted frame into his arms and raised her above his head. He pirouetted with a plastic smile before dancing off the stage. Though the groundlings were in disorder, most of the audience were still cheering.

Something kindled deep within me. Marilena Brașoveanu was Romanian. She had witnessed an incursion, too—and now, tonight of all nights, she had used her own blood to spoil the beauty of the anchor's lies.

A Vigile rattled the bars of my cell.

"Come here, 40."

One hand beckoned me. The other held a syringe. A top-up dose of the drug.

The drug.

Goosebumps covered my arms. Seeing that needle, I realized what I hadn't before, entranced as I was by the Jubilee.

Mental clarity.

My mind was clear as ice. There was no cloud inside it. My vision was sharp, and my gift seethed inside me.

There hadn't been a first dose.

"Come here, girl," the Vigile said.

I stared at my hands. Steady.

Artifice.

Alsafi. He must have swapped the syringes. Hock had shot something into my veins, but it must have been water. And now the building was almost empty; there was only a skeleton staff in the Archon while everyone attended the Jubilee. Until the celebrations ended, only a handful of Vigiles stood between me and Senshield.

Perseverance.

The Vigile drew his gun and aimed it at my head. "Come here," he said. "Now."

"What are you going to do?" I said softly. "Shoot me? Not without the Suzerain's permission."

The gun stayed where it was, but I had stared death in the face once before, looked down the barrel of a gun, and lived. He swore and returned his weapon to its holster. Took his keys from his belt and sifted through them. That was his mistake. Rage was pounding through my body, bubbling in my blood. It had set me on fire, and like the moth I was, I burned.

When the Vigile opened my cell door, I was ready. I sprang at him and slammed my body into his. As we fell to the floor, I clapped a hand over his mouth and nose, squeezed hard, and wrested the gun from his grasp. My arms were shaking, and he was clawing at my neck and hair, breaking skin—but I hit him with the pistol, over and over, bludgeoning his skull with all my strength, until blood glinted and his head rolled to one side. I grabbed his set of keys, hauled his dead weight into the cell, and locked the door with trembling hands.

Footsteps were approaching from somewhere to my left. I ran the other way, keys in one hand, pistol in the other, my bare feet feather-light on the marble.

I would help Marilena Brașoveanu ruin their night of glory. If I had to die tonight, I *would* release the Mime Order.

My head was throbbing as I rounded a corner, hoping against hope that nobody was paying attention to the cameras. I could feel the æther again, clearly enough to avoid the Vigiles patrolling the Archon and to know that Hildred Vance was nowhere near.

I felt for the room with the glass pyramid and found it instantly. Following the signal, I limped across the marble floor, trying to ignore the drumbeat in my bruises. I could sense two squadrons of Vigiles, spread over a vast building. In one corridor, I had to duck into the Minister for Finance's office to avoid a lone one, who I hadn't detected until it was almost too late. I stayed for several minutes behind a curtain, soused in icy sweat. A wrong move could get me hauled back to my cell, and I wouldn't get out again. I might not be drugged, but I was physically weak—I couldn't fight my way to the core.

When I was sure the Vigile wasn't returning, I stumbled out of the office and back into the labyrinth, up the stairs to the next floor. Senshield was somewhere above me.

The central second-floor corridor was empty, dimly lit by sconces. The darkness calmed me, just a little. The signal above me wavered, and I paused briefly to think.

If the core was high up, it was most likely in a tower. The Archon had two, one on each end of the building. Inquisitor Tower was the one that housed the bells. The other one . . .

I sifted through the Vigile's keys. Not one was labelled *Victoria Tower*. But then, only Vance and the blood-sovereigns were supposed to know where Senshield was; no one else would have access.

With fresh resolve, I set off again. Most of the doors I had seen in this building were electronic, but if the Vigiles carried keys, they must also have mechanical locks in case of a power failure—and those locks could be picked.

An alarm began to drill, raising my pulse. Either my empty cell had been discovered, or Brașoveanu's act of defiance had activated some kind of security alert. Metal blinds were scrolling over the windows, and blue-white emergency lighting had sprung up on either side of me. Adrenaline streaked through my muscles, keeping the ache at bay. I avoided a few more Vigiles before I finally staggered into a corridor with a thick ebony carpet, lined by windows on one side. At the end of this corridor was an arched, studded door, and set into this door was a small plaque reading VICTORIA TOWER. My breath came fast as I approached it. The core was now almost directly above me.

I tried the handle, not expecting it to work.

It gave way beneath my hand.

Slowly, I brought my weight against the door, opening it. A trap, surely. Vance wouldn't have left the tower vulnerable while she was at the Jubilee. And yet—whatever lay beyond, it was my one and only chance. I stepped into the darkness and closed the door behind me.

A draft blew at my hair. There were no lights in the tower.

A balustrade was wrapped around a kind of well in the floor; the draft was coming up from there. When I risked a glance, I saw that the well dropped straight down into an entrance hall. A squadron of Vigiles ran through it, shining their flashlights. As soon as they were gone, I hit the staircase, fighting the weakness in my body, my head spinning from exhaustion and pain. I forced myself to continue, gripping the rails to crane myself up every step. My muscles had wasted during my coma and imprisonment; my knees had almost forgotten how to carry me. When I fell the first time, I thought I wouldn't get back up. My hands reached for the next step, but it seemed as if I was at the foot of a mountain, staring up at the distant summit.

You have risen from the ashes before.

I grasped the railing again. One step. Two steps.

The only way to survive is to believe you always will.

When I reached the top of the stairs, I fell to my knees and hunched over myself, trembling uncontrollably. There was light nearby. Almost there. I picked myself back up.

My soft footsteps broke the silence. I was at the highest level of the tower, right beneath its rooftop.

Now I could see that a glass pyramid, illuminated from beneath, made up the center of the ceiling. And there it was, suspended underneath that pyramid: the image I had seen in Warden's dream-scape, stolen from the mind of Hildred Vance. The core. The entity that powered every scanner, all of Senshield. And now I was this close to it, I could sense what it was.

A spirit.

An immensely powerful spirit, somehow trapped inside a glass sphere. The æther around it was in turmoil, alive with vibrations. Our guesswork had been right.

This was it.

"Paige Mahoney."

The back of my neck prickled.

I knew that voice.

A woman stepped from the shadows, into the pale light from above. It made her face skeletal.

"Hildred Vance," I said softly.

She must have devised some way to hide her dreamscape from me. They knew so much more about the æther than we did.

Vance stood with a rod-straight back and no expression. I had convinced myself that I would be able to face the Grand Commander without fear, but sweat chilled my brow as we regarded each other. The iron hand of the anchor, the human embodiment of Rephaite ambition. The woman who was responsible for the murders of my father and my cousin.

A rigor went through me.

She had hunted me across the country. She had used my aura—my intimate and fragile connection to the æther—to enhance her machine. She had shaped my life since I was six years old.

Thirteen years later, she was finally in front of me.

Vance looked from the core to my face. The crow-black eyes regarded me with something I thought at first was contempt, but it wasn't that. There was no heat in the stare. No passion. If Jaxon was right, and we were devils in the skins of men, then Vance had shed her skin already. I was in the presence of a human being who had spent far too much time among Rephaim. Decades too long.

She didn't care enough for my life to feel anything toward me. Not even hatred. Her expression, if it could be called that, told me

I was nothing to her but an enemy war asset that should have been destroyed.

"Even before I saw you in my dreamscape, I knew what you were searching for; what you planned to do. You wanted Senshield." She glanced at it. "I confess, you almost had me fooled. You responded as anticipated to the march on Edinburgh: a replication of the events of the Dublin Incursion, calculated to make you surrender in order to avoid the same bloodshed you witnessed as a child. All went to plan. You appeared broken in mind and body. And yet . . . and yet, I suspected an ulterior motive."

I watched her.

"The Trojan horse," she said. "An ancient stratagem. You presented yourself like a gift to your enemy, and your enemy took you into their house. You realized that, after all your striving, if you were captured, we would take you right to the core—all you had to do was deliver yourself into our custody." Her bony hands clasped behind her back. "Unavoidable civic duty called me away tonight. You used the opportunity to escape. I assume you had help from an ally in reaching this part of the building."

"None," I said. As I spoke, her gaze darted to the core again. "It's brave of you to step out from behind the screen, Vance. And I have something to ask you, if you'll indulge me. Do you remember the names of all the people whose lives you've stolen?"

Vance didn't answer. She must have calculated that there was no strategic advantage to saying anything.

"You didn't just kill my father, Cóilín Ó Mathúna. Thirteen years ago, you killed my cousin, Finn Mac Cárthaigh, and an unarmed woman named Kayley Ní Dhornáin." Saying their names to her face made my voice quake. "You have killed thousands of innocent people—yet when I was in your dreamscape, it was *my* dream-form with blood on its hands. Do you really think I've taken more life than you have?"

Her silence continued.

She was waiting. I was trying to work out why, when I saw her gaze move, ever so slightly, back to the core. That was the fourth time.

She was nervous.

There really was a weakness. It *could* be destroyed.

Time seemed to slow as I looked at the core. I searched it with my eyes, then with my gift.

It took me a few moments to find the ectoplasm. A vial of it, locked inside the sphere, holding the spirit firmly in place and emanating a greenish light. One of Nashira's boundlings—her fallen angels. I could feel the thousands of delicate connections that branched out around it, reaching toward every Senshield scanner in the citadel, in the country.

I didn't know its name, so I couldn't banish it. But surely if I destroyed the casing that imprisoned the spirit, it would disperse its energy into the æther and sever those connections.

Surely.

I raised my gun. At the same time, Vance pointed a pistol at my exposed torso.

"It will kill you," she said, "and achieve nothing. The spirit will continue to obey the Suzerain. It will continue to power Senshield."

I stayed very still.

She could be telling the truth. She could be bluffing.

"You will die in vain," Vance said.

Perhaps I would.

But there had to be a reason she was suddenly talking, *telling* me how Senshield worked. There could be no gain in that. She would only be this free with her information if she was . . .

If she was lying.

And Hildred Vance only lied when it was necessary.

"You know a lot about human nature, Vance," I said, taking my time over each word, "but you made one, fatal error in your calculations."

She looked at the core, then back to me.

"You assumed," I said, "that I had any interest in leaving here alive."

Vance stared into my eyes. And somewhere in their depths, deep in those pits of darkness, was a flicker, just the softest flicker, of something I hadn't truly believed she was capable of feeling.

Doubt.

It was doubt.

I pulled the trigger.

When the bullet struck it, the sphere broke apart, releasing years of bridled energy, and gave up the vial of ectoplasm. It shattered at my feet. I hurled myself to the floor and scrambled away from Vance's gunfire, my fingers slipping through Rephaite blood. Before I could get up, the spirit, freed from its prison, came flying toward me—and seized me by the throat.

A poltergeist. It was enraged, murderous. The Suzerain had commanded it to stay, to power the machine, and I had disturbed it. It slammed me between the wall and the floor. I choked on blood. The gun flew out of my hand.

Vance was a strategist. She knew when to retreat. As she backed toward the door, the spirit cast me aside and raced across the room to slam it shut. Vance stopped dead. She was blind to the æther, unaware of where the threat would go next. Pulling myself on to my hands and knees, I looked up at what was left of the sphere.

She had been right; Senshield was still active. Its light remained as bright as ever.

"You belong to the Suzerain." Vance addressed the spirit, her voice full of authority. "I am also her servant."

I crawled across the floor, toward the gun.

If I was going to die tonight, I would take the Grand Commander with me.

My movements distracted the fallen angel. It whipped away from Vance, pitched me on to my back, and brought its weight to bear against my body. A wall of unseen pressure descended on me like a shroud. Sparks erupted from the wreckage of the sphere and threw wild shadows on the walls as the spirit smothered me inside and out, flinging my aura into a frenzy. Sweat froze on my skin. I couldn't breathe. All I could see was the light from the core.

I didn't know how to fight back. I didn't know how to stop fighting, either. Desperately, I tried to dreamwalk, but I was so weak. All around us, the corporeal world was straining at the seams.

Veins of color glistened behind my eyelids. My dreamscape was on the verge of collapse. As the air was drained from my lungs, I saw Nick smiling at me in the courtyard, surrounded by blossoms, sunlight in his hair. My father, the last day I saw him alive.

Eliza laughing at the market. I saw Warden, felt his hands framing my face and his lips seeking mine behind the red drapes. The amaranth in bloom. And I heard Jaxon's voice:

Perhaps our game is only just beginning.

As my vision darkened, some small instinct made me hold out my left hand, as if I could push the spirit away. My arm was forced back, but I kept my palm turned outward. The scars there felt white-hot, scars I had received in a poppy field when I was a child.

And I felt something change. I *was* pushing it away.

The pain began as a tiny point, a needle pushing through the middle of my palm. As it grew, a wordless scream racked my body—and just for a moment, some of the pressure released. Just enough for me to gasp in one more breath. And with that breath, I whispered, "Go."

What happened next was unclear. I remember watching the glass pyramid shatter. It must have exploded in a split second, but in my mind, it lasted for eternity. I was flung in one direction, Vance in the other.

Then came an arc of blinding white, and the world turned to oblivion.

24

The Crossing

January 1, 2060

New Year's Day

I had woken like this once before, thinking I was dead.

The æther was calling me into his arms, telling me to abandon all my cares, to leave my tender bones behind. My eyelids parted, just enough to see a pale hand clad in shards of glass. The rest of my arm sparkled, armored in diamond and glazed with molten ruby. Even my lashes were frosted with gemstones. I was a living jewel-box, a fallen star. No longer flesh, but crystalline.

Wind howled through the part of the roof where the angel had passed through. Splinters tinkled from my hair as I turned to see the ceiling. The white light had been extinguished. All that was left of Senshield was a cavernous hole in the æther, marking a place where a spirit had dwelled for many years. Over time, it would stitch itself back together.

There was one thing I wanted to know before I left. My hand shook as I rotated it. The fallen angel had carved a word into my skin, joining the fragmented pieces of the scars.

KIN

I lay back in my bed of glass. A friend had once told me that knowledge was dangerous. When I let go, I would have all the knowledge of the æther; this mystery would soon be solved. And I could find the others. Even if they didn't know, I would stay with them. I would watch over them. I would help them win the next stage of the game, the war that had begun today.

Footsteps came through the glass, drawing me back. A moment later, my head and shoulders were lifted into the crook of an arm, and Rephaite eyes were smoldering in the gloom.

"Dreamwalker."

His features gradually sharpened.

"Leave me," I murmured. "Leave me, Alsafi."

He took hold of my left hand and pried my fingers open, revealing the marks on my palm.

"I'm not worth it." I was so tired. "I'm done. Just go."

"Some would disagree with your assessment of your worth." He released my hand. When he scooped an arm under my knees and lifted me, I groaned. My skin bristled with broken glass. "This is not your time."

He carried me through the ruins, pushing the pistol into my limp hand. The fight wasn't over. As he opened the door, I caught sight of Hildred Vance in the corner. Her body was angled away from us, but I could see that she was as broken as I was. She bled just like the rest of us. I wanted to tell Alsafi to turn back, to make sure she was dead, but I blacked out before I could.

When I came round, Alsafi was almost at the bottom of the stairs, and my cheek was pressed against his doublet. When he entered the corridor with the black carpet, I lifted a hand to his shoulder.

"Dreamscape," I whispered. My gift had been weakened, but I felt it. A Rephaite. "Nashira."

Alsafi stopped in his tracks. There was no other way out of the corridor.

"Stay quiet." He spoke quickly. "If anything happens to me, go to the Inquisitorial Office. There, you can access a tunnel that will take you out of the Archon. I have a contact—they are waiting for you there."

"Alsafi—"

"And tell Arcturus—" He paused. "Tell him I hope this . . . redeems me."

I had so many questions, and no time to ask them. Nashira had already swept into view. The hilt of a sword gleamed over her shoulder.

When she saw me, her eyes turned to hot coals. She looked as if she had walked straight out of hell; as if she carried its flames inside her.

"Alsafi."

"Blood-sovereign," he said evenly. "I have come from the tower. The Grand Commander is critically injured, and Senshield is destroyed." He must have been using English consciously, allowing me to follow the conversation.

"I am more than aware of Senshield's destruction." She didn't raise her voice, but something in it terrified me. "The Archon's medical staff will attend to Vance. Bring 40 to the basement at once."

I started to tremble. Alsafi remained where he was, and I felt, rather than heard, the deep breath he took. When Nashira turned back, he lifted his gaze to look her in the eye.

"Is something wrong, Alsafi?"

His muscles were tensing. Nashira took a step toward him.

"I must confess," she said, "I did think it extraordinary that one human, especially one who is in Inquisitorial custody, should be able to cause so much destruction in such a short period of time. 40 has done many things she should not have been able to do. She was able to escape from London as martial law was being implemented. She was able to travel between citadels without detection. She was able to reach the core of Senshield." Another step. "She could not have done any of it without a contact."

Alsafi didn't hesitate. He gathered me close and ran.

Red carpet. Wood-paneled walls. Pain all over my body, tiny sunbursts of pain. His hand tore away a tapestry, turned a key, opened a panel; thrust me into the pitch-black tunnel beyond. My left side crashed against a wall, and a shard of glass penetrated deep into my arm, drawing a scream that seared my throat. Sobbing in agony, I pressed my hands against the door.

"Alsafi, don't!"

A key card came spinning into the tunnel. "Run," Alsafi barked. I dragged myself back to my feet. There was a spy-grate in the door; through it, I saw him draw a sword from underneath his cloak. Nashira's came to meet it. "Go, dreamwalker!"

"Ranthen," Nashira whispered.

Their swords clashed. Iridescent blades, like shards of opal. I leaned heavily against the wall, unable to take my eyes from the grate. Spirits were rushing to join the war-dance of the Rephaim. Immobilized by the fire in my arm, I watched Alsafi Sualocin fight Nashira Sargas.

I could see at once that Nashira was faster. She moved like spindrift around Alsafi, as fluently as Brașoveanu had danced her death ballet. Alsafi used sharper swings, and stayed rooted to one spot, but he was no less elegant. The blades chimed like bells as they collided. Quick as she was, he parried each of her strokes, never changing his expression. I had seen Rephaim fight before, in the colony, though never with swords. I remembered the way their steps resonated through the æther; how the proximity of two rival Rephaim drank all the warmth from the air around them. As if the æther understood their hatred, intensified it, nurtured it.

They circled each other like dancing partners. Alsafi let out a low growl, while Nashira was silent. She struck again, faster and faster, until I could hardly see her movements; just the glint of her hair, the flash of the sword. When it caught Alsafi's cheek, and ecto-plasm seeped from the cut, I flinched.

She was toying with him.

Alsafi's next swipe was harder, and he broke from his position. His blade slashed down, across, up, but never touched her.

Nashira raised her open hand. The rest of her fallen angels came to her from wherever they had been wandering, drawn back to her tarnished aura.

Alsafi spat at her in Gloss. For a long time, neither of them moved.

When the poltergeist attacked him, a tear streaked down my cheek. Slashes appeared across his face, the marks of an unseen knife. He lashed out with the sword, making the thing recoil, before all of the spirits converged on him. Alsafi let out an eldritch sound—a sound of pain—as they tore at his aura like a flock of birds. As his blade clattered to the flagstones, Nashira lifted her sword high. I caught sight of his eyes for a last time, afire with hatred, before she sliced straight through his neck.

I turned away, one hand over my mouth. The heavy *thud* was all I needed to hear.

Nashira stared down at the corpse for a moment—it must have been a moment, but it lasted forever—before her head whipped around, and hellfire flooded her eyes again. And I knew, I *knew* from that look on her face that she would dog my footsteps for the rest of my days, even if I could escape her tonight. A decade could pass from this moment; a lifetime—but she would not stop hunting me. She would not forget. I snatched the key card from the floor and ran.

Dark stars erupted in the corners of my vision. Hot jolts came shooting through my feet as I hobbled across stone, breathing in bursts. I tasted salt and metal on my lips. The throbbing in my arm was making me retch. My legs gave way again, and I curled in the darkness, listening to my fitful heartbeat.

"Rise from the ashes," I whispered to myself. "Come on, Underqueen."

When I rose, my hands left red prints on the walls. I couldn't take much more of this. I would die before I reached the Inquisitorial Office.

Then I saw it. Frank Weaver's Inquisitorial maxim was printed above the doors: I SHALL CAST OUR BOUNDS TO THE EDGES OF THE EARTH. THIS HOUSE FOREVER GROWS.

There was one dreamscape inside. Dewdrops of sweat were forming on my brow. Blood soaked my shift, I was light-headed, and black gossamer was spidering across my vision. I wouldn't stay conscious for much longer. I fitted the card into the lock and shouldered the door open.

The Inquisitorial Office was an ornate room, watched over by portraits of previous Grand Inquisitors. An oak desk, which housed a wooden globe, sat before a floor-to-ceiling bay window. Weaver himself was nowhere to be seen. Silently, I stepped across the carpet.

Someone was standing beside the bookshelf. Red hair flowed down her back, red as the blood that plastered my skin. When she turned, I swung up the pistol. In the faint light from the citadel outside, her skin was waxen.

"Mahoney."

I didn't move.

Scarlett Burnish stepped away from the bookshelf and raised a hand slightly.

"Mahoney," she said, her cool blue eyes seeking mine, "put down the gun. We don't have much time."

Those were the lips that told their lies.

I had threatened the Grand Inquisitor once. Now it was the Grand Raconteur who stood before me, at the mercy of my bullet. Back then it had been about leverage, but I didn't need that now. This was about self-preservation.

Burnish lifted her other hand, as if to surrender, and said:

"Winter cherry."

At first, I didn't understand. It made no sense for her to be using the language of flowers. But then—

Winter cherry.

Deception.

Alsafi's contact.

Scarlett Burnish, the face and voice of ScionEye, who had read the news since I was twelve years old. *She* was Alsafi's contact in the Archon. Scarlett Burnish, a Ranthen associate. A professional liar. The perfect double agent.

Scarlett Burnish, a traitor to the anchor.

Golden light flared into the office. In a movement so fast I almost missed it, Burnish had the letter-opener from Weaver's desk in her hand. It whistled past my head and punched through the Vigile's visor, splintering red plastic. The handle jutted grotesquely from his forehead. Blood wept down the bridge of his nose. He teetered before his dead weight thumped to the floor.

In the clock tower, the bells struck one. The æther heaved with the reverberations of another death.

"Quickly, Mahoney," Burnish said. "Follow me."

More dreamscapes were already closing in. Something made me look up at the surveillance cameras. Deactivated. Burnish pressed the back of the bust behind her, that of Inquisitor Mayfield, opening a gap in the wall. "Hurry," she said, and chivvied me into the space beyond it. She had barely closed the wall behind us before more Vigiles thundered into the Inquisitorial Office. Her hand clamped over my mouth.

We waited. Muffled orders could be heard through the wall for some time before their footsteps retreated.

Burnish uncovered my lips. A *crack* split the silence, and her face was illuminated by a tube of light, making her red hair shine like paint against her skin. Wordlessly, I followed her through a long, unlit passage, just wide enough for us to move in single file.

She hurried me down a winding flight of steps. At the bottom, she held her light toward my face.

"Who do you work for?" I rasped. "The Ranthen? Which—which government, which organization?"

"Good grief, Mahoney, the state of you . . ." She ignored my question, taking in the streams of blood, the glistening crystals lodged in my arms. "All right, stay calm. I can give you medical attention. Where's Alsafi?"

"Nashira." I couldn't control my breathing. "I told him to leave me, I told him . . ."

"No." She started back up the stairs, then seemed to think better of it. Her fist struck the wall, and her face contorted in frustration. "That son-of-a-*bitch*—" The rest of her thought was lost as she seized me by the shoulders. "Did he mention me? Did he implicate me?"

Her grip was like iron. "No," I said. "No. He didn't even tell me."

"Did she capture him, or destroy him?"

"He's gone."

Her eyes closed briefly. "Damn it." One long breath, and she was back to business. "We have to be quick." She whipped off her silk scarf and used it to stanch the flow of blood from my arm, careful not to push the shard in any farther. "Weaver's bloody whiskers, you're freezing," she bit out, but pulled my other arm around her neck. "You had better be worth all this, Underqueen."

A few hours ago, I wouldn't have followed Scion's sweetheart anywhere, but if Alsafi had trusted her, I would have to do the same. It was her or whatever brutal death awaited me in the basement.

We set off into a concrete passageway, me leaning on her as little as I could, but my strength was leaving me. "Stay awake, Mahoney," she said. "Stay awake." As we walked, she took what I thought was a handkerchief from her pocket. As she stretched the thing over her face, it molded to her features, recasting them into those of a woman twice her age. She tapped two drops from a bottle into her eyes and hid her hair inside a woolen beret. I couldn't process this. She was clearly a spy, but who had planted her, and when?

After what felt like years of staggering, Burnish stopped and entered a code into a keypad, and a pair of doors opened. We stepped into a coffin-like elevator that stank of mold and made an anguished death-rattle as it trundled to the surface. When we reached what it told us was street level, Burnish went to a wooden door and unlocked it.

We emerged into thick snow in a dead end just off Whitehall. I wouldn't have given the door a second glance if I'd passed it.

I was out of the Archon.

I had made it out alive.

A truck was parked just outside the cul-de-sac. Burnish opened its back door and helped me climb inside. I registered hands taking hold of my elbows just before I passed out.

". . . was right. She was alive, all that time. I just can't . . ."

The floor shivered beneath me. There was pain at the top of my arm, but it was nothing compared to the sick, steady throb above my left eye.

"Nick," the voice whispered. "Nick, I think she's waking up."

A hand brushed my cheek. As if he were swimming up through deep water, Nick Nygård came into focus.

My senses were still drowsy; it took me a moment to realize, to *see* him. A cut vaulted above his eye, and his face was greased with sweat, but he was alive. I reached out to touch him, to convince myself that he was real.

"Nick."

"Shh, *sötnos*. We've got you."

He pressed me gently against him, resting his chin on the top of my head. The awareness of everything that had happened hit me like a punch to the gut. I tried to speak, but a gate had given way. All I could do was weep. Hardly any sound came out; just broken, straining rasps, punctured with frail sobs. With each shock, my ribs ached and my head pounded and the water beat my lungs apart again. I could feel Nick shaking. Maria rubbed my back, shushing me, speaking to me like you would to a child: "It's going to be okay, sweet. It's going to be okay." I cried until I could no longer feel the pain.

My eyelids lifted again. Now I was on a threadbare blanket, and I couldn't see a thing. My ears felt stuffed with cotton wool, but I could just hear the low hum of nervous conversation.

My arms and legs were a collage of dressings. Someone must have removed the glass. I drifted off again, riding the last wave of whatever sedative I had been given, which soon broke. When my eyes flickered open, I felt more clear-headed, but at the cost of the anesthesia. Most of the left side of my body was smarting.

Arcturus Mesarthim sat beside me, like a sentry.

"You are a fool, Paige Mahoney." His voice was darkest velvet. "A headstrong fool."

"Aren't you used to it by now?"

"You exceeded my expectations."

I sighed. "I exceeded Vance's, too, I think."

He had made questionable choices of his own. It was he who had said that war required risk, and I had chosen to risk my own life.

"Sorry for pointing a gun at you," I rasped.

"Hm."

He glanced down at me, his eyes burning softly. With effort, I moved my arm and laced my fingers between his knuckles. His thumb lightly caressed my cheekbone, skirting around the cuts and bruises. In the darkness of the Archon, I had thought

I would never see his face, feel his hands on me again. And I hadn't truly realized, until now, that I treasured being touched by him.

"What did they do to you?"

His voice was a low rumble. I shook my head.

"I don't think I can—" I breathed in. "I'm all right."

But I wasn't all right. Anyone could see it. I was trembling like someone yearning for a fix of aster.

His hand stroked across my hair, where it wouldn't hurt my wounds. I leaned into it. "You will be pleased to know," he said, "that Adhara, the erstwhile Warden of the Sarin, has come to a decision. Seeing that our human associate had won such a significant victory against Scion, she concluded that human beings may have matured just enough to merit her renewed allegiance to the Ranthen. Consequently, she has decided that her loyalists will be ready to fight for us. We need only call."

I tried to still the heaving in my chest. At last, I had proven to Terebell that her investment in my leadership had been justified. It had all been worth it.

"Where are we?" I murmured.

"We are on our way to Dover."

"Dover." My head felt so heavy. "The port."

"Yes." His hand kept moving over my curls. "Sleep, little dreamer."

I slipped away before I could ask anything more. When I woke again, it took a while to remember where I was. I was lying opposite a fast-asleep Maria, and my head was on Nick's lap. We were close to the back door of the truck. Pain swelled and ebbed in all my wounds with each shunt of the vehicle.

". . . orders at some point in the next few weeks. In the meantime, Mahoney needs to convalesce. Alsafi made a great sacrifice to get her out of there. I expect you to ensure it doesn't go to waste." Burnish.

"Alsafi was my Ranthen-kith." Warden. "I will always strive to honor his memory, but I suspect that Paige will not want to be absent from the war effort for long, even to convalesce."

I stayed still.

"If she doesn't rest, she's going to be too weak to contribute to that war effort." Burnish's voice held a note of vexation. "That won't please my sponsor. She was tortured in the Archon, God alone knows what she had to do to break Senshield, and on top of that, I doubt her injuries have fully healed from the scrimmage. Honestly, I'm surprised she's able to stand up."

"She is possessed of extraordinary resilience. It was part of why we chose her to be our associate."

Burnish made a noncommittal sound. "She's human. Our sanity is a little more brittle than yours. As are our bones." Silence. "She won't see her twentieth birthday if she doesn't rest. She's a vital player in this game, Arcturus. Leaving aside her gift, she has come to . . . stand for something. Hall and the Sargas won't rest until they have her." The truck skimmed over a bump. "My sponsor needs what they call 'fire-setters' to generate waves of revolution in different parts of the empire. They've identified her as a key one. If she wants to keep fighting the Sargas, joining us is her best shot."

"And you think your . . . sponsor is a suitable alternative to Scion."

"Possibly. What matters is that they want Scion gone, and so do we."

"The Ranthen will need to meet them. Whoever *they* are."

"All in good time. They could be just as far round the twist as Scion, but I'm willing to gamble. I won't watch us hand global power to Nashira Sargas."

Warden didn't reply for a while. Then he said, "I will do my utmost to persuade Paige of the sense in resting for a month. But in the end, she must make her own choices, even when they hurt her. I am not her keeper."

"Of course not. But you can be her friend, if you know how. She'll need plenty of those."

One side of my ribcage ached. I shifted my weight off it, hoping they wouldn't notice.

"What will you do next, Grand Raconteur?"

She laughed slightly. "Come morning, I'll be in the Archon's medical room, being treated for shock, having hidden for several hours from the murderous Paige Mahoney."

"That seems a great risk. Someone will suspect you."

"The wonderful thing about living in a morally bankrupt world is that every human being can be bought in one way or another. Everyone accepts a currency. Money, mercy, the illusion of power—there are always ways to purchase loyalty. Trust me: no one will accuse me."

Warden was silent after that.

When the vehicle stopped, a light switched on inside. Scarlett Burnish roused us all and handed me a bundle of clothes. With help from Nick, I eased a dark-blue sweater, an oilskin, and a pair of waterproof trousers over my dressings, flinching at the pain when the sweater covered my left arm. The oilskin was embroidered with Scion's maritime symbol: the anchor wrapped in rope. The hard-wearing fabric felt coarse on my skin, but I could bear it—someone must have topped up my dose while I slept.

"Where's Eliza?" I said.

Nick wouldn't meet my gaze. "She's not here."

My heart quickened.

"Don't say it," I said. "Nick—"

"No, no—she's all right, sweetheart. She's alive." He hitched up a reassuring smile. "She's just . . . with the Mime Order."

"Why isn't she with us?" When he still didn't look at me, I grabbed his chin. "Nick."

It was only now I was this close that I noticed how raw his eyes were. "Burnish made her stay behind, to continue running the Mime Order with Glym. She has more knowledge of London than she does of anywhere else—it made no sense for her to leave," he said quietly. "We had no choice but to comply. Burnish's sponsor wants the Mime Order intact in London and the three of us joining them somewhere—in Europe, I imagine, given that we're going to Dover."

"To do what?"

"To work for them. To continue what we've started." He pulled on his own sweater. "You've done what you set out to do here: united the syndicate and deactivated Senshield. You've given them a chance to survive—more than any other leader has. It's not safe for you to be in the heartland now."

"Scion told the world I was dead," I said. "It should be safer than ever."

"The rumor that you never were will soon get out, and then tracking you down will become even more of a priority. You'll be an embarrassment to them as well as a liability." He zipped up his oilskin. "The Ranthen agreed to send Warden with you, so he can report back to them on what we're doing."

"So we're being shipped off. Because it's what the Ranthen and some . . . sponsor of Burnish's want."

Everything had changed so quickly. Eliza would be distraught at being separated from us. We were her family, and I hadn't even been able to say goodbye. For the first time, I realized how much control I had lost when Scion had broadcast the news of my death.

"Paige," Nick said softly, seeing the set of my jaw, "it might be the best way. Eliza's going to rule jointly with Glym. They can handle things here now Senshield is gone."

It was the end of my reign. I was no longer Underqueen. I had known it, but now it felt real. At least they would have strong leadership—Eliza and Glym were two of the few people I really trusted, and who I knew would keep the Mime Order together in the months to come. If I'd had a say in the matter, they would have been the replacements I chose.

The door lifted, and Burnish returned to the truck, letting in a flurry of snowflakes. She stood and crossed her arms.

"Congratulations." She smiled at us all. "You are now part of the Domino Program, an espionage network acting within the Republic of Scion. Thanks to your newfound employment, you're now on your way out of the heartland, into mainland Europe."

Maria had an impressive bruise on one cheek. "Who exactly are you working for, Burnish?"

"All I'm at liberty to say is that I'm sponsored by a free-world coalition—one that has a vested interest in preventing the expansion of the Republic of Scion." Burnish reached into a briefcase. "Either you do as I say, Hazurova, or I'll just shoot you. You know too much already."

She handed Maria a thin leather dossier.

"There's your new identity. You're going home, to Bulgaria," she said. "You'll receive instructions within the next few weeks."

Maria leafed through the documents, her face tight. The next folder Burnish handed out was mine. "I hope your French is up to scratch, Mahoney," she said. "You and Arcturus are taking a merchant ship to Calais. A contact will meet you there and take you to a safe house in the Scion Citadel of Paris, where the army isn't stationed." She handed me a phone. "Take this. Somebody will be in touch."

Paris. I didn't know what Burnish's sponsor wanted from me, but if there was one place in Scion I could have chosen to go next, it was there. Jaxon had told me that was where Sheol II would be constructed, and that meant a new gray market.

I could stop both.

I opened the folder, which was embossed with the seal of the Republic of Scion England. My alias was Flora Blake. I was an English student who had taken a year out for research. My subject of interest was Scion History, specifically the establishment and development of the Scion Citadel of Paris.

At my side, Nick drew his knees closer to his chest. "I'm not going with Paige?"

"I'm afraid not. I'm sending you back to Sweden, where you'll be of most use to us. You have the language, the local knowledge— and personal experience of how Tjäder runs things there."

He looked through his dossier with a knitted brow. I gripped his hand.

Warden said, "I suppose I am to keep out of sight."

"Correct. And you'll have to think of your own cover story." She checked her watch. "Right on time."

One by one, we emerged from the truck. I looked out at the English Channel, not quite believing that I was heading toward it.

The five of us walked to the seafront, where ships were docking and vehicles were being unloaded. The majority of the ships were ScionIDE property, boasting names like the INS *Inquisitor's Victory* and *Mary Zettler III*. Some of them must have brought the soldiers here from the Isle of Wight. There were merchant vessels, too, freighters that carried heavy cargo between Scion countries and to a small number of neutral free-world states.

"Burnish." I walked alongside her, holding my jacket as close as I could without setting fire to my skin. "Will you do me one favor?"

"Name it."

"One of the Bone Season survivors, Ivy Jacob, is somewhere in the system of sewers that the River Fleet runs through. She's with a woman named Róisín. Can you get them out—subtly, if at all possible?"

After a pause, she said, "If she's a Bone Season witness, I'll make it my priority."

It was all I could do for them now.

After eleven years, I was leaving the Republic of Scion England. I had visualized this as a child, when I was in school or trying to sleep; wished on stars that one day, I would climb aboard a ship and sail into a future ripe with possibility. I just hadn't thought it would happen like this.

Burnish led us into the shadow of a colossal container ship. Letters spelling FLOTTE MARCHANDE—RÉPUBLIQUE DE SCION loomed above us.

"This is yours, Mahoney," she said. "And yours leaves first."

I looked up at it with a pounding heart. It was time. Maria gave me a small smile and held out her arms.

"So this is goodbye, kid."

"Yoana," I said, embracing her, "thank you. For everything."

"Don't thank me, Underqueen. Just tell me something." She pulled away slightly and grasped my shoulder. "Did you see Vance in there?"

I nodded. "If she's not dead by now, she won't be getting up for a while, at least."

Maria's smile widened. "Good. Now go and cause some havoc in Paris, and don't let all this have been in vain. And if you possibly can," she added, "try not to get killed before I can see you again."

"Likewise."

She kissed my cheek and went to join Burnish at the next ship. Nick looked at me, and I looked at him.

I felt as if the ground was slanting. As if my center of gravity was changing.

"I remember when I first saw you." His voice was steady. "In a vision of the poppy field. A little girl with blonde curls. That's how I knew how to find you that day, all those years ago. I remember stitching up your arm after that poltergeist tore it open. How you said you hoped I hadn't sewn it funny."

A weak laugh escaped me.

"I remember," I said, "missing you every day. Wondering where you'd gone. If you remembered the little girl from the poppy field."

"I remember finding you."

My eyes were misting over. "I remember when you told me you loved Zeke, and I thought I would die, because I didn't think it was possible that anyone could love you more than I did." I squeezed his fingers. "And I remember realizing I couldn't possibly die, because you were the happiest I'd ever seen you. And I wanted to see you that happy for the rest of my life."

We had never acknowledged that night out loud. Nick laid his palm against my cheek.

"I remember you being crowned in the Rose Ring," he whispered, and tears spilled onto my cheeks. "And I remember realizing what a wonderful, courageous woman you'd become. And I felt privileged to have been at your side. And to be your friend. And to have you in my life."

He was as much a part of me as my own bones, and now he would be gone. I cried as I hadn't since I was a child. In the shadow of that merchant vessel, we clung to each other like we were ten years younger, the Pale Dreamer and the Red Vision, the last two Seals to break apart.

Warden and I were escorted into the ship by Burnish's contact from Calais, who showed us into one of the freight containers and promised he would be back once we arrived in France. All too soon, a long blast from the ship's horn announced that it was leaving Dover. I sat with Warden among the crates and boxes. Waiting. Trying not to think about Nick, and the ship that would carry him far away from me.

We would find each other. I would see him again.

London would always walk with me; it would live inside my blood. The place my cousin had told me never to go; the place that was my chrysalis, my damnation, and my redemption. Its streets had won my heart, had turned me from Paige Mahoney to the Pale Dreamer to Black Moth to Underqueen, and then unmade me again, leaving me irrevocably changed. One day, I would return to it. To see this land unchained from the anchor.

When we were some way from the port, Warden opened the door of the container, and together, we stepped on to the deck. Brutal wind hacked at my curls as we approached the railings at the stern.

The merchant ship crashed through the English Channel, churning the waves to lace. My hands came to rest on the railings. The ice-cold wind tore at my cheeks, as if it wanted to expose a second face beneath my own, as I looked back at the southern coast of Britain.

I had freed this country from Senshield; I had weakened Hildred Vance's hand. For now, voyants were safer than they had been. They could disappear into the shadows again; they could walk the streets invisibly. But I could do more for them. I would cast off my crown and take up my sword, and I would go to battle. Soon, an unknown woman named Flora Blake would arrive on the streets of Paris, and the theater of war would open again.

And we would meet our new allies. Whoever they were.

"All this time, I thought we were the ones driving this revolution, but this is bigger than we could ever have imagined," I said. "Someone once told me I'd always be a puppet . . . never holding my own strings. Now I'm starting to think they might have been right."

"We all have our strings," Warden said. "A dreamwalker should know better than most that all strings can be cut."

"Then promise me this." I turned to face him. "Whatever orders Burnish or her sponsor sends us, we don't follow them without question. We find out what kind of game we're playing before we show them our own cards. And we stay together." I sought his gaze. "Promise me we'll stay together."

"You have my word, Paige Mahoney."

He stood by my side as we left England behind us. It was the first day of January. The beginning of another year, another life, another name. I looked back once more at the cliffs that loomed along the coast, at the white cliffs of Dover, limned by the promise of dawn.

And I waited for the sun to rise—as it always had, like a song from the night.

SCION: INTERNATIONAL DEFENSE EXECUTIVE
CLASSIFIED INTERNAL COMMUNICATION

SENDER: OKONMA, PATRICIA K.

SUBJECT: AUTHORITY MAXIMUM

Urgent notice to all commandants. Grand Commander VANCE, HILDRED D. has been injured in the line of duty and is unfit for command. In my capacity as Deputy Grand Commander, authority maximum rests in me until further notice.

RDT SENSHIELD has been incapacitated. All units are to return immediately to conventional munitions.

Hostile individual MAHONEY, PAIGE E. has escaped Inquisitorial custody with assistance from at least one espionage agent. We are interrogating all members of the Archon's personnel, up to and including those holding first-level security clearance, to uncover the identity of the collaborator.

Internal and international border authorities have been alerted that MAHONEY, PAIGE E. is at large. All measures must be taken to conceal from the public that this individual is alive. OPERATION ALBION's revised priority is to eradicate her remaining supporters, known as the MIME ORDER, in the capital.

Finally:

Due to the failure of diplomacy with the relevant foreign powers, the need for immediate action in the IBERIAN

PENINSULA is critical. OPERATION MADRIGAL will now proceed with immediate effect. All non-executive communication concerning this operation will be suspended from January 6.

Let us look forward, as a new year dawns on our empire, to casting our bounds ever farther—and onward still, to the ends of the world. This house forever grows.

Glory to the Suzerain.

Glory to the anchor.

Author's note

Although the language of flowers used in *The Song Rising* is based on real nineteenth-century floriography, I have sometimes tweaked the meanings of certain flowers, such as clematis, for the purposes of the story.

Glossary

The slang used by some clairvoyants in *The Song Rising* is loosely based on words used in the criminal underworld of London in the eighteenth and nineteenth centuries, with some amendments to meaning or usage. Other words have been invented by the author or taken from modern English or transliterated Hebrew or Greek.

Æther: [noun] The spirit realm, accessible by clairvoyants.

Amaranth: [noun] A flower that grows in the Netherworld. Its essence helps to heal spiritual injuries. Used as the symbol of the Ranthen.

Amaurotic: [noun *or* adjective] Non-clairvoyant. Also *rotties*.

Archon: [noun] The Westminster Archon, the seat of power in the Republic of Scion. It is the workplace of most of Scion's key officials, including the Grand Inquisitor, and sometimes houses members of the Sargas family and their allies.

Binder: [noun] [a] A kind of human clairvoyant from the fifth order of clairvoyance. Binders can control a spirit (see *boundling*) by marking its name on their body, either permanently or temporarily, or attach a spirit to a particular location using a small amount of their own blood. [b] A name used for a Rephaite with similar abilities, though Rephaite "binders" are also able to make use of the clairvoyant gift the spirit had in life.

Blood-consort: [noun] The mate of a blood-sovereign of the Rephaim. A title previously held by Arcturus Mesarthim when he was betrothed to Nashira Sargas.

Boundling: [noun] A spirit that obeys a binder.

Buck cab: [noun] A cab that accepts voyant clients. Many buck cabbies are employed by the syndicate.

Costermonger: [noun] A street vendor.

Dream-form: [noun] The form a spirit takes within the confines of a dreamscape.

Dreamscape: [noun] The interior of the mind, where memories are stored. Split into five zones or "rings" of sanity: sunlight, twilight, midnight, lower midnight, and hadal. Clairvoyants can consciously access their own dreamscapes, while amaurotics may catch glimpses when they sleep.

Ectoplasm: [noun] Also *ecto*. Rephaite blood. Chartreuse yellow, luminous, and slightly gelatinous.

Emite, the: [noun] [singular *Emite*] Also *Buzzers*. The purported enemies of the Rephaim; "the dreaded ones." They are known to feed on human flesh. Their blood can be used to mask the nature of a clairvoyant's gift.

Fell tongue: [noun] A Rephaite term for any language spoken by humans.

Floxy: [noun] Scented oxygen, inhaled through a cannula. Scion's alternative to alcohol. Served in the vast majority of entertainment venues, including oxygen bars.

Flux: [noun] Short for *fluxion*. A psychotic drug causing pain, hallucinations and disorientation in clairvoyants.

Glossolalia: [noun] Also *Gloss*. The language of spirits and Rephaim.

Golden cord: [noun] A link between two spirits. Can be used to call for aid and transmit emotions. Little else is known about it.

Gutterling: [noun] [a] A homeless person; [b] someone who lives with, and works for, a *kidsman*. Like buskers and beggars, they are not considered fully fledged members of the syndicate, but may go on to become *hirelings* when their kidsman releases them from service.

Kidsman: [noun] A class of syndicate voyant. They specialize in training young *gutterlings* in the arts of the syndicate.

Krig: [noun] A slang term for a ScionIDE soldier. From the Swedish word for war, *krig*.

Meatspace: [noun] The corporeal world; Earth.

Mime-lord or mime-queen: [noun] A gang leader in the clairvoyant syndicate. Under Paige Mahoney's rule, they have become commanders of small "cells" of clairvoyants.

Mime Order, the: [noun] An alliance between London's clairvoyant syndicate and some members of the *Ranthen*, led by Paige Mahoney and Terebellum Sheratan. Its long-term aim is to overthrow the Sargas family and bring down the Republic of Scion.

Mollisher: [noun] A clairvoyant associated with a mime-lord or mime-queen. Usually presumed to be [a] the mime-lord's or mime-queen's lover, and [b] heir to his or her section, though the former may not always be the case. The Underlord's or Underqueen's heir is known as *mollisher supreme* and is the only mollisher permitted to be a member of the Unnatural Assembly. Paige Mahoney is the first syndicate leader in many years to take two mollishers.

Mudlarks and toshers: [noun] Amaurotic outcasts. Mudlarks scavenge for valuables on the banks of the Thames, while toshers forage in the sewers of London. The two communities, while distinct, are closely intertwined and share a leader, who almost always takes the name Styx upon election.

Muse: [noun] The spirit of a deceased writer or artist.

Netherworld: [noun] Also known as *She'ol* or *the half-realm*, the Netherworld is the original domain of the Rephaim. It acts as a middle ground between Earth and the æther, but has not served its original purpose since the Waning of the Veils, during which it fell into decay.

Nightwalker: [noun] One who sells his or her clairvoyant knowledge as part of a sexual bargain.

Novembertide: [noun] The annual celebration of Scion London's official foundation in November 1929.

Numen: [noun] [plural *numa*, originally *numina*] An object or material used by a soothsayer or augur to connect with the æther, e.g., fire, cards, blood.

Ranthen, the: [noun] Also known as *the scarred ones*. An alliance of Rephaim, led by Terebellum Sheratan, who oppose the rule of the Sargas family and believe in the eventual restoration of the Netherworld. Some of the Ranthen's members are currently allied with the clairvoyant syndicate of London (see *Mime Order*).

Rephaite: [noun] [plural *Rephaim*] [a] A biologically immortal, humanoid inhabitant of the Netherworld. Rephaim feed on the auras of clairvoyant humans. [adjective] [b] The state of being a Rephaite; to be Rephaite.

Saloop: [noun] A hot, starchy drink made from orchid root, seasoned with rosewater or orange blossom.

Sarx: [noun] The incorruptible flesh of Rephaim and other creatures of the Netherworld (called *sarx-beings* or *sarx-creatures*). It has a slightly metallic sheen.

ScionIDE: [noun] Scion: International Defense Executive, the armed forces of the Republic of Scion. The First Inquisitorial Division is responsible for national security; the Second Inquisitorial Division is used for invasions; the Third Inquisitorial Division—the largest—is used to defend and keep control of Scion's conquered territories.

SciORE: [noun] Scion: Organization for Robotics and Engineering.

Scrimmage: [noun] A battle for the position of Underlord or Underqueen. A scrimmage is usually triggered by the death of the Underlord or Underqueen in the absence of a mollisher supreme to take over. Paige Mahoney was the victor in the last scrimmage after the murders of her predecessor, Haymarket Hector, and his mollisher, Cutmouth.

Scrying: [noun] the art of seeing into and gaining insight from the æther through *numa*. A *querent* may be used.

Séance: [noun] [a] For voyants, a group communion with the æther; [b] for Rephaim, transmitting a message between members of a group.

Senshield: [noun] The brand name for Radiesthesic Detection Technology. At the beginning of *The Song Rising*, Senshield scanners can detect the first three of the *Seven Orders of Clairvoyance*.

Seven Orders of Clairvoyance: [noun] A system for categorizing clairvoyants, first proposed by Jaxon Hall in his pamphlet *On the Merits* *of Unnaturalness.* The seven orders are the soothsayers, the augurs, the mediums, the sensors, the guardians, the furies, and the jumpers. The system was controversial due to its assertion that the "higher" orders are superior to the "lower," but was nonetheless adopted as the official form of categorization in the London underworld and elsewhere.

Seven Seals, the: [noun] Previously the dominant gang in I Cohort, Section 1-4, based in the district of Seven Dials. The gang was led by Jaxon Hall, with Paige Mahoney as his *mollisher*.

Silver cord: [noun] A permanent link between the body and the spirit. It allows a person to dwell for many years in one physical form. Particularly important to dreamwalkers, who use the cord to leave their bodies temporarily. The silver cord wears down over the years, and once broken cannot be repaired.

Spool: [noun] [a] A group of spirits. [verb] [b] To gather several spirits into a group.

Syndicate: [noun] A criminal organization of clairvoyants, based in the Scion Citadel of London. Active since the early 1960s. Governed by the Underlord and the Unnatural Assembly. Members specialize in mime-craft for financial profit.

Threnody: [noun] A series of words used to banish spirits to the outer darkness.

Underlord or Underqueen: [noun] Head of the Unnatural Assembly and mob boss of the clairvoyant syndicate in London. Equivalent terms in the voyant communities of Manchester and Edinburgh are *Scuttling King or Queen* and *Spaewife* respectively.

Unnatural Assembly: [noun] A collective term for all of the mime-lords and mime-queens in London's clairvoyant syndicate.

Vigiles: [noun] Also *Gillies*. Scion's police force, split into two main divisions: the clairvoyant Night Vigilance Division (NVD) and the amaurotic Sunlight Vigilance Division (SVD). NVD officers are guaranteed thirty years of immunity from justice before being executed for their unnaturalness.

Voyant: [noun] Clairvoyant.

Acknowledgments

This book has been a long time coming. Two-and-a-bit years coming. First and foremost, I'd like to thank you, the reader, for being so patient in waiting for it. Every hour I spent working on this book made it stronger, and the extra time I took to polish it means that I'm truly proud of the story you now hold in your hands. I hope you enjoyed Paige's third adventure, and that it was worth the wait. Onward to the fourth one . . .

The next acknowledgments go to my wonderful editors, Alexa von Hirschberg and Genevieve Herr. I can't express how grateful I am to you both for your patience, wisdom and enthusiasm. I couldn't have pulled *The Song Rising* out of the bag without you.

Thank you to everyone at DGA—most of all to my agent, the incomparable David Godwin, who always has my back—and to Heather Godwin, Lisette Verhagen and Philippa Sitters. Thank you for always championing my writing, and for eating cake with me on that day when I got really overwhelmed.

Thank you to everyone at the Imaginarium Studios for your continued support, especially Chloe Sizer and Will Tennant, whose insight and encouragement has once again been invaluable.

To Alexandra Pringle, Amanda Shipp, Anurima Roy, Ben Turner, Brendan Fredericks, Callum Kenny, Cristina Gilbert, Diya Kar Hazra, Faiza Khan, George Gibson, Hermione Lawton, Imogen Denny, Isabel Blake, Jack Birch, Kathleen Farrar, Laura Keefe, Lea Beresford, Madeleine Feeny, Marie Coolman, Nancy Miller, Nicole

Jarvis, Philippa Cotton, Rachel Mannheimer, Sara Mercurio, Trâm-Anh Doan, and everyone else at Bloomsbury for your dedication to this series. I wake up every day feeling so lucky to be working with you.

Thank you to Sarah-Jane Forder for the thorough copyediting, and to David Mann and Emily Faccini for making *The Song Rising* look just as gorgeous as the previous two books.

Thank you to my translators and publishers worldwide, who work so hard to get my books into the hands of readers who I wouldn't otherwise have been able to reach.

As an author, it's sometimes necessary to write about places you haven't lived in. While I visited Manchester and Edinburgh during the process of writing this book, I am a Londoner to the core, and I knew I could never re-create these two great cities without some help. Thank you to Ciarán Collins, who has once again patiently answered my many questions about Irish; Louise O'Neill for giving the Ancoats scene the once-over; Moss Freed for his insight into Manchester; and Stuart Kelly for being kind enough to be my guide in Edinburgh.

Some other lovely folks whose knowledge has contributed to this book are Melissa Harrison, for bird and tree-related assistance; Paul Talling, of Derelict London, for the tour of the Fleet; Richard Andrew Vincent Smith, whose knowledge of trains is surely unparalleled, or at the very least, far superior to my own—thank you for taking the time to check the Stoke-on-Trent part when you were in the midst of revising; and Sara Bergmark Elfgren, for helping with the Swedish again. Thank you, as well, to the many kind strangers on Twitter who have replied so quickly and willingly when I've asked for help with languages and dialect—you are the people who make the Internet great.

Ilana Fernandes-Lassman and Vickie Morrish—you are the kind of friends everyone deserves. Thank you for always being there whenever I emerge from the tunnel of drafting edits, to eat pizza and laugh ourselves silly.

I've historically been a solitary creature when it comes to my creative process, but over the last couple of years I've learned how much of a lifesaver it can be to share the journey with people who are also experiencing the ups and downs of conveying a story from imagination to page. Thank you to Alwyn Hamilton, Laure Eve, and Melinda Salisbury, and to Team Maleficent—Claire Donnelly, Leiana Leatutufu, Lisa Lueddecke, Katherine Webber, and Krystal Sutherland—for being such great friends over the past year. You are all seriously talented ladies, and it's truly an honor to know you.

Thank you to the booksellers, book bloggers, Bookstagrammers, Booktubers, reviewers, librarians, and other book-loving people who have done so much to support and talk about the *Bone Season* series.

Finally, thank you to my family for putting up with me in my moments of self-doubt as well as my moments of triumph. I might have flown the nest this year, but I wouldn't have been able to start writing these books in the first place if I hadn't had you there to support me following my dream.

A Note on the Author

Samantha Shannon was born in west London in 1991. She started writing at the age of fifteen. Between 2010 and 2013 she studied English Language and literature at St. Anne's College, Oxford. In 2013 she published *The Bone Season*, the first in a seven-book series. *The Bone Season* was a *New York Times*, a *Sunday Times,* and an *Asian Age* bestseller, was picked as a Book of the Year by the *Daily Mail, Stylist,* and *Huffington Post,* and was named one of Amazon's 2013 Best Books of the Year. It has been translated into twenty-six languages and the film rights have been acquired by The Imaginarium Studios and 20th Century Fox. In 2014, Samantha Shannon was included on the *Evening Standard*'s Power 1000 list. *The Song Rising* is her third novel.

samanthashannon.co.uk / @say_shannon

A Note on the Type

The text of this book is set Adobe Garamond. It is one of several versions of Garamond based on the designs of Claude Garamond. It is thought that Garamond based his font on Bembo, cut in 1495 by Francesco Griffo in collaboration with the Italian printer Aldus Manutius. Garamond types were first used in books printed in Paris around 1532. Many of the present-day versions of this type are based on the *Typi Academiae* of Jean Jannon cut in Sedan in 1615.

Claude Garamond was born in Paris in 1480. He learned how to cut type from his father, and by the age of fifteen he was able to fashion steel punches the size of a pica with great precision. At the age of sixty he was commissioned by King Francis I to design a Greek alphabet, and for this he was given the honorable title of royal type founder. He died in 1561.